"He is not dead!"

Jagat's wife went on with quiet fervor. "If my son were dead, I would know it throughout my being. But I live as before. When I wake in the morning it is not to sorrow, but to peace, because he is alive. He may be in prison, or in exile, but he lives. The task is to find him wherever he is."

Jagat rose so abruptly that the dishes on the small table by his chair crashed to the floor. "Moti, I forbade you to—"

She rose also. "Jagat, you will not listen to me. So I must ask help of others. Miss Westley, help me, please—"

"What do you ask?" Brooke inquired. She was aware of a strange tenderness arising in her for this woman.

"That someone go in search of my son."

So it was that Brooke Westley went with Jagat on a journey to look for his son. It was a strange errand for a wife to assign the woman her husband loved....

MANDALA
was originally published by
The John Day Company, Inc.

Books by Pearl S. Buck

A Bridge for Passing
The Angry Wife
Come, My Beloved
Command the Morning
Death in the Castle
Dragon Seed
The Exile
Fighting Angel
God's Men
The Good Earth
Hearts Come Home and Other Stories
The Hidden Flower
Imperial Woman
Kinfolk
Letter from Peking
The Living Reed
The Long Love
Mandala
The Mother
My Several Worlds
The New Year
Pavilion of Women
Peony
Portrait of a Marriage
The Three Daughters of Madame Liang
The Time Is Noon
The Townsman
Voices in the House

Published by POCKET BOOKS

*Are there paperbound books you want
but cannot find in your retail stores?*

You can get any title in print in **POCKET BOOK** editions. Simply send retail price, local sales tax, if any, plus 25¢ to cover mailing and handling costs to:

MAIL SERVICE DEPARTMENT
POCKET BOOKS ● A Division of Simon & Schuster, Inc.
1 West 39th Street ● New York, New York 10018

Please send check or money order. We cannot be responsible for cash. *Catalogue sent free on request.*

Titles in this series are also available at discounts in quantity lots for industrial or sales-promotional use. For details write our Special Projects Agency: The Benjamin Company, Inc., 485 Madison Avenue, New York, N.Y. 10022.

PEARL S. BUCK

MANDALA

PUBLISHED BY POCKET BOOKS NEW YORK

MANDALA

John Day edition published October, 1970

POCKET BOOK edition published November, 1971

This POCKET BOOK edition includes every word
contained in the original, higher-priced edition. It is printed
from brand-new plates made from completely reset, clear, easy-to-read
type. POCKET BOOK editions are published by POCKET BOOKS, a division
of Simon & Schuster, Inc., 630 Fifth Avenue, New York, N.Y. 10020.
Trademarks registered in the United States and other countries.

L

Standard Book Number: 671-78098-0.
Library of Congress Catalog Card Number: 73-111648.
Copyright, ©, 1970, by The Pearl S. Buck Foundation.
All rights reserved. This POCKET BOOK edition is published by
arrangement with The John Day Company.

Printed in the U.S.A.

MANDALA

A schematized representation of the cosmos, chiefly characterized by a concentric organization of geometric shapes, each of which contains an image of a deity or an attribute of a deity. A symbol representing the effort to reunify the self.

I

JAGAT, THE MAHARANA OF AMARPUR, India, was wakened as usual on this summer morning by the flutter of pigeons outside the window of his bedroom. It was no small noise, for thousands of pigeons had nested, generation upon generation through the centuries, in the corners and crannies of the ancient palace. Each morning, as long as he could remember, he had opened his eyes to the first soft stir of the early pigeons, who then roused the multitude of their fellows until the beat of their wings rose into soaring, accelerating rhythm. He sat up in bed, naked under the white silk sheet, and he yawned mightily. Across the wide space of the room, he caught sight of his reflection in the immense mirror attached to the wall opposite his bed, a pleasantly handsome man, he observed with satisfaction. He closed his mouth, and smoothing his curling dark hair, he gazed into his own lively dark eyes. Then he smiled at himself, tossed aside the covers, and walked toward the casement windows opened to the morning air. As was his habit, he leaned upon the windowsill to gaze at the landscape, while from the distance across the lake he listened to the slap and beat of the wooden paddles of women washing clothes on the marble steps of the water gate of the small city.

It was a scene he loved. Beyond the lake the hills rose in semicircles of desert brown, bare and round as women's

1

breasts. Their smooth surfaces were dotted with low desert shrubs, and in the valley, as wide as a plain, the city of white marble shone in early sunshine. The hills were stored with marble and the houses were built of marble. On the edge of the city and facing the shore of the blue lake, the white marble palace spread for a quarter of a mile, walls and gold-tipped turrets and minarets, the palace where his family had lived for centuries, Rajputs of Rajasthan. He, the Maharana, and his wife, Moti, the Maharani, and their two children lived in the modern western wing which he had built while his father, until his death, had continued to live in the vast rooms of the palace proper. Between rose the great edifice of audience halls and passages and libraries.

Thinking of Moti, he felt a familiar warmth surge in his loins. They were still young, he and she, though their daughter Veera was old enough to be married, and indeed would be married in the coming months to a young prince of Limbdi, and their son, Jai, was in an English preparatory school near Mussoorie and destined for Oxford, where Jagat himself had taken honors at the age of twenty-two. Yes, they were still young, he and Moti, he just reaching forty and she just past thirty-eight. They had been far too young at their marriage, but it had been an arranged affair, she the daughter of a statesman and man of inherited wealth, Sir Ramakrishna Prasad. It had taken time to fall in love, even after the first required consummation of the wedding night.

He glanced at the German clock hanging on the wall over the door. The palace was full of clocks, amusing gifts from visiting plenipotentiaries of Europe throughout the centuries. This one he had chosen for his own because he liked its quaint Gothic aspect, a cathedral of gold with a spire of silver whence, upon the hour, four small figures came out to execute a spasmodic priestly dance. The doors of the cathedral were wired back, however, for the convenience of a pair of brown wrens who built their nest there, season after season. One of them flew over his head now, bearing in its mouth a dried bit of grass. It entered the cathedral busily, its tail moving up and down.

"Aha, little one," he exclaimed. "You are early. Where is your mate?"

As though in answer, a second wren flew past him. Argument took place between the two small birds, a confusion of twitterings and cheepings, to which he listened, amused. Here in India the line between human and non-human was finely drawn, if indeed it were drawn at all. His people were wise, he believed, in their acceptance of animals as part of the living family upon the globe. The animals reciprocated. Cows, sauntering along the streets of cities, fancied themselves human, and gray monkeys, swinging over the rooftops, knew no difference between themselves and man. Even the lesser creatures—mice, chipmunks, squirrels, and such minute varieties of life— deserved the respect and tenderness they were given, although they could be annoying in their trustfulness, taking over anything as their possession if it suited their convenience. His own father had once given up sitting on his gold throne for days until a mongoose had reared her family upon the crimson velvet cushions. In the face of this self-confidence on the part of creatures never harmed, his people had come, through ages, to accept them at their own value.

Such musings diverted Jagat only momentarily. He had not forgotten the disturbance in his loins and he considered whether to yield to it. Moti would still be sleeping. The one disharmony between them that remained after the years was the matter of timing. He fell into drowsiness early after sundown, but she was wakeful beyond midnight. At dawn it was he who woke, but it was noon before she opened her eyes. Whether to disturb her now! The air floated in from the lake, soft with the mists of spring, while he hesitated. Suddenly the daring music of a bird's song smote his ear and hastened his decision. Let her wake, let her wake to his need! He walked with impetuous step across the room, snatching a garment as he crossed the passageway to her room. At her door a serving woman slept and he pushed her aside with his bare foot and entered.

Moti was sleeping. He went to the low couch of her bed

and stood looking down on her. She slept with her right hand under her cheek, her face pale and peaceful, the long dark lashes on her cheeks, her dark hair tumbled in curls. She was fair-skinned and slender, a Kashmiri, and her bones were delicate. Her white sleeping sari had slipped from her right shoulder and left bare her right breast, as round and firm as the breast of a young girl. The sight of it quickened him and he knelt beside her.

"Moti," he whispered. "Moti, I am here!"

She opened her eyes at this and gazing at him in gradual recognition, she smiled. Then she turned on her back with both hands and pushed her hair away from her face. She had beautiful hands. Once a young sculptor from Paris, a friend Jagat had made in his student days, had stayed a week in the palace, and refusing to visit the sights of Amarpur, he had spent his time carving in local marble Moti's clasped hands.

He leaned above her now. "Moti, it's a perfect day!"

He spoke in English as they did by habit, for his language was not hers, and it was in English that their deepest thoughts and then their love had been expressed.

She sighed. "Jagat, you promised me you would not wake me before ten."

"But it's such a day! The wrens are building their nest in the clock again."

"They put it into your head to come here to my room?"

"Does it belong in my head?"

She laughed a pleasant gentle laughter, and moving, she made room for him on the bed. There was no need to lock the door. The serving woman would stand guard when she saw it closed. He threw aside the loose garment he had wrapped about him, and lying beside her, he took off her sari slowly, enjoying the rising power in his loins. Love was still the sweetest pleasure in life, the total communion which made them one, however brief the hour, and drove away the difference in their minds. They said not a word, not he, not she, a silent duet, a routine familiar and unfailing in its pleasure. Suddenly it was finished and as swiftly as he had come he was ready to leave.

"My thanks," he said, and stooping, he kissed her full upon the lips and went away.

Her presence followed him, nevertheless. This girl, this woman, to whom he had been married since he was eighteen years old, was still intimately unknown to him. They conversed sometimes, exploring the hidden meanings of Hindu scriptures, of poetry and history, of modern democracy and Chinese communism. He knew the habits of her mind, although he could not always follow its pathways, and he was enjoyably familiar with the contours and intricacies of her body. Yet he did not know, and perhaps would never know, the hidden feelings of that body, even as he did not know the secret thoughts of her mind. Did she respond to his robust and frank physical excitement? If she did, she controlled its expression, and lay seemingly passive. He had once listened to a vulgar young Englishman, a cinema director in Bombay, expounding upon the defects of Indian women.

"They look beautiful but they are lousy lovers," the fellow had said and had proceeded to describe the contradiction.

"They give in at once. But that's all they give—they don't know anything about the art of making love."

He had not replied to the vulgar chap, repressing his anger that any Indian woman had yielded to such crude demand. Perhaps none had. Perhaps it was wishful male boasting, but he declined any further conversation—indeed, had never met the man again. Nor would he agree that Moti was not a good lover. She had most tender and gracious ways of receiving him, even with welcome, if welcome meant not refusing. But it was an accommodation rather than a harmony. Or was it? Yet he preferred it, on the whole, to the falsely romantic gestures of professionals in Paris or London, those experiences of his youth, which in his maturity he had given up from sheer distaste. Yet could it be possible that he had never known the full joy of a woman?

He stepped from his shower and put away such thoughts. Moti was his beloved wife and she made no complaint, not even now, when his princely income was cut in half by the new government. The wives of some of the princes who were his friends in neighboring states had complained bitterly. How, they wailed, how could they pay the costs of their families, buy the saris and jewels they needed, not to speak of the maintenance of the palaces, if half their income were sliced off? There was also the matter of the land. It too had been taken away, that is to say reduced, until there was no leeway for needy royal relatives, who after a lean year at Monte Carlo must come home to recoup their fortunes. In other times a prince could simply tell his tenants that he must have a larger proportion of the harvest than last year and send his steward to sit by the threshing floor until the winnowed grain was divided according to the royal landlord's command. Thus it could be, and had been here in this very state that he had seen his father so decree on behalf of his gay younger uncle who had been sued for millions of francs by a French mistress when he left her. That year, when the grain tax was taken from their many hydes of grain, one fifth of the harvest was all that had remained to the farmer who had plowed the earth and sown the seed and cared for the fields of wheat.

No, Moti never complained. In her quiet, graceful way she had only listened while he told her of the new regulations, her large eyes dark in her cream pale face, her face that somehow just missed beauty. In her silence he had continued.

"Moti, I shall have to think up a business, or something, because there will be still less for the children, since the decrease goes on with each generation until eventually there will be nothing. Yet somehow it's fair, or so I feel, after all these years of taking from the people and giving nothing back. It's odd, though, to realize that I am no longer the ruler in my own state."

She was wearing the soft white sari which was her usual habit and they were sitting after dinner on the spacious marble terrace that his grandfather had built on the west face of the palace, the year he brought home the Greek girl with whom he had been infatuated. He had built it around a huge neem tree that spread its shadowy leaves above them, and a fountain played at its roots, a fountain where a statue of the Greek girl stood naked in pale green marble. She had died soon, for those had been the days before clever Swiss scientists had discovered the remedy for sudden dysenteries—or had she hanged herself? Palace gossip!

Moti had replied thoughtfully. "Something is gone, of course, Jagat, now that you are no longer the ruler, and in a way I suppose the people will miss it. Your father was a figure of glamour and excitement in their rather dull lives. Even his sins were glamourous. As for your grandfather— it must have been very lively when the Greek girl was here. Even you, darling, are quite glamourous, though without Greek girls, I am thankful to say. But your tiger shooting—by the way, I'm afraid a moth has got into that big tiger's head on the wall between the windows in the salon. Will you take a look at it?"

"But do you not mind having your allowance for jewels and saris cut in half?" he had inquired.

She had shrugged her delicate shoulders. "I have hundreds of saris and more jewels than I can ever wear. You are so generous, Jagat. I've already planned to give Veera some of my jewels when she marries. And I daresay it will be exciting for the peasants to have more to eat—at least as exciting as Greek girls and maharajas wanting their weight in gold on their birthdays."

She had laughed suddenly. "What an inducement to obesity that must have been! Still, your grandfather kept his figure—I suppose he had to choose between gold and the Greek girl's love, or whatever it was. She was young enough to be his daughter, wasn't she? And he was so foolishly mad about her. I can't bear to go into that little room where she hanged herself."

Upon this she had risen and walked away with her unvarying grace, a grace so slow that it might have seemed indolence but he knew it was not. She was an inveterate student, not only of Indian religions but of Catholicism, her Catholic teacher for many years an aged French abbot who had taught her a pure Parisian French. But Father DuBois had died last year, and when he felt death approaching he had tendered her into the care of a young English priest, Father Francis Paul, a handsome bearded ascetic whose father had been a Protestant earl and highly indignant that a son of his should be a priest in a rival form of Christianity. On any evening nowadays when Jagat came home to his palace the tall black-robed figure of the young priest might be seen sitting in a comfortable chair on the terrace, while near him, but not too near, Moti lay in her long chair, her head leaning upon the cushions, the wind blowing her hair softly away from her face.

Thus it was he had found them last night. They welcomed him as always, Father Francis Paul rising to stand silent, his fine thin hands clasped in front of him, his handsome head bowed, the brown beard clipped, and the brown hair worn slightly long. Whatever the two were discussing they ceased, and when they sat down the priest waited for the Maharana to speak before he made his own pleasant comments, suited with gravity or levity to what might be said. He was well educated, his cultivated mind his means of approach to a prince.

In spite of a secret prejudice against Catholicism, Jagat enjoyed conversation with Father Francis Paul. There was nothing quite like the keen English mind, cogent and cool even when it was clouded with religious mysticism. But mysticism was natural to the Indian mind, though corrupted, it was true, by superstition. Even he, Jagat, would not begin a new enterprise or undertake a journey on a day declared unlucky by a fortune-teller, nor was he ashamed to confess it. Indeed it was in his mind to consult the fortune-teller this very day concerning a project of which he had not spoken to anyone, not even to Moti. Then he decided against it. A good day, it was a good day, the air clear and dry and the lake shimmering in silver points of light under the sun.

Suddenly now as he dressed himself, a bird whose like he had never seen flew into the room, a white bird too small for a pigeon, too large for a thrush. It entered through the open window, direct as an arrow, circled twice beneath the high ceiling, and settled on the massive gold frame of the painting he most valued. The walls of his room were hung with old masterpieces depicting Rajput and Mogul history, and this one the white bird had chosen was a portrait of Jagat's ancestor, the mighty Pratap, who regained the great fortress of Chittor after it had been seized by the Mogul invader Akbar. Until Chittor was regained, Pratap declared that none should use gold or silver dishes but all should eat only from leaves of trees and none should sleep on silk or cotton mattresses but only upon beds of straw and men must leave their beards uncut until such time as the Mogul invaders were driven away. For so long was this command obeyed that Jagat's grandfather, though he ate from gold and silver dishes, had placed green leaves under his plate in token, and straw was laid under his bed. And why did this old memory return now? The white bird brought it back again. For on the morning of the great repulse such a white bird had flown into Pratap's tent. A good omen indeed, Jagat told himself now, for his own contemplated adventure!

In her rooms Moti sat reading a new book by Jean Paul Sartre. She read English and French with ease, and it pleased her to travel thus into the minds of westerners, since long ago she had made up her own mind that she would never cross the Black Water and leave her own country to visit another except through mind and imagination. She looked virginally young, in spite of Jagat's early visit, or perhaps because of it, though this thought she never allowed herself. After it she had bathed herself meticulously and had then eaten her usual vegetarian breakfast, for she ate no meat, in spite of Jagat's persuasions.

"A good slice of roast beef will put color in your pale cheeks," he had reiterated throughout their married years, but as steadfastly she had refused. She did not believe in taking life, not even by eating an egg, which contained the germ of life, and especially did she loathe tiger hunts, the sport which Jagat so enjoyed. Yet she did not protest when he commanded their son Jai to accompany him into the mountains to one of the many shooting boxes which generations of princes had built there. Jagat alone had shot and killed more than a hundred tigers, the best of which were stuffed or their heads mounted and the palace's walls were decorated with them. Others were skinned and their coats made into rugs to lay upon the marble floors. But she would have no animal skins or heads in her own rooms.

She sat reading through the morning hours in graven stillness and no one disturbed her, although more than once a servant came to the open door, looked in, and went away again. She closed the book at last, placing a white satin marker between the pages, and continued motionless in thought. She could not, she reflected, accept the transitoriness of this new western philosophy. To live as though no more than the present moment were all—no, here in the abode of history this was not possible, although the weight of India's past was at times an inheritance almost too heavy to bear. Perhaps that was why young persons like Veera and Jai seemed idle and purposeless. It was impossible to create a present commensurate with so glorious a past, impossible to equal one's ancestors in prowess and daring. But how explain Jagat in that case? Jagat had never been idle or purposeless. From the day of their marriage he had always been busy about something. Thank the gods that at least it was not about women!

She had been betrothed at sixteen and married at eighteen and in the two intervening years her mother had prepared her for what she supposed a husband must be.

"Women are sad." With these words her mother usually began her homily. Then she continued. "The cause for this basic sadness is that women allow themselves to dream of faithfulness in love. It is only a dream and dreams are always dangerous. For men cannot be faithful. Their nature forbids it. When a dog sees a rabbit his jaws quiver and his saliva runs. He cannot help it. Similarly when a man sees a young and pretty woman, however he may wish to be faithful to his wife, his jaws quiver and his saliva runs. You will be foolish if you allow yourself to be hurt."

It was true that in her girlhood Moti had dreams of

MANDALA • 11

love. "How can I prevent being hurt?" she had asked her mother one day. She could see herself now, a young girl oversensitive to tenderness, to delicacy, to beauty, and given to dreaming.

"Try not to love your husband too much," her mother had advised.

"But is it not my duty to love him as much as I can?" Moti had inquired.

"I give you my secret advice," her mother replied. "I know very well that if you allow yourself to love him, you will assuredly be hurt. Read your books, study your music, learn languages, do anything to occupy your time and your mind, but keep from loving your husband too much—or any man."

"What other man could I love?" she had asked in her innocence.

Her mother had appeared confused. "Of course there is no other," she had replied.

Now, however, she understood that love could not be so easily controlled. Yesterday she had been startled to discover that had Father Francis Paul not been a priest she could love him. The young Englishman understood her troubled inquiring mind, he dealt tenderly and delicately with her doubts, and he comprehended the complexities of her life as the mistress of this vast palace. No one ever before had been concerned with her personally as a soul and she responded inevitably but sinfully, she now agreed with herself. The priest was her spiritual guide—her guru, she would have called him, had he been Indian.

She had not allowed herself to love even Jagat fully until now, when she found herself very much needing to love him. When Veera was married and Jai in college in England—or in America perhaps, for Jagat was talking about Harvard, and America was much farther away than England—then she would have only Jagat. And he had never loved another woman. If her mother were living she would go to her and tell her.

"Mother, Jagat is not like any other man alive. He has been faithful to me, as his wife. May I not love him?"

Her mother was dead, however, and there was no one

else to whom she could possibly say such a thing, certainly not to her older sister, married to the prince of a neighboring state who kept a harem of dancing girls, as indeed Jagat's father had done. Therefore how explain Jagat? When he assumed rule, he had dismissed all the dancing girls who, like a flock of loud-voiced birds, had kept the palace noisy with their laughter and quarrels. When they were gone, paid off and gone, the quiet of history had descended upon the palace and the lake. In this peace she had lived, had been the Maharani and mistress of many servants, had reared her children, had been Jagat's wife without allowing herself to love him until now.

At this moment there was a knock on the door, already open, and when she called permission to enter, Veera came in, followed by a woman servant in a gray cotton sari bearing a silver breakfast tray.

"It is time for you to eat, Mamu," Veera said. "And I have ordered your toast as you like it—very crisp and brown—though how you can eat this Indian imitation of English bread! You should taste the bread we have at school, real bread!"

She was a slim tall girl in a pale yellow sari, her dark hair long and braided down her back. She looked like her father, her eyes lively and brown, her skin fair, her features clearly marked, the nose slightly aquiline in profile, her mouth sculptured and Greek, the corners deeply cut and the lips delicate but full. Alexander of Greece and his men had left something of themselves in north India when they came there as invaders long ago.

"I am accustomed only to our Indian bread," Moti replied.

"And I do think," Veera went on, sinking down upon a red satin floor cushion, "that you ought at least to have an egg with your breakfast. You should see what we have at school—porridge, fruit, eggs, kidneys, and bacon, and I eat everything."

Moti laughed. "Spare me—I couldn't possibly! Don't try to reform me, child. Tea and toast are enough for me and I eat fruit at dinner."

"But you are always pale."

"I don't live on mountains as you do at school."

"Then you should."

"No, I shouldn't. I don't like mountains. They frighten me. I wish your father would fetch you back and forth to Mussoorie instead of being always too busy. I am terrified, especially by that narrow final road to your school—a ledge above a precipice, without guard rails! I can't think why no one has fallen into the gorge."

"Because we know we must be careful!"

"I daresay."

Silence fell while the serving woman poured tea and presented toast.

"Thank you, Saira," Moti said. "Now you may go. Veera will take care of me."

The woman withdrew, her hands lifted palm to palm in respect, and the door closed.

"I suppose," Moti said to her daughter, "that you have things on your mind. Else you would not be up so early."

"Yes, I have." Veera paused and went on resolutely. "Mamu, must I be married?"

Moti looked at her daughter, startled. "Yes, of course you must. Your father has arranged everything. Why do you ask?"

"Mamu, the girls in school who come from Bombay say they are allowed to choose their own husbands nowadays."

"Indeed! But you come from Amarpur, not Bombay. And your father is the Maharana, not a Bombay merchant."

"But Jai will choose his wife, perhaps in England—or America. At any rate in Bombay!"

"Does he say so?"

"He wrote me that he would."

"I must speak to his father. I would not like an American daughter-in-law, or even an English one. I like the western people but that does not mean taking them into our family."

"Is he to choose his own wife, Mamu?"

"I have not heard of it."

does he not marry before he goes across the
...r?"

...eve your father has decided against it. He does
...eve men should be married too young."

...ut he was married young."

"Yes."

"Why should I be married young and not Jai?"

"You are a girl, my darling, and there is the difference. You are a responsibility. Strange things happen to girls that do not happen to men. It is safer for girls to be married young."

"Like you?"

"Like me."

"Did you ever wish you were not married, Mamu?"

"No. I never think of such things. It was my karma to be married to your father."

"How do you know?"

"Did it not happen?"

Veera gazed at her mother thoughtfully. There was no answer to this. She began again. "But how do you know Raj is my karma?"

"It has happened. We consulted the astrologers, we compared your horoscopes, the elements, the present stars—everything."

"Except Raj—and me."

"Well, darling, you saw him, didn't you? In my generation I wouldn't have been allowed to see your father."

"Yes, I have seen him—once."

"Handsome?"

"Yes, I suppose so—if you like the big burly type. He is probably hairy all over. He has hair on the rims of his ears!"

"Veera!"

"But Mamu, I don't like hairy men!"

"You must not allow yourself to have such thoughts. Really, Veera!"

Here Moti roused herself to earnestness. She put aside the breakfast tray, first washing her hands in a small silver basin and drying them on a linen napkin.

"You are too much like all Indian girls nowadays. You don't know how fortunate you are that your life is so pleasantly arranged for you. You need not, as the western girls must, devote your time and thought on how to find yourself a husband. I am told that between the ages of fourteen onward western girls and women can accomplish no good, wholehearted work because of the difficulty of finding husbands for themselves. Of this responsibility we, your parents, relieve you. Raj is a fine young man, well educated, of our own caste—"

Here Veera sprang so swiftly to her feet that her sari slipped from her shoulder. She adjusted it impatiently. "Mamu, you really are too old-fashioned! You know the government has abolished caste."

"Yes, darling, of course, but still it's wise, nevertheless—convenient and all that—to marry within one's caste."

"If I loved a man I'd marry him whatever his caste."

"Then I can only say you would be foolish," Moti said with decision. "And now, darling, I think you had better go to your practicing. That Debussy piece sounded very beautiful yesterday. I hadn't liked Debussy before."

"You want to get rid of me, Mamu. Is your beautiful young priest coming today?"

A flashing look passed between the two women.

"You never used to be impudent, Veera," Moti said coldly.

"Well, but he is beautiful—isn't he?"

"I don't think of such things. And he'll soon be going away. He's volunteered for a hill station."

"Does Bapu know?"

"Yes. As a matter of fact, he promised Father Francis Paul the skin of the last tiger he shot—as soon as it is sent back from Mysore, where it's being 'fixed,' as your father puts it. Now go, Veera."

"Yes, Mamu."

The willful child blew her a kiss from the tips of her fingers and went away. But left alone, Moti put aside her books and sat long in deep thought.

"Highness, the American has come."

Jagat was in his office, a vast square room whose floors, walls, and ceiling were all of white marble. Upon the walls were embossed in gold the portraits of his ancestors. He looked up from the huge ancestral desk which now was his.

"Ask him to enter."

The bearer turned obediently and was stopped at the door.

"Wait," Jagat commanded. "How does he look, this American?"

The bearer turned again to face his master. "Highness, he is young."

"Well?"

"Highness, what can I say? He is a man with two legs, a head, two arms."

"Two eyes, I suppose."

The bearer grinned and wagged his head left and right in assent.

"Very well, tell him to come in," Jagat ordered again.

He turned to his desk but in an instant the door opened and the American came in. He was indeed young, still in his twenties, Jagat surmised, and he had a kind face, alert blue eyes, red hair cut short, a wide smile, the American smile. His right hand was outstretched and ready.

"Are you—what do I call you: Mr. Maharana, or what?"

To that ingenuous western smile Jagat could not refuse response, nor could he ignore the waiting hand. He took it into his own for an instant. It felt young and hard and warm and he dropped it.

"Call me what you like, and sit down, please."

The young man sat down, continuing earnestly. "No, but I mean it. I tried to get your man to tell me what to call you and he wouldn't. Should I say sahib or something?"

"Oh, not sahib," Jagat said, laughing. "That is what we used to call the British."

"Haven't you a family name, sir?"

Jagat reflected. "It's odd, you know," he said at last.

"Family names here aren't the same as with you. We have two principal family names in this state. Like most peoples, we have a legend that we go back to the Sun and the Moon, and so we call ourselves Suryavanshi, or the Race of the Sun, and Chandravanshi, or the Race of the Moon. I am head of the Suryavanshi."

"Then do I call you Mr. Sun?"

"You may call me what you like," Jagat said.

The young man gave a hearty roar of laughter. "So long as I get on with the business!"

"So long as we get on with business."

"Correction sustained. Will you tell me what you have in mind, sir, in making over the lake palace?"

Jagat hesitated. He had not told even Moti of what he had in mind. He had told no one.

"I have in mind to be a businessman," Jagat said at last. He made his tone firm. "One has to do something nowadays, you know, Mr.—do I have your name?"

"Call me Bert," the American said. "My name's Bert Osgood."

Jagat avoided both names gracefully. "As you know, since 1947 we princes have had little more than our titles in this new India. We were absolute rulers in antiquity and very nearly so throughout the British period, but now that we have our own central government we have yielded our thrones—quite voluntarily, on the whole, I must say. I say 'voluntarily' in the sense that we approve the change, with varying degrees of enthusiasm. The Nawab of Bhopal, for example, has found it—well, difficult! Many of us have taken jobs in government and business or the professions. One maharaja makes soft drinks and is piling up money; another raises white tigers for western zoos. They're very rare and are to be found only in his state. I'd thought of conducting tiger hunts for tourists—no, no, I'm joking. Still, I must do something. My income has been cut in half but not my patriarchal duties. I still have palaces and temples to maintain because we have always done it and there's no one else to do it, so I have to conduct religious festivals—and feed hordes of relatives and dependents of all sorts. It's expected, you know. We have all the old responsibilities and obligations to the people, but not the old wherewithal to do it. Well, that's that!"

He paused to examine the fresh young face opposite him and discerning no sign of boredom, but on the contrary a look of absorbed interest, he continued, "My father, had he been alive, would certainly have found it impossible to give up his rulership here. There were about seven hundred rulerships, you know, varying from great states to little holdings of a few acres. Something had to be done, of course, to unify the country after independence. Still, there were tempers and all that. One maharaja actually drew a pistol during the negotiations. But I was in favor of giving up my rulership here. One thing the British did for us, you know, was to give us a sort of umbrella of government. I doubt there'd ever been a united India before they came—or most of the time while they were here. But they left us a united people—barring the Muslim-Hindu situation, of course, but then we could never be religiously united, not really, not in heart and soul, in spite of living side by side in comparative peace. Too many old memores of Muslim conquest—this whole state of mine was under attack three times, major attacks, but the people never yielded, not really. Well, they did, I suppose, in fact but not in spirit. The old fort there beyond those mountains—Chittor it's called—they swore they'd never even visit it until it was theirs again, and it wasn't theirs until after independence. Then of course we had a ceremony and the Prime Minister came and handed it back, symbolically—wonderful place, Chittor Fort! It was the capital of the ancient former state here in my region."

"Could it, too, be made into a hotel?" Bert Osgood asked eagerly.

Jagat laughed. "No, no—it's ruins, mostly. I've had some of it restored—the lovely palace of Padmini, and a few of the buildings."

"It could be a tourist spot," Bert suggested.

"Perhaps." Jagat rose abruptly. "I've talked too much. Let us go and see the palace I have in mind, see if it's possible. I want to make a marble palace into a luxury hotel for Americans—and Europeans, of course. I don't know why I think of Americans first, nowadays. Everyone seems to—"

He led the way through a huge entrance hall, and then through marble corridors and into spacious rooms whose marble floors were strewn with tiger skins and from whose walls the heads of tigers looked down in jungle ferocity. Osgood stared about him.

"Doesn't it give you nightmares to live in the midst of all these wild beasts?"

Jagat laughed. "No, it only brings back memories. This chap here—" He paused beneath a huge and menacing tiger's head. "This one gave my father and me a bad time, I admit. I was very young—it was my first hunt. We were hunting one autumn after the rains stopped in the forests near the Jai Samand lake—lovely lake, man-made for a reservoir, as it happens, by an ancestor of mine. Anyway, there are beautiful islands and small fishing villages and so on. We were in my father's shooting box and the bearers reported one evening that a huge tiger was prowling about in the forest not far away. My father ordered them to beat up the game within shooting distance and we went outside, expecting it would take some time. Well, do you know, the tiger was stalking *me,* if you please! He'd come right up to the box. I saw two gleaming green-gold eyes close to the ground not twenty feet away. He was crouching to spring. I'd hardly time to aim. But I shot him straight in the right eye. Great fun!"

"You call that fun?"

"Oh, yes—one has to have one's wits about one. I like that. It's exciting. I got a taste for it after that. My son goes with me now—only he doesn't enjoy it, I'm sorry to say."

They were walking through the endless halls and passages of the old palace.

"How long is this marble monument?" Osgood asked at last.

"Only a quarter of a mile long," Jagat said cheerfully. "And it's not all marble. The foundation under water is granite—built for eternity. My ancestors couldn't conceive of an age in which our way of life might cease to exist. I confess I too find it difficult to believe even now, at times."

"Everything changes," the American said cheerfully. "Good thing it does, too—good for business."

"I hope to find it so," Jagat said gravely. He led the way to a flight of marble steps leading down to the lake. "Here's the boat house. I keep my motor yacht here."

He ran lightly down the steps to a shelter where the yacht waited. Two boatmen appeared in silence, greeting him with palms pressed together before their faces.

"Mind your head," Jagat told the American. "The ceiling is low."

They sat down. The motor started smoothly and the yacht moved out into the lake.

"My god," Osgood said with reverence, gazing back at the marble palace they had just left. "It makes the White House look like a doll house. And there are hundreds of them, you say?"

"Every maharaja had a palace, probably several," Jagat told him.

"Who paid for them?"

"The people."

"Patient people!"

"I'm glad it's ended. Except for my private wing, the palace is open now to the public. When my father died, I gave it to the city. They don't know what to do with it, exactly—but people come and see it and guides make a little money from tourists."

"It's a grand tourist sight."

They were silent for a while as the yacht cut the calm water cleanly. The sun was high and the lake reflected the blue of heaven. From the distant steps where the city gate led to the water's edge came the rhythmic beat of women washing clothes. They dipped them into the water, laid them upon the stones, and flailed the water out of them with short sticks.

"That's the palace I want to make into a hotel," Jagat said suddenly.

Osgood turned and stared across the lake. There in the center of the blue water stood a gem of white marble. He whistled softly under his breath.

"Man, it's a natural—I can just see it! A folder with pictures: the lake, the palace, and those mountains behind, sand-colored—sort of gold, aren't they? And the dark green trees on the shoreline! Wait—I'm writing the publicity. 'Lake Palace—old-style princely elegance, modern comfort in a setting of unparalleled beauty. Pleasant year-round climate, convenient plane service from Delhi. Road and rail to Ahmedabad and Bombay, Continental and Rajasthani cusine, radio and telephone in every room.' And this lake—boating, fishing, water-skiing, houseboats. There aren't crocodiles, I hope?"

"There are," Jagat confessed.

"We'll shoot 'em," Osgood said with enthusiasm. "There won't be a crocodile by the time we get electricity here."

"The people won't want them shot—they're supposed to bring some sort of luck. They're sacred."

"There won't be luck for anybody if a tourist gets his head bitten off," Osgood retorted. "No—no—forget the crocodiles. Or, say, we could pen them up at one end of the lake and the tourists could feed them. It would be one more activity."

"Here we are," Jagat said, laughing.

The motor died slowly and the boatmen tied a rope to an iron set in the marble post. A long flight of marble steps led to the palace and Jagat mounted them to the triple doors of bronze set in marble and carved as delicately as lace. An old watchman folded his palms as they passed him and entered into a huge marble loggia, beyond which were courtyards overgrown with weeds and bent trees. Fountains stood dry and mute, and birds, startled by their entrance, whirled about their heads.

Osgood exclaimed in excitement. "I can just imagine it all! Fountains playing, indirect lighting, marble cleaned up and shining white—wonderful place to dance—the bar over there."

He walked toward the first courtyard and was stopped by the pattering of the watchman's bare feet behind him and a pull on the tail of his coat, accompanied by an outburst of crackling words in Hindi.

"He says the two old cobras are drinking milk in the

courtyard," Jagat explained. "It is the hour at which they are fed."

Osgood stepped back hastily. "We can't have cobras! They'll have to be cleared out."

Jagat hesitated. "They've been here a long time. They're supposed to bring luck, too."

"They won't bring us any luck," Osgood insisted. "Just let one of 'em bite a tourist and you'll get sued. Have 'em killed." The two men looked at each other.

"I'll have them moved to another island," Jagat said.

"Do you mind if I don't go back with you?" Jagat asked. They had spent the day in the lake palace, their luncheon brought to them from across the water. They had covered sheets of paper with figures and sketches.

"You're not spending the night here, are you, after a day like this?" Osgood exclaimed. "Man, you need a rest."

"I want to think things over and there's no better place than this palace in the middle of the lake. After all, I'm undertaking quite a project, you know. One has to be spiritually ready for such a change—moving the cobras, for a symbol! It's been their palace, too, for centuries."

"Well, if you're financially ready, it's all I ask," Osgood replied. "It will stand you a quarter of a million dollars I should say—a couple of million if you were in the United States, but you don't have inflated labor costs here."

"I shall have to get all sorts of government permissions but I can get them if your firm can guarantee dollar profits," Jagat countered.

"Guarantee! I don't know about that. Americans will have to be persuaded to come to this remote place. But they'll go anywhere, I guess, if they have a good hotel. Nothing's remote if you sleep in a good bed at night and eat good food and have a bar to sit around for a while. Of course you have to have activities—belly dancers and so on. How're your Hindu girls?"

Jagat did not reply. This was an aspect of American human nature of which he had heard but about which he preferred not to think. There was a street of prostitutes in the city of Amarpur where women looked out of their

cages and called invitations to the passersby. They were
not really in cages, but the barred gates gave the illusion
of women imprisoned. He avoided the street, understanding at the same time the reason for its existence. He
avoided reply now.

"The yacht will take you back to shore," he said quietly.
"My car will be waiting for you at the quay. You will have
time to catch the next flight to Bombay—the only flight
each day, as a matter of fact. When we are ready for guests
I have been promised two more daily flights. Don't be
alarmed if the plane seems shaky. It's an old Viscount, but
they keep it quite well patched up. Our record for accidents
is no higher than your jets and not as devastating."

"Thank you, sir," Osgood replied, and recognized the
return of the prince. "I'll have the necessary information in
your hands by the end of the month, down to the last item.
I'm a little worried by one thing—will you have enough
bedrooms to carry the cost? You've kept a lot of space for
the luxury suites."

"Those are the guests I want," Jagat said. "I want all my
luxury suites filled by people who come here because this
will be the finest hotel in the most beautiful country in
the world."

Osgood laughed. "Guard them against mosquitoes,
then!"

"No mosquitoes," Jagat retorted. "The lake is full of
fish. It used to be that they could be caught only for my
ancestors. Now they'll be fed to Americans."

"You're going to be a great success."

The two men shook hands and Jagat stood watching the
yacht as it cut its way through the water, golden under the
light of the setting sun. In the silence a sudden loneliness
fell upon him, a darkness of the spirit. He was at the
threshold of a new life, a new age. Until now he had lived
the sheltered life of his ancestors, sure of wealth, sure of
leisure, accustomed to worship and to power. Now he had
been stripped of power and half his wealth had been taken
from him. Whatever power he could accumulate for the
future must be of his own making, the power of his own

personality, his integrity, his rectitude. For he would not be forgiven if today he pursued the old easy arrogant ways of his ancestors. His grandfather, and his father before him, had only to send for a beautiful girl whom he chanced to see in passing, and she was his. It was a privilege they had taken from the conquering Moguls, who had been so rapacious that Hindu women had learned to cover their faces if they went into the streets. That necessity had passed but the lesson of antiquity remained deep in the hearts and memories of women. Even in Moti, perhaps! She did not cover her head, but her heart was cool, or so he imagined. And she would not say she loved him. In all the years of their marriage she had never put into words her love for him, evading him always with excuses.

"Why do you ask me to say what you already know?" Thus she would reply to his demand.

She would not object, he supposed, to his making the summer palace into a hotel. She never expressed objection to anything he said or did. If she felt inner unwillingness, she withdrew still more deeply into that place of silence where she lived, into which he could never enter. To withdraw was her reply, leaving him always with the sense of being essentially alone. To this he was accustomed, and he had relieved it by physical activity—hunting, usually. There was nothing more absorbing than tiger shooting. But this, this was a new loneliness. They were all suddenly solitary, these princes of whom he was one, these kings without crowns, leaders without portfolio. In the stillness of the marble palace he was aware only of ghosts. Here his father and his grandfather had passed gay summer holidays in a life that was perpetual holiday. Even as a small boy he could remember the vast white spaces alive with girls in brilliant-hued saris, he could hear the echoes of their laughter and their songs. His grandmother and his mother had been tolerant of young creatures who came and went while they themselves remained secure and unchanging. Men must be amused, they believed, and to amuse a man was dreary business for a woman. Let the girls come, and when they went let others come. The old big family life had seemed eternal. Now all was gone. His parents and grandparents were gone, and their way of life had followed them. Weeds were growing in the gardens, the marble walls were gray with mildew and birds nested in the carved ceilings. Only he was left and he must make all things anew.

"Perhaps even myself," he muttered.

When evening came, he was glad to hear the engine of his yacht draw close to take him back to shore. As he stepped aboard, the sun dropped, violent and crimson, into the lake.

Moti looked the length of the dining table to Jagat at the other end. Breakfast she took alone and they seldom met for luncheon, but usually they dined together. She never felt smaller than at the foot of this table. It was of solid teak, one great spread of polished wood, twelve feet long and four feet wide, cut lengthwise three centuries ago from a vast teak tree, so that the wood would not crack or curl. There were no such trees nowdays. Elephants had dragged the last of the great virgin trees from the forests of Aracan. Above the table a vast and intricate chandelier of glass, made in Czechoslovakia and bought by Jagat's grandfather, shed a sparkling downward light into the dining hall. The Goan butler and two footmen served master and mistress and then withdrew behind a great carved screen of ebony inlaid with semiprecious stones, through whose interstices they could watch the table and be ready to appear with dish or drink.

Moti sat in silence, which Jagat now broke.

"And what did you do today?" he inquired as he helped himself to curry from the silver dish the butler was offering.

His voice was kind, his eyes were absent. He bent his head above the plate of rice and curry as he ate. Moti replied, her voice soft and calm.

"I? Nothing, really! I read for a while in the morning. I wrote a letter to Jai. It will be the last until after his holidays. He is coming home next week, you know."

"I have not forgotten. Well, how do you suggest that he occupy his time?"

She considered. "I thought we might ask Father Francis Paul to be a sort of tutor to him. He has been assigned a new mission to one of the hill tribes, but he might get a stay, just for the summer, if it were known that we wish it."

"What will he teach our son, pray?"

"Well, to perfect his English, perhaps."

"Jai speaks very good English."

"His accent is rather Indian, don't you think?"

"He is Indian."

"I know, Jagat, but we have always spoken English with a good Oxford accent. And there are so few opportunities now for us to meet the right sort of British."

She helped herself to milk curds from a crystal dish which the butler offered. When Jagat did not reply and she perceived that he was no longer listening, she continued.

"Veera asked me an odd question today."

He lifted his head, always alert to his daughter's name. "What was that?"

"She asked me if she must marry the man we have chosen for her."

"Does she object to Raj? If so, she is very foolish."

"How can she object when she does not know him?"

"She has seen him."

"That's not quite enough for her, it seems."

Jagat pushed his plate aside. "How can she expect to know a man until she is married to him? Any other knowledge between man and woman is superficial."

"Will you talk to her?"

"Certainly not. It would be most embarrassing."

"Have you ever talked with Jai?"

"About what?"

"Marriage—or even women."

"Why should I? He probably knows more than I do."

"Oh, Jagat, really you can be very tiresome."

But she spoke these words sweetly, half laughing, and he laughed with her. They rose together and walked toward the terrace.

"I speak only from experience, my dear. I never knew anything about women—not really—until I married you.

Any other relationship is nonsense and only skin deep. All my father's relationships were nonsense except his relationship to my mother; that's why I got rid of his harem, at what cost, too—a greedy lot! I could do with that money now. And I haven't told you, have I, but today an American chap came to see me. I met him when I was in Delhi last month. Moti, what would you say if I made the lake palace into a hotel?"

She sank into her accustomed seat with unaccustomed suddenness. "What are you saying, Jagat?"

"My dear, we can't possibly live on our government allotment, especially when we have all these relatives, cousins, and old aunties and uncles who have never worked in their lives and would simply be bewildered if I insisted on it now. And all these palaces to keep up, besides! I thought I'd begin with the one in the lake and if it's a success, I could do something with the others— after all, Amarpur is one of the most beautiful places in the world. Well, I met this American when I was in Delhi last month—he belongs to one of the great hotel chains and is contemplating a hotel in Bombay. I forgot him, of course, until the idea came to me of making a hotel myself, and then I remembered he'd given me a card, so I telephoned him and he came in from Bombay on the early plane. We spent the day at the lake palace looking at everything. He thinks something can be made of it and he's to send me estimates and plans."

She was silent for a moment, then spoke. "I'm not sure I shall like strangers about."

"Why not? You have simply to be yourself. They'll be charmed to meet a real Maharani of Amarpur."

"You mean I'll be one of the sights?"

"I mean you are to be exactly what you are, my dear —that distinguished lady, the Maharani of Amarpur."

They were interrupted by the butler bringing wine, the *gulah* wine distilled from the wild rose petals of Haldighati. His face was closed and calm, but he had heard. What would it mean if foreigners came flooding into Amarpur? He moved about the terrace, his face impassive, his sandaled feet silent and smooth. Then with palms pressed together he left the presence of his master to enter his own private world, the world of J. Rodriguez, of Goa.

He had married a young Goan girl many years before, Inez, a girl of his own caste, and she had died only a year later at the birth of their first child, the child dead with her. Whether it was personal sorrow or anger at his Portuguese employer that compelled him to leave the narrow enclave of Goa he did not know, and perhaps it was something of both. At any rate, he had left the ship's chandlery shop where he had first found employment after he left the Catholic school where his parents had educated him. It had been a sudden action, the result of an accumulation of small insults by the fat Portuguese shopkeeper who drank too much and harried too many Indian girls. During Rodriguez' service there he had ordered his own sister never to come to the shop even to bring a message from their aging parents or from Inez.

"This fat man is a pig," he had told Inez.

It might have been easier for him had he not been to school and learned too much about the past, about which nothing can be done in the present. Thus he had read in history books how it came to be that even when the British left India to herself and independence, the Portuguese did not leave Goa. It all grew out of a quarrel between two European nations, it seemed, Spain and Portugal, and hundreds of years ago. For Columbus, the fool, thought that he had found the Indies, when all he had found was a small island on the other side of the world, and this mistake excited the Europeans and especially those two nations, Spain and Portugal, and Portugal was jealous of Spain and set out to find her own way to India, the lands of jewels and spice. Meanwhile the Pope, fearing a war between the contending nations, divided the world, except Europe, in two parts, and the year after Columbus landed on his island, this Pope drew a line of his own imagining north and south a hundred leagues west of the Azores, and announced by a papal bull that the Portuguese were to have all the heathen—that was to

say, the non-Christian—lands east of this line and Spain
was to have all the lands west of it.

In this way, Goa had been established, a foothold upon
the coast of vast India, but a foothold that Portugal
refused to remove until the great and good Prime Minister
Nehru forced it off. On the day that Goa was freed and
brought back into India, where she belonged, Rodriguez
had declared his own independence by eating meat on
Friday and resolving never again to make confession to
any priest. It was difficult for him to keep this decision
secret, especially when Father Francis Paul visited the
palace, but he managed to serve the English priest with
his usual calm detachment. He had been in India for thirty
years by this time, serving the Maharana of Amarpur for
twenty of those years; he had left Goa on the day that the
Portuguese had called him Indian swine because he had
refused to carry a message to a young girl whom the
Portuguese wished to entice into being his mistress. He
had left Goa that same night, and by foot he had traveled
to Bombay and had taken service with a Parsi family,
from which place he had been lured by the old Maharana, who fancied the way he prepared lamb curry. Twenty
years ago he had come to Amarpur and to this palace
and now only the gods could know what was about to
happen. He disapproved strongly but secretly of the action
taken in Delhi against the princes and so long as he lived
he would continue to revere the Maharana. The gods
create the great as well as the small, and who is man
that he should defy the gods by declaring all men equal?

"Nevertheless," he told the servants as they sat ringed
about him that evening, squatting so that their buttocks
hung from their knees without touching the ground,
"nevertheless, what can I say when our own master says
he will open the lake palace to any foreigner who can pay?
At least it is the lake palace and not the island palace
where the mighty Shah Jehan spent his years of exile and
where in a dream he planned the noble Taj Mahal in
memory of his faithful wife who had died as she gave
birth to his fourteenth child. I tell you we should not
allow the foreigners to enter. Five hundred years ago, the

Portuguese bit Goa out of India's westward thigh and for centuries clung there like leeches, sucking our blood, however we tried to pluck them out. The earliest one, named Albuquerque—hateful his memory—was called Viceroy of the East and he killed how many thousands of our people, not sparing women or children! I tell you they come as tradesmen, these foreigners, and they stay to rule. No, no, His Highness, our Maharana, is inviting the devil to come again into our heaven."

He sighed heavily and then observing the new moon rising over the palace, thin and pale, empty as a bowl, he said abruptly that he was tired and would go to bed, his lonely bed, for he had never married again.

Veera was wandering in the rose gardens. She was restless, the school holiday was too long, yet she did not wish to return to school. She missed her schoolmates yet she felt impatient with them. Three months from now she would be a married woman. In two months she would have her diploma and then there would be a month of preparation, the buying of saris from Karachi and Benares, the jewels and furniture and all that makes a marriage. She wanted to be married and she did not. Sleeping and waking, she dreamed of Raj, the handsome young man from Bombay, and was afraid of him. He was the son of the Maharaja of Limbdi, but he cared nothing for being a prince. Instead he laughed at his own father and she had thought it bold and amusing of him, the only time they had met, but now she was not sure that she liked it.

"My father wears homespun suits instead of satin nowadays, for the sake of the new economy," he told Veera, "but the buttons are of huge diamonds, as usual. It would not occur to him that buttons are not necessarily jewels. You know what a friend calls our princes? He's a writer chap. He calls them 'bejeweled, breathing fossils of feudalism.' "

"My father is not that," she had retorted.

"Oh, well, your father," Raj had granted. "He's been in England. England changes everyone, especially Indians. We're never the same afterwards. I'm not, myself. You'd never have wanted to see me if you'd known me as I was before I went to school in England. I was awful, really. Why, I even wore a dhoti!"

Veera had laughed "How do you know I want to see you now?"

He had looked solemn for a moment—his cheerful face for the first time without a smile.

"I say, I hope you don't mean anything by that. I think you are beautiful, you know. And of course, it's a good thing that the princes have joined the nation. A friend of mine whose father used to have ninety-nine elephants as a matter of course has given them all up except three he's especially fond of. And another friend's father, a Nizam, was said to have taken two hundred concubines with him when he visited a neighboring prince for one night. He said the ladies didn't get out much. Well, they don't get out at all now."

It was impossible not to join his laughter. Remembering it, Veera laughed again, but softly. There was something lovable about Raj, yet could she ever be in love with him? But did she want to be in love? The girls at school talked a great deal about love, they studied old Hollywood magazines and dreamed over the love lives of western beauties, but these were only dreams. Such love did not exist in India, perhaps. Yet love could be a sorrow and a burden as well as joy. Suppose she loved Raj someday and he did not love her? The thought was insupportable. She would drown herself then in the lake. She leaned pensively on the deep windowsill and gazed down into the sunlit water lapping against the granite wall of the palace foundations. It would take courage to kill herself. She was not as brave as Padmini of old had been, that lovely lady of Chittor, who when the enemy Moguls came to conquer, assembled her ladies and with them descended into the cellars of her marble palace, there to build fires into which they threw themselves. She had visited the palace often, for her father loved the ancient fort of Chittor with its towers of victory and its ruined walls. She had even wished to descend to the chamber of immolation, and was stopped by caretaker, guard, and guide.

"It is not safe," they insisted. "It is becoming a place of death, inhabited now only by cobras and the ghosts of the dead ladies. They are equally dangerous."

Why, she mused, was the ghost of a lovely lady dangerous? And had Padmini led her ladies to death for love's sake or pride's sake? Impossible, of course, to yield one's person to a man one did not love, an enemy! Yet if she, Veera, did not learn to love Raj, was this not what she would be compelled to do? What exactly was this yielding of the person? Girls spoke of it in whispers, with fear and awe and a strange sort of longing. How could one long for that which one feared? Except that one did!

At this moment her father's yacht came puffing out of its shelter beneath the palace. She leaned far out of the window and saw a foreign man and her father descend the marble steps and board the yacht. Then the boatman headed the vessel toward the lake palace, the water dividing into two silver-edged lines of rippling water. Her father was entertaining a foreign friend today, but for what purpose? As for that, what purpose had her mother in making a friend of Father Francis Paul? Was there something fascinating about western men? A few of the Bombay girls liked foreign men, too. She left a longing for school again, for someone to whom she could talk. It was only with her own age group that she could really talk. With parents she had always to be quiet and yielding and graceful. The pain in her breast was perhaps only loneliness for her school home, although when she was in that high mountain fastness where the British in days of empire had sent their children out of the damp and torrid heat of the plains, she became equally lonely for her palace home and these two rooms of hers, where she lived most of the time when she was here, with no one except her old ayah who had taken care of her since she was born. If she were still lonely after she was married, then really there was no cure for loneliness. And was her mother always lonely? If not, then why did she spend so much time with Father Paul? It was a question not to be answered, like so many other questions to which there were no answers. Or was it only women who found no answers to their questions?

A flock of pigeons, hundreds of them, flew from under the roofs and out of the turrets of the palace. They soared upward in a living cloud, circled in widening waves of flying wings and settled into the palace turrets and cornices again. There they had lived for centuries and there they would continue to live.

The door opened and her old ayah came in. "My little one," she exclaimed. "Why are you leaning so far outside the window? Some man looking up might see you."

Veera drew back and threw herself on the cushions piled on the crimson carpet.

"What is a wife?" she asked.

The old woman peered at her from under shriveled lids. "A wife, little one? A wife is what a man comes back to. He wanders—oh yes, it is to be expected that he wanders —but she must not upbraid him. She must only say in a gentle small voice, 'Darling, how have I failed you?' Since she is a good wife, he will be angry at himself, and so he will speak angrily to her. 'Shut up,' he will shout. 'Don't say anything.' But when he has had his affair and he is finished with the other woman, he will come back to his wife and he will ask her forgiveness."

"And will she forgive him?" Veera inquired, intently listening.

"She will forgive him," the old woman declared. "She will say, 'Darling, I love you, I will always love you.' This is her duty."

"But will he love her?" Veera persisted.

The old woman deliberated for a long moment.

"He will respect her," she said at last.

Young woman and old looked at each other, the one with doubt, the other with pity. Then the old ayah knelt beside her mistress and caressed her slender soft hand.

"Little one, your husband will love you. He has such virility. And you are pretty as a rose of Kashmir."

"How do you know Raj is virile?" Veera inquired.

The old woman came closer. "Have you not seen his

ears? He has a frill of black hair on each ear—as long as that!"

And she measured an inch on her bent thumb.

Far away in the desert hills, in his three-room house, Father Francis Paul was reading his mail. The door was open, and the wind blew fine sand in a shallow drift across the floor. The desert was on the march again now that summer was here, borne on the power of the wind across the eighty thousand square miles from the great Rann of Cutch to the valley of the Sutlej. For hundreds of years the Rajputana desert had been on the march, "choking the right lung of India with salt and sand," the old Maharana had said bitterly. Today's wind from the northeast was still mild in comparison to the high and steady gales that in summer and monsoon seasons would carry vast burdens of dust across the wide northwest. Father Francis Paul put down his mother's letter and gazed at the desert framed by the open door. His mind's eye saw his mother in the sitting room at her desk in Rickford Castle, the rose-scented air stirring her short white curls. Across the lawns the noble forests stood green against the English sky. They had been his childhood joy, his favorite place for dream and adventure, and now more valuable than ever in his memory. How could he impress upon the Maharana the treasure a forest could be? Here the mountain growth was merely part of the village communal estate, to be used as fuel and fodder. Last year he had visited the hill stations and had discovered that even the majestic eucalyptus trees of Nilgiri and Mount Abu were being cut.

He sighed and put away the letter. He would make it a matter for prayer. The small bare room in which he sat would have been unendurable this morning were it not that the wind, still dawn-cooled, had risen with the sun. It would last only a few hours. By noon the air would not stir and a pall of fine sand, roused anew by the padding feet of camels, would hang under the sky. The camels—someday he must make a study of those travelers upon this landscape, beasts as unchanging as monuments, native through centuries, each camel ancient, whatever its age. He had spent much time involuntarily, it is true, studying their curious shape. Waiting for the ramshackle bus to carry him from a stay in the palace to the hills where he now lived, he gazed at the camels as they passed in long, slow procession or rested while their drivers stopped for bottled soda water and curried rice. The camel frame was unique, a skeleton built like the hull of a ship but resting on four angular legs ending in enormous pads of feet, the fetlocks a clever shock-proof device that served equally well for soft desert sand or rocky paths through the hills. The low-swung neck balanced the high, humped back, and at the end of the neck sat the small melancholy head, the mouth loose, the lower lip mobile and hanging, the eyes heavy-lidded and sad. From these eyes a strange camel soul peered out at a world it did not care to understand, and which it could accept only to a degree. Were the camel too heavily loaded, or were its feelings hurt by some indifference on the part of its driver, the beast was capable of lowering itself gently to the earth and remaining there immobile in protest until it died. Yet camels were not all soul and gentleness. In sudden wrath a camel could blow out its foul breath at the offender, until a man fainted with the stench. And only yesterday, although Father Francis Paul would have said he knew all about camels, he had seen a camel make a strange performance. Inside its enormous bulk a deep roaring grumble had echoed like thunder in distant mountains to issue at last through who knew what tubes and channels to the throat and then to the mouth, from whence there appeared a pink balloon of membrane two feet in diameter. He had been aghast.

"What is that?" he had asked the Bhil camel driver squatting half asleep in the dust after food and drink.

The Bhil had yawned and scratched his head. "Who knows? It is his private amusement."

So it seemed to be. He watched while the camel, its mighty belch erupted, withdrew the membrane again into its mouth. This ancient land, he reflected, this India, was rich in surprises, large and small. No day was empty of new sights and sounds and smells. Now at this very moment, for example, as he sat between open window and door, facing the village street, without turning his head he saw this daily scene changing as continuously as pictures upon a film screen. A small nearly naked girl, dark-skinned and with tousled hair, was balancing upon her head a brass pot brimming with water which she had just drawn from the village well. In an open doorway a young mother held her baby, sheltering it in the crook of her left arm while it suckled at her breast. A ragged bearded old man led three small dusty monkeys on a string across the street. Above his head among the rooftops and the branching neem trees a crowd of gray wild monkeys chattered, looking down at the captive three in obvious curiosity and pity at their plight, while a deer, tied to a post by a doorway, turned its head to watch. At the end of the street a crane, feeding at the edge of a marshy pond, spread its immense wings and rose in slow majesty to escape the village din.

Father Francis Paul recalled himself abruptly. It was all too easy to become absorbed in the world outside his door, but today he had no time. He had promised to be at the palace for dinner to celebrate the fortieth birthday of His Highness, the Maharana. The bus left its station at two o'clock and he had barely time to take his usual light lunch of curried rice and curds. True, food would not be served until shortly before midnight, but he knew the royal family and especially the Maharani would be expecting him soon after sundown. His lips twitched in a reminiscent smile. The first time he had been invited to dine at the palace he had not known that conversation would continue for hours and the meal not be served until eleven o'clock, after which he would be expected to retire promptly. It was the usual custom of India, as he now knew, but then he had sat half starved, waiting. Now knowing, he enjoyed the long preliminary evening leading to the climax of dinner, and after the full meal, departure for sleep.

Indeed, celibate and ascetic though he was, Father Francis Paul enjoyed the luxury of the palace. That evening he was met as usual by the turbaned bearer at the door and escorted to his rooms in the west wing. The Maharana often insisted that he stay the night, and in a sense this spacious bedroom, with its private sitting room opening to the western sky and the white marble palace in the lake, had become a haven for his spirit. Each time, in anticipation, he prayed that it was not a sin to enjoy beauty so deeply, and he continued to enjoy.

"Does Holy Father wish anything to drink?" the bearer inquired.

"Nothing, thank you," Father Francis Paul replied.

"Nor to eat?"

"Only the fruit on the table yonder, thank you."

"His Highness bids me to ask Holy Father's forgiveness because he will be late this evening, but Her Highness will be waiting as usual for Holy Father on the western terrace at eight o'clock."

"Thank Her Highness and say I shall be there."

"Meantime, bath is drawn for Holy Father."

"Thank you."

The bearer made pranam, his hands folded palm to palm, and touching his forehead before he went away, he closed the door softly behind him. Father Francis Paul went to the window and stood in meditation, his fingers on his rosary. Such beauty was God's free gift, and surely not to be found in greater abundance than here in Rajasthan. It was a desert beauty, the lake a glittering blue by day, and now a mirage of blending colors through which the setting sun made a bold path of ruddy gold. The white palace was reflected in pale gold and beyond it the dark green of the farther shore made a firm base for the mountains of Aravalli, bare and rocky but misted now in pale rose. In the gardens of the palace the mango trees stood massed and black. The royal palace was the heart of history here in this small city, not an old city as India goes, founded only in the sixteenth century in the ancient state of Mewar, and yet how much life had been lived here, and was yet to be lived! He was reminded that tonight he must ask the Maharana about the smaller island palace a mile or so to the left, where Shah Jehan had been imprisoned for some years—how many years?—while he dreamed of the tomb at Agra for his loved wife. Was it older than the larger lake palace?

It was at this moment that Father Francis Paul made a

decision which he had resisted for at least five years. It concerned the writing of a history of Rajasthan, this region where so much of India's history and legend were woven about the lives of heroes, among them Rana Sanga, ruler of Mewar in the sixteenth century, who fought the Muslim invader, the Mogul Emperor Baber, and died with eighty-one wounds in his body. Rana Sanga, the willful and beautiful, the lord of lords, who, defeating his enemy, the king of neighboring Malwa, had then, with his habitual careless grace, freed that captive king, and with an armful of flowers had returned to him half his lost kingdom! And those mountains, now fading into violet night, were still dotted with the forts and battlements of the beloved Rana Pratap, who had so long defied the great Mogul Akbar through years of stubborn rebellion. After the great fort at Chittor was lost—ah, that day of loss before this marble city was founded, when Chittor was the capital, and the royal forces were compelled to surrender to the invader, that day when the fort was three times sacked by the Moguls, and Rajput men went out in saffron robes, to die fighting while their women, three thousand in number, flung themselves into fire, preferring death to the dishonor of yielding themselves to the victorious enemy!

Father Francis Paul, dreaming, had sunk down upon the cushioned seat underneath the open windows. Now hastily he recalled himself and looked at his watch. He had little more than half an hour before he must meet the Maharani, and by now his bath was cold, doubtless. No, not quite—the day had been hot and the water in the vast marble tub was only pleasantly cool when a few minutes later he stepped into it. He allowed himself a brief luxury, for his usual bath was no more than water poured over himself from an earthen jar in the corner of a small bare room in his house. Now he was submerged to his shoulders in clear, soft water, so clear in fact that he was somewhat embarrassed by his own nakedness, his long legs white and thin and his feet surprisingly large. He was not accustomed to his own bare maleness, and he rose dripping out of the tub. Tonight he put on his white robes, freshly washed in the brook that ran near his house by an old woman who came twice a week to tend his garments, this in itself a luxury, he sometimes feared, but it would not have done for him to deal with such matters himself in India. Since he was a lone missionary priest and had no fellowship with others like himself, he had a man to look after his kitchen and three rooms and hoped that he was not living in ease as a priest should not. To beware, he had always been careful to eat the simplest food and, in deference to his Hindu parishioners, to eat no meat. Nevertheless, he reminded himself severely now as he combed his beard that he must not take advantage of the Maharana's liberal mind. Meat would be served tonight, as it always was, and the Maharana would eat with healthy appetite, as he always did, while the Maharani, who ate no meat, took her usual vegetable meal. It was ten minutes to eight when he was ready in his fresh white robes, his rosary about his neck. He took a last look at the darkening sky. There would be no moon until later, and then they would watch it rise from the terrace. Even now the Maharani was waiting for him. How delightful this life! He hoped such enjoyment was not a sin.

When he entered the open doors of carved teakwood she did not rise from her chair. She waited for him, immobile while he came near. How handsome he was, she thought, graceful and yet strong, his dark beard clipped to a point, his dark hair smooth, his skin fair. There was something striking about blue eyes—one saw them in Kashmir, of course, but in an English face they held power. She missed the English. In spite of approving independence one did miss them, somehow. It was a pity so many of them had refused to stay in India. She had grown up in Bombay and had made friends of English girls when she went to school with them. Father Francis Paul was before her now and he stooped to take her hand. Sometimes he even kissed it, and he did so tonight. She felt the soft brush of his beard upon her hand before she withdrew it, lingering a few seconds.

"How are you?" she murmured. It was increasingly difficult for her to call him Father. They were almost of an age, he and she, at least she so supposed, for she had not asked

him and now did not want to know. If she were a few years
his senior, she did not want to know.

"Sit down, please," she said in her soft voice.

He sat down near her. "I never saw a finer sunset," he
said.

She had forbidden him to say Your Highness to her. "Do
not," she had begged. "It makes such a distance between
us."

"Yes," she said with seeming indifference, "the sunsets
are very fine at this time of year."

Such emotion filled her breast that it was difficult for
her to speak. Her unutterable loneliness, her longing to
love someone, really to love someone before she grew too
old, her need to be near some human being were well nigh
unbearable. Yet since all in life must be borne she spoke
the more calmly.

"His Highness is sorry to be late."

"I suppose His Highness is very much occupied now
with this new scheme of the hotel. We have heard of it
even in our mountains."

She lifted a newspaper from the small marble table at
her side. "He is also busy just now at this—"

He took the paper and saw the bold headlines. MAGNIFI-
CENT MAHARANA OF MEWAR.

"Read on," she commanded.

It was the sports page of *The New Delhi Times,* and he
read on. "The Premier Prince of India continues his
prowess at the royal game of cricket. At the head of his
own Amarpur team he has made ninety-seven runs off a
crack New Delhi team. It is to be remembered that he
once led his team at Cambridge and represented his
country there. This he might have continued to do, except
for the war. Now he leads his state, the land of kings, no
longer on the red field of battle but on the green cricket
pitch."

Father Francis Paul returned the paper, smiling. "His
Highness is as young as ever, and I am glad to see him so.
He looked particularly fit when I last saw him. I admire
him more than I can say. I daresay there are not many

princes who would have chosen classical music to dancing
girls upon the occasion of his last birthday dinner."

She replied with the same soft indifference. "Jagat is
very English in some ways. And tonight we are dining
quietly."

"Has he shot any tigers lately?"

"Yes, quite a big one, he tells me. I wouldn't look at it.
You know how little I like that sort of thing. He took Jai
with him against my wishes. I do so dislike killing things,
even tigers. I'm glad Jai didn't kill anything. Jagat speaks
of hunting in Sikkim before the snow falls."

He knew her moods so well that he could discern the
inner restlessness behind the controlled composure. "Why
are you sad?" he asked quietly.

She resisted him, as she always did. He penetrated her
too easily. She longed for his understanding and dreaded it.
Alone she reminded herself always that he was a priest and
it was his duty to care for souls. Yet it was distasteful to
be thought of as a soul, especially as one among many
souls, most of them only the mountain Bhils among whom
he lived.

"You like to hide yourself from me," he went on. "You
would have me pursue you like the Hound of Heaven and
coax you. Very well, I will do so."

She wished to deny this hotly, but she could only turn
her face away so that all he could see was her pale Kashmiri profile outlined against the sky. Some men, he
supposed, would not call her beautiful, since she had not
the sultry charm of the usual Indian woman. But to him
she was very beautiful, her delicacy, her pallor, her
melancholy, all in all an invitation he could not have
resisted except that long ago he had learned to control the
impulse of the flesh. He wondered now if the impulses of
the spirit and the mind separated from the flesh were not
the stronger for their subtlety.

"How are those Bhils of yours?" she asked suddenly.
"How you can continue living with them I do not know—
a man of your learning and family!"

"Perhaps those very facts make the Bhils the more
interesting to me. No, it's their need that attracts me as a

priest. Indians like you have access to the world, but the Bhils live as they did hundreds of years ago."

"I have access to the world?" she repeated. "Locked in this palace?"

"You speak English, French, German—and I don't know what else. Nothing locks your mind here."

She did not reply, and gazing at her pale profile, he went on.

"Have you ever talked with a Bhil?"

"What would I have to say to a Bhil?" She did not turn her head.

He did not reply directly. Instead after a moment of silence he began to speak as if to himself. "They do not seem strange to me, those hillfolk. In some ways they make me think of Highlanders of Scotland, my own people, with all our small clans. Bhils don't marry within their clans, either, and they've the same resourcefulness, too, as we have, in small practical ways, though they look so different."

She turned her head now to glance at him. "The Bhils are certainly not beautiful. They're almost black and their noses are thick and broad and they are hairy, like animals."

He ignored this. "Yesterday I went to a small chapel I opened about a month ago in a distant village. The road winds hither and yon among the hills, and I still take my Bhil guide with me, though I've been there many times. We stopped to rest, and of course the guide wanted a smoke. He was proud of having a few matches, but he wasn't skillful with them and he used them up. He was quite calm about it, however. He took a piece of tow from the fold in his loincloth, one end of it set inside a hollow bone for a handle. Then he picked up a couple of bits of that marble of which our hills are made, you know, and he struck them together and caught the sparks in the tow. He blew hard upon it and in a moment had a flame. Alas, he next found he'd forgotten his pipe. But it was quite all right. He broke off a twig from a bush and thrust it into the ground and dug out a small hollow. Into it, as into a bowl, he pressed his tobacco and set his flame to it. He covered the tobacco with earth, drew out the twig and curved his hand about the hole and sucked in the smoke as well as though he had a pipe. I could not but admire him."

She laughed. "You and your Bhils! Confess that you love them."

"Of course I do. At least I love their souls."

"Well, I don't love them. I don't like black hairy people who wear nothing but a loincloth and a piece of dirty white cotton cloth about their shoulders even when it's cold."

"Ah, my friend, don't say you are prejudiced against a people because of their caste!"

"Why not, when I am? Still, that is not to say that I wish them harm. Let them keep to their villages and I will keep to my palace."

Unknown to them, Jagat, having washed and put on a fresh white suit, had come to the door. He stood there, not wishing to break into their conversation. Now he came forward.

"Moti, I have never heard you speak so. Don't believe her, Father! She is merely being moody. She knows very well that by law caste no longer exists."

He sat down, opened his jeweled case and lit a cigarette, his every movement quick and sure, and continued in his usual firm fashion. "I myself have a very high respect for our Bhils. I don't forget they were here before my own ancestors were. As a matter of face, we Rajputs still recognize their priority. It's become a form, of course, but we take permission from them when we buy land, a token gesture and all that, since we are no longer in power, but tradition holds."

"Jagat likes the Bhils because they are savage hunters," Moti said.

"They are fine hunters," Jagat agreed, "but not savage."

"All hunters are savage," Moti argued.

"Oh, come now, Moti," Jagat retorted. "The Bhils hunt to eat. Most extraordinary, you know, Father, the way they disappear into the landscape! I was on my way to one of my shooting boxes a few weeks ago—in your territory, by the way—and I heard a man's voice call a greeting. I looked about and saw no one until a bit of the landscape seemed to move and I saw one of my own Bhil runners. But before he moved I could not see him. His dark skin and homespun dhoti simply lost him against the desert hills.

"And something very interesting—he was hunting for a lion he swore he'd seen. Very rare, if true! One doesn't see them—not in a lifetime. They're not native here, you know. When the Muslim invaded India ages ago they brought African slaves, who brought lion cubs with them. These cubs stayed here in Rajasthan and begat their kind, of course. There are some to be seen in Jungadh, where there's a game preserve, but I never saw one in the wild, nor do I believe my Bhil had seen one. Anyway, I soon lost him in the thorn bushes—simply couldn't see him!"

"The women can surely be seen," Moti said with a slight malice.

Jagat laughed. "Undoubtedly! That is why they wear bright blue skirts and red shawls and clattering anklets and bracelets—a cheerful lot they are, independent, too."

Moti drew her white silk sari about her shoulders. "A dirty lot! I simply won't have a Bhil woman in the palace. And you may call it independence. I say they are unteachable."

Father Francis Paul intervened peaceably. "Ah, I hope you are wrong. I hope to make good Christians of the women so that they will help me make Christians of their men."

Jagat made his ready laughter. "You Englishmen, you never give up hope! Why not leave the innocent Bhils to be happy in their villages? Let them enjoy their heathen ways! They believe in some sort of god whom they call Mountain Father; they worship their ancestors in a vague sort of way, and snakes, too, I believe. They even accept some of our Hindu gods, don't they? I have seen Ganesh's elephant head here and there among the hills and sometimes a hint of Siva. And they reverence our Hindu Trinity."

"I hope they will not accept Hinduism, Your Highness,"

Father Francis Paul said bluntly. "Left to themselves my hillfolk are free and independent and honest. But when they come under Hindu influence they doubt their own souls. Your people despise them and the Bhils feel it. And let me take this opportunity to say what I have wanted to say this long time. Pray take it kindly, Your Highness, but I must protest that your under-officers are not always just to the Bhils. Your men demand grass and firewood far beyond what is right, and while I admire your zeal in building the new dam, I wonder if you know that Bhils are doing forced labor on it."

"No, I do not know it," Jagat said. "If it is true, I will see that they are paid."

Moti shivered in the night air, now growing chill. "Must you have the dam, Jagat?"

"Yes, I must," Jagat said. "How else shall I get power for electricity in my lake palace?"

Father Francis Paul intervened again, not so peaceably. "Then let me tell you now, as a discourteous guest, that it is no wonder when a Bhil takes revenge by thievery and even by an occasional murder. While you build your palace hotel to honor millionaires from the West, the Bhil country remains as undeveloped as in the dawn of its history. There are no roads, no schools, no hospitals, no irrigation for the fields. Your men use the Bhils when they can be useful, that is all. And the Bhil villages are worse than those of the Hindus, although their very structure shows the independent spirit of the mountain people —the houses not crowded together as they are in the Hindu villages but each house, though made of mud or rough stones and mud, and roofed with jungle grass, set upon its own low mound and surrounded by thornbush."

For a moment Jagat was tempted to reply with anger. Instead he rose, crushing his cigarette in a gold ashtray on a small marble table at his side.

"I agree with you, Father," he said lightly. "Now let us dine. You look as hungry as a sadhu. But then you always have a lean and hungry look, you priests."

He led the way, as was his right, and after him Father Francis Paul waited for the Maharani and then followed.

At the table however, after the Goan butler had served the first dishes, Jagat returned to the Bhils.

"You know, Father, I do not at all feel as my wife does about our primitive peoples. If for nothing else, I repeat that I admire the Bhils as keen sportsmen."

Father Francis Paul smiled, eager to meet his host's mood.

"How do you define a sportsman, Your Highness?"

"A sportsman"—Jagat was thoughtful, considering the sport of kings—"is one who kills not only for food but, first of all, for the joy of the hunt. Ours is not a great game country, as you know, and that is why sometimes I have gone elsewhere in India when I wanted the best game. But we do have tigers, and for tiger hunting I find that Bhils are the best beaters. They can smell a tiger far away, and see it when it is invisible even to a hunter as experienced as myself."

"They kill the tigers for their skins," Moti argued.

"Granted," Jagat said. "But so do I. Skins and heads, too, and if they are fine specimens, like those two at the door, I have them stuffed and mounted."

"Love my Bhils for any reason you like," Father Francis Paul replied, "but allow me to love them as human beings with souls."

Jagat sat back in his chair, his head back. "Come, come, you are accusing me of not believing they have souls! Of course they have, not quite of the same texture as yours or mine, perhaps, a bit simpler in the grain, you know, but souls all right. I'm not sure they'll be accepted in your British heaven, but I daresay we Indians will put up with them in our heaven as we do here on earth, and they'll be more comfortable with us than with you."

Moti interrupted. "Jagat, I wish you wouldn't be irreverent."

"I shan't argue with Your Highness," Father Francis Paul said. "But then I have the advantage of you. I pray for you every morning."

Jagat laughed. "Do you indeed? Kneeling, I daresay on the bare earth! I must give you a tiger skin for a prayer rug, to spare your poor knees. I shouldn't want you to shorten your prayers for me."

He rose as he spoke, the meal concluded, and led the way to the terrace again. The young moon was silver pale in the sultry darkness of the sky, but lanterns hung in the branches of the great neem tree, and coffee was waiting on a garden table. A turbaned manservant poured and another placed the delicate English porcelain cups on small side tables. From afar a wailing music rose and fell in the soft night air and a gentle wind wafted the scent of tuberoses from the garden, their heavy sweetness made delicate by distance.

For a few minutes no one spoke. Moti, often silent, sat wrapped in the soft white folds of her sari, and Father Francis Paul did not speak as he sipped the strong black coffee. Suddenly Jagat began to talk, half musing, half in soliloquy, with brief apology.

"I say, I must bore you, but you're the only Englishman about nowadays, Father, and I can't talk to Americans in quite the same way. There's one here now, a foreigner who really doesn't know the least thing about India, history or anything. At least you English share centuries with us even though we were on the opposite sides of the road, in a manner of speaking. Yet we princes were on your side, you know. My old father could not believe to the day of his death that things must change and I'm glad they didn't while he lived. He could never have changed. The talks started in the last year before he died, but I'd begun to act for him, and I never told him. He sat there, as he always did, on piles of satin cushions—he couldn't sit on a chair without tucking his feet up—and under the cushions the wall-to-wall carpet of tiger skins—seventy-one tigers, and he had shot them all and had the skins sewed together and in each corner was a huge mounted head. He was proud of that room, and I never told him that I'd shot a hundred and one tigers—a hundred and eleven now. No, he'd never have lived through the change and if I'd told him that I was making his summer palace in the lake into a hotel, well, he would have had me punished somehow, whatever my age. He had his cruel side. Once I saw a Bhil beaten, at his orders, until his black skin fell away in strips and showed the red underneath. The wretched chap looked like some sort of human zebra. I've never forgotten. But I miss my old father. And I'm sure even the Bhils miss him—in spite of everything. There's no one to dance for now. Though I suppose the tourists would enjoy the old folk dances. Yes, that's an idea. D'you know, Father, it's no small task to change the palace into a hotel. It's symbolic of the profound change in my life. I used to run about those marble corridors as a child—I can still remember how cool the floors felt to my bare feet. And the fishing—our people won't like other people fishing in the sacred lake, but they must get used to it. I'm planning to put a swimming pool and tennis courts on the next island, and make the palace where Shah Jehan lived into a ballroom and amusement place. It will take most of my capital but Osgood swears it will pay. I suppose so— at any rate it gives me something to do. That's the damnable part of not being the ruler anymore. There's nothing to do. Of course the village panchayat elders come to me still when there's a problem somewhere. But I know I can't do more than advise and someday they will know, too—if they don't know now, pretending, perhaps!"

"I am sure they are not pretending," Father Francis Paul said, "and I am sure you can help them. Their whole experience is of looking up to someone—it's not easy suddenly to begin functioning on one's own and it will take time."

"That's true of the individual man. I was restless enough under my father's command, and yet when he died very suddenly one day—of eating too much in the heat, poor old man—I felt terrified, even though I had been acting for him for three years and more and half the time didn't even tell him of what was going on. What was the use? He was living in another era. Still, it was a shock when I knew I'd never see him sitting there on his cushions again."

Moti spoke out of the shadows of the neem tree. "I miss him every day."

"Ah yes, you were always his favorite, Moti. In a way you're somewhere between the eras, I suppose. Father

Francis Paul, what do you think of a woman who won't
go to America when I offer her the opportunity?"

"America?"

"I shall have to be going there one day to study the
hotels, at least in New York. Osgood tells me of such
extraordinary things that I can scarcely believe him. I shall
want to see for myself, if I can persuade the government
to give me the permission to leave—the dollar is far too
precious, alas, but if I can prove that my hotels—yes,
there'll be many of them before I am through—will bring
a harvest of dollars, they will let me go. I might take my
son with me."

"Oh, no!" It was a cry from Moti.

"Oh, yes," Jagat retorted. "I know he's supposed to be
going to Oxford in the autumn if he passes his exams
properly, but it might serve us better if he goes, say, to
Harvard."

"I don't know any Americans," Moti murmured. She
shivered slightly and drew the end of her white sari over
her head like a scarf.

But Jagat was gazing up at the moon, his hands clasped
behind his head. "Ah, you'll have to get to know them, my
dear, whether you like it or not. Have a liqueur, Father—
our famous rose liqueur."

Rodriguez, the butler, was there with a silver tray upon
which stood liqueur glasses as fragile as flowers, and
Father Francis Paul took one and held it to his nostrils
and breathed in the rich fragrance.

"I never taste this elsewhere than here in the palace,
Your Highness."

"Because it is only here—a secret of our family."

They were talking with difficulty tonight. There were
long pauses. Father Francis Paul was disturbed to find in
himself a longing to be alone with the Maharani. Why
should he feel this need? He felt restlessness in her mood;
he could not divine its cause and he was troubled. But
Jagat sat on, lapsing into silence and abstraction.

"If you will excuse me," Moti said suddenly. She rose
and gave her hand to Father Francis Paul. For an instant
he felt the slim coolness against his palm and then it was

withdrawn. She walked across the terrace with smooth grace, the rising night wind stirring the folds of her sari, and disappeared into the palace.

A silence fell between the two men, each hiding his thoughts from the other. The priest had only once been in love with a woman and now would never be again. Long ago when he was a lad, dedicating himself to the church, he knew that a certain door must never be opened lest, once open, it could not be closed. The prince had known many women, one of them his wife, and he remembered each of them from the first creature that his father had sent to him when he was sixteen, "in order," the old Maharana had said, "that you will be a decent man, staying clean and away from prostitutes." Of them all only Moti remained vague in his mind, his wife with whom he had lived since he was eighteen, and by whom he had had his children. He wished that he could speak to the priest about her, not so much to ask advice, but only to talk, to explore the nature of a woman who kept herself secret, who gave her body not unwilliingly so much as indifferently, who was not cold so much as withdrawn. But what could a priest know of women and how could a man in decency speak of his wife even to a priest?

Yet so urgent was the need that he was forced to meet it obliquely.

"I envy you religious men," he said abruptly.

"Do you indeed?" Father Francis Paul replied. "In what way, Your Highness?"

"Well, you are able somehow—I can't think how—to live free of—of entanglements. We Indians have our sadhus and holy men and so on of course, but one can't say—for example, it seems impossible that a man like you, virile and young, should be without passion—for women, I mean. I am too curious—forgive me!"

"We are not without passion," Father Francis Paul replied. He tasted the liqueur again and felt it on his tongue richly sweet.

"Then—what do you do with yourselves?"

"I can speak only for myself. What do I do? I pray! If that does not suffice, I go out into the villages and do my work. Your Highness must know that I am endeavoring to establish a school and clinic in every twenty-five-mile area in my parish. The government has been wonderfully helpful with its encouragement of the panchayat system."

"Then you have no personal private life?"

"Not in the sense you mean."

"Do you never long for it?"

"I do not allow myself to long for earthly happiness. But you—surely you have every happiness, Your Highness. Your family, your position—the excitement of new India everywhere, your own plans—"

His voice died away. One could not say, "And your beautiful wife."

Jagat rose abruptly. "Yes, you are right. I have every happiness. And now, Father, if you will excuse me—"

Father Francis Paul rose to his feet. "Of course—it is thoughtless of me—it's always difficult to tear myself from this place—and your company. My Bhils are good to me, but—"

Jagat laughed his strong, hearty shout. "But they are only Bhils! Come often, Father. You are always welcome."

He led the way to the door and delivered the priest to the night guard and went to his own rooms. There, leaning from the open window, he saw that Moti's light still burned. She was reading, he supposed, as she often did, far into the night. Why should she be sleepless when she had no worries? Surely she lived in peace. The moon shone upon the waters of the lake and happened by chance to make a path of light to his marble palace. An omen, perhaps, and a good one, he hoped. His mind was entangled again in its problems and he left his bedroom and went into his private sitting room. A light burned on the great pink marble table which served as his desk. His papers lay there, the plans, the figures, the estimates, the order sheets. He slipped off his white linen jacket and sat down in his short-sleeved shirt. The night wind had died down and the air was steaming hot, damp from the lake upon which the sun had burned all day. When he put in electricity for the hotel, he would put it here, too, into this wing of the palace. Meanwhile he must make do with the punkah. He clapped his hands and the servant, always waiting outside his door, appeared, his palms together before his face.

"Punkah, boy!" Jagat said shortly.

The servant jerked his head left to right in assent and disappeared and in a moment the ancient punkah began to stir the air above Jagat's head. He turned to the sheets of plans, frowning. That priest, always talking about the Bhils as if he, the Maharana, had not enough on his mind! Let the government take care of the Bhils, since princes were no more! And the government had done a great deal, let it be said! He was loyal, as most of his generation were, and loyal also to the British who, departing, had left behind them a solid structure of government, based upon human rights. Yes, and they had left the English language also, a unique means of communication between East and West, as well as among the many-tongued peoples of India. There was a great stir, of course, between liberals and conservatives among his own people, the conservatives wanting to do away with English as a foreign tongue, but the liberals, among whom he was coming to be a leader, believed as he did that they were fortunate in having English as a language not only between hemispheres but between the differing groups of their own people. Twelve to fourteen main languages within the one country, and who was to say which should be the national tongue? No wonder the President addressed parliament in English, and the Prime Minister himself, when he answered the questions flung at him every day in the two Houses of Parliament in Delhi, used English as a language common to most members! Hindi, the Hindus insisted, should be the national tongue, but think of Telugu and Gujarati and all the others who did not understand Hindi! No, no, India, mother of Asian culture that she was, belonged to the modern world, and for this the British could be somewhat thanked, especially when one considered the vastness of China, where the very structure of government had been destroyed and a vacuum made for whatever was taking place there. Look at Tibet! The Tibetan refugees were still pouring down over the Himalayas, through snow and ice.

Here Jagat withdrew his thoughts firmly. To the variety that his own country provided, he simply must not allow himself to add the Chinese and the Tibetans. He had his own immediate problem. He had a marble palace to make into a modern hotel, lest his grandchildren, when he had them, might starve like common beggers.

"The most important aspect of hotel management," Osgood said, "is the food. It's better to have a superb, even though limited, menu than a lot of dishes of poor quality. Speaking for Americans, they'll expect the food they're used to."

"Indians will also expect the food to which they are accustomed," Jagat said.

"Sure, but don't have it so spiced that it will burn the skin off American tongues. I ate something called chili the other night which sounded cool and was hot as hell. I haven't been able to swallow anything but ice water since. That's the sort of surprise you must see to it your guests don't get. Another thing you have to have is thoughtfulness toward each guest. It's good policy. Like hooks in the closets and sending fruit and flowers to the rooms! Then when folks go away they will tell their friends how nice it was in your hotel. Of course there will always be people you can't please. You should keep a card catalogue of that kind and when they want to come back tell them you haven't any room. You planning a golf course? You must have a golf course."

Jagat's eyebrows lifted. "Here in the middle of a lake?"

"You could have it on shore somewhere. You can't expect American business executives not to play golf."

"But they play golf at home."

"That's why they'll want it here. In a good hotel the clerk asks if the guest plays golf and if they do he hands them a card to the golf pro and telephones the golf personnel. The golf personnel then call on the guest and offer their services and say they'll be glad to give him an appointment if he needs the attention of the golf pro. It's things like that which make people come back. You'll have dancing, of course—you've got a grand place for that in the old audience room—you could take the throne away and make the dais wider for the orchestra. You could have a movie theater put in the old Maharana's sitting room." He frowned and pinched his lower lip between thumb and forefinger. "I don't know what you'll do about guests dancing barefoot. In the best hotels in America guests can't take off their shoes in the ballroom. Here I don't know—your girls kick off their sandals anytime."

Jagat laughed. "Let us meet that problem when it arises!"

Osgood grinned. "Well, I'm just telling you! Now as to the linens. You should have three sets of sheets and pillow cases to every bed, one on the bed, one in the laundry, one on the shelves. Let me see—if we count on four hundred guests that will be—"

He figured silently for a moment, then went on talking. "I'll contact the distributors who specialize in linen and china and silverware. Best thing will be to write the embassies in New Delhi and ask for recommendations from different countries, like I did for the Ashoka."

"The government will insist that we use Indian goods as far as possible," Jagat reminded him.

"Oh, sure," Osgood agreed. "But all this comes afterward. First thing is to get a good architect to do a layout for you. Then interior decorators—I can get those for you. They'd better be American."

"I shall want Indian decor," Jagat said.

"Of course, but chairs and beds? You won't find people willing to sleep on the floor or on charpoy cots. And it's very important to have the best people for advertising and public relations if you want to get the right kind of people here. It doesn't pay to get the wrong kind, the riff-raff type, the dollar-a-day tourist. Advertise that this is the land of kings, and the hotel is a palace where only princes have lived."

He stopped suddenly, and Jagat, surprised, followed the line of his gaze. It led to Veera, standing at the door, wrapped in a sari of soft rose silk, her long black hair braided down her back.

Jagat felt a vague displeasure. "My daughter," he said briefly. "Veera, this is Mr. Osgood."

Veera came in, sinuous and graceful, and sank down on a cushioned gold chair. "Father, I have a letter from Jai."

She cast a look at Osgood from under her long dark lashes.

"Well?" Jagat raised his eyebrows. "Is it necessary that I be interrupted in business because you have a letter from your brother?"

"Because he asks me to tell you that he has left school, Father."

"Left school!"

"Yes, Father. He is volunteering for military service."

"Military—"

"Yes, Father, because the radio is saying the Chinese are massing on the border and a lot of the boys are leaving school. Jai says it is our tradition as warriors and Kshatriyas. He says he is sure Grandfather would want him to go if he were alive."

"Oh, idiot," Jagat muttered.

"Indeed I think Jai is quite right, Father." Veera's enormous dark eyes sparkled points of light. "And I shall be angry if Raj does not go, too."

She lifted her eyes now and bestowed upon Osgood a long liquid look, daring and pleading together. Will you understand? the look inquired. He replied by a blush that came from his suddenly melting heart.

He turned to Jagat. "I must say I admire your son, sir."

Jagat would not be appeased. "Nonsense! The Chinese aren't massing. It's one of their provocative incursions. It's been going on since 1954, when the Prime Minister pointed out that their maps showed an inaccurate boundary alignment. They promised to rectify it, but it hasn't been done. Still, we do have the signed treaty of the Five Principles of Peaceful Coexistence. They can't repudiate that."

"They can do anything in my opinion," Osgood declared. He could not remove his gaze from the beautiful girl in the gold armchair by the door.

"Father, it's been announced on the air," Veera insisted.

"The Chinese have already crossed the border in the eastern sector of Longju and they've penetrated half a mile into our territory at the Roi village. Worse than that, they're advancing their patrols in Ladakh, in the Chip Chap area. Jai telephoned me, too."

"Idiot, idiot," Jagat insisted.

Veera rose. With a graceful gesture she drew the end of her sari over her head and stood, the image of a young virgin madonna in spring. "Don't be angry, Father," she said in her sweetest voice. "All the best young men will be wanting to join our armed forces. We should be proud of them."

Jagat ignored this evidence of nationalism. "Did he say he was coming home first?"

"Yes, Father. He will come home tomorrow."

"Have you told your mother?"

"Yes, I have told her. She has gone into meditation and wishes not to be disturbed. May I go now, Father?"

"Yes, go by all means, since you have ruined my day. See that Jai's rooms are made ready."

"Yes, Father."

Her eyes rested quietly upon the American for a few seconds. Then she smiled and went away.

Silence fell. Jagat bent his head over the blueprints, endeavoring to collect his thoughts. He cleared his throat.

"I hope you realize, Mr. Osgood, that we must exercise the greatest economy in all this. I want everything done in the best taste but there must be efficiency and no waste. I am investing capital."

When there was no answer he looked up inquiringly and met Osgood's stupefied gaze.

"I simply have never seen such a beautiful girl. I—I hope you don't mind my saying so, sir! I really have never seen—well, she's just—you know—"

"My daughter is still a child, a girl at boarding school, her education unfinished," Jagat said coldly.

"What are you educating her for?" Osgood demanded. "She doesn't need education. She's already got everything."

"She is engaged to be married," Jagat said bluntly.

He was displeased and he rose as he spoke. "If you will

excuse me now, Mr. Osgood, I am disturbed over the news about my son. I should return to the palace and to my son's mother. She is distressed or she would not go into meditation. I will telephone my son and forbid him—another day, Mr. Osgood. Will you return to the city with me?"

"I'll stay and finish taking measurements."

"Very well. I'll send the boat back for you."

He nodded and left the room. A moment later he was swiftly crossing the water.

"Good morning, Father," Jai said.

He had slept later than he intended, but it had been well past midnight when he arrived. At eighteen he looked twenty-five, his beard black underneath his shaven skin, his eyes shadowed by thick black brows. Along the edge of his ears were delicate fringes of fine black hair.

"Come in," Jagat said.

He was sitting behind his office desk, the one that had belonged to his grandfather, a desk of English design but made of Indian rosewood.

Jai sat down on a straight chair near the door. He was in western dress, a suit of light surrah silk, but he wore no tie and his collar was turned back from his strong neck. Jagat glanced at him and away again. He had no intention of showing softness toward this wayward son and he continued his work on the papers which lay before him, marking certain figures with his gold-handled pen.

"Very encouraging increase in our industrial production," he said, not looking up. "Glass and cement, salt, cloth, yarn, ball bearings, electric meters, khadi production—all better than last year. We're undercapitalized, of course—I shall have to find a loan somewhere—float it, if I can get my government to agree with me. The Gang canal is finished, thank God, but irrigation must keep up its pace—especially the Rajasthan canal. Meanwhile you, my only son, want to go and get yourself killed by the Chinese!"

"I can't see myself just going off to England or Amer-

ica, Father, while the Chinese start war on our borders,"
Jai said.

"I can send a hundred men in your place," Jagat said.

"None of them I," his son retorted.

Jagat put down his pen. "Do you want to break my
heart?"

"No, Father. Do you want to break mine?"

"How can I? Your heart is of marble."

"Then it's a Rajput heart, straight out of our mountains.
I don't forget our ancestors. We lead the whole of India,
don't we, Father? If we don't lead the resistance, who will
fight?"

Jagat did not answer, and Jai continued impetuously,
"I'd be ashamed not to be the first among the chaps at
school to volunteer. They expect it of me. I'm a Rajput.
I've had officer training. They'll follow me but I follow no
one."

Jagat sighed. "Like my old grandfather who died before
you were born! I remember him well enough—I was almost your age when he died in nineteen thirty after making a great fuss over meeting the Prince of Wales at the
Coronation Durbar. He upset the whole family—the whole
of India, as a matter of fact. Absolutely refused, of course,
to follow the Nizam in being presented to the Prince! The
Sol Batristi would not allow him to do so and he was
always guided by our House of Parliament, the Lords
being the sixteen highest Rajputs Amirs and the Com-
mons the thirty other Rajput Amirs. Do you know what
the Sol—?"

Jai grinned. "Why do you think you need to tell me
what the Sol Batristi is?"

Jagat sighed. "God—to think that's all gone! At any
rate, an officer of high rank here saw that my old grandfather must somehow meet the Prince and he persuaded
him to go to Bombay to do so. The government there was
adamant, too, and the English Prince was the one who
solved the problem. He received my grandfather on board
his ship, which was technically English territory, and my
grandfather left immediately afterward. Did I ever tell you
that story?"

"Yes, Father."

"Oh, I did, did I?"

"It helped me to decide to join up, Father," Jai said, smiling.

Jagat turned his eyes from that charming smile. "Fighting the Chinese is unnecessary! We shall carry on negotiations as we have been doing since nineteen fifty-four, when their maps began showing the inaccurate boundary alignments. After all, we are not westerners who throw themselves into wars with such delight. Our traditions are different."

"Yes, and what do the Chinese say?" Jai demanded. "They say the maps are the old Nationalist maps and they have not had time to revise them. Well, they lie! They have had plenty of time. Besides, they complained that same year in July, Father, that our troops were in Barahoti in the Uttar Pradesh. That's south of Niti Pass and it's always been our country. And a year later in spite of our government refuting what had been said, the Chinese troops invaded."

"You know your history," Jagat said grudgingly.

"I do know my history, but I remember, too," Jai replied. "I listened to you talking with the Prime Minister, when you took me to New Delhi with you. And I remember two years later when the Chinese Prime Minister said that his government had agreed to the old McMahon Line in Burma. But three years ago, after all those years of talking—talking between our governments—that same Chinese contended that the boundaries had never been fixed and the McMahon Line had never been recognized and the maps needed no revision! With such people, what can we do but fight? They've laid claim to fifty thousand square miles of our territory! Shall we endure this? Some of our patrolmen have lost their lives. Meanwhile the Chinese have finished the highway linking Tibet and Sinkiang, and it runs straight across the Aksai Chin region of northeast Ladakh—our land! And what has come of all the arguments during this past two years? We've presented three times the amount of evidence that the Chinese have and do they care? They are full of lies, I tell you, because they're determined to have that territory. This is the year of the showdown and I want to have my part in it. They're in Ladakh again in the Chip Chap region with their patrols. It's got to stop."

"You have camel dung on your shoes," Jagat said. He had let his eyes drop while his son spoke and he now observed the soles of the smart English shoes his son wore over his white socks.

"What!" Jai exclaimed. He bent hastily to examine for himself. "Good God, Father—the state of our streets! Really you should do something. I walked only a few yards outside the palace gate. I wanted to stop by the lake and see if my motorboat was there. It's not to be used by anyone except you. What shall I do?"

Jagat pressed a bell on his desk. Immediately a servant entered and made pranam. Jai extended his right foot. "Take off my shoe and clean it."

"Yes, Sahib."

The man squatted and removed the shoe gently and went away.

"I'd better throw the shoes away," Jai complained. "Camels are such stinkers."

Jagat laughed. "What will you do on the battlefield, you fastidious young fool? I'll tell you another family story while you wait for your shoe—if your mother hasn't already told you. The Rana of Sadhari, who was a Jhala chief under one of the maharanas here, became such a favorite with the Maharana that the old man gave him one of his daughters for his wife. The bride came to Sadhari in great state, and the Rana waited to see whether she came as a good Hindu wife, in gentle submission, or as a princess. In the evening when she was alone with him on the terrace he asked her to bring him a bit of charcoal from the brazier to light his long pipe. She declared immediately that she would never do the work of a servant. The Rana insisted; whereupon she rose, got into her waiting chariot, and ordered her people to take her back to her own people.

"The Princess, at home again, told the story to her mother, who, very indignant, went to the Maharana him-

self and asked that permission for the marriage be withdrawn. The Maharana was like your grandfather—I dare
not say like me! He said nothing but he went to Sol
Batristri, and the Rana of Sadhari, who was one of them,
was summoned. By that time I fancy he was rather sorry
for all the commotion he had caused, and he came in a
humble mood. My old grandfather, however, invited him
to the narrow corridor—you remember it, the place you
loved to hide in when you were a boy, and where only one
man at a time can pass—and through it they went into
the courtyard which was then in full sight of the women's
zenana, which is now no more. My grandfather had ordered some slippers to be placed there in a certain spot.

" 'Put on your slippers,' " he told the Rana.

"The slippers could not be found, of course, and so my
grandfather went and found them himself and dusted them
off and presented them to his son-in-law, who was horri-
bly embarrassed and made all sorts of apologies. But my
grandfather was quite calm! 'We are not master and subject here,' he said. 'You are my son-in-law and according
to our scriptures I must treat you with respect, which I
do.' Of course the Princess was watching all this from the
windows of the zenana and she at once declared that she
could not be better than her noble father and so she
came out and went home with the Rana and did her duty
as a wife."

Jai listened to all this with his slightly superior smile.
"My mother has also told me this story."

"Then you were very courteous not to interrupt me,"
Jagat replied.

"I am leaving tomorrow for the front," Jai said softly.

Father and son exchanged a long straight look.

"Very well, my son," Jagat said. "Now go to your
mother."

Moti was sitting on the terrace under a pipal tree which
some ancestor had planted three centuries earlier. It was
enormous, the diameter of its trunk a matter only to be
conjectured since no one had the energy to measure it and
besides it was more interesting to guess than to know. She

had risen earlier than usual today for she knew that Jai had arrived in the palace and would call upon her sooner rather than later. She was eating today one of her occasional European breakfasts of coffee, croutons, and conserve—a habit she had learned from a French governess in her girlhood—to which she added only fresh fruit in season.

She sat alone, not considering the servants as presences, and thoughtful as usual, she reflected upon a woman's relationship with a son who had become a man. There was no doubt that Jai was now a man. Her women had brought faithful news of him, and while she believed he had no sentimental attachments, it was true that when he was in Bombay he had met a pretty actress at a party in a Juhu Beach hotel frequented by theater people and that something had happened. Something between man and woman meant of course only one thing. She felt no jealousy, merely a withdrawal. She had done her best to rear the willful little boy into a good man, although she was not sure of the definition of goodness in a man. For a woman, goodness was simple, its limitations being chastity before marriage and faithfulness afterward. She felt rather sorry for men, always at the mercy of their physical instincts. Alas, poor Jai, impulsive and downright! Did he love her anymore? It was difficult for a son to sort out his feelings about his mother as a woman. They had not been in close communion for years, certainly not since he had been in school, especially in an English school where customs and traditions were those of the English upper class.

Then she saw Jai standing in the doorway and was astonished to perceive how handsome he had grown. The beard of course was a youthful affectation but it was somehow becoming. His face still tended to a childlike roundness, the pale olive of his complexion ruddy on the cheekbones. He had fine hazel eyes, large and expressive, the lashes extravagant and the brows clearly marked.

"Come in, my son," she said.

He came in, pausing to put his hands together in

pranam. "Good morning, Mother. Are you as well as you look? I hope so."

"I am well, thank you."

She gestured to a servant to put coffee before Jai, but he refused. "Thanks, no—I've never learned to drink the stuff. I'll take a cup of tea."

The servant disappeared and he continued to look at his mother with appreciation. In the flickering shadows of the pipal tree her delicate face took on a liveliness that, not quite natural, was becoming. He had never thought of her as a woman, or even as someone separate from himself. Now it occurred to him with a slight sense of shock that she had an existence quite apart from him, a life of her own not connected with his. His sense of justice compelled him to realize that this was entirely within her right as an individual, and especially since he had no particular need of her except as someone to be in the palace when he came home. Once a year she returned to her girlhood home in Jaipur to remain for one month and at such times he missed her.

"Jai," she said suddenly, "do you not plan to marry?"

"No, Mother."

"Why not?"

"I want to go to the front quite clear and free."

"And what if you are killed and your father has no heir?"

"Does it matter, now that we are no longer rulers in India?"

"It matters to your parents."

He did not reply. She was peeling a fig daintily with a silver knife.

"I really cannot have my mind disturbed at this moment," he said at last.

"How cold you are," she said. "At a time when you should be thinking of love, you think of war and killing! If you come back and tell me you have killed even a Chinese, I shall not want to touch your hand."

"I am sorry, Mother. I shall try to kill as many Chinese as I can, before they kill me."

"I dislike this conversation," she said abruptly and put down the fig.

But a moment later she took it up again and began eating it in slices. He could feel her mind arranging arguments against him.

"The government is saying that they still wish to hold discussions with the Chinese at any level. Why then must you take responsibility on yourself to delay your education and become a soldier?"

Jai could not sit still. He stood up and began to pace back and forth before his mother, throwing words at her over his shoulder.

"Mother, you read only what you like to read in the newspapers. Do you not know that only four days ago, on the eighth of September in this year of 1962, to be exact —an historic date, Mother, and that's why I emphasize it—the Chinese intruded into Thaga La—"

"Of course I know"—her voice was impetuous and her eyes were suddenly flashing—"but I also saw that in the Ladakh region where, after all, the major clashes are taking place, the government suggests that both sides withdraw in order to avoid further difficulties."

"Rejected by the Chinese!" He paused before her. "Today our government declares that no talks can take place until the positions the Chinese have taken by aggression are corrected. Can't you see, Mother, that the Chinese have no intention of retreating?"

She gave up eating the fig, once and for all. "But why?"

She was defeated, he could see. Fire died in her eyes and her fingers trembled as she dipped them in a crystal bowl and wiped them on a linen napkin.

"You are your father's son," she said. "You will do exactly what you like. I don't see why I trouble myself about either of you."

She wished him gone. As soon as he was gone she would go to her rooms and write one of her long, self-searching letters to Father Francis Paul. She would ask what duty a woman had toward a man who had been her son but had reclaimed himself. Had she not done all she could? When he was a child she had tried to teach him gentleness toward all living creatures. Even the birds, she had taught him, must not be disturbed in their nests. They must be allowed to build and to lay their eggs and hatch their young, though it was inconvenient, as, for example, when swallows chose the great crystal chandelier over the dining table it had certainly been very inconvenient.

"Mother, why are you smiling?" Jai inquired. He was eating figs now, peeling them with his fingers and putting them into his mouth whole.

"I was thinking of those swallows that built in the chandelier in the dining hall. Do you remember?"

Jai laughed. "How could I forget? One never knew what was coming next until old Rodriguez hung a mosquito netting under the chandelier. But no, you wouldn't let anyone touch the nest. I can assure you, Mother, that Rodriguez never let it happen again. The next spring he saw to it that the swallows understood they were not welcome."

"Was that what happened? I wondered why they did not come back. I think I felt rather hurt."

"You see, Mother," Jai said, his mouth full of fig, "it's all very well for ladies like you to have these sweet principles but the fact is that the rest of us have always to think of ways of making it possible for you to continue to believe as you do. Someone must stop the birds secretly, someone must kill the mosquitoes and snakes and shoot the tigers and fight the Chinese, if any of us are to live. Rodriguez could do it secretly with the swallows, but I cannot go to war in secret, Mother. So give me your blessing and let me go. I don't know when I shall see you again."

She rose, unable to speak for the tears tightening her throat, and putting her palms on his cheeks, she drew down his head and kissed his forehead in blessing.

When he was gone she felt a loneliness so intense that it was not to be borne. Was this a presage of evil? Of Jai's death, perhaps? No, absurd! He was in perfect health. It would be weeks before he would be in danger, weeks of training and preparation. The war might even be over. Yet this new loneliness was different from her habitual sense of being alone. There was a primeval depth to her present misery, as though a part of her own being were gone, as though now she no longer had her own self. In the whole world she had none to whom she could speak. Surrounded by people, she was solitary and no god was near. She longed for a single god such as Christians had, for among the multiple godhood of the Hindu it was difficult to find the central identity she craved. In the sacred trinity of Siva the Creator, Siva the Preserver, Siva the Destroyer, where was she? There must be one spirit more definitive, less comprehensive, one to whom she could pray quite simply for guidance. It was attractive to believe as Father Francis Paul did, that there was a Father, a God supreme, who took heed, as she did herself in a small way, even of a swallow. But would she have felt this necessity if she had never met Father Francis Paul? For it was true, and she was never one to hide the truth from herself, that until Father Francis Paul came to the palace that first evening she had not thought of herself as solitary. She had not thought of herself very much as anything, merely one who had her place in the complexity of palace life. What had Father Francis Paul said to make her realize her own being? Indeed they had talked very little until she had begun writing him long vague letters, and now when he visited her, they discussed only such questions as she had asked in her last letter. Nor did she write often, for she was still diffident with him, being by nature shy and likely to escape into silence or even into one of her abrupt withdrawals. And sometimes he hurt her in ways that she could not understand as, for example, when he praised Jagat to her. He never allowed her to blame Jagat, not even for his love of hunting tigers and wild boar.

"His Highness must make his own decisions," Father Francis Paul said.

It was always "His Highness" when he spoke of Jagat, and though she could not imagine what other term he might have used, yet to say "His Highness" was almost a rebuke to her, as though she had somehow failed in proper respect, and she could not bear rebuke from one so gentle as Father Francis Paul. Ah, that was it—he was gentle to the point of tenderness, and tenderness was what her life lacked.

Upon the impulse the word gave her, she rose and drifted off to her own rooms, her white sari flowing about her. There she closed the door and went to the desk of inlaid rosewood and took up her pen.

"What shall I do?" She wrote, as usual without salutation. "My son is going to war—my only son!"

Upon leaving his mother, Jai had gone straight to Veera. He found her in her own sitting room, eating a substantial breakfast of English bacon and scrambled eggs. She was in English dress, a summer frock of Indian muslin, as green as a new leaf. She was pretty, he granted, and with some surprise that he had never thought so before. He sat down in the most comfortable chair.

"Are you happy about Raj?" he asked abruptly.

"Why do you ask?" she replied. She spread Indian orange marmalade on a bit of toast.

He scrutinized her. "You look as though you were in love."

"How do you know how a girl looks when she's in love, pray? I wish we had good English marmalade again!"

"How unpatriotic you are—just when I've decided to join up!"

"Have you told our mother?"

"Just! She's unhappy."

"Of course. You're her darling."

"Nonsense. She hasn't any darling. If she has, it's you."

"That's really nonsense. No daughter is ever her mother's darling. That spot is always reserved for the son. What made you decide to join up?"

"I don't know. Yes, I do. It's something definite that one can do. It's difficult to find anything definite now. Everything's a hodgepodge of old and new, like Father's making a hotel out of the lake palace! Have you seen the American?"

She gave him a look at once merry and shy.

"He's seen me."

"And?"

"Nothing."

"I take it he liked what he saw?"

"I daresay."

"And Raj?"

"Can I help what Raj thinks? Besides, he doesn't know."

"Is there something to know?"

"Of course not. How could there be?"

"Then what are we talking about?"

"Nothing."

"Nothing definite. That's what I mean. Nothing is ever definite in India."

He rose restlessly and went to the window. The view was what he had seen all his life but today it struck him as beauty he had never seen before. The lake, rimmed by the desert-gray mountains, was blue beneath the blue sky, and in its midst the marble palace glittered whiter than Himalayan snows. He remembered the palace as a child, when his grandfather had spent the summers there surrounded by his concubines, his wife, the old Maharani remaining in the palace—for the sake of peace, she had always declared. The amazing patience of those ladies of old India! What woman nowadays would accept so amiably the antics of man? Yet the strange passivity of even the modern Indian woman was perhaps to be explained by that inheritance. A woman waited for life to assail her. It did not yet occur to her to shape life to her own demands. Not even Veera! He thought of other girls he knew; he thought of Sehra, when they had last met in Bombay, where he always went, if possible, for at least a part of his holidays, staying at the big new hotel on Juhu Beach. He had met her there one Sunday, with her family, of course, her stout good-natured mother, her father who was chief of some government bureau, her younger brothers and sisters. On Sundays it was usual for families to leave the city and go to Juhu Beach, and the wealthiest came to the hotel for luncheon. He had been swimming that day and on the way back to his rooms he had seen Sehra, a tall beautiful girl in a rose-pink sari. When he came down again in a fresh suit of tan linen, he had sat down at a table outdoors, near Sehra's family, and had made some excuse to introduce himself. After that he had twice gone to her home, a big house set in gardens facing the sea.

"Are you in love?" Veera asked now.

He turned, startled at the accuracy of her thrust. "It is what I am asking myself."

"Who is she?"

"Sehra Lall."

"I don't know her."

"I scarcely know her myself. She's rather beautiful, though."

"Indian fashion?"

"Yes—but new India."

"Delhi or Bombay?"

"Bombay."

"Do you want to marry her?"

"No, although I might if I weren't joining up. I mean —it's too soon under ordinary circumstances. Besides, I'd be going abroad."

"Our parents want you to marry before you go anywhere, don't they?"

"It's not so important as it used to be when it was a matter of succession."

"Ah, we're not royal anymore—not really! Do you miss it, Prince Jai?"

"Yes, in a way. No—because I feel free."

"Shall you see this Sehra before you go away?"

"I think so—for my own sake."

He sat down and they looked at each other for an instant, a frank interchange. Then he spoke.

"I wish you'd tell me if you really love Raj."

She flung out her left hand impatiently and the enormous diamond on the third finger glittered. "The question is whether I can love him when I have the chance."

"He's not repulsive to you?"

"Why should he be?"

"Those hairy flanges on his ears!"

She laughed. "Oh, that—"

"No?"

"Jai, why do you press me? Look at your own flanges!"

"I'm rather fond of you, you know."

"Must we be sentimental? We never have been."

"No, but I'm sensitive just now, perhaps. I'd like to go away thinking everything's all right with everyone."

"How do I know whether everything is all right? I'm finishing one part of my life and beginning another, since this is my last year at school."

"When do you plan to marry Raj?"

"Soon, I suppose—unless I decide not to—"

"Possible?"

"No, I think not. There's no one better—on my horizon, at least."

"You've excluded the necessity of love?"

"Oh, I'll love him, I imagine, once I'm married to him and there's no other possibility."

"Is there the possibility now?"

"How do I know?"

It was a conversation singularly unsatisfactory and he put a stop to it. "I'll be on my way, Veera. Write to me."

He rose and came to her side and she clung to his hand with both her own.

The sun was setting in the Indian ocean when Jai came out of the smoothly flowing waves to join Sehra Lall. She sat with her parents at one of the small tables on the terrace of the hotel under the palm trees.

"You wait until the last moment, always," she complained as Jai accepted a robe from a waiting servant and seated himself beside her.

"Excuse us," Sehra's father said, "we will take a short walk."

He jerked his head at his wife and she followed him, a large silent woman in a white sari, her graying hair pulled back from her pallid face.

Sehra laughed. "Poor parents nowadays! They are so anxious to be modern—and so reluctant to give us our freedom—always within limits, of course! Jai, tell me why you like to frighten me when you swim."

He wiped his salt-wet face on a towel the servant handed him. "Are you frightened?"

"Of course I am. You know how dangerous the bay is. Once the tide turns, you'll be swept out to sea. No one can swim fast enough to make the shore. It's the wickedest tide in the world. Yet you swim out so far, and barely make it back to shore. I could see the water pulling against your legs when you walked out of the water."

"It's good of you to be frightened."

"I can't help it."

The moment became suddenly meaningful. Now was the time for him to speak the words that would bind him to her, give him something of his own to come back to, and if he never came back, someone of his own to mourn for him. Sehra was beautiful today, more beautiful than usual, the damp salt wind curling her dark hair about her face. If he were sure that he was to die in battle, he would immediately speak. He would put out his hand and take hers. But he could not be sure of death, and if he lived to return he was not sure that she was the one to whom he wished to return. Yet the fact of his departure in a few hours lent urgency to their meeting. He could be alone with her for only a very little while. Whatever he could say must be said now. He leaned his arms on the small table, his face near hers.

"Sehra, I am so nearly in love with you."

He paused and she waited, her eyes large and dark.

"I need very much to say that I love you, perhaps because I am going away, not knowing whether I shall come back. But it wouldn't be fair to have you waiting for me. I don't know what I'll be if I come back, someone quite different from what I am now, I'm afraid. You might not like me."

She spoke, her voice low. "I'll always like you—no matter. I'll always—love you."

He could not reply. How does a man refuse a gift? She had offered him her heart, a human heart, a woman's heart. In these last days he was searching for some meaning for his life. Surely there was meaning beyond a skirmish with the Chinese in the mountains of the borderland! Perhaps meaning lay in no more than the good common ways of men and women. If he came back to Sehra, she would make him happy in those ways. They would have children, lovely children with great liquid dark eyes and dark curls. If he came back safely, that is—

And suddenly he knew it was not such life that he wanted. He put his hand gently on hers.

"Thank you," he said. "I shall never forget what you have told me."

Before she could reply, her parents returned and he withdrew his hand.

"Come, Sehra," her father commanded. "The night wind has risen out of the sea, and your mother will have a chill."

They went away, Sehra turning to give him a long yearning look. The swift twilight fell, he felt the wind cold on his flesh and a premonition of ill crept into his heart, but he refused to accept it. Tomorrow morning at dawn he was leaving for the camp. Six weeks of basic training and he would be thrown into battle in Ladakh. Six weeks!

"I am not pleased," Jagat said.

Weeks had passed since Jai had left for the front. Autumn harvests ripened in the fields, and autumn winds cooled the desert air. It was hard to believe that Jai was fighting in Himalayan cold. He threw down the compact book which the Director of Economics and Statistics had sent him a few days before.

"Sir, it has been a very dry year," the director said.

Jagat took up the book again and read aloud.

"Rabi cereals down ten percent from last year. Kharif cereals down five percent. Pulses no better than last year. A drop in total food crops. Oilseeds lower. Fibers lower."

"But Miscellaneous brings the record up," the director urged. He was a small fat man in loose white cotton dhoti and shirt and his round face was sweating with anxiety. It made no difference to him that nowadays the Maharana had been deprived of power. The habit of traditional conscience compelled him to submit reports to the no longer ruling prince. Nor did Jagat see any inconsistency in this attitude.

"The trouble is that the irrigation projects are falling behind," he complained. "Look at this—only the Gang Canal is completed. No figures again this year for Mahi or the Rajasthan Canal—"

"Look at Chambal, please, Highness, also Bhakra Nagal!"

Jagat closed the book on his desk. "Don't call me Highness! Ah, forgive me, old friend! The truth is, I am worried about my son. He is on the border—and fighting has broken out straight to the Burmese frontier. Peking has ordered its troops not to restrain themselves to the McMahon line. This morning's radio news says that Lumpu has been captured. That's ten miles south of the McMahon line! My son complains that their weapons are antiquated, that nothing is ready, supplies short, and yet they must proceed to battle. We've been lulled ino unpreparedness on every hand—and no one is more unprepared than young men like my son, the very flower of India, sacrificed—"

He broke off. The director sighed and wiped his eyes with the tail of his shirt. "My two sons also, Highness—"

Jagat put out his right hand impulsively and clasped the director's right hand and shook it in downright British fashion, then dropped it hastily. It felt soft and damp and he was slightly ashamed of the impulse. It was not an act his father would have understood. That was the trouble with these complicated times. One had modern democratic impulses which merely embarrassed the recipient. The director would have blushed had he not been so dark. As it was, he looked hot, small rivulets running down the sides of his cheeks.

"Well, well," Jagat said, very gruff. "See that the irrigation works."

The director put his palms together before his forehead in pranam, gathered his papers, and went away. Jagat sat for a few restless moments behind his great rosewood desk with its red marble top, looking at the trophies of his hunts. Ah, those beautiful nights he had spent in his shooting box in the Aravalli hills! Hour after hour he had paced the flat roof, pausing to gaze over the moonlit landscape, listening for the sound of the beaters. When the moment came, when he saw the golden eyes of the wild beast gleaming through the underbrush, what care and skill were necessary to shoot to the heart, if possible, and not to destroy the beauty of that feline skull! He was a passionate man and he had loved women, but no moment of passion ever equaled the pure pleasure of the moment when his bullet went true to its target and a beautiful animal lay warm and dead upon the earth. He had trained Jai to be a fine sportsman in the English manner but based upon good Rajasthan tradition, and was this now all to be wasted at the hands of a fanatic Chinese?

Ladakh—he had often been to Ladakh, first with his father and then alone to inspect the tea plantations on the lower slopes of the Himalayas. The lands were ancestral, bought by his great-grandfather, and they had been enormously profitable. They might now be destroyed, those beautiful hanging tea gardens, planted upon slopes so steep that he marveled always how the tea pickers kept their footing, a sight to see in season, when hill men and women made harvest, their bright garments glittering in the hot sunshine. Alas, the Galwan valley post in Ladakh had already been lost to the Chinese and on the twenty-fifth day of October, after bitter fighting, radio news said, Indian troops had withdrawn from Tawang and civilians had been asked to evacuate for the last stand. The brave people, men carrying their old parents, mothers carrying their infants, had left their homes and belongings in order that Indian armies could wage war unimpeded. Thus the battle at Chushul began and was even now being waged. Somewhere in that bloody fray was his only son. Bloody he knew it was, for the Chushul post was of immense importance, a gateway to India, and the Chinese were using every means to overrun the post, pouring in reinforcements, thousands of their bitter-faced men, hardened and ruthless.

"Oh, Jai, my son, my son—"

The groan burst from Jagat's heart and he could not endure the pain. Yet he could do nothing, nothing but wait for news of the battle. It must go on for days, it might go on for weeks, for the Indian armies were fighting, stubborn and brave. And how selfish of him to think only of Jai, when all over India men and women were enduring the same agony because of their sons! He got up from the chair of ebony and silver which had been the gift of a viceroy to his grandfather, and walking to the marble-latticed windows, open to the lake, he saw the white palace, shining in the blue waters, a scene always incredible in its beauty and peace. On the marble steps of the city water gate, women in bright saris bathed themselves and washed their clothes, the rhythmic pounding muted by distance. Suddenly a small motorboat put out from the quay of his own palace, directly beneath the window where he stood, and he saw the American, his arms loaded, seated in the stern near the noisy engine.

Jagat determined to follow. It had been some twenty days since he had visited the reincarnated palace, his time occupied by the usual autumn business of his agents, the reckoning of harvests, and the division of rents in grain. True, since the lands had been given to the people, it was no longer as huge a labor as it had been in his father's time, when every harvest center must have its royal representative to assess, record, and receive the portion due the royal family. Nevertheless, certain lands still belonged to him as the prince, and he had need to know his assets, now that they were so seriously reduced. He was indeed in a strange and ambivalent state. He approved the relinquishment of royal power and the yielding of princely states. A modern nation could not be built upon a foundation of ancient autocratic rulers. Yet he was accustomed to being such a ruler, and had continually to check his undemocratic impulses, a task the more difficult since his people persisted in treating him as their ruler and coming to him for advice privately after the panchayat meetings of the village elders, designed by the Indian goverment as modernized tradition.

Only yesterday he had sat in at such a meeting in a village ten miles from the city. He had risen early, before dawn, and had traveled by horseback over the rough road, with him his groom and one aide. When he entered the village the people were already awake, the women stirring in the earthen-walled houses, while the men, wrapped in their white cotton shawls against the morning chill, squatted in a row along the one street of the village. He was accustomed to the early morning dejection of villagers, and he shouted greetings, awakening thereby the gray monkeys still asleep in the big banyan tree that surrounded the village well. His shout stirred the villagers as well and they rose to give him dim smiles and scattered replies of welcome. Then, encircling him, they held discussion of village affairs, and especially the crimes of a landlord who could not or would not realize that he was no longer the old zamindar, with all but power of life and death.

Yes, tradition still worked in the deep old ways of family and life. Thus yesterday, when business was finished at noon, he had been urged to attend a village wedding about to take place and had yielded to the presence of eager dark hands on his arms and shoulders.

"Stay with us, Rana," voices besought.

He stayed and was amazed to discover how little the old customs were changed. The sword had already been sent to the bride's home, after Rajput custom, and she was married to the sword and was being brought to the bridegroom's house for the religious ceremonies and the fasting. Her procession was met by the bridegroom on horseback, who descended and entered the bullock-drawn chariot of the bride to sit beside her behind the curtains that concealed her from the crowd. The groom was very young, and there was a commotion at the last minute when he could not be found, his horse waiting and impatient. At last he was discovered, flying kites with a

friend on a hill behind the village, and hurried to the bath
to be cleansed and dressed in his wedding robes.

Throughout all this Jagat had waited, amused and reflecting, for in the village nothing was changed, while here
in his palace all was changed. He felt the deep changes
in himself now without understanding their depth, and he
was restless. He clapped his hands and when a servant
appeared he gave his command.

"I go to the palace hotel."

A few minutes later he was in his motorboat, moving
swiftly across the smooth and glittering waters. At the far
end of the lake he saw the dark snouts of crocodiles
thrusting out to seize food which a man threw to them,
and remembering a command he had given a few days
before, he turned to the boatman who was tending the
engine.

"Did I not say the crocodiles are no longer to be fed?
I wish them to die."

"Highness, you did," the man replied, "but if they are
not fed they will not die. They will eat our children. They
will even snatch our women while they bathe and wash
clothes. You remember, Highness, in your father's time a
crocodile died in a drouth and when he was cut open to
see if he had valuables inside him, he was full of jewels and
gold trinkets."

Jagat continued to be impatient. "We must be rid of
these monsters before the hotel is opened to guests. One
American eaten and it will make such a noise around the
world that we shall be ruined."

"Yes, Highness," the man agreed peaceably.

No more was said, but Jagat knew that nothing would
be done unless he himself shot the old and sacred crocodiles. Yet he, too, would do nothing, and knew he would
not, until compelled by some mischance. Meanwhile the
crocodiles would be fed and he knew that, too, with a sort
of despair. In the midst of all change, there was something unchanging and unchangeable in himself as well as
in his people. He moved to another irritation.

"Has the wood been gathered for brewing the rose
wine?"

"I will see to it, Highness," the man replied in his usual tranquil manner.

Jagat did not reply. A sudden wry memory crossed his mind. The English priest, Father Francis Paul, drank the rose wine with frank pleasure, and it occurred to Jagat now that this rose wine contained a concentration of aphrodisiac so expensive that even in his grandfather's time, when money was much more valuable than now, a single bottle would have cost two hundred rupees if they had bought it instead of making it. He considered telling the priest on his next visit the danger in the wine. Was not celibacy difficult enough for a priest? And should he allow a priest who visited his own wife to provide her with spiritual consolation at the same time to drink a liquid so aphrodisiacal in its power as the famous rose wine of Jam Vibhaji? This Jam Vibhaji was the same man of old who, besides his other food, gnawed sixteen marrow bones for dinner. For him, too, the milk of two buffaloes was given to another buffalo, and the rich milk of that third one was given to Jam, who drank it with relish, although if any ordinary man drank such milk, it violently emptied the bowels. The rose wine had been created for Jam, and Jagat himself was careful how he drank it, lest he turn too savagely upon his own wife. Better to deny the rose wine to the priest, or else order it secretly diluted!

Before he made a decision the motor died down and the boatman pulled the boat to the marble steps of the palace, and Jagat stepped out. The guard came out to meet him.

"Where is the American?" Jagat asked.

"He is on the great terrace," the man replied.

Jagat entered the hall and mounted the marble staircase to the open terrace on the next floor. In the center of rooms opening upon a colonnade was this vast marble terrace whose ceiling was the sky. Here Bert Osgood was at work, standing in the hot sunlight before a wide table, his body bare to the waist, his eyes hidden behind dark glasses.

"Good morning, Prince," he called in his loud and

cheerful voice. "You came at the right moment. I'm designing the luxury suites around the garden. Want a look?"

"I suggest that you put on your shirt," Jagat replied. "This sun is dangerous even for me."

"I'm used to it," the American drawled.

"I suggest that you are not," Jagat retorted.

Bert did not hear him. He was shuffling a sheaf of papers. "Here's the detail of a suite. I'll use all Indian stuff for curtains and upholstery. Boy, they're beautiful! I spent last week in the Bombay shops. No need to get materials anywhere else, except here in your own storehouses, though! I'm sending to a New York firm for a couple of interior decorators, people I usually work with. They'll handle all the details. Do you know what you've got in your ancestral cellars? Chests, tables, beds, all sorts of European furniture, most of it still in the crates—your ancestors really knew how to spend money, didn't they, though why they never used the stuff—there's a bedroom set from Paris, gold enameled, as good as the day it was shipped a hundred years ago, not even unpacked until I opened it."

Jagat smiled slightly. "They preferred their own ways, I suppose, when it came to living."

"Then why buy all that?"

"Just to know it was there, in case they wanted it. Or perhaps no one bothered. Who knows?"

"Well, lucky for you, Prince, it will save you a lot of money. Now here's the detail of management and so forth. I've put down a few ideas of what Americans like in a hotel. We want to keep all the native charm, of course, all this Indian atmosphere, but with it they'll want—"

Jagat interrupted. "Indian guests may prefer something new. After all, we've lived in all this Indian atmosphere for some thousands of years."

Bert threw down his pencil. "Did you hire me to tell you how to make a hotel for Americans, too, out of this Indian love nest? Or am I dreaming?"

Jagat laughed. "Please tell me."

Bert tried to look stern. Impossible not to smile back at this charming Indian face!

"Prince, I forgive you. Now, as I've told you before, haven't I, I notice that in the new hotels you Indians like, in Delhi and Bombay, you're careless about small things. But small things show thoughtfulness—for example, making the toast in the bedroom if room service sends up breakfast. As I've said, Americans remember things like that and tell their friends. It's important to keep up standards, especially with Americans. Jackets in the dining rooms, and no taking off shoes on the dance floor—that kind of thing, like I said."

Jagat listened to this, his dark eyes dancing. "There are many interesting sights here in Rajasthan. The region is full of history. The fort at Chittor—"

"Oh, sure, you'll need to set up tours and all that," Bert said. "But Americans will sure want what they're accustomed to having—you know, like dancing and golf, movies, and swimming and fishing. You might even get conventions here once in a while."

"Conventions?"

"Yes, Lions or Elks, or something—maybe even—"

"Animals?"

East and West faced each other in mutual incomprehension.

Bert looked blank. "Who's talking about animals?"

"You said lions."

"Oh gad," Bert groaned, then broke into raucous laughter. "It's a fraternal society—we have lots of them."

A bearded servant in high white turban appeared at the head of the stairs. He carried a silver tray upon which was a sealed envelope.

"Telegram, Your Highness," he said.

Jagat tore open the envelope. Inside was a slip of thin paper, upon which a few words were scrawled in English.

"Killed in action," the words declared. There was something else, "conspicuous bravery," but Jagat grasped only the one eternal fact. His son was dead.

"Excuse me," he muttered. "I have had news. I must go at once to my wife."

"I knew he would die," Moti said.

"You could not have known it," Jagat replied. He was ashamed that he was impatient with her, especially in the presence of the servant who was packing his bags. He had chartered a helicopter to fly him to Ladakh, as close as possible to the border town of Chushul, where the Indian troops were still embattled.

"I will take only the one bag," he told the servant.

"But, Highness, it is very cold in Ladakh."

"I will wear what I need," he said.

"You will be very hot before you reach Ladakh," Moti said.

He wished she would cry, but she did not. Not one tear had she shed since he came to her an hour ago, the tears streaming down his cheeks and the telegram open in his hand. She had taken it, read it, and then looked up at him from where she sat alone on the terrace, wrapped in her white sari. As he gazed at her, expecting her to break into sobbing, she had seemed simply to wither away, her eyes growing larger and more dark. She gave him back the telegram and did not move.

"Come," he had said at last. "Help me to pack. I must leave at once."

She followed him, and did not help. Sitting here in his room, she merely watched, tearless, while he directed the servant. He turned on the radio now, to get the news. The Prime Minister's voice came into the room. He was speaking in English. "On this fateful day we face the greatest menace that has come to us since our independence. Yet let us gird up our loins and face this menace. We have behind us the strength of a united nation. Let us rejoice because of this and apply it to the major task of today, that is the preservation of our complete freedom and integrity and the removal of all those who commit aggression on India's sacred territory. Let us face this crisis not lightheartedly, but with seriousness and with a stout heart, firm in the faith in the rightness of our struggle and with confidence in its outcome."

The beautiful voice faltered, paused, and then went on. "I invite all of you, to whatever religion or party or group you belong, to be comrades in this great struggle that has been forced upon us. I have full faith in our people and in the cause and in the future of our country. Perhaps that future requires some such testing and stiffening for us."

The voice fell silent. Involuntarily Jagat had paused to listen, and he did not notice that Moti had left the room. Now she was back again, her sari caught up in front with a heavy load of some sort. She came close to him, faced him, and let free her sari. The load she carried fell at his feet, an array of gold, all the gold jewelry she possessed, the collars of gold, the earrings, the bracelets, the finger rings, her bridal treasure. Until now she had resisted yielding it, although the Ministry of Finance had besought women to give up their gold trinkets to help pay for the defense. Moti indeed had paid no heed to such demands. It was as though she had not heard, had not felt herself a part of the people. More than once Jagat had thought of speaking to her, saying, "But, Moti, it is because you are the Maharani that you should be an example to the women of Rajasthan." He had refrained out of a sort of delicacy, doubling his own contribution of money.

Now, seeing the glittering mass on the marble floor, his very heart was torn. He put his arms about her and pressed her close to his breast. Half dressed, he felt her cheek wet against his bare flesh, and looking down, he saw that she was weeping at last, with terrible restraint but weeping.

"Cry, cry, my dear," he urged again.

And suddenly, hearing his plea, she yielded to great tearing sobs. Against the wall the turbaned servant stood with his back to them that they might have the courtesy of privacy. Then, unable to endure, he was overcome with his own weeping and he ran from the room.

Alone with his wife, Jagat felt her being one with his in sorrow as they had never been even in the passion of married love. That which they had created together, their only son, was now no more. What must it mean? The question forced itself into his mind. Would this oneness of sorrow continue after the weeping passed, or would it, too, pass as all things pass, leaving them eternally separate?

He pressed Moti to him in a new agony.

"Weep on, my dear," he whispered. "Weep on, for your own comfort and mine!"

The helicopter descended. Jagat stepped out and gazed upon the vast high desert of Ladakh, surrounding Lake Spanggol. Far in the upper distances he saw the outline of the cruel mountains of the Himalayas. From their crests in the clear sunlight of noon, a mighty wind was blowing spumes of snow, visible though many miles away.

A guard in a torn uniform approached him and presented arms.

"Highness," the man said, "I am waiting for you."

"Where is my son?" Jagat demanded.

"Highness, your son's ashes were scattered over this lake with those of the other dead," the guard said.

His slender dark hand lifted, the fingers fluttering like a bird's wings.

Jagat gazed into the blue intensity. The lake was one of many in the region of Ladakh, a hundred miles long, the largest. Why should Spanggol be the resting place of Jai's ashes? He had scarcely hoped to find Jai's body, for the journey had taken too long, but he had hoped, nevertheless. He walked the short distance to the shore now, and stooping, he dipped his hollowed hand into the water. It lay in his palm, translucently clear and bitterly cold. Winter had already crept over these high plains. The short summer began in May and ended in September.

He stood up and brushed his wet hand against his coat. "You are too cold in that thin uniform," he said to the guard.

The man was a dark fellow from the south and his skin was an ashen purple with cold.

"Highness, we have been given no winter garments," he replied.

"Did my son have only these cotton clothes?" Jagat demanded.

"We are all treated alike," the man said. He hesitated and then burst out, "The Chinese wear padded khaki, warmly padded. And they have good weapons—very new, modern, automatic guns."

"Russian-made," Jagat said.

"No! Chinese," the man argued. Thin rivulets of mucus trickled from his nose and froze on his upper lip.

"Come," Jagat said. "You are shaking with cold. Where do you sleep? Take me there. We cannot talk in this wind."

The mountains in the distance loomed white against the blue sky but there was no snow on the sandy plains. The incessant winds swept them clean, day and night.

"There are a handful of us left," the man said. "We escaped, running away, it is true, but only after fighting until nearly all of us were dead. We have no good guns, Highness—only these, thirty years out of date."

He showed his gun and then walked ahead of Jagat, talking over his shoulder.

"The Chinese have everything, Highness—artillery, machine guns, everything—"

"The wind tears the words out of your mouth," Jagat shouted. "Wait until we are in shelter!"

Shelter was in a small ancient temple in the hills beyond the village of Chushul. Two aged lamas in yellow robes were lighting incense before a Buddha, and a pair of cow's-fat candles guttered in brass holders. They turned, startled to see Jagat.

"His Highness, the Maharana of Mewar," the guard said. "He is come to find his son."

"Alas," the elder lama replied. He was a tall thin Tibetan, his face a leathery brown from sun and wind.

"Alas," Jagat repeated.

His hands were aching with cold, and he walked to the altar and held them close to the flaming candles. A bleak chill, smelling of ancient dust and old incense, pervaded the temple.

"Come into the inner hall, Highness. It is warmer there," the younger lama said.

He was a small pale creature in robes of coarse orange-colored wool, his face peaked between his outsized ears. He led the way as he spoke, and Jagat followed, stooping when he walked under the low door. Inside the hall a brass brazier burned, and around it sat five Indians, three of them wounded. They tried to rise but Jagat gestured and they sank to the earthen floor again.

"Sit on this cushion, Highness," the elder lama said. "I will fetch you hot tea."

An immense weariness fell upon Jagat. He sank on the cushion, his legs folded under him, and held his hands over the brazier. The guard sat next to him. For a time all were silent, the men in respect, Jagat in desperate weariness. The lamas brought in bowls of buttered tea, and Jagat drank the rich hot liquid. The warmth crept through his veins, restoring him to a partial vitality. He put down the bowl on the red lacquered tray and looked at the circle of watching faces.

"Tell me," he said, "tell me exactly how my son died."

They looked at one another, each waiting for the others to begin. At last one spoke, a young man, an Indian, whose wounded leg was bound in a bloody rag torn from the olive green uniform of some dead Indian soldier. His dark face was haggard.

"Highness, it is not to be told in one day or one incident."

"Begin where you please," Jagat commanded.

The man drew a raucous cough from deep in his lungs. He spat into the earth, and scraping sand, he covered the spittle.

"The Chinese have been playing a game with us for two years," he began. "We have faced each other many times in small posts over a vast territory, Indian posts always smaller, perhaps a hundred and fifty men, Chinese posts always larger, four hundred, five hundred men. With the Chinese everything is always well planned. They are very tightly knit—our Intelligence cannot break their codes. We have few interpreters. So we are never prepared. We live only from day to day, waiting. Food is short, water is short, ammunition not enough. Everything comes by air, sometimes too late. And you know, Highness, we Indians are not men of war, while the Chinese are warriors for five thousand years. They have studied strategy of every sort and they have good leaders. This is their technique—"

He drew a circle upon the sandy earth. "Here is their post—at the Galwan river post, even two years ago, it was like this. We faced them so—like this, until now. While we waited they surrounded us secretly with their superior forces. When we discovered them, we protested. They did not reply. They sat on high ground and waited while we starved. Then they made gestures to us, shaking their fists so—"

He raised his bony fists above his head and shook them. "They put on loudspeakers and shouted that we must surrender. We refused. Starving and without water, we refused. At last the helicopters with food and water came near and dropped supplies—not enough, but something."

Jagat interrupted. "Did the Chinese allow this?"

He asked but his heart put its own question. What of Jai? Had he died in hunger and thirst, he who had never in his short life known hardship, he a prince's son?

The man moved his head left and right. "They did allow it. We never knew what they would do. When they allowed it, we supposed it was all part of the cold war and that it would go on like that. And it did go on. You remember, Highness, we established the post in July so that we might cut the supply line to a new Chinese post there on the Galwan. You remember, for it was printed in the news, that we stood firm in spite of all their jeers and threats. They came to within fifteen yards of our post and we said we would shoot if they came nearer. They halted then, and our two governments exchanged notes. Then they withdrew. Again we supposed that this was all part of the cold war. Then the order we had been given not to shoot first was rescinded. This was a comfort to us. How could we believe, though, that here at Chushul the same tactics would not be played? Alas, it was not the same. It did go on from July to October, but on the twentieth day of October they attacked in full force. We resisted but they wiped out our post. Of all the men at the post only I escaped. Not that I ran away—no, I went suddenly sick and I leaned behind a rock to vomit and they missed me.

When night fell I found my way through plains and hills
to Chushul. It was many days later."

"It was different at Chushul," the guard put in.

An older soldier turned on him. "It was not different!
Exactly as has been said, the Chinese had planned everything. You know that Chushul may be divided into three
parts, the airfield, the mountain that overlooks the airfield,
and the village. You'd think, Highness, that the Chinese
would take the airfield or at least the village. No, it was
not their plan. They planned to take only the mountain,
and this they did take and from the rear while we faced
the lake. The mountain is sixteen thousand feet high. Why
did the Chinese take it? Because it lies within the territory
they claim. Chushul village—what is it? Why should they
take it? Fifty houses or so, three hundred to five hundred
people living in huts, illiterate, meat-eating fools! Tibetan,
Mongols, barterers, intermarrying—"

"We grow wheat," the younger lama said.

"Well, a little wheat," the soldier granted, "and you
catch wild horses and shoot birds."

"You resisted the Chinese?" Jagat asked.

"Of course we resisted!"

More than one voice spoke but the youngest soldier
took over the story again. He scratched a line on the floor.

"We had no chance, Highness," he said. "The Chinese
have collapsible boats but they did not come over the
lake. They came overland from Tibet on a motor road
they had built. The road is on the great vast plateau they
had already claimed. They came in force, four thousand
men, and took the mountain in two days. The village was
on our side, but what could we do? We fought hand to
hand against their new modern weapons. They are tough,
the Chinese! They value hardship. Their goals are clear—
there is no confusion. They are deliberate but swift. On
the twenty-second and the twenty-third of October they
established the line they claimed and they ceased fighting.
Everything according to plan—their plan!"

The elder lama interrupted. "Ah, that was how they
came into Tibet! Everything was according to plan. First
they deceived us with good words. Then their soldiers

came in force. They knew all our secrets. They had maps even of the sacred Potala. Our god-king barely escaped."

The old soldier broke in. "All the time they were quarreling with us these last two years over the boundary lines, they were planning. 'Our line is five thousand years old,' we said. 'Ours is eight thousand,' they said. Bitterness on both sides! But we never thought then that they would attack."

Jagat sat listening, his eyes fixed on the dying coals. "At what hour was the attack?" he asked now.

"At dawn," the young soldier said. "There were always one of two times of attack—at dawn or dark, both the hours of failing sight. They came rolling down the road they had made at our rear—first the artillery, then the men marching, all well clad. We had no winter clothing and not enough troops. Your son, Highness—"

His voice fell to a lower key. He stared into the coals. "I see your son now. He stood for an instant, not believing. None of us believed. Intelligence had not warned us. Then he shouted. It was he who shouted first of all 'The Chinese are coming!' That was the cry that waked us. We were huddled together for warmth here on this very floor. He shook us by the shoulders, running everywhere at once to waken us. He was the first."

"When did he fall?" Jagat asked. His voice came out tight and weak.

"At once," the young man replied in a whisper. "He fell at once."

"Dead?" Jagat asked.

The young man moved his head in assent. "At once," he repeated. "There was no pain."

"The wound?" Jagat asked, his mouth dry.

"The back of the head—blown off! Only the face was not touched—like a beautiful mask—of death itself."

Jagat asked no more. Jai's brow was high and fine, his eyes large and dark beneath. He would never tell Moti that her son's head had been half blown away.

A Ladakhi woman came to the door with a sick child wailing in her arms and a man followed. Now the man came forward and addressed the elder lama, speaking in a language Jagat did not understand. Man and woman were dressed in Tibetan clothes, straight robes, girdled with a sash. They looked strangely alike, their faces wind-beaten and brown, their dark hair in braids, the man smooth-faced, lightly bearded, as Mongols are. The old lama rose and led them into the temple.

"Our captain was brave, also," the young soldier was saying. "He was wounded at the end of the first day, but he kept on directing us, lying on a heap of straw. At noon the second day he died. We fought on until night. Then we surrendered. But not until some of us retreated to the small hills here, bringing our dead—those we could find. Each buried according to his own religion."

"You have done all that you could and bravely," Jagat said.

The dawn was breaking and he rose and went outside. The early light shone across the sky and struck the distant snow-covered mountains with a rosy splendor. Once before he had seen such beauty, once when he and Moti had taken the children, then young, on a holiday journey to Darjeeling. He had roused them early one morning, coaxing them to go with him to Tiger Hill and see the sun rise on the Himalayas. Moti and Veera would not be coaxed. The rooms in the small British-built hotel were comfortable and warmed by burning coal in the iron grates, and his womenfolk would not leave this comfort. But he and Jai, wrapped in coats and sweaters, had climbed into a jeep and in the darkness had been driven to Tiger Hill to behold the dawn rise over the mighty Himalayas. Through the darkness and bitter cold they had waited in the small enclosed tower set on a hill. Never could he forget that moment when, Jai's small hand clutched in his, they had seen the first pearly outlines of the snow-covered mountains etched against the sky, so high they seemed to hang at the zenith. In silence he and his son had stood watching while the light grew bright and brighter until at last the Himalayas stood in their full magnificence against that dawn-lit sky. In silence they climbed into the jeep again. And now Jagat remembered what he had forgotten. The roadway hung on the edge of cliffs so high that the bottom was not to be seen. Suddenly he felt Jai's palm press his, and he realized the child was trembling as though in a chill.

"What is it, my son?" he had asked.

"I am afraid," Jai had sobbed. "I am afraid—afraid!"

He had clasped his son in his arms then and hidden the little face against his breast.

"I will not let you fall," he had promised. "You are safe, my dear."

The scene came back to him now in its full portent. Had Jai some strange prescience even then that he might one day die in the presence of such mountains upon the far side of a high plateau like this?

He turned to the waiting men. "I will fly back to Delhi," he said. "I will make my personal report to the Prime Minister."

The Prime Minister sat behind the great desk when Jagat entered. His head, wearing the white Gandhi cap, was sunken upon his breast. He rose when he saw his visitor.

"Come in," he said. "I'm sorry you were kept waiting even for a moment. I know of your loss."

Jagat felt the clasp of the firm delicate hand.

"As it was, Mr. Prime Minister, I felt apologetic that you sent for me this morning ahead of so many others who have come before me and are still waiting in the anteroom."

The Prime Minister gestured toward a chair, and seated himself again as he spoke. "This shocking business—to imagine that China can push India about is silly. To imagine that India can push China about is equally silly. We must accept things as they are. It is fantastic to talk about war, but—"

He broke off. "Tell me how he died."

Jagat described briefly the manner of his son's death. So often had he repeated it in his own mind that he told the story almost without emotion. It was the Prime Minister who wiped tears from his own cheeks with his white linen handkerchief. Then, controlling himself and making no attempt to comfort Jagat, he went on to speak of the nation's plight. The thrusts of the Chinese were totally unexpected. Most of India's army of half a million men was stationed on the border of Pakistan and the men were not prepared for the attack on Ladakh. Indeed there was still only one Indian division there, not more than fifteen thousand men at most, and the passes were guarded by not more than forty thousand men, bearing only old weapons.

"I know," Jagat said. "I am told that our men had no good rifles, whereas the Chinese had automatics, or semi-automatics, and Soviet mortars that fired a hundred and twenty millimeter shells."

The Prime Minister sighed and went on. The Chinese supply system was also superior. It had been thought that it would be impossible to carry supplies up the narrow paths clinging to the steep cliffs, but the Chinese had accomplished the impossible. Their soldiers had been supplied with every service by means of trucks and mules, jeeps, laborers, and porters.

Jagat interrupted. "In the Ladakh area, sir, their laborers built roads, and with such speed that trucks came to within a few miles of their position while our men had to march a week to get to a base or airport."

The Prime Minister sighed again and went on. What could he do except what he had done? On October the twenty-ninth he had sent an urgent message to the American President and to the British Prime Minister for speedy military aid. Both had responded. The Americans were sending five million dollars in small arms, and only yesterday he had been promised planes to transport troops to the front.

"The twenty-ninth of October?" Jagat broke in. "It was the day of my son's death!"

The Prime Minister gazed into his face, his dark eyes sad. Before he could speak, a clock struck. He looked at his watch and rose hastily. "I am due at this moment in the Lower House. The matter of this alliance between Pakistan and China is to be discussed. Our enemies are now allies against us, it seems. I shall be fiercely questioned by the members. But the war can't last. Pakistan will make peace."

He nodded briefly and left the room. Jagat stood watching the slight, bowed figure in white trousers and knee-length black coat walk down the corridor until it disappeared, and a door opened to a garden of flowers, freshly watered and shining under the hot sun. Why was he here? No one could do anything to bring his son back. Jai was no more now than a handful of ashes, scattered upon wind and water. The thought was unbearable and Jagat left the great buildings which had once been the seat of British empire and walked out to the street. It was glittering in the sun, the buildings a sultry red, the pavements hot, women in bright saris shielding their heads from the heat. He stopped a taxicab and got in.

"To the Ashoka," he said.

When he entered the hotel the vast lobby was swarming with people but the air was cooled, a relief after the midday sun. In the midst of the crowd he paused, overcome by a feeling of desolation, of personal need. To whom could he go? He had always been the strong one to whom others turned, and he must be that again as soon as he went home. Moti would want to hear everything; he must tell her and then be ready to comfort. And Veera—what could he say to her? With these heavy thoughts he could not face the loneliness of his hotel room and the hours which must pass before he could catch the airplane for the airport nearest Amarpur. Instead of entering the elevator, then, he went to the salon beyond the lobby. A grand piano stood in a far corner and someone was playing. Ah, music might bring relief! The salon at this noon hour was almost empty and walking its length, he chose a seat near the piano. Now he saw that a woman was the musician. He did not know western music and hence did not know what she was playing, but it was something with a melody, haunting and yet powerful. She was an American, he was sure. One could always tell an American, especially an American woman, afraid of nothing and of no one. She was playing as though she were alone, her head bent in absorption. He could see only her profile, pure and fine, and she wore a simple white dress of some sort, crisp and close-fitting. Even her shoes were white, and a narrow white band held back her bright fair hair.

She brought the music to a close, holding the keys so that overtones lingered upon the air.

"That was very beautiful," Jagat said.

She turned her head and he saw a lovely face, tranquil and strong. For an instant he thought he had been wrong about her age, so secure was her loc' 'ut no, her eyes, clear and reflective, proclaimed maturity. She w.. young, but no longer a girl.

"Do you like music?" she asked.

"I know very little about western music," he replied.

"That was a Chopin prelude."

"Very sad music," he observed.

"Yes. In the center of his being he was always sad."

"Is there anyone who isn't?" Jagat inquired.

She looked at him directly, and then spoke as though she perceived his grief. "No—not one."

It was a new experience, this direct talk between two strangers. He knew no woman well, not even Moti, he sometimes thought. Should he ask this western woman's name? He considered and decided against it. There could be no purpose in knowing. He rose and gave her his thanks.

"For a few minutes you have made me forget. Thank you."

He went to his rooms and the next day woke late after a restless night. The sunlight of mid-morning beat against the shaded window and in dismay he snatched his watch from the bedside table. He had missed the daily flight to Amarpur! For an instant he was remorseful, then he had a feeling of respite. There was one day more before he must return to Moti with the detailed description of Jai's death—a useless sacrifice, for what had his son been taught of killing except how to shoot a tiger, between the eyes if possible, so that the skin might not be marred? Had Jai shot a Chinese between the eyes? If so, he had not lived to tell it. While he bathed and dressed he brooded upon the manner of his son's death. The Chinese, he had heard, came into battle with a frenzy of singing and shouting and noise. He was not sure this was true. Probably it was not. Else how could they have crept upon the sleeping Indians from the rear? For that matter, how could they have made a motor road across the desert in secret? Yet they had done so.

Such thoughts tortured his brain until in despair after his breakfast, brought to his room, he telephoned the offices of the President himself and asked to speak with him. He was put through at once and heard the gentle cultivated voice of the old scholar whom all India respected.

"Mr. President, I have just returned from the front where I went to learn how my son died."

"I know," the old voice replied. "I gave orders that you were to be allowed to go in search of him."

"I must speak with you," Jagat said.

"Come at once. I will postpone my appointments."

In an hour Jagat sat facing the aged statesman in his office in the presidential palace, where once a British Viceroy had ruled. In spite of his years he was erect and alert, his spare figure elegant in black knee-length coat and white jodhpurs. On his head, above the thin dark face of an ascetic, a large white turban sat like a churchman's miter, enhancing by its whiteness the brilliant dark eyes.

"Pour out your heart," he said to Jagat.

"My son is dead, Mr. President. It is no use to speak of the past. Let me speak only of the future. Yet how can we know the future unless we consider the past? My son's death and the deaths of other young men like him will not be useless if we learn."

The wise old man listened in silence. The patience of years of human stress and confusion surrounded him like a garment and his lined face did not change its benevolent peace.

Jagat went on. "Let me speak of our country, for which my son died." He leaned forward in his chair, his gaze fixed upon the aged and tranquil face.

"India, China, Pakistan, we form a triad of enemies, a

veritable trinity, like the Three-Faced Deity in the Elephanta Caves, only it would be hard to designate which of us is which, since each would claim to be the Creator, and none would accept the role of the Destroyer, and how can any one of us claim to be the Protector? Alas, in life nothing is so clear as it is in stone, for we change, we change! At any rate, Mr. President, when Pakistan failed to make its case regarding Kashmir in 1959 before the Security Council of the United Nations, she turned to China, in revenge or desperation—who knows which? At any rate, her talks with China reaffirmed her own sovereign rights in Kashmir. At that time China was careful, you remember, and only after the conclusion of her conferences with us did she agree to meet with Pakistani delegates. But you know, Mr. President, as I do, that these talks between the Chinese and the Pakistani were only a sign of further recent agreements. How else explain the fact that only last spring Pakistan gave to China almost six thousand square miles of her own territory? Our military pressures upon the desert of Aksai Chin forced the Chinese to realize they could not have Aksai Chin and so could not use that area as a passage-way between Tibet and their own province of Sinkiang. At any rate, all this has led Pakistan to draw away from us—indeed, from the West—and lean toward China as a revenge. China is now central in the whole Kashmir problem. Yet the mountains in Kashmir are a necessary bulwark, both for Pakistan and ourselves, not only against China but against each other. Gilgit and Baltistan especially are essential for Pakistan, and if we Indians lose Ladakh, there will be a great hole in our defenses. And Soviet Russia, too, concerns herself in Kashmir. She has supported us even against China; she is sending Russian instructors to teach our Indian air force pilots how to fly in those formidable mountains, and she has promised us jet fighters more modern than those sold to China, if I am to believe today's newspapers. To what purpose, Mr. President? I think of the Chinese province of Sinkiang, of course, so rich in minerals and a strategic point between herself and China—her own borders there are undefined. Sinkiang is the prize. But for us?"

The President moved in his chair and glanced at a clock on the wall. Jagat made haste to come to an end.

"Ladakh has become important to China now as a passage to Sinkiang. She will insist upon Ladakh. You are aware of this, Mr. President?"

The old man inclined his head and Jagat rose.

"Of course you are, sir, but for me Ladakh is my son's grave. He died to serve the ambitions of China—that is, he so died if we yield that territory."

"We do not yield."

The old man's voice was firm. He put out his hand and Jagat shook it. It was frail to the touch but strong in its clasp and he went away somewhat comforted. There was nothing new in what he had said. It was obvious that the old man had thought of everything, and knew everything.

It was evening when he entered the hotel lobby. Above the din of guests coming and going, he heard again the distant strains of the piano and an old loneliness, only deepened by his son's death, now overwhelmed him. He went to the salon where people from every country sat in small groups at tea or cocktails and passing them by, he took again the seat nearest the piano. Yes, it was she who played. She looked up and smiled as she continued to play, and he listened to the music, slow and powerful, that flowed from under her hands. She brought the chords to an end at last in a final resonance, and looked toward him. It was a summons, was it not? He rose and came to her side.

"I am leaving early tomorrow morning. I hope you enjoy your visit in India. Where do you go from here?"

"I stay here for some days yet—how many I cannot tell. I don't know my plans."

He hesitated. This was a beautiful face, upturned to his, still younger perhaps than he had thought, and yet somehow old with a sort of inner sorrow. Loneliness, too, perhaps? What was a woman doing here alone, so far from her own country? He was curious about her, foolishly, for she was a stranger and must continue so.

"Are you free this evening?" he asked impulsively.

She did not seem surprised. "Yes, I am. I'm always free. I don't know anyone."

"I might be able to show you a bit of India."

"I'd like that. I've been wondering when it would happen."

"You have no friends?"

"No."

"You make me curious."

"I have nothing to tell, really. I'm simply—traveling."

She sat there, her hands resting on the keys of the piano, her face turned up to his, an honest face with all its beauty. It occurred to him to wonder why he had spoken to her. Perhaps it was sheer sorrow at Jai's death and a necessity for the relief of a new experience. He was not accustomed to personal sorrow and he did not know how to deal with it. Perhaps it was only the need to delay facing Moti with the tragedy. Perhaps—perhaps—

"I'll meet you here at eight? We might dine together," he said.

"I shall be here—over yonder in that gold chair. It looks comfortable, but there's always someone else sitting in it." She glanced at him with a glint of humor in her grave blue eyes.

He laughed. "This time it will be you."

"Yes."

She had a lovely smile, wistful yet gay, and it changed her face to a girl's face. She began again to play as if she had forgotten him. He went away then and the echoes of her music followed him.

That evening he waited for her in the lobby, half wishing that he had not made the appointment. He knew no western women, beyond the few he had frequented years ago when he was at Oxford. This woman was not one of those. He had heard that American women were independent and free, and that they did not easily fall in love, but he imagined that in fact women were the same everywhere in the world. There were the available ones and those who were not available. She belonged to the unavailable. He looked at his watch impatiently. The evening must not last too long. He should be on his way to Moti in the early morning.

Then he saw her step out of the elevator and walk toward the gold chair gracefully and without haste. She had put on a black dress ankle length and clinging. The neck was low but the sleeves were long. She wore emeralds in her ears and one huge emerald on her left hand. No wedding ring, he noticed. All this he saw in the few seconds before their meeting.

"I am not late, I think," she said, as he approached her.

He realized for the first time the quality of her voice, soft and intensely feminine.

"No, I am early. I beg, are you really American?"

She laughed. "Yes, really! Why? You don't like us?"

"I don't know you. As a matter of fact, you're only the second American I've ever talked to. The other one is a brash young redhead who's turning one of my palaces into a modern hotel."

"Then should we not introduce ourselves?"

They were sauntering now toward the dining room. "Yes, of course, and I must apologize for not taking you somewhere else to dine. The food is not always good here but there's air conditioning."

"It's delightfully cool—and that's more important than food."

They entered and were led to the table he had ordered. In a silver vase a white rose faced her.

"For you," he said. "I told them not to put the usual yellow marigolds between us."

She smiled at the rose. "Thank you."

He continued. "And I have taken the liberty of ordering some Indian food for you. It may not be the best, but it will be different. I didn't want to present you with tough beef, and our Indian lamp chops are absurd. They're goats, really."

"Such dainty little goats," she said. "I've seen them scampering about the country roads. I couldn't bear to eat them. And I've never had Indian food. What better time to begin than now, with you, a gentleman of India?"

"You've never been here before?"

"No, never."

"Shall I introduce myself now?"

"Please."

"I shall spare you the titles. My father was the ruler of a province in northwest India. In the natural course of history—very ancient—I would have succeeded him. But these are modern times and there are no more princely states. My name, simply spoken, is Jagat."

She did not ask what she was to call him and he did not tell her. If they were companions only for the evening she need call him nothing. If they met again—and perhaps again—then she could choose the name she liked best.

"And your name, please?" he asked.

"Brooke Westley."

"Brooke," he repeated. "I have not heard that name. It suits you. Miss—is it Miss?"

She hesitated for more than an instant. "Yes—"

Something difficult hung between them, a sudden impulse on his part to inquire, on her part he imagined a reluctance. In this brief interim the food arrived, and he busied himself with explanations.

"I have not ordered our usual bread. In my opinion it is too heavy. Oh, yes, I eat it, Indian fashion, tearing the cakes apart—it's like an English pancake, but thicker—and sopping up the curry—but it's not a particularly pleasant procedure if one's not used to it. These are chapati, much thinner and more delicate. And that's rice of course, only yellow with saffron. Eat it with this curry and here are the condiments. I ordered a vegetable curry. I'm afraid our chickens are the dainty sort, too—bantams—ah, they've put chicken into it in spite of me! But try it. And prepare your plate so—"

The white-turbaned waiter served her but Jagat himself dipped the chopped nuts, the shredded cocoanut, the mango chutney and piled them on the rice upon her plate.

"And this," he went on, "is milk curds, designed to cool the tongue if the curry bites too sharply—as it will the tongues of all who are not born to it."

She listened with the air of amusement and began to eat. He watched her. What a beauty she was, the long dark lashes—oh, he was accustomed to long dark lashes, but not to these surrounding violet blue eyes and beneath the dark blond hair. Tonight she had swept her hair upward into a loose coil that outlined the noble shape of her head. He liked the cleanness of her profile, the features delicate yet defined, the face oval, the bone structure subtly strong. He was used to the lushness of beautiful Indian women and in fact liked it, but this was something new, the skin so pure and pale, the lips a delicate pink. Yet her mouth was unexpectedly sensuous.

"I like this food," she said, tasting it.

He was ridiculously encouraged. "Good, now I can enjoy my own food."

He was hungry, and they ate for a few minutes in silence until she put down her fork.

"There—I can eat no more."

"You won't like the dessert," he declared. "Osgood—that's my hotel chap—says I'm never to serve Indian desserts. It's almonds crushed in cream and sugar."

"I often like what other people do not," she replied. "And it's not a contrariness of nature, either. I think perhaps it's because I like something new—food I've never tasted, people I've never known."

"Ah then," he said in triumph.

He considered what to suggest after dinner. Not dancing —it was too soon after Jai and he had not the heart for it. Yet he wanted to be in her company. Somehow by her composed beauty she relieved the darkness of his soul.

"Will you forgive me if I make the most obvious invitation after dinner?"

"If it is what you wish," she replied, smiling.

"Have you seen the Taj Mahal? By moonlight?"

She laughed. "No! And I agree it's obvious. I daresay I'm the only American in India who hasn't seen it. And it's been suggested by every guide and cab driver. And I've refused."

"Ah then, something else?"

"No, not something else! Because I've been waiting for the right moment and the right person and I think I've found both. Otherwise I would have gone at last quite alone—or never have gone."

An exchange of looks passed between them, silent and exploring.

"It's overrated, you know," he told her defensively. "Not in beauty but in—well, romance. The Shah's wife bore him fourteen children and died in the last birth. Not much romance left, I imagine!"

"It is for beauty that I want to see it," she replied. "And perhaps one doesn't need romance after the first one. Perhaps love—or remorse—or anything that's strong enough to move a man's soul, or a woman's, takes its place. Love is not the only force."

He listened, trying to divine her meaning. How much was contained in those words and what was therein contained?

"Then let us go," he said.

He directed the waiter to summon a cab and was glad that he did not have his own car and chauffeur here waiting for him. What would the man have thought of such a jaunt? By roundabout gossip the news would have reached Moti—the chauffeur to the cook and the cook to the women servants and they to Moti's personal ayah—idle talk, for probably they would never meet again. Brooke! Of course he could not call her by her name, now or perhaps ever, but it held a smoothly flowing music. In the car, winding its way among the evening crowds, it occurred to him that she had said nothing of herself.

"I say," he began, "after all, I told you who I am. You have given me nothing of yourself except your name."

They were leaving the city now and entering upon the highway to Agra. She seemed not to hear him.

"What are those black knots hanging in the trees?" she inquired.

"Those? Ah, they're vultures, waiting hopefully for a car to run over a dog lying asleep in the dust. Then they'll swoop down and consume it. Of course what they really long for is an accident between human beings."

"I wonder you endure them!" she exclaimed.

"They are good scavengers," he replied.

She made no comment to this, reflecting upon what he had said, without criticism apparently. The Indian scene was simply another way of living.

"So," he resumed, "what are you?"

She considered, as though she did not know. "In a way," she replied, "you might say I am no one in particular. I was born in a quiet old city on the eastern coast of the United States. My parents were wealthy, I was an only child, and they died when I was young. I scarcely knew them. They left everything to me and not having the inspiration of work, I have pursued music and been pursued by it. Other than that, I have not made connection with life."

"You have not married?"

"No."

"Why not?"

"I have not seen the man I wished to marry."

"You have had too much independence," he suggested.

She looked at him quickly and then away again. "Perhaps that is my handicap."

He longed to ask her whether she had ever been in love and denied himself, for he had not the right to ask—not yet, and perhaps never. With an Indian woman, a modern one, he would not have hesitated. Sex was direct and there was little else to talk about between man and woman. But this beautiful human being, sitting beside him and yet at infinite distance, was a person as well as a woman. He did not believe she was cold. The lines of her mouth, the liquid warmth of her eyes, the cadence of her voice, the voluptuous softness of her hand when it had clasped his in greeting, the roundness of her slender body, all conveyed their message to his strong maleness. And yet, and yet!

The car stopped. "Have we arrived?" she asked.

"Yes, This is the entrance. I want you to pause for a bit as we enter, and absorb the proportions of beauty."

He bade the driver wait, and he led the way through the great tunnel gate and to the farther exit, facing the mausoleum. They were not alone. Some scores of people moved about, the women in saris bright even in the moonlight, the men in white, the children linking them together. The lagoon, a path of moonlit water, led between marble walks on either side. Far at the end the marble building stood translucent in the night.

He turned to speak to her and saw that he must not speak. She was standing motionless, head lifted, hands at her sides, the night wind blowing her hair softly. Her eyes were luminous in the moonlight, her lips parted. When she spoke it was as if he were not there.

"This is the first thing in my life that I have ever seen which is more beautiful than I dreamed."

"Then I am happy you have found it in India," he said gently.

He spoke very little to her after that, beyond guiding her about the place so familiar to him. He mentioned the jewels with which the filigreed marble had once been set, and which long ago the conquering British soldiers had dug out of their sockets and sold. Yet as an aristocrat himself he gave full credit to the English nobleman and viceroy who had ordered the thievery stopped and had even replaced some of the stones albeit with those of lesser value. She listened gravely and in silence, pausing sometimes to follow a pattern of the carved marble with the tips of her fingers, feeling out its beauty. At his side she descended into the crypt where were the tombs of the wife and the husband.

"The Shah dreamed that he would build a marble tomb for himself as well," Jagat told her, "but it was to be of black marble. Alas, his greedy sons forbade it. They deposed him and made him their prisoner. In his old age he could not prevail."

"It is better not to have sons," she said.

He received this bitter truth with shock. How could she know that he had lost his only son? She did not know. She had spoken out of divination. He made no reply, but when they had returned to the hotel, he took her aside into the now deserted salon and motioned her to be seated. She obeyed, leaning back as though in weariness, but she was not weary. She was only prepared, as he saw, to listen. He drew his chair near to her, facing her. They were alone in the great room, the guests gone, the servants drowsy at their posts.

"We are strangers, you and I," he said. "We are strangers from different parts of the world, and perhaps from different ages in time. Much of our life here in India is still medieval. Yet I feel at this moment as though I have known you before. Tell me—" he leaned forward—"why do you say it is better to have no sons? It is the strangest thing that can be said to an Indian, and no Indian will believe it, except perhaps I, at this special moment. I am in grief for the loss of my only son. He was killed in Ladakh, thirteen days ago, by the Chinese. I shall never have another. Can you still say it is better to have no sons?"

She received this with silence, as though it were a communication from another planet. After a time she replied, her white and narrow hands clasping the carved ends of the arms of her chair. "I think it is better for you also to have no sons. Now you will complete your life in your own way. You will fulfill yourself because you have no one else to fulfill it for you. When a man—and a woman—have children, they divide themselves, they also excuse themselves. See what I have done, they say, I have replaced myself. If I do not complete my entire duty to my generation, my son will do it for me in his time. It is said very often in my country that children are the hope of the future. To me that is evasion and nonsense. They will do no better than we do. Your son, had he lived, would have done no more for his generation than you have done for yours—or will do, for you are still a young man."

"I am in middle life," he told her.

"Then you have no time to beget more children," she said quietly.

He gazed at her with doubt and wonder. Was she right? She was not shaken by the penetration of his dark eyes and she met his gaze without question.

"Is this why you have never married?" he asked.

"I told you—I have never seen the man I wished to marry."

"If you did, would you marry him?"

"Yes, if he wished it."

"If he did not?"

"Then I would arrange my life to be near him—forever."

He received this and put it into his memory to think of again and again. Now he rose.

"I leave tomorrow morning very early, so good night is good-bye—unless you feel inclined to come to Amarpur. You might be my first guest in the Lake Palace Hotel. Will you accept this as an invitation?"

"Perhaps."

"May I see you to your room?"

She hesitated. "Will it disturb the guests if I play the piano?'

"I am sure it will not."   ..

"Then good night."

She put out her hand without rising and he took it between both his own. It felt firm and cool between his burning palms. He left her and when he looked back at her she was already at the piano and she did not turn her head. She had forgotten him? He put the question to himself and then he remembered. She had said good night and not good-bye!

"Moti!" he said.

She was in her room, lying on a chaise longue, and she turned her lusterless eyes toward him.

"Why have you delayed?"

"It was necessary that I stop in New Delhi and acquaint certain persons with what I learned at the border."

Her ayah had followed him into the room.

"My mistress eats nothing except a handful of curds, a little fruit."

"Go away," Moti said impatiently. "Leave us! What does it matter whether I eat?"

The ayah, frightened at such impatience in one habitually mild, shrank back into the shadows outside the door.

"What did you discover?" Moti demanded.

Jagat sat down. Her rooms, usually fresh with the scent of flowers, were strangely desolate. All flowers had been removed, the potted orange trees and lemons, the roses cut from English tea roses imported from gardens in Delhi, the scentless blossoms of the local dessert. Vases were empty, and floors and furniture were dusty. True, the high winds had blown fine sand everywhere during these last days but Moti was fastidious and during such seasons she usually kept her women busy. She observed now his wandering gaze.

"I have not been able to endure my stupid women running hither and thither."

"You are killing yourself," he told her. "You want to die. I command you to live."

Her eyes were sunk in pools of shadows. She had lost much weight in the days he had been away and now she sat enshrouded in her white sari, her delicate bones a mere framework for the thin covering of pale flesh.

"How can I eat?" she asked restlessly. And then with her new and unaccustomed impatience she pressed him. "Tell me what happened to him."

He sighed at the task. "How do I know? He died with scores, hundreds, of others. The attack came from the rear—"

Thus in halting sentences, bit by bit as he drew upon his memory, he recounted what he knew. When he came to the part that told of old weapons and scanty clothing in the midst of bitter cold, she could not listen quietly. She rose and paced the room, hither and yon, now by the door, now at the far end where the windows overlooked the lake. Agony compelled her to motion. He was astonished at her swiftness, she who could sit by habit through hours of stillness.

"Did you not complain when you were in Delhi?" she cried at him. "Did you not tell them there that they have murdered our son?"

"Full reports had already been made, Moti. It was not necessary for me to repeat them. We are asking aid from the United States, from England—the latest weapons have been promised, the utmost in defense."

"Of course, now that he is dead—"

"Moti, you forget yourself. Our son was not the only—"

She turned on him from the opposite side of the room.

"He was, he is, the only one for me! But how can you understand a woman? You have never understood me! I have lived here a score of years and you know nothing of me. Why should I expect comfort from you now? Reports! Did the reports say the word *murder?* Whose fault was it that Jai had an old weapon that he could not use to save his own life? Where are the warm clothes he should have worn to save him from the cold? He hated the cold—I don't forget how when he was a little boy he hated snow. That he should die in the cold! I cannot forgive you. Go back to Delhi and tell them that Jai, the son of Prince Jagat, has been murdered!"

"Moti, they would call me insane."

"Let them! Does it matter what they call you?"

"Moti, listen to me. The Chinese have said they will withdraw when—"

"Oh, don't talk of the Chinese! Will their withdrawal bring back my son?"

It was useless to speak. He sat immobile, his eyes fixed upon the marble floor while she accused him, sobbing out her anger and grief. Suddenly he could bear no more. He rose and walking to where she leaned against a pillar exhausted with herself, he put his arms about her, and lifting her, he carried her to her bed and laid her down against the pillows. How light, how frail she was in his arms! She fell back, her eyes closed, silent now except for the sobs.

He beckoned to the serving woman who came out of the shadows.

"Soothe her," he commanded. "Rub her temples and brush her hair. When she is quieted, bring her a bowl of milk."

He went away then to his rooms and considered his own loss. Until this hour his days had been busy with travel and talk and the meeting with the American woman. Now he was alone. Here in the palace of his ancestors, his birthplace, and his son's, he was utterly alone. The endless stream of his family history had passed through these walls. Now abruptly it was stopped. He was the end. Who tomorrow would inhabit these rooms, from whose walls his forefathers gazed at him, a procession of princes surrounding him from the day of his birth? When he died, the rooms where they had all lived would be empty. He and they would be no more and there was not one to follow them.

For him this was the hour of Jai's final death.

In the night, in the darkest night, when sleepless, he lay in his bed tossing and turning this way and that, he heard someone at his door. Immediately he lay still and listening. The door opened, its hinges creaking. Then it closed softly. He thought of thieves, of assassins. Once in this very room an ancestor prince had been killed by an unknown man. The murderer was never found, but it was said that he was the husband of a beautiful young woman whom the prince had taken into the palace. But that was long ago, and Jagat had committed no such crime.

Had be been afraid he would have shouted, but he was not afraid, only curious. Who came in so silently, so stealthily, and who was even now crossing the marble floor? In the darkness he imagined a form.

"What do you want?"

He spoke in his ordinary voice, neither loud nor low. He scratched a match and lit his bedside candle and peering into the darkness, he saw Moti coming toward him, the ends of her white sari dropped from her shoulders and clasped in her hand. He cried out.

"Moti! Are you ill?"

She did not reply. She drew nearer until she was at the side of his bed. Then she sank to her knees and there in the candlelight he saw her supplicating face.

"What is it, Moti?"

He saw her eyes burning. Her narrow tongue ran out of her mouth and wet her lips.

"Jagat!"

"Yes? Are you afraid of something?"

"No . . . Yes—of you."

"Of me?"

"Afraid you will refuse me."

"But what do you want of me?"

"Jagat, I am still young enough."

He stared into her eyes so dark in her pale face. "Moti—"

Suddenly he understood her presence and he could not go on. Not in all the years of their marriage had Moti come to his bed. It was always he who sought her, never she who sought him. This he had accepted, thinking it the behavior of a modest woman. Now here she was, seeking him. He felt a strange embarrassment, a shyness, as though she were not his wife. She was no longer Moti, the silent girl who had submitted to him as a bride, as a woman, as a wife, the mother of his children.

"Moti—" he repeated.

"Give me another son, Jagat!"

"Moti, I—"

"That I may give him back to you, and so fulfill myself! You know a woman cannot live—or die—without this duty. Jai must be born again in his brother. Your family has no heir. Why else have I lived except to give you an heir?"

Once he would have rushed into passion had she come seeking him. He would have swept her into his bed and crushed her with his ardor. To be sought, to be loved, to know her body urgent with his urgency, would have been a power sweet and new. For so long she had filled his physical need and had given him nothing more, the more he had never had from her. Indeed, he had never had it from any woman, for what sweetness is there when love is bought from a stranger?

She was kneeling at his bedside and yet he could not lift her up. To her supplication he felt his soul and body give refusal, inexplicable refusal.

"Moti, I—"

"Take me, Jagat!"

"I cannot—"

His voice was only a whisper, but she heard. In the dim light of the candle he saw her rise to her feet and stand there beside the bed, looking down at him with dark, dark eyes. Her hair flowed down about her face and fell to her waist in darkness. He had not seen her hair like this since their wedding night.

"You will not!"

It was exclamation, not question.

"I cannot."

"Then you have been with a woman. Oh yes—" She leaned over him, supporting herself with her hands outspread upon the sheet. "That is what you have done. It is what men always do when they are sad. They hurry to a woman and relieve themselves. They cannot be sad for long. Especially you, Jagat! You have always used me for your own purpose. Now, when I ask you to—to—do you think it is easy for me? I am ashamed. I despise myself even while I beg you. But it is for Jai—it is because we have no son."

He took her left hand and pulled her down.

"Sit here beside me, Moti. Listen to me! I have not been with any woman. I have come straight from the battlefield. I stayed only a short two days in Delhi and then came home. How could I have the heart to go to any woman, Moti? I am no longer a young man, I do not —I have no need to—to—merely for—for—"

She bowed her head over their clasped hands and he felt the warmth of her hair flowing over his bare arm.

"Shall we never have another son?" Her voice he could scarcely hear.

He took his other hand and smoothed the hair away from her face.

"Moti—not like this—never like this—"

She sat silent and very still for a long moment and then as silently as she had come she left him, a white shadow drifting away.

He put out the candle then and lay alone in the soft black night, thinking and wondering. Why had he not accepted her? Had death made the change in him? In these days of shock and sorrow had a vital part of himself died with his son? In his loins now there was only quiet, in his loins where he had been wont to feel a life almost separate from himself in its willfulness. Night or day he had felt that life ready and quivering, the seat of desire and independent from his being, urgent and quick to respond to any woman young and beautiful. He understood very well the unceasing necessity which had kept this palace gay with women, the thirst which his father and his father before him had never seemed able to slake. That he himself had not brought girls into his own rooms was simply that he had been of different stuff, as virile but more fastidious. No, he had not even been more fastidious. It was Moti who had made it impossible for him to take another woman after marriage, her pale gentleness, her patient submission, her invariable yielding which was never response, so that she left his eternal question eternally unanswered. Was she unable to respond or did she find him somehow distasteful? His male vanity could not accept the latter possibility and yet could not answer the question. He had continued to woo her gently, but sometimes with force. His male vanity! Was he vexed because she had come to him now only for the sake of a child?

Reflecting thus upon himself, he was led to reflect further upon Moti. Let him remember that she came of high caste and as befitted so noble a birth she was a modest woman, uncovering herself with reluctance when he demanded it. He had found this reluctance enticing and lovable, her chasteness a proof of her nobility, and remembering her as she had been an hour ago, seeking him instead of being sought, he felt her in some vague way lower than she had been. Unfair, unfair, he told himself, for at least she had come not for her own sake. Suddenly he understood his refusal. She had not come to him out of her own need. Her heart was not his, if indeed she had a heart. She had not come to him crying, "Oh, Jagat, love me!"

Yet could a woman nobly born ever lower herself to such pleading for her own need? He remembered an ancient tale of Vyasu, who wrote the mighty book of the *Mahabharata,* and how when he chose a wife among his three nieces, he made a test of them so that he could be sure that he did not choose the one who had been fathered by a slave. This test was that each of the three princesses should walk before him naked. The eldest was so ashamed that she closed her eyes, the second, being also ashamed, covered herself with yellow ochre, but the third princess walked without shame, parading her nakedness before him. Seeing this, he knew her to be of common origin and he rejected her, making his choice between the other two.

Against his will Jagat recognized in himself the ancient prejudice toward immodesty, although he understood that grief and despair had made Moti change herself. In such confusion of his mind he wondered if there were a secret flaw in Moti somewhere that she could so far forget herself. He even allowed himself for a moment to give way to an old question hidden in his mind regarding the English priest. Never before had he permitted this question to rise to the surface of his mind. Now here it was in all its bareness. Was there something more than spiritual need in her when she accepted the presence of the bearded young priest? A priest is still a man.

Yet strangely at this moment he felt no jealousy. Should he not properly feel jealousy? Had he allowed himself the question before Jai's death certainly he would have been jealous. Yet here he was, his heart as calm as a bird in its nest, and now he wondered at himself even more than he wondered at Moti. Death had disturbed their separate beings, and to what measure he did not know, except that for him this night sleep was impossible. Nor did he rest for the next seven days, not as he usually did, sleeping deeply through the night. By day he wearied himself in many ways while he mourned for his son and in spite of all he could not rest, while night followed day for seven days.

On the morning of the eighth day he rose early and went to the lake palace to see what progress had been made there.

"You have a guest," Osgood said. He was living in the palace now in order to superintend the changes there. Jagat leaped from the boat to the marble steps of the landing. "What guest? And how can you put him up in this confusion?"

Workmen were everywhere, the birds were distracted and flying out of their nests in cornices and candelabras, and the noise of pounding hammers and shouting men spoiled the stillness of the afternoon.

"It's a woman," Osgood said.

"A woman!" Jagat repeated, unbelieving.

"She says you invited her."

"I?"

"So she says."

Jagat smiled wryly. "In a manner—"

He knew of course who the woman was. He had thought of her many times in the past week, a strange week at that, for he and Moti had scarcely spoken to each other. The days had passed in a strained silence, she more withdrawn than ever.

"Shall I not send for Veera to be with you?" he had inquired last evening when they had sat in silence at the dinner table.

"Why should we add our sadness to hers?" she had replied. "Let her remain with her school fellows."

Looking at the pale face, he had felt it impossible that she had come to him that night, seven nights ago. In those seven nights he had not approached her. Never before since their marriage had he remained so long continent. He was still without desire.

"Where is this guest?" he now asked Osgood.

"In the small room opening on the upper terrace. I'd been using it myself but I turned out when she showed up. It's the only room yet with a bathroom. I can't ask her to take a dip in the lake—which is what I'm doing in spite of the crocodiles!"

"The crocodiles are all at the upper end, as I told you. Besides, I doubt they'll eat you—all that red hair!"

Osgood laughed.

"When did she arrive?" Jagat asked.

"Last night. She appeared as cool as you please at the landing. I saw a boat coming across the lake in the moonlight and I thought it was you. Then I saw a woman step out and the boatman with her luggage. I went down, of course, and there she was. Her name is Miss—"

"Ah yes, now I remember." Deceit, for he had never forgotten! "Miss Westley, an American also. She was in the Ashoka."

"You might have warned me," Osgood said.

"I didn't think she'd take me so literally."

"Lucky I'd fixed myself up with a decent room and bath! How long is she staying?"

"How can I tell? I have not seen her."

They were talking over the dusty debris of men at work.

"She's up," Osgood said. "I sent breakfast to her room. That's another thing. I'm only set up here for one person. I brought my own cook from Delhi. What am I to do?"

"Tell him to serve her as well," Jagat said. "She's your countrywoman, not mine."

"Yes—well, I've no time for entertainment." Osgood retorted. "I have another job in Bombay scheduled for next month, and things must be well under way here. I ought to fly to the States some time between and get what I can't get in India."

"Fly, my friend—I shall be here," Jagat said.

He controlled his desire to hasten his steps and indeed almost wished she had not come. The days of formal mourning past, he longed to plunge himself into the work of this hotel and the administration of the lands he still had left. Much of the land was gone, but much was left. His princely family had been rich in lands, since they had of old desired to be paid in land rather than money. With the land went the villages, independent and yet belonging to the earth by centuries of endurance and toil. Only this morning he had risen early to ride horseback to the central village, where he maintained a sort of office, to meet with the village elders, the panchayat. To them he had reported in brief detail the manner of his son's death. Strangely, he had not felt it was he who rode through the cool morning air. Instead he saw everything through Jai's eyes, Jai who never again would gaze upon the crystal mountains gleaming in the dawning sun, and never again breathe into his living lungs the pure high air of the desert. With Jai's eyes he saw the caravan of camels padding through the dusty country roads, and the herds of small dark goats, pursued by little angry boys, shivering half naked in the early air. With Jai's eyes, too, he saw the villagers in their white cotton shawls sitting bleakly along the streets, waiting for the sun to rise to warmth. With Jai's eyes he saw the swallows flying from their nests of mud, encrusting the village walls, and the cows, wandering in search of food. All this was Jai's heritage as profoundly as were the great cities of Bombay and Calcutta and Madras, and the great industries of Tata in the eastern province, as profoundly, too, as the history of thousands of past years or the brightening days of tomorrow. All, all was Jai's heritage and now never could be claimed.

The village elders rose when he entered the low-roofed mud building. They greeted him with folded hands and bowed heads in deep silence. When he had seated himself upon the cushion on the earthen floor, polished with cow dung, they sat also and he told them, controlling heart and voice, of how Jai had died, and why. While he spoke he looked at one weathered face and another, bearded old men with turbans, shaven old men with gaunt cheeks and thin sinewy necks. The scene was that of the centuries and he knew as he spoke that when he was gone it would never be repeated. Even had Jai lived, he could not imagine that he would have sat here among these elders.

His story was cruelly short and he made it so, lest he weep. "Thus died my only son," he told them, and pressing his lips together to make them firm, he went on. "Death is meaningless unless we who live give it meaning. Especially is this true of the young who die before their time. There are many in this war who have died, and many more like them will die. Who can foretell the end of the age? Let us therefore try to fulfill in our lifetime what these would have done had they lived."

With this said, he had gone on to speak of reforms

that he planned in their region, the building of schools, especially technical schools, the improvement of cattle and crops, the establishment of hospitals and clinics.

One old man had called out a question. "Is it true, is it true, that the lake palace is made into an inn for people from across the Black Water?"

He had explained that in a way this was so, and he told them how his revenues had been cut that they might have more and that he had therefore to seek ways of support for himself and his family, since he remained a prince, but a prince without a realm. They had listened, and with sighs had pitied him, and yet he imagined he saw the glint of greed in their eyes. It was all old and well known, archaic as the barren desert and mountains, and made more so now by the glitter of new metal and the fresh whiteness of the marble walls of the palace. Telephones here took the place of shouting servants and electric lights replaced the candles in the old crystal chandelier imported long ago from Europe. And nothing was as different and as new as the sight of the slim straight figure of Brooke Westley walking toward him, down the marble corridor at this very moment.

He went toward her. "I am glad you have come, although I did not expect you so soon."

She did not put out her hand but their eyes met. "I felt compelled."

"Are you in trouble?" he asked.

"No," she said.

"Then how are you compelled?"

"I follow a sympathy," she said.

Her eyes did not waver as she spoke these few simple words. He had never met so frank a gaze. There was no coquetry in her, no pretense.

"I do not know what you mean," he said.

"And I cannot explain," she replied. "Therefore let me live here quietly for a while. I shall not be a trouble to you. I shall be quite happy, waiting."

"For what?" he asked.

"I shall have to find out," she said.

Now she put out her hand. "Don't feel responsible for

me. I take care of myself. I shall find my own way. I am not afraid. I've never been afraid in my life. I've always been alone."

"But you puzzle me!" he protested.

"Don't be puzzled. Accept me as I am, whenever we meet, or if we meet. You will let me stay? At least for a while, until I find out why I've come—"

He hesitated. "Well, it's far from comfortable, you know. We've only just begun."

"It's wonderful, living in the middle of a lake. That's new. I've lived in encircling mountains and I've lived in the middle of the city of New York, encircled again. But I like this. The water is quiet."

She spoke in a soft rush. Now she put out her hand and he found himself holding it. He did not quite know what to do with it, aware of its warm softness and yet—

She pulled it away gently. "I like your Mr. Osgood. Of course I know I've put him into consternation. Think of finding a man here so—so American! I like that, too. It makes me feel oddly at home. And yet I don't feel strange with you, either. That's another oddness!"

"But you'll be very lonely," he said when she paused.

"Oh, no, indeed, I'm never lonely. You see, I scarcely knew my parents, as I told you. I grew up with my grandmother in a big old house in the country, and another big old house in New York. And there are other reasons—"

She had turned away and now she had glanced at him over her shoulders. "Does the name Westley mean anything to you? It's rather well known—"

He shook his head. "I don't know Americans."

She interrupted. "Why should you—living in this heavenly place? That palace—" She waved her hand toward the palace across the lake.

"You must come and see my wife," he said.

She stood quite still for an instant, gazing at the palace, its marble roseate in the light of the setting sun.

"Will she like me, do you think?"

"I am sure she will. Just now she is very sad because of our son. But in a week or so, perhaps, it will be good for her to know someone new. I have a daughter, too. She will want to come home as soon as she knows— about her brother, I mean."

She did not reply at once. Then she said, slowly and thoughtfully, "It's strange. I come here alone, knowing no one, and suddenly I have friends—many friends."

II

"SUDDENLY I HAVE FRIENDS—many friends."

She heard her own voice speak these words and instinctively she drew back. She was not yet ready for friends. Indeed she had not come to India to find friends. She had come upon impulse, drifting as she had drifted all her life, yet not aimlessly nor helplessly. In search of beauty she drifted, caught upon her dreams as an empty shell drifts, floating upon the waves of the sea. She was conscious of emptiness, and she was conscious of need to be filled. Surely the meaning of need was capacity. Her capacity was for reality, but reality was still vague and she could not define it in words. She had learned, however, that reality was not always beautiful. Sometimes it was harsh and rough, sometimes it was poverty and darkness, sometimes it was power and fear. Sometimes it was only music, clear and uncomplicated. She judged by her own appraisal. Whatever reality was, it was truthful, it had no concealments, it made no pretense. It was life, deep and slow-growing. She had come to believe at last that reality was to be found only in a very old country, the oldest of countries, and so she had approached India, the mother country of ancient Asia. Here she would live at least for a while, she told herself; here perhaps she would find her own being, who had all her life been lost, for she had no home. Guided by none but herself, she had discovered these words.

"The antipathies and sympathies of Today, the sudden affinities like falling in love at first sight, and the sudden hostilities that apparently had no sense—all were due to relationships in some buried Yesterday, while those of tomorrow could be anticipated, and so regulated by the actions of Today. Even to the smallest things—"

She had read these words one day last summer in her grandmother's house in Edgartown, upon the island of Martha's Vineyard, and suddenly guidance had come to her own mind and soul. Until then there had been no guidance. She had, she felt, merely walked through the days of her life, accepting the events which formed the pattern of her grandmother's life, the ordered events, set in motion many years ago. She had gone to private schools, had been graduated, had been presented to society, had been a debutante noted for her beauty but accused of coldness, had never lived, in fact, until the day last summer when she had walked the seashore at Edgartown, as she so often walked, wondering if this were to be her whole life, this unawakened calm, neither young nor old, this waiting for no one and for nothing. The sun, she remembered, was setting across the inlet, and she had turned toward her grandmother's house. Dinner was always at six, an early dinner because her grandmother went to bed at nine. It would not have occurred to her to be late for dinner in her grandmother's house.

She walked back to the house over a stretch of sand and then across the terraced gardens. The evening air was mild and the glass doors to the drawing room were open. Her grandmother was there, sitting in her chair by the chimney-piece, where a fire burned, and dressed as usual in her long dinner gown, black and long-sleeved, but with white at her throat and wrists. Sarah, the maid, was serving sherry.

"Good evening, Brooke, my dear," her grandmother said.

The book she had been reading slid to the floor. Brooke stooped to pick it up.

"Algernon Blackwood," she read. "I don't know him."

"Ah, you should," her grandmother said.

Her eyes had lingered upon the page where the book opened when it fell and she read the words which had given her sudden guidance, those words which she repeated now to herself, softly, as she stood on the marble courtyard outside her room in this strange and beautiful marble palace, set in the midst of an emerald lake in India.

"The antipathies and sympathies of Today, the sudden affinities—"

She had taken these words, written by an Englishman now dead, and had made them her own. From that day, that evening in Edgartown, she had avoided the antipathies, she had followed the sympathies, and they had brought her to India and now here, she did not know for what purpose.

Jagat smiled when she spoke of many friends.

"Let me be the chief among them," he said gracefully, and then they were interrupted. The American, Bert Osgood, called to him from a stairway at the end of a corridor.

"Hey, Your Highness! I have a question of logistics."

"Your Highness?" she repeated, her eyes questioning Jagat.

"I am only Jagat, nowadays," he replied. "Highnesses are out of fashion. They belong to yesterday. Will you excuse me, Miss Westley?"

"Brooke," she said upon impulse.

He did not speak her name. Instead he left her standing there, and now half an hour later, she was not to see him again, it seemed. But he remained one of the sympathies. She had recognized him at once in the Ashoka, in New Delhi. She had descended from the jet in New Delhi two days before this meeting and she had simply stayed in the hotel, awaiting guidance. She had not of course explained to her grandmother about antipathies and sympathies. They were not on such terms of communication. On that evening in Edgartown they had proceeded as usual to the dining room. There were only the two of them. Twice a month her grandmother invited a few guests, old friends, men and women who came to Edgartown year after year. Several times each summer when Brooke came home from school her grandmother inquired courteously, "Have you friends, my dear, whom you would like to have for the weekend, or for dinner?"

"Thank you, no, Grandmother," she always said.

She had friends, but none of them were close enough to invite for a weekend. What would they talk about, here in this environment of a great silent house, near the vastness of the sea?

That special evening, however, the evening she now remembered, her grandmother had made an unusual effort.

"I feel, Brooke, that you are lonely," she had said.

She could remember the exact moment, Sarah serving the roast lamb, when her grandmother had so spoken.

"Oh, no, Grandmother," she had replied, surprised. "I am never lonely."

Her grandmother persisted, again unusual. "I worry about you, nevertheless. When I am gone, as in the course of nature I must go, who will be near you? I have been selfish, I fear. I have let you lead my life, instead of insisting that you build your own."

"I am quite happy, Grandmother," she had replied.

"Then it is because you do not know unhappiness," her grandmother said with decision. "There is a difference. You will know happiness when you have it."

"Perhaps happiness is just not being unhappy?"

She put this in the form of a question and her grandmother had lifted her eyebrows. "You are either very wise or very young."

To this she had only smiled. Later, that same evening, when dinner was over and they were again in the drawing room, the fire blazing afresh for the evening was cool, her grandmother began the revelation. The house was silent except for the pounding of the surf on the sands.

"I have a premonition of my death, Brooke, my dear," she had begun almost cheerfully, as though she were announcing a journey she had in contemplation. Brooke

herself was sitting on a cushion on the floor by the fire
and she looked up, startled.

"How strange, Grandmother," she said under her
breath.

"Not at my age," her grandmother replied with her
usual calm.

"Tell me about it, Grandmother!"

Her grandmother set down her small coffee cup. A generation ago, perhaps two, the cups had been brought from
China by a seafaring ancestor. The house was rich with
such gifts from Asia. Across the room a showcase held a
collection of jade snuff bottles, jade of every shade and
hue glowing softly in the lamplight. When she was small
her grandmother on rainy afternoons had sometimes
opened the glass doors and allowed her to handle the
smooth, cool jade.

"It has not been sudden," her grandmother was saying.
She gazed into the flaming logs. "The immanence has
been growing in me. I believe I shall die very soon. I
shall not leave this house again. I was born here, you
know, on a summer's day, and here I would like to die.
My only concern is you, my child. I want you to promise
me that when you are alone you will immediately set
upon a journey. Where, I leave to you. But I would like
you to go to a country you do not know. Be guided only
by your own inclination. If I have learned anything in my
long life it is to be grateful for every occasion when I
followed my sympathies and avoided my antipathies."

She had hesitated again for an instant and then had
proceeded without further pause.

"Since I am near the end of this life, and ready to
begin the next, I would like to tell you of men whom I
have loved—and shall always love."

Here in India, so far from that evening, she remembered vividly her sense of shock, perhaps embarrassment. Her grandmother in love? She had felt shy.

"Oh, Grandmother, really," she had murmured.

Her grandmother had laughed gently. "Do you think
it impossible? What you don't know, child, is that the
heart never grows old. I've watched with amusement my

aging body, knowing that the eternal flame in my heart does not so much as flicker. Yes, after your grandfather's death, twenty years ago, I have been in love several times —three times, to be exact, three times really in love, and other times, too many to remember, on the brink of love. You need not look shocked, my child—it was intentional, constantly intentional, and I was never unfaithful to your grandfather, my husband, who remains the love of my life. Indeed, it was he who told me to keep loving. We had a long last talk—at first I could only cry, and then he actually grew impatient with me. He scolded me—"

Her grandmother here paused to laugh softly. "Oh, the darling! He knew me so well! I was too young of course, when we married and he was old enough—almost—to be my father.

" 'Stop crying,' he ordered me. 'I haven't much strength and I know that without me you will feel lost. And you're too young not to fall in love. Listen to me! I *want* you to fall in love—as often as possible. I want you to know that wherever I am, I'll *approve*. I don't want you to be what's called faithful to me. You'll be faithful to me by doing what your heart desires. I'm not afraid of your doing anything stupid and tasteless, because you are intelligent and a woman of taste. And I don't want you, above all, to feel what's called a sense of sin. Love can never be sin. It can be only a blessing. Even if you're not loved in return—though I can't imagine that—to love is a proof of life—indeed, it's the only proof, for once you can't love another human being, you're not alive.'

"That is what he told me, Brooke—such wise, wise words! He gave me my freedom. Of course I told him I'd never love any man again, and he just smiled.

" 'When you do,' he said, 'remember, I'll be glad.' "

Her grandmother had fallen into silence then, gazing into the fire, a tender smile on her lips.

"Did Grandfather die soon?" she had asked.

"He died that same night," her grandmother had said quietly, "and I can't explain, child, but those last words he spoke, which I've remembered exactly as he spoke them, and I have never repeated them to anyone before, gave me the strangest sense of comfort. I didn't need to love anyone else, I didn't even want to love anyone else, and for several years I thought I never would. But what he had said somehow gave me freedom—not to find anyone to take his place, for that would be impossible—but freedom to be myself, to enjoy people, to find companionship. And after nearly three years I did love someone—a man older than myself, who brought me comfort, because he was wise and because he was lonely and I was able to comfort him. We loved each other quietly, like father and daughter. And when he died, I loved a man my own age, a musician whose name you would know if I spoke it. We still love each other, though we are no longer lovers. And these two were true lovers. The third one—well!"

Her grandmother had laughed softly. "That love was a playful one! I knew he was not to be trusted, that he was enjoying life too much to be depended on, but then I had no need to depend on him. And it was good for me to laugh and be made much of, and teased and taken care of, and told how beautiful I was—oh, it was very good for me."

Her grandmother was laughing again. "And of course I didn't demand faithfulness of him, or expect it, or even want it. We were playfellows until—"

She was suddenly sad; though still smiling, her eyes were sad.

"Until what, Grandmother?" Brooke had asked softly.

"His plane crashed one night in a storm, when he was on his way here," her grandmother said.

"Grandmother," she had murmured.

"Yes, child?"

"Why are you telling me all this, Grandmother?"

"Because I want you to know that you must follow your sympathies," her grandmother had replied. "Because I want you to know what I was told by the man I loved best of all. It is love itself that is important—the ability to love, no matter whom you love. For when you can no longer love anyone, you are no longer a living person. The heart dies if it loses the capacity to love."

Her grandmother's voice ceased, and they sat silent for a time, gazing into the fire. While they had talked, a sudden storm had rumbled out of the sky and she heard the soft spatter of big raindrops against the closed windows.

"Do you still love a man, Grandmother?" she had asked at last.

Her grandmother had seemed to change before her very eyes. When she spoke thus of love, her face had softened, her eyes glowed, she shed her years and became young again. She smiled as she continued to gaze into the fire.

"It is always possible," she said. "Thus I am suspended between love and love. I am happy that my body will die before my capacity to love is ended."

They had fallen into long silence then, and she had sat remembering the years of her childhood and girlhood when men had come to this house as guests and had stayed sometimes for days and gone away again. Or, when she had been away at school, how often her grandmother had traveled abroad or to some distant state to come home again for the holidays. She understood now what her grandmother was trying to tell her, that she was following her sympathies, whatever and whoever they were, and thus following, she had found joy in living, instead of sorrow and loneliness.

"It is getting very late," her grandmother said suddenly. "And I have said all I wanted to say."

She rose with these words and, bending, she kissed her granddaughter's hair and with her hands she smoothed her cheeks and then she left the room. In the night she had died. The day after the funeral Brooke left for India. Why India? Because it was far away on the edge of the world and because it was utterly unknown.

And here I am suspended, she thought.

Outside the door of the room that Bert Osgood had given her as her own the corridor opened upon a wide marble terrace. The balustrades were banked by marble seats, cushioned in red velvet. The heat was already

intense, even at the early hour of the morning. The sky
was a clear hard blue above the golden sands of the
mountains. She had been waked as usual by the washer-
women on the marble steps of the city water gate across
the lake. When dawn broke, the pounding of the wooden
sticks upon wet clothing beat out the rhythm of the day.
Useless to complain of the hour, Osgood had told her
last night.

"They've been at it for centuries. You can't stop them
now."

"I shan't try," she had said.

He was not one of her sympathies, she knew, and yet
he was not an antipathy. He hovered somewhere between
both extremes, a simple and comforting presence in this
place. When he left Amarpur on one of his sorties across
the world in search of modern conveniences to insert
somehow into this marble edifice without damaging its
beauty—for in his way, she discovered, he had a nice
sense of maintaining ancient beauty—she felt slightly
bereft. He was, she realized, a bridge between her present
and her past, and she was not yet prepared to sever the
link. Or, putting it in other words, she was not sure
enough of herself to feel entirely at home alone in India,
and she was glad when he returned.

She saw Osgood approaching her now in the distance,
and she seated herself at the small marble table where
she took her breakfast. Soon, but indefinitely soon, a
turbaned houseboy would bring a silver tray with the
necessities. Osgood approached.

"Is that fellow late again?" he inquired.

"It doesn't matter," she reminded him. "I have no
schedule to keep."

"Well, *he* has," Osgood replied. "Promptness is a lesson I'm trying to teach here. You can't have American
guests and forget the clock. People won't stand for it.
And don't you spoil him, please! You're his first experience of an American and it's important that you
help *me,* not India!"

"Calm yourself," she said. "He is coming."

Down the corridor indeed a slight figure appeared,

white-clad with a wide red belt, a tray balanced on his turban. He walked in measured steps, not hastening, and as he came near he lowered the tray skillfully.

"Good morning, madam," he said in cheerful English. "I am late—sorry, indeed!"

Osgood looked at his watch. "Five minutes. That's ten minutes better than yesterday. Make it on the dot to-morrow."

"Yes, Sahib." A wide smile flashed across the dark face. He poured coffee, added sugar and milk, and then broke two small brown eggs into a cup while Osgood watched with stern eyes.

"Thank you, Wahdi," Brooke said. "That will do nicely."

"Thank *you*, ma'am."

He bowed and went away.

"Have you breakfasted?" Brooke asked.

"Hours ago," Osgood said.

He leaned against the marble balustrade and stared across the lake. "Queer country—queer people."

"I'm the one that's queer," Brooke said. "I don't feel in the least strange here. I've been here before, I think."

"What do you mean?"

"Just that. Yesterday I went walking in the town."

"I wish you wouldn't go alone."

"How else can I go?"

"You can wait for me."

"Oh, come now—"

"I mean it."

"I like being alone, I think."

"You mean you'd rather be alone."

"Perhaps."

They paused. Then Osgood began again.

"Well, what did you see?"

She peeled the orange on her plate and ate its segments slowly, talking between bites.

"I saw a small naked girl with long tousled hair. She carried a big brass water jar on her head. She was waiting to cross the street. She looked about four years old."

"Probably was ten," Osgood said.

"Probably," she agreed. "And I saw a young mother in a blue cotton sari sitting on the curb of the street, nursing her baby. She had lovely breasts. The traffic was crowding by and no one looked at her."

"You can see the likes of her any hour, any day, anywhere," Osgood said. "Ancient Asia—eternal mother. Bosoms? Go to the marble steps yonder across the lake and you'll see the women bare to the midriff washing themselves, sari and all. It's clever—they take a bath and do the laundry at the same time—wrap the wet sari around themselves and saunter home again."

She laughed. "Really? I must pass that way one of these days." She went on remembering. "And I saw a ragged, dusty man with a long matted beard leading small monkeys on a leash across the street, weaving his way between the carts and the automobiles. Oh, and I saw a spotted deer tied to a post outside someone's door. It was plump—not thin like the children."

"A pet," Osgood said. "These people will do anything if they love a creature."

"All that in the town," she said, "and outside on a desert road I saw cranes flocking in the sandy shallows of a dry riverbed. I went quite near them but they were not afraid."

"Animals are never afraid here," Osgood said. "Look how I try to get rid of the damned birds in the lobby! They've nested for centuries in the chandeliers—gorgeous glass things brought long ago by maharajas wandering in Europe—"

"Those ancient desert mountains," she mused, not listening, "worn to their marble bones! And the banyan trees, putting down their manifold roots in search of the earth! I stopped to rest on a wooden bench under a banyan tree in a village at the foot of a mountain and a row of yellow-necked crows sat on a vine and stared at me. And a sad little monkey joined me. And a huge construction work was going on, a highway being made, and the loads were carried by tiny donkeys. There wasn't a truck. And I saw a cow eating a brown paper bag. Cows here like paper bags, I'm told. And the restaurant keeper told me, too, that cobras are friendly and he says they won't attack unless you hurt them. They'll even play with children."

"Don't try it," he warned.

She went on. "And monkeys can't swim, he told me, and that's why they had to learn to jump so far. And betel nut grows on a vine in the shade and it has to be picked by men because the vines wilt if women touch them and the nut spoils. And snakes love the vines so one must be careful. Sometimes their poison contaminates even the leaves. And there are many kinds of betel, he told me. Small leaves come from Benares and big ones from Mohoba and Poona, and long ones from the south. Betel leaves are four annas apiece in Bombay, he said, and I saw such a lovely tree in the desert, all bare with great bunches of brilliant orange flowers."

"The pallas tree," he said.

"How do you know so much?" she asked.

"I don't know half of what you already know," he said. "Only, what will you do with all these unrelated items?"

"Relate them, somehow, someday," she replied.

She finished the eggs, so small they were like pigeon eggs and tasted the bacon and decided against finishing it. The flavor was strong and the meat was tough. Then she put the question she had wanted to ask all along.

"When is the Maharana coming back?"

Osgood turned his head for a quick glance. "He's never been away."

"You mean—"

"He's been in his palace across the water there."

She put down her napkin, her appetite suddenly gone. "Does he stay away from the hotel for weeks at a time like this?"

"He's in mourning for his son, I suppose. Besides I hear the Maharani has been ill."

"Have you ever seen her?"

"No."

"Then you don't know if she's beautiful?"

"No. Not important to me, anyway. I have a job to

do. All the same, young lady, if you'd let me, I'd take you around—Chittor, for example."

"What's that?"

"An ancient fort, wonderful place. Someday, perhaps—"

He looked at her and she turned her head away.

"Well, so long," he said. "I'll tell the boss if he shows up today."

"Tell him what?"

"That you asked about him."

To this she did not reply, and he laughed and went away.

Day after day she sat under the marble canopy and waited, though for what she did not know. And why, she did not know, except that waiting without desire she was at peace. Across the lake the royal palace stood white and silent. Suppose she simply plunged into the country beyond, climbing the bare sandy mountains, visiting the caves and ancient forts and palaces, the shooting boxes and the dak bungalows the English had left behind them? She was not afraid for she had always been alone. But she had no impulse to wander again beyond the surrounding lake—not yet, at least. She was in a strange state of suspension, as though she had finished one life and waited to begin a new one. Her former life grew daily more remote, its events slight, its emotions shallow. She seemed on the threshold of the new life, though presently contained within the marble walls confined by the waters of the lake. She was alone and yet not alone. The place was busy with workmen, but they let her walk past them usually in silence. A dark face here and there looked up and smiled as she passed, but it was seldom that anyone spoke.

Slowly and alone she became aware of a new awareness, a conviction, which stole into her heart with a sense of deepening peace. She was beginning to feel the marble palace was her home, its uncounted rooms a dwelling familiar to her. Never before had she known this feeling of being at home in a place, although she had no com-

munication with anyone beyond. Letters reached her from
banks informing her of money received on her behalf
from her grandmother's estate and she did not answer
them. Money was there and she used what she needed
and left the rest idle. Those whom once she had thought
of as friends receded into shadows. Literally now she
knew no one. Bert Osgood was gone on one of his
business trips to the West, and now she did not miss him.
She spent her days in seeming idleness but in inner activity. She read, discovering one book after another,
strange books of the East which were not strange to her,
and a vast library of books of the West. Here in this
building set in living water, she discovered a meeting
place of the two halves of human history, East and West,
but in books. Who had collected them here? She did not
know. She found in the books of India—translated into
English and set side by side with the originals in half a
dozen languages, in Urdu and Tamil, Gujrati and Hindi
—that in India there was no tragedy. The modern books
of the West, which she had read since her adolescence,
had been filled with tragedy—tragedy in the Greek
sense—but here in India there were no uphappy endings,
for there was no end.

There is no end, she thought, because in India life
never ends. It goes on into some other realm. And this,
she thought, surprised, is modern truth, for if science
teaches any precept, it is that there is no destruction but
only change. She found immense comfort in the discovery
that here in this oldest country, in this most ancient
culture there was a truth as new as today. And then,
reading a book she ordered from London, she found the
report of a speech made by the Prime Minister of India,
that most modern man, in which he had quoted a saying
from the wandering saint of new India, that spirit of the
past made flesh today, and they were the words of
Vinobe Bhave: "Politics and religion are obsolete," the
saint declared. "The time has come for science and
spirituality."

And upon this, the author, an English scientist, had
thus continued: "Truth—that is of course the key word;

for what does science mean except truth? And of all
human activities the quest for truth is the most noble, the
most disinterested, the most spiritual."

Truth, she thought, truth is reality—about myself,
about the world, and life, and past and present. Reality
is what I want. I shall not rest in the pursuit.

"Sit down," a Huxley had written a hundred years
ago, "sit down before fact as a little child, be prepared
to give up every preconceived notion, follow humbly
wherever and whatever abysses nature leads, or you shall
learn nothing."

It was as a child that she had come to India, and was
now here, a child with simplicity and nothingness, except
a child's sharp readiness to see and to accept. Why India?
To this question there was no answer except that she,
born into the newest of modern nations, had come to the
oldest people in human history, in order to discover
reality. What truth she did not know. But she came as a
child. As a child now she began to explore even the
palace which housed her. As a child she wandered about
the marble corridors, she entered the many rooms, she
lost herself in the courtyards and the pavilions, she descended into the caverns buried beneath the waters of the
lake.

It was in these caverns, the foundations of the palace,
that she discovered one day the treasures of the past. In
boxes, in great crates, now opened, she discovered crystal
from a Europe of a century ago, jewels from a Paris that
belonged to the age of kings, paintings from the Italy of
Michelangelo, tapestries of the Medici, goblets of silver
and gold from Elizabethan England.

"Be careful, dear one," an old servant implored her,
when he saw her entranced among such treasures. "Though
we see no cobras here because of the surrounding waters,
yet who can say that there are no cobras? Their ancestors
may have laid their eggs in these caverns in the days
when this was part of the land."

"How long ago?" she asked.

"Long, long before the days of Shah Jehan," he said.

"For Shah Jehan was imprisoned on the island next to us, and that was in another age."

She was learning almost unconsciously the language of the Rajasthani, hearing it daily and with her extraordinary facility absorbing its meaning. But she found no cobras. The cellars under the water were strangely dry, impervious even to damp through some thick substance painted on walls and ceilings and floors, a substance which she was told was now forgotten, so that none could duplicate it.

When Bert Osgood comes back, she thought, I shall tell him what I have found. He must use these gifts from another world. This French satin must be hung as curtains and these Chinese brocades must cushion the chairs and divans.

She laughed when crates opened earlier by Bert revealed the set of furniture made all of glass, a huge bed and chests, tables, and chairs, upholstered in crimson velvet and made in Czechoslovakia a hundred years ago, the velvet as fresh as today and the glass pure crystal. Oh, how absurd, she thought, and so beautiful that it must be used.

She could not wait for Bert's return. She suggested to servants the crates be unpacked and taken upstairs to a square room that opened upon a secret courtyard, given over to birds and small animals, its fountains choked and dry. She ordered the courtyard cleaned, the birds and animals coaxed to other parts, and the fountain made to flow again. When the walls of the room were cleaned, she found that they were built of mirrors, and even the ceiling was a mirror. What prince, long dead, had devised this means of manifolding his infatuation? She imagined a lovely girl, naked in this room of glass, repeated a hundred times among these walls. And as she imagined, she seemed to see the girl alive again, her face, half turned away, her dark hair swinging like a cloak over her left shoulder. Suddenly she saw, or imagined that she saw, that the girl was herself, again and again herself. Had she once been born in India?

Alone in the room of glass she was suddenly afraid

and ran as if pursued, and that day, at that moment, saw
Jagat at the head of the marble stair.

She had forgotten how handsome he was. He stood
there high above her, dressed in a western suit of a light
tan silk.

"Who pursues you?" he asked, looking down the stairway.

"No one," she said, her face upturned to him, "and
yet I feel I am pursued."

"Ah," he said, comprehending. "The palace is full of
ghosts. I shall drive them out when the guests begin to
come. You will see them walking briskly about, asking
for the swimming pools and golf courses, Americans
instead of ghosts."

"I cannot imagine it," she said.

"Will you come up, or shall I come down?" he demanded.

"I will come up."

She mounted the marble steps slowly, conscious of his
observing eyes, her head lifted, her lips smiling.

"I was told you had gone away," he said.

She took a step higher. "Is that why you came, thinking I am no longer here?"

"No. I was sorry when I heard you had gone."

"But you came."

"This Osgood chap wants me to send him the measurements of the entrance hall. He thinks we should have a
carpet."

She was three steps away from him now and she
paused. "He is wrong. There must not be a carpet. The
floor is too beautiful. If he insists, then I beg that you
will use one of the Persian rugs that I found in the great
boxes below."

"So you concern yourself!"

His eyes, his voice, were pleased and amused.

"I concern myself," she agreed.

She was one step away now and he put out his hand
for hers. She felt his hand supple and strong, the palm
warm and hard.

"Your hand is cool and soft," he said, not letting it go.

"In spite of tennis and skiing and horseback riding?"

"You do all these things?"

"I was brought up to do them," she said, and drew her hand away.

They were side by side as they walked the marble halls, she tall for a woman, but he was a head taller. She had forgotten how tall he was. Where had he been all these weeks? She bit her tongue and would not allow herself to ask. He looked younger than she remembered him. His olive skin was smooth, his dark eyes bright. Magnificent eyes—but she had seen such eyes even in the faces of begger children here in India. His features were Caucasian, however dark his skin, but the people of India, she had read, were Caucasian.

"Where are you going now?" he asked.

"I am going nowhere," she replied. "I am simply here."

"Then let us climb to the roof and see the sunset."

"Has the day ended?" she asked in surprise. "I have no idea of time. My watch stopped days ago and I have not wound it. And there are no clocks in the palace, are there? I have not seen one. I begin the day with the sound of the women flailing clothes on the marble steps across the lake. I end the day with the moon and the stars, and the cry of someone calling. I don't know what he calls."

"It is the call for evening prayer at the mosque."

"But you are not Muslim?"

"I am not religious. My wife is very religious but Hindu. She also takes instruction from a young Catholic priest without intention of becoming a convert."

"I also am not religious," she said.

They were walking side by side, and she felt the same ease in his presence that she had felt in the Ashoka. He held her elbow lightly when they faced the second flight of stairs and she was aware of his touch against the bare skin of her arm.

"Is this region like the rest of India?" she asked.

"No part of India is like any other," he said. "Yet everything is here, poverty and riches, desert and mountains, forests and rivers, white-skinned folk and black. We are all here, separate but mingled, united but apart. I am a Rajput."

"Rajput—what does it mean?"

"Translated it means the Son of Kings. But it is not I alone. We Rajputs are all sons of kings."

"A clan?"

"Yes, in a fashion. We are Kshatriya by caste, a warrior clan, but the lines are not sharply drawn between us and the Brahman. We Indians are not a race, for our origins are mixed. Thus we are often ruled by Brahman who then become Kshatriya. We are aristocrats, yes—descended perhaps from the Scythians of Tod, but long ago —oh, very long ago. We Indians bear the heavy burden of past greatness. It gives us an inferiority complex now, I sometimes think. But I am talking very seriously with a beautiful woman—too seriously."

They were on the roof now and in the presence of such landscape that she could not reply. She walked to the marble balustrade surrounding a roofless balcony and stood looking toward the mountains. They were violet, shading from the palest purple to blackness in the valleys. The crests of the mountains were gold in the light of the setting sun, now just over the horizon, and the gold was reflected in the still waters of the lake, and the royal palace on the shore was tinted with rose.

"I am interested only in serious things," she said after silence.

She turned her head to meet his curious gaze. She looked away again and continued. "I came to India because I was weary of my own generation, I think. I was weary of smartness and cleverness and repartee and beat music and rhythm and silly dancing. Above all, I was weary of not caring about anything—not life, not death, not the past, not the present, not even about the future."

"Are you speaking of your own people?" he asked.

"I am speaking of them because they are the only people I know," she answered. "I am weary of them. I tell myself there must be other kinds of people. It is not possible that the world is full of people like the ones among whom I grew up."

"Your parents?"

"They died before I can remember, as I told you. I grew up with my grandmother. The night she died she told me to follow the man I love."

"But if you do not know who he is?"

"I think she will let me know somehow, when she thinks I need him."

"But if she is dead?"

She gazed into the distance. "She is probably alive somewhere—if any of us lives."

"Reincarnated?"

"I don't know. I thought perhaps I could find out about such things here."

She turned to look at him again. "I don't mean I want to see her, particularly. She was always remote, though kind, you know, and I think she loved me in her fashion. I suppose her real emotions were divided."

"How do you propose to find this man you love when, or if, you need him?"

"I'll happen on him by chance—as I did upon you." She was gazing again into the sky. "I have never seen such a sunset. Is this unusual? See how the rose and the gold pour over the marble crests of the mountains! I'd think it was snow if I did not know it is marble."

"The only sight that surpasses it is near Darjeeling. Have you been there?"

"No. Should I go?"

"Someday."

"Will you tell me about it?"

"I'd rather you see it straight and fresh with your own eyes."

"Alone?"

"I hope someone will be with you."

There was a look in his eyes, warm and understanding, and she turned away. That look in a man's eyes! She had seen it before and had been warned. Impossible dream nowadays, the dream of love! Love had been offered her many times, inevitable for a girl as beautiful as she had heard herself described, and the only heir to a family fortune. But each time she had felt none of her synpathies. Once or twice there had at least been no sympathies. Once or twice there had at least been no become her habit.

"I am really happiest when I am alone," she said, and realizing what she had implied, she withdrew again quickly. "I don't mean you, of course, nor just now. Truly I think it was because of you that I came. But not you, exactly, and perhaps not you at all. I am looking for someone who can open the gate to me."

"The gate?"

"The gate to India. I have no key."

"There is no key to any country except through a person," he said. "And this is especially true when it is for India."

They were speaking in strangely quiet tones, slowly, the words far apart, each searched for and then lingered upon.

"Is it difficult to know your country—your people?" she asked.

"Yes, and no. We are various, so many of us, each different. We look as different, one from the other, as we are. We believe in many gods, and yet only in one. And each man is convinced that he is the most beautiful man in India, and his people the best. Each group clings to its own ancestry and none is absorbed. Witness the Parsis, who came here centuries ago from Persia and, imbedded now in India, are part of us and yet separate. Even in Bombay, where they center, they are apart. We do not absorb each other, as the Chinese do. We keep our blood-streams separate and pure."

He was gazing into the afterglow and she saw his profile as dark, as strong, as that of the mountains themselves.

"And you?" she asked. "You believe in this separation of the blood?"

"Yes," he said, and turning his head, he looked at her

with a look so powerful that she refused its meaning, whatever it was, and parried.

"And you think yours are the most beautiful people?"

He laughed. "Of course!" The moment was broken. He sat down on the marble balustrade, his back to the sky. "I remember once I was giving a press conference in Calcutta. As a matter of fact, I was with my father, the old Maharana, and since he would never exert himself I had often to speak for him. He was simply lazy, I'm afraid. Well, the people of Bengal are not among our most beautiful, physically, let us say. The press conference was long and even I grew somewhat weary, especially as the reporters tended toward a certain quarrelsomeness which is perhaps a quality of the mercurial Bengali. At any rate, to vary the procedure, I said, 'Now that you have all asked me many questions about difficult subjects, let me ask a question. Why do the Bengali think they are the best people in India?' "

He paused, smiling to remember.

"Why?" she asked.

"Well, when I asked the question," he went on, "a very small, very black, spidery little man rose impetuously to his feet. 'Because,' he piped in a high little voice, 'we are the most beautiful!' It was a lesson for me! Even he—"

She laughed with him. "That's rather sweet. I like him."

"Then you will like us," he said.

The sun was gone now, even the afterglow fading, and the air was suddenly chill. She shivered, and he was concerned.

"You must not get cold. This desert air can be treacherous at night, after the heat of the day."

"I am never ill," she protested, and was loath to leave the landscape, darkening under the evening sky.

She went nevertheless following his lead and allowing him to take her hand and place it on his arm.

"The stairs are dark," he said. "The marble is polished by centuries of footsteps and very slippery."

In the silence of twilight they walked to her rooms. At

her door they paused, each searching for words to suit the moment. He looked at her, his eyes dark and luminous.

"It occurs to me that I may be the key for which you have been looking."

"It is possible," she agreed.

He hesitated and then went on. "In that case I would like you to meet my wife. We have had no guests because of our son's death. But you will not be considered a guest. I have told her about you. Will you dine with us tomorrow evening?"

"Thank you."

"I will send a boat for you at sunset."

He put out his hand for hers and she felt his firm swift handshake, as English as though they stood on a London street.

In preparation for the evening, she chose to wander during the whole of the next day. She called for a boat in the morning and was floated across the lake to the shore. Steps led up the embankment and to the left was the palace gate, its arch looming. To the right was the street that led through Amarpur. She turned to the right, passing a park where flowers bloomed in a mass of hot color. Here she paused—curious mélange of flowers, she thought, English marigolds and daisies, roses and larkspur, growing sturdily amid flowers that were strange to her, orange and purple and red. A few people strolled the paths and stared at her, though kindly. She was a stranger and so felt herself for the first time. Then she was recognized as foreign. An ancient gentleman in a white shirt and dhoti, a white turban wound about his head, approached her. His genial brown face wrinkled into smiles.

"You are English?"

The voice was gentle, the accent pure.

"American," she said with an answering smile.

"American," he mused. "I have not seen one before."

"I have not been here long."

"May I walk by your side?"

"If you please."

Side by side they proceeded along the path. His feet were bare but sandaled.

"What shall I tell you about our town?" he inquired.

"Whatever you like."

She had the sense of ease, of former acquaintance, that was becoming familiar to her. Among strangers she no longer felt strange, although she had never before seen this old man. He waved a hand toward the houses surrounding the square of the park.

"Have you heard that last night there came here a band of robbers?"

"No one told me," she said.

"Ah, yes, we have evil as well as good. But they were mannerly robbers. They observed the custom. How do I know? Because the man they came to rob is my brother— a very clever man."

"He knew they were about to rob him?"

"Ah, yes, it is our custom, a courtesy, you understand. The robbers sent word in order that my brother could prepare. He waited until midnight, he and his household. Then they heard music."

"Music?"

"Ah, yes, our robbers always approach with music. With music they came, and my brother went to the door to meet them. He invited them into his house and they played a game of betting."

"A game?" She was mystified indeed.

"Ah, yes, but my brother, as I said, is clever. He won the game and was allowed to keep his goods. The robbers went away courteously."

He pointed a finger to a house at the end of the walk. "It is my brother's house. You see it is quite peaceful this morning."

She saw a house of stone and white plaster. Upon the front was painted in bright colors the figure of a traditional god, seated upon a life-sized elephant.

"It is beautiful," she observed.

"We think so," the old man said.

Children were gathering about them as they stood ad-

miring the house. One girl, very small, in a dirty pink
sari, smiled at her, eyes enormous and dark.

"Good morning," she said in staccato English. "What
is your name?"

"Brooke," she replied.

"Brooke," the child repeated.

"My granddaughter," the old man said with compla-
cency. "I teach her English. Would you like her?"

She was mystified again. "Of course I like her. She is
pretty."

The old man looked pleased. "Then you may have her.
I have plenty more."

He pulled the child to him and wiped her dusty face
with the end of her sari. "Go, dear one. She wishes you
for her own."

"Oh, no," Brooke cried. "I didn't understand! I don't
mean—I don't want to—oh, please!"

"Take her," the old man said with a noble gesture of
his thin, beautiful hand. "She is yours."

"I'm sorry—I'm very sorry," she stammered. "It
wouldn't be possible."

The old man shrugged skinny shoulders. "It was a
gift," he said simply, and pushed the child away, but
gently.

"I'm sorry," she said again. And then to divert him:
"How is it you speak such beautiful English?"

He replied as amiably as before. "I was four years in
England. I am a Cambridge honors. In English literature."

"And you teach?"

"No, now I am resting. You see I am very old."

She glanced at his smooth and cheerful face. "But you
have many years to live, I think?"

"I've already lived," he replied, "and not only in this
life but in others. There is no end to my living. Whatever
I was before, whatever I am now, I shall proceed into
another life."

He paused before a squalling baby on a doorstep. The
mother was washing the naked infant, rubbing soap over
his fat wriggling body.

"See this child? He does not wish to be clean. It is

antipathetic to him. You will think it only natural. But it has meaning. Everything has meaning. Who can tell? Perhaps in his last life he was drowned. Naturally he hates water."

Before she could inquire, a procession drew near. A young girl, indeed a mere child, bedizened in a gay sari, sat in an ox-drawn cart. Behind her walked a group of young women and girls all singing.

"A wedding," the old man explained. "And yonder comes the groom."

She saw a young man, very young, scarcely more than a boy, sitting on a horse, a heavy turban wrapped about his head. He wore a suit western in cut, this in honor of the occasion, but it was made of bright blue brocaded satin. Before him on the saddle he held a little boy.

"For luck," the old man told her. "So that he may have a son very soon."

Two boys followed on horses and behind them came again a group of singing girls and young women.

"Ah yes," the old man said, wagging his turbaned head. "The women are happy. They have snared another young man. How gay they are! It is natural."

They were gay indeed, their saris bright orange and pink and draped over full skirts swinging about their ankles. Shoulders and upper arms were concealed in tight bodices that did not cover their bare and lovely breasts, firm and round. Their arms were covered to the elbows with bracelets of silver and glass.

"No longer gold," the old man said, observing her eyes looking at such decoration. "Our great Prime Minister has called upon our women to surrender their gold for the war effort against the invading Chinese. We are very patriotic!"

He pointed to a wall and there she saw a huge likeness of Nehru, appealing to his people with palms outspread. At its base there sat, oblivious, a boy, perhaps of twelve years, although it was difficult to tell for the children were slender and underfed. He was crouched on the ground, patiently feeding wisps of grass to a bony horse.

"Ah yes," the old man said. "The child knows that his horse may have been his friend in another life, or perhaps even his father."

As he spoke, a man came out of a house and threw into the street a heap of green leaves for a cow to eat.

"And why," she asked, "do your people allow these cows to wander about the streets?"

The old man paused to watch the cow as it slowly chewed the leaves. His eyes were tender as he spoke to the beast.

"Dear mother cow, enjoy your food!" He turned to Brooke. "As for your question, let me tell you that I am a modern man. I do not venerate the cow. Moreover, I come of Muslim ancestry. Muslims like to eat meat. But we also consider the feelings of our Hindu brothers. As one of your great Christians said many centuries ago, 'If eating meat makes my brother to offend I will eat no meat while the world stands.' Or words to that effect. I remember the Archbishop of Canterbury one day preaching upon this subject in London and I have not forgotten. I myself have eaten no meat since the Archbishop preached for my benefit."

While he was speaking they arrived at a diversion of the street, and here he took his leave. Bowing slightly to her, his hands palm to palm, he went to the left while she continued on her way back to the lake. The sun was already at its height when she stepped into the waiting boat and she was glad to be shielded by the red and white striped awning above her head. The water shimmered as it rippled on either side of the bow and the boatman, his engine puffing, laid his head on his folded arms and went to sleep waking at the exact moment, nevertheless, as they approached the marble wharf. She stepped ashore and mounted the steps into the lobby. Already it looked like the entrance to a modern hotel. Behind the desk a clerk waited.

"Will you have luncheon now, please, madam?" he inquired.

She recognized Bert Osgood's training. "Yes, thank you."

"In the dining room, or upstairs in your rooms, please, madam?"

"Upstairs, thank you."

Half an hour later, washed and cool, she ate a luncheon of thin lamb chops, green salad, and a sliced melon that might have been served her in New York. No, not quite—the chops were miniature and the bones were dark. The green was not lettuce but some other leafage and the melon she could not define. Like all else in India, it was familiar and yet entirely different. She ruminated upon this likeness, this difference, and while she drank her coffee, which did not taste like coffee, she gazed thoughtfully through the open door. The sun blazed white hot upon the marble plaza outside her shadowy room and glittered upon the marble minaret in its center. Muslim, certainly, this minaret was, and yet the marble lace that fringed its roof was delicately Hindu and so were the gold tips upon its points. Meditating, she was overcome by drowsiness, but she was becoming accustomed to this afternoon exhaustion. The sun beat down upon the white houses in the distances, the desert shimmered with light, and the lake was a mirror of glass. She set the tray outside her door, closed it, and undressing, she lay upon her bed. It too was of marble, and not even the foam rubber mattress could make it soft. But she liked the inner hardness and the soft surface and she fell asleep to wake at sunset.

Jagat was waiting for her at the palace dock. She saw him there, a statuesque figure in a white linen suit. Handsome, she thought, but more than that—much more. He had the look of a prince, the son of kings, and yet he was as modern as any Englishman. He stepped forward as the boat touched the dock, he put out his hands for her, and helped her ashore.

"The steps are wet, and you must take my arm," he commanded.

A flight of steps led upward and she lifted the long skirt of her white evening gown. It was not the first time she had dined in a palace. In Athens she had met her grandmother's friends, King Paul and Queen Frederika, and twice she had visited in Stockholm, always with her grandmother, to dine with the old Swedish king, now dead. Once she had even played tennis with him, he then being more than eighty years of age but still agile and gay.

"Call me Mr. X," he had told her. "For the moment we will forget the 'majesty.' "

But would this Indian prince be like those of the West? He was guiding her through a long corridor up still another flight of marble steps.

"We will have cocktails on the western terrace," he was saying. "My wife is waiting for us and with her is the English priest, Father Francis Paul. I thought it might be pleasant for you if we were more than the two of us. I wish my daughter were at home. She is about your age—perhaps a bit younger. Veera is her name. I have not seen her since my son's death. Indeed, this is the first time we have seen anyone."

"It is very good of you to allow me to come," she murmured.

She was surprised to find herself shy. Alone with Jagat she had not thought of shyness, so direct was he, and so easy in manner. Now, approaching the terrace, she saw a lady in a soft white sari and a tall man in the black robes of a priest.

"Moti," Jagat said, "this is Miss Brooke Westley. Miss Westley, this is the Maharani, my wife."

Brooke put out her hand and felt another hand laid within it, a slim cool hand, so soft as to feel boneless. It was swiftly withdrawn.

"Miss Westley," a low voice murmured. "You are welcome. My husband has told me very much about you."

"And this is Father Francis Paul," Jagat said.

She looked up into a pale white face, the dark beard trimmed to a point beneath dark eyes. It was the face of a Christ, and had he, assuming the likeness, emphasized it purposely by the beard and the somewhat too long dark hair? But the voice was very staccato, very English.

"Miss Westley, how do you do! Welcome to our town!

We don't see many guests, and seldom indeed an American. I've heard of Bert Osgood, but I've not seen him."

They were seated and she looked from one face to another. A serving man in a white costume stood waiting.

"Well, what shall we have?" Jagat inquired.

"Nothing for me, thank you, Jagat," the Maharani said.

"Oh, come now," he exclaimed. "A martini? Ranjit has learned to make them very well."

His voice was edged with impatience and she bowed her head and was silent.

"A martini for the Rani," Jagat ordered, "and—why not the same for all of us? Come, come—"

"I shall wait for your rose wine, Your Highness," Father Francis Paul said, dark eyes smiling.

"Well, I'll excuse you, but three martinis, Ranjit."

The serving man bowed and went away. Almost immediately he returned with the three glasses and set them on the small marble table. In spite of what her husband had said, the Rani did not touch her drink. She looked at Brooke, her dark eyes plaintive, and made an effort at conversation.

"And how do you like our town, Miss Westley?"

"I can only enjoy so beautiful a palace," Brooke replied.

She took her glass as she spoke and sipped the martini. It was excellent, very dry, and with a flavor she did not know. Suddenly she decided to cast aside her shyness and be herself.

"What is this flavor?" she inquired to Jagat. "It is like flowers, but not any that I know."

"It is a citrus that long ago was brought here from Greece by my grandfather," Jagat replied. "It bears a small bitter fruit, but when pressed this bitter fruit has an extraordinary essence, a flavor that is more like flowers than fruit. We make the essence every year and bottle it—at least I suppose we do—it's more in Moti's realm than mine, eh, my dear?"

"I believe that Ranjit makes it," Moti said indifferently.

"It is famous, Miss Westley," Father Francis Paul said.

"My grandfather imported more than a citrus," Jagat continued, smiling. "He also imported a beautiful Greek girl. As matter of fact, I believe it was she who brought the citrus tree. She had a scent made from its fruit and the legend is that upon meeting her he noticed this scent even before he saw how beautiful she was, whereupon she showed him the little bitter orange. It seems she used it on her skin."

The Maharani stirred. "But we Indian ladies have long used oranges, Miss Westley. Our women pound orange skins and mix the pulp with fresh cream for our skins. I have even heard that some of your famous cosmeticians in the West have taken the recipe—modified it, of course, and made the ingredients more lasting and less dependent on the daily efforts of servants."

Her voice was sweet but somewhat colorless and she spoke slowly, articulating each word perfectly.

Father Francis Paul laughed. "These matters are beyond my ken, Highness, and certainly must be beyond my interest, alas! Miss Westley, changing the subject, how did you happen to come to Amarpur? No tourist comes here as yet, although when the lake hotel is finished, I suppose we shall be a tourist center. I'm not looking forward to it, I must say. But I shall be safe enough in my hill home. I'm a missionary to the Bhils, Miss Westley, a fascinating group."

"I don't know them," she said. "In fact, Father, I don't know anything about India. And I'm not a tourist. I've come here in a sort of existential mood, taking each experience as it comes—"

"But why Amarpur? It's a small place—in fact, the word *pur* means *town*. We're not even a city."

She looked at Jagat, pleading. He responded promptly. "I met Miss Westley at the Ashoka in New Delhi. I was feeling very low and sad. I'd been under tension about Jai, and then, knowing the worst—well, it was my first hour alone—I mean, away from people I knew. And she was playing the piano in the salon—she's a fine pianist—"

He turned to his wife. "Which reminds me, Moti, my

dear, we must have one of the pianos moved to the lake palace so that Miss Westley can have her music."

"Of course," Moti murmured.

"Well," Jagat continued, "so we introduced ourselves and I told her about the lake palace and she grew—what shall I say—curious, about Amarpur, and came here. I must say it was a surprise to me, for I didn't take it seriously when she said she'd like to come—or I thought she'd wait until the hotel was finished, but Osgood gave her his room and bath—it's the only bath that's completely working."

"It works perfectly," Brooke said. "And I'm quite happy and comfortable. I find something new every day in the lake palace, and something new every day in Amarpur, too."

Father Francis Paul persisted. "You haven't yet told us exactly why you came here, though, Miss Westley."

"I don't know," Brooke said. She faced him with honest eyes. "I don't know and I shall stay until I find out."

A servant in white costume and a broad red sash appeared at the door. "Dinner is served, Your Highness!"

Jagat rose promptly. "Very well, Rodriguez! Moti, my dear, we must break him of calling us Highness."

She rose. "But what can he call us, Jagat? It's what he's used to—"

"Let him continue," Father Francis Paul advised. "Let him keep to the good old customs."

Moti put out her hand. "Miss Westley, please—we will precede the gentlemen this evening. We'll be very western."

And clasping Brooke's hand lightly, she led her away from Jagat and into the dining hall.

Afterwards Brooke remembered nothing of the evening except the moment when the Maharani, she whom Jagat called Moti, spoke. They had dined in a vast hall, at a vast table, a servant behind every chair, and they waited while Father Francis Paul spoke his silent grace for himself. Moti bowed her head in courtesy but Jagat sat erect and unbending. The priest crossed himself and then, grace over, he lifted his dark head and smiled at them. Immediately the servants presented food. Moti refused all meat and Jagat explained to Brooke.

"My wife is Hindu. She will eat no meat, however it is served. She is also Christian, but only to an extent. She believes, in spite of all that Father Francis Paul does to convert her altogether to the one faith, that it is possible for her to be religious on all fronts."

"I also follow Mahatma Gandhi," Moti murmured.

"The Rani is a good Christian," the priest said, comforting. He turned to Brooke. "Are you religious, Miss Westley?"

"I don't know," she replied. "What is religious?"

Jagat interrupted. "Let us not spoil good meat by talk of religion! Try the roast lamb, Miss Westley. It is Southdown English and not Indian goat. I have a farm of sorts up in the foothills."

She helped herself, smiling an apology to Moti. Jagat helped himself largely, continuing to talk. "I grow good English beef and mutton. The climate is hot for them, but at least I have some eatable meat. And don't let them feed you lake fish! They taste of mud. They're fit only for the crocodiles. As for our hens' eggs—"

"Now, now," Father Francis Paul said. "I feed on local fish and local eggs! They are quite palatable."

"Defend us!" Jagat rejoined. "We need it. But I am not deceived. Our food is execrable unless it is cooked in Indian fashion and all the flavors hidden in chili and pepper. No false patriotism for me, if you please! I am quite aware of our weaknesses as well as of our strengths. I prefer English food."

The meal was English, except for the crisp Indian bread, thin cakes of wheaten floor fried in vegetable oil.

"I find these delicious," Brooke said.

"*Popodom*," Jagat told her. "Yes, they're good, but scarcely food. Delicacies, perhaps?"

Such small talk, desultory and difficult, had lasted through the meal and had been brought to an abrupt end by Moti, the Maharani. She had been eating vegetables in silence. Now, placing her knife and fork neatly together on her plate, she looked at Brooke with dark and searching eyes.

"We will have coffee and the rose wine on the terrace, Jagat," she announced.

He looked up, surprised. "Very well—"

He had led the way, thus, to the terrace, and directed their seating in his arbitrary manner.

"Miss Westley, you will have this chair. The view across the lake is very fine, especially now since we have electricity in the lake palace. The indirect lighting and so on—"

"Beautiful," Brooke murmured, sinking into the cushioned chair of carved teakwood.

"Moti, in your usual place—under the neem tree. I know you don't like the moonlight."

She sat down in a cushioned chair. "I feel it in my bones. It is more subtle than the sunlight, and more dangerous."

"And you next, Father," Jagat was directing.

He seated himself last beside a small table and lit a cigarette. Silence fell upon them all. What, Brooke asked herself, what was to be said, who was to speak first, if speech was necessary? She sat relaxed and waiting, gazing at the scene before her. The evening was translucent, the desert air clear, the moonlight soft but cold upon the mountains. On the huge terrace the shadows cast by the neem tree were black and Moti sat in their darkness. Father Francis Paul was near enough to hear her when she spoke. The whiteness of his face, the blackness of his beard and hair were startling in the half glow of the shadowed moonlight. But Brooke turned to the landscape. She could see the full sweep of the mountains beyond them, pure marble city and the soft glitter of the lake. She continued silent, overcome indeed by the magnificence of the scene, the towers and many windows of the marble palace extending in vast wings on either side of the terrace.

Only Jagat was restless. He had sat down and now got up again; he walked up and down the length of the terrace; he perched himself on the balustrade, swinging his legs outside and drawing from Moti at last an irritable protest.

"Jagat, can you not be still? You destroy the illusion of the night. And if you fall from that height, you will lie in pieces on the stone courtyard!"

"It would be pleasant," Father Francis Paul said, intervening for peace, "if we had some music."

Brooke turned her head. "Yes, it is a night for music. I was wondering what we lack. Music!"

"Fetch your sarod, Highness," Father Francis Paul said. "I have not heard you play for a long time."

"For a reason," Jagat said.

"It would be a pity if you gave it up, Highness," Father Francis Paul observed. "So difficult an instrument, and so few play it well nowadays!"

"I have no time," Jagat said indifferently.

"Nonsense," Moti said. "You have plenty of time. Who is there to tell you what you must do and not do? You are your own master."

"And I have not heard the sarod," Brooke said. "What is it?"

"It is an instrument resembling a huge banjo," Father Francis Paul explained. "His Highness plays it very well. In fact—correct me if I am' mistaken, Highness—but I believe you were taught as a youth by the greatest sarod player, Ustad Allaudin Khan."

"Who gave me up," Jagat retorted. "He said I did not practice enough. He himself practiced for hours, many hours every day, and yet would not consider himself a master—or an Ustad, as we put it—until he was forty-eight years old. I once thought I might become an Ustad also—but there were other things I liked better than sarod playing."

"Killing tigers," Moti said out of the shadows.

Jagat laughed. "Playing soccer!"

"I wish to hear the sarod," Brooke said definitely.

Jagat hesitated and then clapped his hands. A turbaned servant appeared.

"Sarod," Jagat commanded.

The man wagged his head and disappeared to return in a moment with a large shapeless mass. He unwrapped it carefully, laying aside the double coverings of quilted yellow satin and black velvet, and gave the huge instrument to Jagat. Brooke rose, went to his side, and put her hand on the smooth, polished body.

"Like satin," she murmured.

"I was given this sarod by my father when I was nine," Jagat told her. "It is made from a teak tree on my grandfather's lands, an old tree, so thick that the body is carved whole. Twenty-five strings, as you see, and this plectrum is made of a polished coconut shell. Twice I lost it, but my father would not buy a new one and I had to find it. The whole house was upset, searching. I play only ten strings with this plectrum, and the other fifteen repeat the sounds in echo. But I don't like to play it alone. It's meant to be accompanied by drums or a sort of gourd instrument, the tamboura. I check my sarod by it—but, well, I shall have to do my best unless you, Moti—"

"Very well," she said quietly. "Have the tamboura fetched."

He clapped his hands again and again the servant appeared, like a genie, Brooke thought and did not say, and upon command produced the tamboura and gave it to his mistress. She took it in both hands and played upon it, and listening to the drone it gave forth, Jagat corrected his strings.

"This is court music," Jagat said before he played. "In the past the people were not allowed to listen to it but today—well, Ustad Al Akbar Khan gives concerts even in America. It was his father who was my teacher. I'd be ashamed to play before either one of them now. His father would not allow me to hear western music until I was nine. Then my own father insisted, and so I was allowed to have a few classical records. I like Bach best. His music makes me think of our own Indian raga."

"I like tala better," Moti observed.

"That's only rhythm," Jagat said with contempt, and so continued. "But Indian music is nothing to make a fuss about. We have only seven basic melodies. All other melodies are simply combinations, permutations, harmonies between the tonal qualities of our instruments—that's all. We'll have nothing new until we get infusions from western music. As in everything else, we Indians can't escape our own traditions. The past is still our prison."

"Do begin, Jagat," Moti said impatiently. "Why must you always talk so much before you do anything?"

He began to play, then, with a strong, lingering touch and suddenly the evening was filled with echoing music. And Brooke, watching his absorbed face, saw a man whom she had not imagined existing, a warm poetic passionate man, alien to her but profoundly attractive. She felt a premonition, a shudder that was half fear. All that, in her terminology, was neither more nor less than falling in love, a state of mind and emotion which she feared, because it was, she knew, beyond the range of reason.

It was at this moment that Moti spoke. "I suppose you have been told that our son is dead." Her voice was silvery quiet.

Brooke was startled. She gazed into the dark eyes, so large in the pale face in the shadows of the neem tree. "I know—I have heard how tragic—"

"Not tragic at all," Moti continued. "For, you see, he is not dead. I have positive evidence that he is alive."

Jagat put down his instrument. "Now, Moti—"

She held up her narrow pale hand, glittering with rings. "Please, Jagat! I must speak. I have waited to discover Miss Westley. To some persons one may speak, to others, never. I may speak to her. She is in sympathy. You see, Miss Westley, I know he is not dead. I have explained this to Father Francis Paul. You understand, don't you, Father?"

"I understand *you*," Father Francis Paul said gently.

"Yes," Moti went on with quiet fervor. "You do understand me. You see, Miss Westley, there is something inexplicably close between a mother and her son. If my son were dead, I would know it throughout my being. But I live as before. When I wake in the morning it is not to sorrow, but to peace, because he is alive. He may be in prison, or in exile, but he lives. The task is to find him wherever he is."

Jagat rose so abruptly that the dishes on the small table by his chair crashed to the floor. Servants sprang forward but he paid them no heed.

"Moti, I forbade you to—"

She rose also. "Jagat, you will not listen to me. So I must ask help of others. Miss Westley, help me, please— I beseech you!"

She clasped her hands together in the act of beseeching. Brooke looked at Jagat and spoke to Moti.

"What can I say, except that if I know how to help you I will do it?"

"No one can help her," Jagat said bluntly. "What she asks is impossible."

"What do you ask?" Brooke inquired. She was aware of a strange tenderness arising in her for this woman.

"That someone go in search of my son. It is all that I ask—that someone go in search of my son!"

Jagat lost patience anew. He leaped to his feet and gave the carved chair in which he had been sitting a great push so that it overturned.

"Let us leave this place, in God's name," he exclaimed. "Miss Westley, if I had known my wife would have put this absurd request to you, I would never have invited you here. She knows our son is dead. She is simply not willing to believe it."

"But how do you know it is absurd?" she asked.

"What do any of us know about life, and about death!" Father Francis Paul murmured.

They were all standing now, each looking at the other. Jagat spoke again, resolving the moment.

"Come with me, Miss Westley," he commanded. "Let us walk through the palace. I would like to show you the room where my father reigned. Please excuse us, Moti— and your pardon, Father."

He held out his arm for Brooke and she could only obey the command. Yet when they had left the room, when they had entered one great hall after another, it was not of these that he spoke, nor even of his son.

Instead he spoke impersonally of the Chinese, who were still pressing on the borders of the north and the east.

"It is nothing new, this Chinese invasion. That is what my wife cannot understand. She looks on it as something momentary, a single attack from which peace will proceed as a matter of course. What she cannot comprehend is that we have always had this pressure, reaching downward through Tibet upon our Indian borders. It has been a disintegrating force through the centuries. I daresay it would have destroyed us had not Britain taken command over us. That we have had a few centuries of peace is only because China during the last century has been in a period of decline. Whenever there is resurgence, the pressure begins again upon Southeast Asia and therefore upon us. We recover during her periods of decline—that is to say, between each dynasty—but when the resurgence begins with a new dynasty, in the inevitable pattern, we are again facing her on our borders. A hundred, nearly two hundred years before your Christian era a horde of nomads came out of western China and settled on the borderlands of India. Their descendants ruled India. They were odd-looking men, by the way, tall, big noses, pink skins, not at all the sliteyed Mongolian type. God knows where they came from, that Yuechi tribe!"

She listened, knowing that he was talking against some inner fear of his own and she broke across that fear.

"Do you think there is any chance that your son is alive?"

He paused, his hand resting upon the head of a huge stuffed tiger. "It is true that I did not see him dead," he replied.

In the night she woke and was aware of wailing music from across the water. She rose from her bed and went to the open window. The curtain was closed and she drew it aside. The moon was setting and a long shaft of golden light shimmered upon the lake. She watched that setting moon with a sadness she could not explain. Why was moonset more sad than sunset? The pale glow, the uneven orb, the knowledge that the moon was old and was dead, whereas the sun blazes with the fires of youth, these made her conscious of the shortness of her own life, the evanescence of her youth. How much longer must she wait for whatever was to come? Yet what could she do but wait, when there was nothing to which she could return? Solitary wherever she was, she was less solitary here than elsewhere in the world. The lake contained the palace and this palace contained her self. People by the millions lived not far away, but still beyond. And there in the marble palace across the water, its towers white against the sky, Jagat lived. Jagat! Who was he in her life, what was he to be? She had refused all questions, all answers, when she thought of him. Let time reveal! But she must recognize the revelation. In her entire life, she had never met a human being who was so strong a sympathy as Jagat. Without loving him—surely she could not be so foolish as to think of love—she knew that she must be near him, at least until she knew what the sympathy could mean, must mean, if she were true to herself.

She waited until the moon sank behind the horizon, illuminating in black shadow edged with gold the lonely island and the palace built there so long ago, to serve as a prison for Shah Jehan in the days of his youth, the empty palace and the ruined garden. When the last glimmer of light was gone and a soft darkness had descended she went back to bed and slept. And in the morning was awakened not by the sound of the women's flails, beating upon wet garments spread on marble rocks, but by a soft scratching on her door. She knew by now that this took the place of a knock. She rose, and putting on her robe, she opened the door.

A serving man stood there. "Dear One," he said coaxingly. "I have waked you. How can I help it? His Highness has come across the waters to speak with you."

She looked at him with eyes still heavy with sleep. "But I am not bathed nor dressed, nor have I breakfasted—"

"He also has eaten no food this morning. He says, if you please, he will join you here on the marble plaza for the early meal."

"Tell him I will be ready in twenty minutes."

He wagged his head from left to right and right to left, signifying consent, and then disappeared down the long marble veranda. And she closed the door and locked it, for in their zeal the serving folk sometimes entered without a sound. When she had protested gently, they were hurt.

"But, Dear One," they said, "we come to help you, we who love you!"

What protest could she make against their love? None, except to draw the small brass bar across the door and then hasten to dress so that she could draw it back again before they knew. So now she made such haste, bathing herself quickly, slipping into the few clothes she wore, her legs bare and her feet thrust into sandals. To brush her long straight hair took but a few minutes and then she opened her door again. Jagat was already there, seated at the small marble table in the minaret where she took her meals. He rose when he saw her.

"I must beg your forgiveness, I have come too early, but I have been sleepless. After you left, Father Francis Paul and my wife together beset me. As you learned, she is convinced that our son lives, and whether she has convinced the English priest or whether he is moved by her importunity I cannot decide. Perhaps he himself cannot say."

"Please sit down," she said and seated herself.

The serving man appeared with the breakfast tray and in his presence they were silent. He was about to depart when Jagat spoke. He cast a quick imperious look over the table.

"Stay! Is this English marmalade?"

"H-Highness," the man stammered. "How do I know one nation from another in marmalade? I am only a poor Muslim."

Jagat took a small spoon and tasted the contents of the glass bowl in its silver stand.

"It is English," he announced, "Crosse and Blackwell. You may go."

The man wiped his sweating brow, bowed, and tottered away. Brooke laughed. "Must you terrify him, Your Highness?"

"Of course I must," Jagat retorted. "If I do not keep him in terror of me, he will cease to obey me. And here I am still master, if not Highness. Please, Miss Westley— no more titles! Let us be friends. I am in sore trouble. I have no one with whom I can talk from my heart. Will you call me Jagat?"

"If you will call me Brooke."

"That will be difficult. We Indian men are not so easily —what shall I say? Well, never mind! I will do what you wish. Now eat while I talk. For myself, I have no appetite. My wife was troubled and weeping all night long. In fact, by this time—what time was it? I don't know, but the moon was setting."

"I woke, and I went to the window and drew aside the curtain and saw the moon sinking—such an old moon! It made me strangely sad. I still feel the sadness, although it is such a bright and beautiful day. How the town shines in the sun!"

"Ah, you see, there must have been a communication! It is one of our sympathies, is it not? Perhaps we knew one another in some other life."

"Do you believe in that?" she asked, instantly alert.

He shrugged his shoulders. "How do I know what I believe? I am a man of modern India."

"Is there a modern India?" she inquired.

He gave a short laugh. "I don't wonder that you ask, having seen here only the most ancient India. We are not changed, you would say—nothing except this symbolic modern hotel, made from an old palace where kings spent their summers. I came as a child with my grandfather, and my father. They brought their concubines here—my grandmother and my mother stayed in the palace then on the mainland but it was understood that— well, that the other women came here. The Greek girl— she—I don't know whether I should tell you, but you have her room and this was her plaza and my ancestor built this minaret for her so that she could sit outdoors and enjoy the breeze and be shaded from the sun."

"I am glad you told me," she said. "Now I know who it is that I sometimes feel is here with me."

"Do you believe in such possibilities?"

"I never did until I came here. But now—I have strange new feelings. I say new, but they are only new to me. They seem very old feelings, consciousness rather than knowledge, and I come into it—or move out of it."

"Then you know," he said. "You know the weight of the past upon me. It is the ancestral pressure of our old, old country, our many millions of people, alive and dead, the past as crowded as the present. One feels it in all old countries. I remember the visits I made to China—"

She lifted her head. "I have always wanted to go there, but now I cannot, since I am an American."

"Yes, I was there more than once. My grandfather, who was sent by the British with a note to the old Empress Tzu Hsi, was the first of our family to visit China. But I was there twice with Sardar Patel, in the days when he and the Prime Minister were trying to maintain cordial relations with the Chinese Communists. It was before the Chinese seized Tibet, of course. The Prime Minister found it hard to believe that they could do such a thing, although he had most reluctantly to accept the fact. I suppose he has compensated by receiving the Dalai Lama in exile."

He sat frowning and forgetful for a moment, then slapped the marble tabletop with the palm of his hand. "Well! That is bygones. How quickly the present becomes the past! To speak again of my son—I don't know what to do. It would be futile to search for him, of that I am sure, and yet how to placate my wife—no, comfort her is the word. I do want to comfort her—please her in some way, at least—although of course he is dead. I know that."

"I think you should go," she told him. "I think it is your duty to comfort her in any way you can."

They looked at one another. Her eyes did not falter before his dark and piercing gaze.

"I cannot explain why I feel I have known you for a long time," he said at last.

"Nor I," she said, "for I feel the same about you."

He rose, walked to the balustrade of the terrace, and gazed across the lake at his ancestral palace. The flag of his clan was flying from the highest tower, fluttering and waving in the dry desert wind.

"I have forbidden that flag to fly," he said, "but my people persist in wanting it there. I've told them I no longer have the right to a royal flag."

"They need to believe in you all the same," she said.

"You are very intuitive." Then silence was long between them, and rich with unspoken thoughts. He turned to her at last somewhat abruptly.

"So I must go on a fruitless search!"

"Don't you think so?"

"Yes—if for no other reason than that I shall have no peace until it is done. She will not complain or press me, but she will slowly pine and die. That is what Father Francis Paul told me last night when she left us alone at midnight. He is not my father confessor, you understand —I confess to no one—but he has perceptions about her that—well, lucky for him that he is a priest and not a man—"

She did not reply to this moodiness. Instead, she put her own question.

"If I say I would like to go with you, what would you think?"

He sank down upon his chair. He leaned his elbows on the table and faced her. "You cannot mean it!"

"Would it be possible? No—first of all, would you let me?"

Amazement was plain on his dark, expressive face. "I—what can I say? I cannot imagine letting you or not letting you. If you were an Indian girl, it would be impossible. But you would not think of it if you were Indian. I don't know what she—my wife—would say. Yet she felt an unusual warmth toward you."

"Would you like me to go with you? For me—it would be a wonderful way to see India—apart from finding out anything new about your son, of course."

He hesitated. "I do dread going alone. Of course there'll be servants and bearers and all that, but—"

He broke off, brooding.

"May I ask the Rani myself?" she persisted.

He looked relieved. "Yes, that is best," he said. "Since you are an American, nothing will surprise her. She will not be shocked. For this we may be grateful to your female compatriots who have the reputation of doing exactly what they please. But I must warn you, it will be a difficult journey. And I do not know where it will lead."

"Let it lead where it may," she replied.

"It is very good of you," Moti said. "I do not know why you are willing to do it."

"I don't know, myself," Brooke said, "except that I am led by my sympathies, and somehow my sympathy is toward you—what shall I call you, ma'am? I would like to say Your Highness, if you will let me."

She spoke truthfully, for there was something that prevented familiarity. She was therefore the more surprised when Moti put a hand on hers, a very soft hand, she knew, as she felt it upon her own.

"Please call me Moti. It is my true name. It means pearl. I have always liked it."

She did not move away and after an instant Moti withdrew her own hand.

"Please," she repeated.

"I will try," Brooke said, "but forgive me if it is difficult at first. I'm rather a remote sort of person, I'm afraid. At least my acquaintances say I am. Perhaps it's because I've always been an only child, brought up by a rather formal grandmother. In a strange way, I suppose, that's why I am in India. I'm not quite at home in my own country—nor anywhere, for that matter. I search the world."

She paused, discerning upon Moti's face a shadow of sadness. She began again.

"At the same time, I don't want to—I wouldn't for anything hurt you or put something between us, a reluctance or anything like that, which I don't feel. Moti—it's pretty—perhaps I can—"

Moti interrupted, "Ah, no, only if it seems natural! I thought perhaps—since there is something between us that is sympathetic—do you know, it's easier for me to speak to someone quite foreign than it is for me to speak to one of my own people? We Indians seem to share such an immense experience. We've all been taught the same ways and the same thoughts and ideas, depending upon religions and castes, of course. One has no chance of expressing one's own self, for if one does, one becomes too different and there's no use in starting a great argument. I don't know if you've noticed how we all tend to argue and disagree immediately someone gives an opinion, and we're always doing it—expressing opinions, I mean—and yet because nothing we say is ever really new, it's all puddling about in the same ancestral puddle. But you've not been in the puddle with us, and so it seems purifying somehow to communicate with a stranger, though as I said I don't feel you are a stranger. Have I seen you in a dream, I wonder?"

All this came pouring from Moti as though a barrier had been removed from her soul.

Brooke waited for the pause and then spoke. "I don't feel you are a stranger, either. I don't feel anything strange here in this beautiful place. I seem to have seen you all before—you and Jagat—"

Here Moti broke in. "You say 'Jagat' so easily. Why do you not feel as easy with me?"

"You are very different, you and he—"

"More different than being just man and woman?"

"Oh, yes, not because of that."

She felt Moti's dark, searching eyes upon her face. "Do you believe in dreams?"

"You mean sleep dreams?"

"Yes."

"I seem never to dream when I sleep."

Moti clasped her slender hands together, "I dream every night. Not always important dreams, but—"

She broke off.

"What is an important dream?" Brooke inquired.

"One I cannot forget—the one, for example, that makes me believe my son is not dead, though I am told his body was burned and the ashes cast upon waters. Shall I tell you why I believe he lives? Oh, I must tell you so that you will understand."

Moti paused again. She frowned in concentration. The huge room in which they sat, her private sitting room, was silent. The windows were open but it was near noon, and people were in their houses, sheltered against the rising heat. The doors to the rooms were open and only the flutter of an occasional bird, flying in and out again, broke the stillness. The room was gold and white, the furniture covered in white satin, the walls white and paneled in gold. The decor was western, the chairs and settees French, the paintings Italian and English. Only the scent was Indian, a faint, too sweet perfume of citrus and sandalwood. Moti, motionless, her hands folded upon her white sari, began the telling of her dream.

"I distinguish between the small dreams and the others. The small ones are only of small daily troubles. The large ones, the others, are entirely new to me. I am in places I have never seen, among people I have never known. On a certain night, and I am sure it was the night when my son was said to have been killed, I had such a dream. I dreamed that I was lying on the bed in my bedroom, as indeed I was. I lying on my back, with my hands folded on my breast. I felt very weak, not ill, but weak. I was not sleeping but I was aware that I was doomed to die. Someone, a doctor, had told me that I was about to die. I lay there considering my death, which was near and was, I had been told, inevitable. Suddenly, as though light broke into the dark room, I felt my will rise up.

" 'I will not die,' I told myself. 'Who can tell me that I must die when I will not?'

"Upon this decision I dreamed that I rose from my bed, and just as I was, in my night garments, I ran out of the room, out of the palace, no, not so much ran, as simply I was outside. I found myself in a landscape I had never seen before. It was not Indian. I was on a hillside and I ran down the hill toward the valley. On the way I passed through a ruined temple. This was Indian, the temple. It had pillars instead of walls, and the tiled floor was crumbling. Someone lay on the floor, dead. It was a young Chinese man. He had been shot. It was he who was dead, not my son. I did not linger but ran on. Down in the valley there were children playing. The sun was bright on a rippling brook. I was suddenly very happy. I was young again, I was strong, and I, too, had escaped death. Then I woke. This dream stays with me, as though it were only last night."

She came to the end, and sat gazing at Brooke anxiously and in question.

"A lovely dream," Brooke said, "but I never understand dreams."

"It means simply that my son did not die. A young Chinese died. But somewhere Jai lives. If he had died in the dream, I would have died, too. But we live."

"If he lives, we will find him," Brooke promised.

She rose and put out both hands. Moti clasped them and then put them to her cheeks.

"You are my daughter," she said, "and Jagat is your father."

"I hope you don't believe Mamu's nonsense," Veera said.

Brooke rose from the long chair in which she was lying. She was on the marble plaza, resting after a walk through the town. She had returned to the hotel after her visit with the Rani. No one was to be seen except the workmen, neither Bert Osgood nor Jagat, and she was restless and puzzled. Was the Rani as innocent, as naïve as she seemed, a woman so childlike, so cloistered for a lifetime as to accept without question a long journey that her husband proposed to take with a young and foreign woman? She pondered the last words: "You are my daughter." Surely the meaning of these few words, so succinctly spoken, was that a daughter could be trusted. A daughter could be trusted, yes, to devote herself to her brother Jai, and to behave toward Jagat as to a father.

And I don't want to involve myself, Brooke told herself.

Restlessly then she had wandered through the streets of Amarpur, the town of Amar, shining like a gem in the bare desert. She soon reached the end of the houses crowded one against the other, and there the dusty street led to the edge of marshland, dry now until the rains came. Four silvergray herons rose at her approach, their tails and necks white, their heads scarlet, and their wings of enormous spread silver in the sunlight. Cows, too, wandered to the marsh in search of water, the ubiquitous cows of India, lowing in disappointment.

Three camels passed her as she walked on. When their driver paused to rest in the shade of a high thorny cactus tree, she paused, too. The camels' feet, she observed, were equipped with natural shock absorbers, a loose tissue of muscle which rose and fell like springs under their body weight. The driver, an ancient man, his flesh burned to blackness by the desert sun, carried a goatskin of water over his shoulder. When she drew near he grinned at her from toothless gums, and offered her water. She shook her head, smiling her thanks, whereupon he drank from the neck of the goatskin, a long gurgling drink that ran down his gullet and splashed audibly in some remote region of his being. She laughed involuntarily and he joined her in laughter, without knowing that he himself provided its cause. A lovable people, she thought, warmhearted and easily amused. She was beginning to feel at home with them. A horse-drawn tonga painted with bright floral designs against a background of yellow passed by. She hailed it and climbed in and rattled back to the town, and thence to the lake and then found a boat waiting to take her to the hotel, feeling rested and reassured as she always did when she went among the people.

She had bathed and put on a fresh white garment and was lying on the long chair on the terrace, half asleep until now she had heard her name called. Opening her eyes, she beheld a beautiful Indian girl in a green sari.

"I am Veera," the girl said, "and my mother, the Rani, has told me about you."

Brooke sat up, but Veera put out her hands and pressed

her shoulders. "No, please! You are not to get up. I will sit here."

She seated herself, and then abruptly spoke of her mother, and her mother's faith that her brother lived.

"Is it nonsense?" Brooke inquired.

"I think so," Veera said.

Her hair, a shining chestnut brown in the late sunlight, fell to her shoulders in loose curls. Her skin was a pale cream without flaw. Her eyes were golden brown.

"I thought all Indians had dark eyes," Brooke said irrelevantly.

Veera smiled. "I am sitting in the sunlight. Therefore my eyes are light. In the shadow they are dark. It is my Kashmiri ancestry. There are many of us fair here in the north. The very dark people are in the south, sprung from the Dravidians. You should have seen my brother Jai. You might have taken him for English—except for his ears."

"His ears?"

"Yes. On the flanges of his ears he had fringes of soft black hair an inch wide. It is considered a sign of virility. But I think Jai never knew a woman. He was singularly pure."

"You believe he is dead?"

"My father so believes."

"You always agree with your father?"

Veera gave her a sidewise look from under her long lashes. "I think so."

"Tell me more about your brother."

"What shall I say? He was very handsome. When he was at school, the same boarding school where I go now, not far from Mussoorie, the girls were mad about him. They still talk about him. But they said he cared only for his studies. Yet as I knew him he was gay, a fine dancer, very modern, very English."

"What did he want to be?"

"I don't think he knew. Or perhaps he knew and put it aside. Sometimes I think he had a premonition that he would die young. He took such intense pleasure in life— as though every day were his last. But he was different with everyone. I daresay if you asked my parents, each would give you a contrasting picture of him. And his friends—they never agree about him. I suppose none of us really knew him. Then suddenly one day he went off to battle, as casually as though he had known all along that he must go. He hated it, too, for he loved the Chinese, actually. He'd studied their language, and he knew their history. He was very sad when they took Tibet in such cruel fashion, and for a long time he could not believe it—not until he went to see the Dalai Lama in Delhi and heard from his own lips all that happened. Then he visited the refugee camps in Mussoorie and Darjeeling and heard still more. I remember he wept when he told me about men and women carrying little children on their backs through the snow and over the terrifying passes of the Himalayas."

Brooke listened to the lilting rhythmic flow, so characteristic of the Indian who has never lived abroad. Veera spoke English perfectly but it was Indian English, the consonants softly blunted, the ends of sentences never quite dropping to conclusion.

"He wept?" Brooke repeated, incredulous.

Veera flung back her hair with both hands. "Yes, he wept! Does that shock you? Let me tell you that our Indian men are not cold like Englishmen! When they are sad they weep—not woman-tears, either, but man-tears, for it is man-sadness. We don't conceal our feelings as you do—no, I don't mean you, for you aren't English. But I haven't known any Americans—not well, at least, just tourists in hotels in New Delhi and Bombay. I can see that you're not like them or the English but I don't know what you are, really!"

"I am not like most American women," Brooke said quietly.

"How are you different?" Veera demanded.

"I don't know," Brooke said.

"Then how do you know you aren't like the rest of your countrymen?"

"Because I don't feel at home with them. It's as if I were of a different family."

"Are you happier with us?"

"I don't know you well enough. But—"

"Yes?"

"I have a feeling that I knew your father before, and this I had at the very first time I saw him in the hotel in New Delhi."

She faced Veera's scrutinizing, skeptical eyes.

"If you were an Indian woman, that would mean just one thing," Veera said.

"I am not Indian," Brooke replied, "and I don't know what it means. I only know that I follow my sympathies, and somehow I am led by my sympathies, which include your mother, to go in search of your brother, though he is dead. Call it—whatever you like."

Veera rose. "You are very honest. I'll be as honest. My father sent me a letter asking me to come home at once. He is puzzled by your wish to accompany him. He is confounded by my mother's insistence that my brother is not dead."

"I am glad you came," Brooke said. "I would like to include you in my sympathies. Perhaps I am only looking for a family where I can belong. I don't know—"

"Now what does that mean?" Veera inquired.

"Nothing, perhaps—except I long for a few people in whose presence I am—happy."

She was surprised by Veera's quick response. For now this slim tall girl leaned over her and kissed her cheek. "Welcome, sister," she said clearly. "My father is your father."

With this she walked away, her head high and the evening breeze fluttering the ends of her green sari. Left behind, Brooke pondered the subtle sarcasm of those final words.

"You are putting yourself in a very delicate position, Miss Westley," Father Francis Paul said.

He had come upon her in one of her wanderings, a few days later. She had not seen Jagat, or Moti. Neither had she seen Veera or Bert Osgood. She was in the bazaar, a narrow street into which the relentless morning sun poured its livid heat. Her skin was burned brown and she was thinner than she had ever been. When the priest approached her this morning she was standing beside an old sword-maker as he pounded a complex design into the brass handle of a narrow-bladed sword. When it was finished he would slip it into a cane. He stopped now to pour water on a revolving whetstone, and against the wheel he held the fine-edged blade.

She was startled by the high English voice. "Oh—it's you, Father!"

"What are you doing here?" he asked.

"I learn so much from the people on the streets."

"Ah, yes, wonderful people! You must see my Bhils, sometime."

They turned away from the sword-maker, and side by side they walked down the narrow street, followed by a straggle of small naked children. She did not reply to his remark, and after a silence he began again.

"The Rani's daughter Veera told me of your plan to accompany the Prince's search for his son. She seems troubled—after all, he's her father—and the rules governing men and women in this country are so—"

She interrupted. "I am not a woman of this country."

"Ah, but you are an American, and that is even more important. One must consider the influence one exerts. 'If eating meat causes my brother to offend,' and so forth."

"Do I offend, Father?"

"Not me," he said. "I am beyond offense. But—"

"Please!" she said impatiently. "It is not necessary for you to say more. I will go away alone somewhere, Father. Please tell His Highness I shall not accompany him. I am quite accustomed to traveling alone. Last year I climbed the Andes in South America. And I've always wanted to explore the border countries between India and China. Perhaps I'll go to Nepal—or perhaps I'll simply— go home."

She stopped, turned to him, and put out her hand. "Tell them all," she said, "tell them I do not wish to offend."

Father Francis Paul released her hand limply and stared down from his narrow height, bewilderment in his simple and good face. "You are a strange young woman," he murmured, "a very strange young woman."

"I am sure I am," she said. "I'm very sure I am. I've been told so before."

With this she left him standing in the middle of the dusty street, the naked children swarming about him, nor did she look back. She had been too impatient, of course, but she had an old impatience with gods and priests. When her grandmother lay ready for the coffin, a Protestant priest had prayed above her dead body.

"Father in Heaven, forgive this woman her sins. Remember that they were the sins of love and not of hate."

She had interrupted his prayer. "Can there be sins of love?" she demanded.

He had answered as sharply. "Your grandmother was a strange woman. Seeming so pliant, she reserved certain areas of her life totally for herself. She never gave herself wholly to God."

"You mean she loved men," Brooke said abruptly.

He looked at her from under his frowning brows. "I am sorry she told you," he said. "Now you will remember her in sin."

"I will remember her as she was," Brooke said. "She had the courage to follow her sympathies. So shall I."

Remembering now as she walked the dusty roads of India, she could have wept for new loneliness, and would not. For she did not wish to be anywhere else in the world rather than where she was. This—this was to follow her sympathies.

III

"BETWEEN THE TWO OF YOU," Jagat said bitterly, "you have driven her away."

His wife and daughter sat mute. They had been talking together in half whispers when he stormed into his wife's sitting room. Modern as they were among Indian woman, they relapsed into the past when he was angry. They became submissive, they did not look at him. Each sat in her place, Moti on her usual white satin sofa, Veera in the red velvet armchair which some ancestor had bought long ago in Belgium. Each bowed her head and waited for the storm.

"You two," Jagat shouted, "you conspire for ends that I can only guess. Veera, why do you stay at home? Is it a school vacation? I have not heard of it!"

Veera summoned her strength. "Raj told me that—that—"

"Raj!" he bellowed. "Is he my son-in-law already? I have not seen a wedding ceremony! If this is how it is to be even before you are married, Raj interfering in my business, and you, Veera, plotting with him against me—"

Veera lifted her head. "Bapu, I did not plot. I came because you asked me to, to help my mother."

Jagat refused to be placated. "Against whom? Against me now, it seems! Of what am I suspected? Your mother invites a young American woman to help her discover a dead son! Is this my fault? Veera, you have put silly suspicions into your mother's head!"

"O Jagat," Moti murmured. "Don't call Jai dead!"

"What else, Moti? You are unreasonable. But all woman are unreasonable. So now I must go in search of an American woman who is looking for my son!"

Veera summoned all her courage. "Perhaps she has simply left India and gone back to her own country. She is very strong, Bapu. Indeed she is strong. She is accustomed to doing what she likes. She has no family."

It had not occurred to Jagat that Brooke could have left India. He felt anger drain out of him and dismay chilled his veins. Nevertheless he tried to continue with fury.

"Did she say to you that she wished to leave India? If she does, I don't blame her! Beset by the two of you, it is no wonder that she is altogether confused. By now she must be in Delhi or Bombay—from whence she will fly —east or west, God knows! Did she say nothing?"

He looked from one face to the other, for an instant aware of the peculiar expression on both faces. It was a look of question, of doubt, of a certain patient female cynicism.

"Why do you stare at me?" he shouted.

The two women bowed their heads again. Neither answered. He waited a long instant and then sprang to his feet, muttering.

"You two—you two—"

He left the room, slammed the door, and marched down the long marble corridor leading to his own quarters. There he entered and closing the door, locked it. Servants watched his every movement and, unless the door were locked, within minutes a man would bring him coffee or fruit. At this instant he wanted no one in his presence. He must face himself alone. For he understood completely the look upon the two faces, his wife's, his daughter's. Without spoken accusation, but with a cool comprehension, he was accused.

"Of what?" he shouted aloud to the room, empty except for himself.

His eyes fell upon the portrait of his grandfather, the Maharana who had been knighted by Queen Victoria for extraordinary loyalty to her throne during a period of local rebellion when several Indian princes had endeavored to free themselves from the pervading control of the British empire. Among those princes who had complained that their so-called independence of the British was merely nominal, his grandfather had maintained that the princes fared better with the British than they could have done alone, one state against another, each prince dealing with his own complaining subjects. But this same grandfather had maintained a harem, and now he remembered also his grandmother and her patience as one woman after another, each younger and more beautiful than the last, was added to her household. No wonder Indian women inherited a cynicism regarding their men! Though he himself might not deserve it, he could not escape such punishment for the sins of the past. In a curious way, the Americans themselves were suffering the same vicarious guilt. Americans had never built empires in Asia, nor had they claimed territories or enforced unequal treaties. Yet now, merely because they were a white majority, they were blamed and even hated for all that other white men had done. It was fate that the innocent must share in the expiation for past guilt. Men die, he thought bitterly, but guilt lives after them until it is somehow expiated. He had taken a new interest in America since the evening in New Delhi when he had discovered the beautiful American woman. Indeed, though he was no reader of books, he had visited the palace library and had read two books of American history, from which he had gathered information new to him, the fact, for example, that the seizure of India had coincided with England's loss of the new colonies in America.

"You Americans owe us a debt," he had told Brooke quite gaily.

"Many debts," she had replied, "but which?"

"I doubt you could have freed yourselves so easily had we not offered Englishmen a greater booty—thirteen poor little colonies in a wilderness in comparison to our riches of gold and gems and fine merchandise."

She had smiled her lovely smile, which remembering now caused him a dart of pain. She had continued then:

"You also gave other gifts to our Emerson and Thoreau, who returned them to your Gandhi, from whom Martin Luther King receives again—a practical interchange of the spirit!"

But what had all this to do with him now, except to add to her endearing charm? She was the first woman with whom he had ever communicated except through the body. He was himself no intellectual, a man of business, he often said, but it was somehow pleasant to be able to talk with a woman freely, without regard, he would have said, to sex. Yet his was a logical mind, as he very well knew, and he knew his position in his own household. He would never be able to convince Moti and Veera that he had no romantic interest in the young American woman. She was merely a traveler, a sort of tourist, however different she was, a guest in his hotel only by chance. He was pacing the room, making arguments for himself. Suddenly, blindly impelled by angry desire, now frustrated, he went to the window and stood gazing at the scene, so familiar and yet today become significant. The sun glittered on the water and under the intensity of its light the marble palace standing in the middle of the lake shone as though by inner illumination. Workmen were moving here and there on the verandas, the plazas, the steps. He saw Bert Osgood's small motorboat dart from the dock beneath his window to puff its way across the still water. Bert was alone and in a hurry as usual. The wake the boat left behind spread from violent waves into widening ripples that splashed against the women washing on the city steps. Strange how empty that palace seemed—strange —strange!

Suddenly he was struck by a new and overwhelming comprehension. It was empty because Brooke was not there! Day after day, aware of no urgency, he had stood at this window and had gazed at the rooms which were hers, the plaza where she took her meals or sat for the outside air. Each day he had brought her near through his German binoculars so that without her knowledge he could examine her face and figure, even the shape of her hands. It had not occurred to him that this was an invasion of her privacy. If she wished to be private, he would have said, let her stay behind the closed doors of her rooms. She became his property when she was outside. He realized dimly that he was being very Indian, but he was Indian and did not wish to be anything else—Indian and a prince. Now and then when he was restless in the night, especially if there were moonlight, he had risen from his bed and through his binoculars he examined the palace. Twice he had been rewarded. Twice he had seen her in a long white gown, walking on the terrace. And once she had stopped walking and had gazed across the water as though she saw him. The moonlight, clear as it was, did not illumine her face, but he seemed to feel her eyes upon him, those dark violet eyes, set in their dark lashes, and her fair hair hanging to her shoulders.

Now she was gone. He had lost her. He turned from the window and groaned. Surely he was not in love! It would be too foolish, too upsetting to his entire life. Yet never before had he felt this half-angry, half-dismayed need for one woman. Of a woman, yes—he had had his women, he had even known infatuations, but never this deep hunger, this sense of deprivation because she was not there, this intolerable demand, not merely for a woman's body, but for her self entire, whole and unchanged, whatever she was and as she was. If this is love, he thought half-angrily, it is very uncomfortable! A simple physical need was easily satisfied and forgotten, but how could this confusion in himself be resolved when he did not even know what it was? It was a monstrous invitation—a woman had no right to be both beautiful and intelligent, and when she was both, it could only bring confusion to a man. And, in addition, to be American, one of the people least to be understood and among all the earth's peoples the most opposite to his own people! He had recently developed a healthy hatred for Americans, partly because of their criticism of the beloved

Prime Minister. The matter of Goa, for example, when American newspapers had rushed to accuse Nehruji of oppression—what hypocrisy when for eleven years the aging statesman had tried every other means of restoring to India the enclave which Portugal had seized and held for hundreds of years, although Goans had clamored to be restored, as old Rodriguez, the butler, had told him!

"In fact, Highness," Rodriguez had said, "I could no longer tolerate the stupid Portuguese. Oh, yes, I waited, because I knew Nehruji had even asked the Americans to intercede with Portugal and beg them to withdraw as Britain did, with honor and respect from all. But Americans failed, and I left my house. Now I am Indian."

And why was he thinking of all this now when the only inquiry he must make was whether he loved an American woman? But it was her quality which compelled him, her total appeal which troubled mind as well as body. Yes, for the first time in his life he was in love and the knowledge cut into his heart of flesh and gave him agony.

"Must I endure this also?" he muttered.

Indeed of the two, death and love, it was love, this love, that was the more insupportable. He found it so. For death was an end. It must be accepted since there was no recall. But love? It was alive so long as lovers were alive. Now he felt an assuaging joy, pervading and wild. She was alive! Wherever she was, she was living and so was he. He rushed to the door. But stay—did he want to find her? What would happen to him if he found her, what disarrangement, what disturbance, what overthrow? That she was an American could only be catastrophe. An Indian woman he could simply have added to his household, somewhat shamefacedly, perhaps, since he was a modern man. Or as a modern Indian, he could have maintained a separate establishment for her in Delhi or even at safe distance in Bombay, where he had business interests in a motion picture studio his father had once bought and forgotten. But Brooke he could not put into a separate establishment. With a different woman, one of another sort, it would have been easy, indeed natural. But with her, with Brooke, her sensitive, active mind forbade such disrespect. Moreover, let him face himself, wherever she was, that place would become the center of his life. He recognized her unique and peculiar quality, the aristocratic bearing that was the outer expression of inner hauteur and spiritual aloofness. Whatever his relationship might be with her it would be formidable. Did he want to begin it? Better to let her pursue her own way, better to let her remain an episode unfulfilled!

The idea was intolerable. He hastened from the room, and descending the wide marble steps at the same pace, he opened the door to the lower dock, leaped into an empty motorboat, and wrenching the engine into action, he roared his way across the lake, meeting Bert Osgood halfway.

"I must talk with you!" he shouted.

"Your Highness," Osgood said, "I don't know where the lady went. Seems she rented a car to drive her to the airport."

"Get on the telephone," Jagat ordered. "Find out what flight she took, and where."

Bert was dazed. "Sure, Prince. If that's what you want. But maybe it's her own business?"

"Do it!" Jagat ordered.

He followed Bert into the room he had made his hotel office and threw himself into a chair, his ears alert for what Bert's questions might convey. During the tedium of operators he stared about him impatiently. All doors were open and from where he sat he could see an amazing change in the lake palace. Walls and windows were finished. Decorators had moved in. He saw two Americans, man and woman, measuring bolts of brocaded satins for windows, still unpacking crates of furniture. He should have been here to see what was going on. Had he been here every day Brooke could not have escaped his knowledge. But he had been afraid of himself, he could see that now. He had made secret arguments against himself. Twice he had chartered a helicopter to take him to Jaipur to visit a courtesan with whom he had maintained a vague relationship for the past four years.

"Whom are you loving?" she had inquired in the night.

"Is it not you?" he had answered.

"Not I," she had retorted. "I know you too well, Highness. You are loving a stranger, someone you are afraid to love—or one who does not love you. Do not think you can deceive! Love is my business and men are my clients."

"Then I don't know her name," he had said. He had lifted a lock of her dark hair and let it fall again—once he would have put it to his lips.

"You do know her name, very well," the woman had persisted, "but you will not speak it even to yourself because you are afraid. Tell me, is she fair?"

He had laughed again and proceeding to passion, had refused her further questions. Now he knew of course whom he loved, and yes, she was fair.

"On her way to Bombay," Bert was saying. "But not directly—connections not good. Luggage checked through the Juhu Hotel."

Jagat leaped to his feet. "Enough," he shouted. "Expect me back when I tell you!"

The two women, mother and daughter, sat together in Moti's sitting room. Neither spoke for a while after he had left them. Then Veera ended the silence, her voice calm and determined.

"Mamu, I shall not go back to school again. Let me stay with you. I have been away too much. I need to learn that which I can never learn in school. Raj's family is all Indian. Though they live in Bombay, they are not new Indians. I think Raj wants me to be an Indian wife. I think I wish it also."

Moti did not lift her drooping head. "How can I help you?" she murmured. "Everything is changed now—more changed, even, than when the British were here."

Veera knelt at her side. She took the narrow, listless hand into her own warm young hands and smoothed it.

"Let me stay at least until we know about Jai."

"But I do know," Moti said, suddenly alert.

Veera did not reply, continuing to gaze into her mother's face.

"If he were dead," Moti said, "I would know it here, in my womb, where he was conceived and created."

She withdrew her hand and pressed it against her body, and suddenly the door opened and Jagat stood there again. He was in a whirl of haste.

"If I must go on this search for Jai, then I must go," he shouted. "Ranjit is packing the bags. He will accompany me. I don't know where to begin—New Delhi first, to search military records. Perhaps Bombay—the hospital where the captain of Jai's regiment lies wounded—lost both legs. Veera, since you've left school and it's so near the summmer holidays, you'd better stay with your mother."

He paused to frown at them and pull at his full lower lip. "Look here—you might keep an eye on Osgood and the decorations. I've been distraught—I don't know what they're doing—hauling all sorts of things out of the cellars. I want everything Indian in decor but American in comfort—modern, that is—"

They dared not answer, subject to his flashing eyes and darting brows.

"Do you hear me, Veera?" he thundered.

"Yes, Father," she said.

"And surely," Moti put in gently, "we must postpone the wedding."

He turned on her. "Wedding?"

"Veera's wedding."

"Oh—yes, of course. Unless Veera—"

"I don't mind," Veera said. "Raj will understand. He is coming to see me next month, as soon as he's got his diploma. He was going to England after we were married. We can wait until he comes back."

"You'll have to wait," Jagat grumbled, "now that I'm off on this foolish expedition."

He felt guilt in the bottom of his being, and to hide it, he was arrogantly impatient with the two women. Let them dare to protest any decision he made! Above all, let them dare to mention Brooke!

Yet it was Veera, to his surprise, who did dare.

"Will the American lady go with you, Father?" she asked.

He glared at her too innocent face. "Why do you ask such stupidity? I don't know where she is."

"Why?" Moti murmured.

"Someone offended her, that's why," he retorted. "She is offended and she has gone away. You know that!"

He had betrayed too much and Veera seized upon him. "And does it matter that she has gone away, Father?"

He flashed his dark eyes at her. "No—except that she is my first guest at the hotel. She has connections. She is rich. She will tell people to come here or not to come. What did you say to her?"

"Nothing, Father—just—idle talk."

"It is women's idle talk that ruins business!"

He had left them both and in this evil mood. Behind his back they sighed, and spoke of other things. In an hour Veera left her mother to rest and then finding herself restless, upon impulse she ordered a boat to take her to the lake palace.

Bert Osgood was in the glass bedroom of the lake palace, unpacking an immense chandelier, bought a century ago in Europe and left in its box in the cellars. Dusty and irritable with the heat, he was grumbling to half a dozen Indian helpers and to the American decorators who had come from New York to finish making the palace into a modern hotel.

"Of course no one will use this glass bedroom," he was saying. "It's so obscene it's funny. Imagine some old maharaja with his latest love here in this huge, absurd glass bed, magnified by these mirror walls, and the mirror ceiling—O lord, can you see the pair of them visible above and below and on all four walls—"

He was interrupted by a silvery voice from the open door.

"She was probably very beautiful."

He looked up. Veera stood in the doorway, wrapped in a silk sari of a pale pearl pink, edged with silver to match the silver of her sandals. He recognized her at once and blushed.

"Miss—Miss Veera!" he stammered. "You've caught me in an awful moment. I'm—filthy—as you see—oh, this is Alpha Barron of New York and her husband— they're our decorators."

Veera nodded, smiled, and leaned against the door-frame, looking cool and indifferent. "I've never seen this glass furniture—but I've heard about it. My grandfather bought it for his Greek concubine but she hanged herself before it could be unpacked. Fancy it's being brought out of the cellars now!"

"We aren't using it," Bert said. He was wiping his face with his handkershief, smearing it hopelessly. "That is, we shan't use it except for exhibition purposes. This part of the palace is to be a sort of museum. I've put everything here that has some amusement value."

"Beautiful things," Alpha put in breathlessly. She was young and smart, her dyed blond hair piled high, her skirt well above her knees. She habitually forgot her husband until suddenly she remembered him and drew him into the conversation. He was a roundfaced young man in tight trousers and a plaid sport shirt.

"Don't you think so, Ronnie?" she said, remembering him.

"Oh, very beautiful," he agreed, staring round-eyed at Veera.

"You'll simply love the suites," Alpha went on, always breathless. "I've done them in that heavy brocaded satin —bolts of it in the cellars—French, you know!"

"My grandfather was often in Paris," Veera said, indifferent, as always, with strangers. She turned to Bert. "What became of your first guest?"

"Miss Westley? She told the desk clerk, it seems, that she was going away for a few weeks."

"Will she be back?"

"She said she might be—or might not."

"Did she say where she was going?"

"She said something about Bombay."

"Did she say why?"

"No. I didn't ask. But it was sudden. She didn't say a word about leaving until suddenly she was all packed. Is His Highness around, Miss Veera?"

"He was with us an hour or so ago," Veera said.

She allowed her gaze, under the heavy fringe of her lashes, to rest upon Bert's dust-streaked face, daring him in the silence to think his thoughts but to put no further question about her father. What she saw in his eyes was only a simple and naked admiration of herself and she drew the edge of her sari over her head, holding the silver edge lightly, concealing nothing but adding a frame to her beauty. He was not thinking of her father, as she could see, and pretended not to see.

"M-Miss Veera," he stammered. "C-could you—would you—like to see some of the rooms we've finished?"

"I would, indeed," she said. "I've heard my father speak of what you're doing."

"Then—please, Alpha, you and Ronnie go on with this —I'll be back very shortly. If you'll excuse me just a minute, Miss Veera, when we reach the other wing—if I just wash my face—I'm so embarrassed to be caught like this—"

He was piloting her, his hand on her elbow as he talked, and at the entrance to the wing he left her standing in the corridor while he darted into a door. She heard the sound of running water, and in a moment he emerged, cleansed and ruddy, his red hair on end, and his usual cheerful smile on his face.

"There—I feel better—I ought to change my shirt, but I don't want to keep you waiting. I've so hoped—you see, I really want your opinion of all that I'm doing. I want the decor to be Indian, but the utilities to be American— modern to the last touch, every comfort and convenience but all done with style—Indian style. Now whether I've achieved—Alpha is rather extreme sometimes—it's so essential that nothing be overdone—and we're lucky to have found these fabulous things in the cellars—still packed in boxes, most of them, and preserved from decay. It'll be fabulous, the whole place—"

He was babbling, but she found his youthfulness charming and his adoration touching. Raj never adored her. He would have considered it beneath him. But American men, she had heard, were like this one. They adored women, beginning with their mothers. He was staring at her, his jaw hanging.

"Are you home on a vacation, Miss Veera?"

"No," she said, suddenly deciding. "I have finished my education. I shan't go back to school."

He hesitated. "I was awfully sorry to hear about your brother. I only saw him twice—"

"Yes. I'm staying home partly because of that. My mother has not been herself since—we heard."

"Nor has your father, if I may say so. He hasn't taken the same interest here—"

She avoided answer for an instant. Then she decided to tell him. "My mother is certain that my brother is not dead. She insists that my father go in search of him."

They stopped in the middle of a narrow corridor.

"Oh, I say—" he stammered, staring down into the pretty face. "Do you think it's possible—"

"I don't know," she said, looking up into his honest blue eyes. "We Indians are odd. We do feel things sometimes! But my father is going—has perhaps gone."

"Where will he—has he any idea—"

"I don't know," she said. "We shall have to wait."

They stood looking at each other, very close in the narrow passage. She seemed entirely passive, as though she were expecting, or waiting, for him to make some move toward her. He did not know Indian girls, not one like this, at any rate, and a man did not just take a princess into his arms as though she were a common—a common—

"We'd better—there are steps here—let me—"

Ahead of them marble steps descended, and walking ahead of her, he paused and took her little hand to help her and felt his head swim.

When she was gone, and he watched her boat as it drove across the calm waters, he was aware of a necessity, heretofore unknown to him, to go alone into an empty room, and there, hidden from the eyes of others, to discover exactly what was taking place in his being. Until now he had considered India merely a new place of business where he could exert his powers of salesmanship. He was an American of so pure a caliber, so simply constructed, so local by nature, that he was at home anywhere in the world merely as an American. On the streets of Amarpur he came and went exactly as though he were on the main street of the small town in Ohio where he had been born and had grown up. He behaved toward the people in India as he behaved toward his own people, to their mystification, amusement, and delight. They loved him extravagantly without understanding what he said and forgave him everything because he made them laugh. Intensely human themselves, they perceived that he was as human as they, and children followed him the moment he crossed the lake and set foot on the steps of the great marble water gate.

All this he comprehended and repaid by growing fond of the people here in a vague sort of way, granting them their puzzling difference from the people he knew back home. Never had it occurred to him, however, that he could possibly look on an Indian female as a woman. When he had last been in New Delhi, out of a curiosity which he considered normal but adolescent, he had visited the Street of Prostitutes and had been shocked by the spectacle of women in cages, one cage after another, and all exposed to the stares and judgments of passing men. Some of the women even had children with them. In the back of every cage was a curtained corner, to which a male customer repaired when he had chosen his woman. Though prostitution held a certain fascination, Bert could not stomach this sort of indulgence and he had walked away in considerable indignation, after having given a rupee to a small boy in one of the cages and roused the woman's smiling invitation. He had shaken his head brusquely as he walked away.

But this girl, this Veera, she was a real princess. He found himself remembering the glance of her dark liquid eyes, the deeply cut corners of her lovely mouth, her soft beguiling voice. There's something about her, he thought, something that invites a man, but innocently. He stood transfixed by the thought, and then shook himself like a dog.

"Steady, Bert," he muttered. "You didn't come here for anything but business."

And he returned to his drafting board.

As for Veera, she returned to the palace and her own rooms, and opening the chest where she kept her saris, she began to count them. Her old ayah, always mindful of her whereabouts, came to find her.

"Dear Little One," she exclaimed. "Why are you counting your saris? I can tell you how many there are—one hundred and twelve."

"I want to see them," Veera said. "I shall give some away to your daughter. I want at least a hundred new ones when I am married."

"How my daughter will rejoice," the ayah exclaimed, and putting her hands palm to palm, she made the gesture of thanks.

Veera smiled without speaking. Whether she married Raj or whether she did not, she could amuse herself with new saris. She had liked the look of stricken admiration in the blue American eyes. It held an element of worship which she had never seen before, certainly not in Raj's eyes, black and lively, appraising to be sure, anticipating perhaps but never reverent. There were no goddesses in India, none to be given worshipful love, at least. Kali could be worshiped in fear, but her vengeful, cruel face could not be loved.

"You are not to take any of these, the gold and the silver," she told her ayah. "Nor may you take the ones of pure white."

That night to her mother, as they sat on the terrace, alone except for the punkah boy in the distance, she spoke as though she were breathless with the heat of the night.

"I do really wish to postpone my marriage, Mamu!"

"Why?" Moti asked.

"I wish to wait until my heart is cleared of sorrow. I

would like to go to my wedding with joy. It seems more fair to Raj."

Moti considered this. "At any rate," she said at last, "we can do nothing until your father returns."

"When does he leave?"

"Tomorrow before dawn."

"When will he return?"

"Who knows?"

Silence fell and grew more heavy until Veera could not bear it. She rose from her chair.

"Let us go to bed, Mamu. Even the moonlight seems hot tonight."

"Good night, my child," Moti replied.

She held out her cool slim hand, and Veera, stooping, put it to her cheek.

"Good night, Mamu."

He found Brooke in the sea at Juhu, after an hour's search. No one could tell him where she was although everyone in the hotel knew her, it seemed. The desk clerk reported that she was not in her rooms. Yes, certainly she was registered but she never answered the telephone. A servant was sent to the seventh floor with a master key. He opened the door of her suite and returned to announce that she was not there, although her luggage was unpacked, her clothes hanging in the closets. On the terrace a waiter reported that she had breakfasted there but two hours ago. It was the bath boy who, hearing the discussion, called from beyond the fringe of cocoanut palms that she was swimming in the surf, and that he was growing anxious because the tide was due to turn in less than half an hour, and she would be carried out to sea, although she was a good swimmer.

"Find me bathing trunks!" Jagat shouted. "I will go after her."

The beach boy pointed to a dot far off from the shore, and Jagat had plunged into the tepid sea and had then forced her to swim ahead of him to land.

"How can you be so foolish?" he gasped, the bitter

water choking in his throat. "You know how dangerous this bay is!"

She threw herself on the sand. "How did you know I was here?"

"I inquired at the hotel, of course. But why Bombay?"

She turned over on her back. "I wanted to get away by myself, and I don't know anyone here."

She looked up at him frankly and he examined those violet eyes, the dark lashes wet with seawater.

"Have I done something to make you hate me?" he demanded.

She shook her head. He continued.

"Has it anything to do with me that you are here?"

She considered the question. "The answer is yes. But the importance is—how much?"

"How much what?"

"How much it has to do with you."

"How much has what to do with me?"

"My wanting to escape."

"Escape?"

"Yes. I'm a moon child, born under Cancer."

"You don't believe that nonsense!"

"Not really. But moon children withdraw themselves by instinct."

"When?"

"Whenever they can't answer their own questions."

"You are saying that you wish to escape me."

"Yes."

"So you throw yourself into the sea!"

She laughed. "Not quite that—I was trying to feel the exact moment when the tide changes."

"Suppose you were too late—after all, this is an Indian sea. How do you know its pulse?"

"That's what makes it exciting."

"Does this excitement apply also to human beings?"

"Not in general."

"To me in particular?"

There had been white women in London and Paris, but it was not her whiteness now that invited his interest. It was not even her beauty. He saw the strong slender grace of her body, the smoothness of her skin, the perfection of the detail of her frame, but beyond these diversions he felt the power of her being. He had not been drawn before to inquire of the person contained within a woman, but now, to his surprise, he thought of her apart from her womanhood.

"Yes," she said at last. "To you in particular."

He had been standing above her, but now he flung himself down beside her. What should be said? Lying there upon the hot sand, his heart still beating from the struggle with the sea, he felt himself faced at this moment with the insurmountable force of her personality. Calm as she appeared, detached and almost careless, he knew that she had none of these qualities. And she was talking in a low, concentrated tone, to him and to herself.

"You are a stranger to me. I have no wish to know you and yet I long to be with you wherever you are. I don't even understand what sort of man you are, because I don't know your country or your language and yet I know I have been looking for you all my life. I don't know how you feel toward me, and I ought to care, but I don't. My half of the world is not yours nor yours mine, and yet until we know each other in some way I don't comprehend, we'll never be whole. You're old—yes, you are, because the age of your people is in you, and I'm young, because my people are young and youth is all we have, but until we teach each other whatever it is that each does not know, we can't know enough to live—perhaps even to survive. And I don't know what I am saying or why except that wherever you are, there I must be."

He listened to this as though he heard only a voice in the darkness, so completely was all else excluded from his consciousness. The sun shone on water as blue as the Mediterranean, but he did not see it. A magician wandering by and crying his tricks paused to stare at them but Jagat was not aware of another presence. When he spoke it was with a banality that horrified him when he heard his own voice.

"I have a wife and children."

She struck back at him. "I do not ask to be either your

wife or your child. Whatever I am to be to you—if it is anything—is someone entirely separate. I make my own place."

"But what place?"

"How can I tell when I don't know?"

"Do you mean—love?"

"Not as you mean it!"

"There is only one love between man and woman."

"I don't know whether what I feel toward you is love. I can only call it a sympathy, a stronger sympathy than I have ever known before. And I follow my sympathy. Where you are, there I am, in spirit, if not in body."

He rose to his feet and stood looking down at her. She was sitting up now, her feet curled into the sand, her lovely face upturned to his, her face as frank and honest as a child's. He put out his hand to lift her up.

"You will come with *me*," he said firmly.

They walked side by side along the beach and mounted the steps to the terrace. There they paused, she waiting for his direction.

"Let us leave in the early morning," he said. "This afternoon I must visit the hospital where my son's captain lies wounded. Shall we meet for dinner—say at seven o'clock?"

"Yes," she said.

They exchanged a look and gravely they parted. She went to her rooms and bathed and dressed and packed her bags, in a mood strangely calm. He had come to find her. That was what she had expected and feared. If he comes she had told herself, it will be a sign of recognition. He knows me, as I know him. If he does not come, then I am mistaken and I will go on my way—where? Anywhere, perhaps to another country, seeking my own, finding where I belong.

She was not surprised when out there in the blue sea suddenly he had appeared. It occurred to her at that instant that she had expected him. She was in fact sure of him. So strong a sympathy as she felt for this man could not be hers alone. Its very power assured a reciprocity.

"But it's not love," she insisted aloud. "It is something deeper and stronger, as though we'd known each other a long, long time."

She wanted to be alone, and she telephoned for luncheon to be sent to her sitting room. There before the window, closed in the air-cooled room, she ate with good appetite and at peace. She had been honest with him, and would be, always. Coquetry, byplay, the games of love, were impossible between them. She would hide nothing from him. She would make no pretense.

The hospital was crowded with wounded soldiers. It was a full half hour before Jagat found the young captain. Very young he was, almost as young as Jai himself. He was lying on his back in his bed, staring up at the ceiling. An ominous flatness below the hips revealed that both legs were gone. His face had the skeletal pallor of suffering.

Jagat put out his hand. "I am Jai's father."

The thin face brightened. "I heard that you were in Bombay, Your Highness, but I did not dare to imagine your coming to see me. Alas that I could not come to you." He motioned to his lower body. "They had to be taken off, after all. Gangrene set in."

"I am sorry," Jagat said, aghast.

The young captain refused pity "Oh, I daresay I'll learn to do without them. After all, I'm not a centipede. But let's talk of Jai. We got to be friends, he and I— somewhat the same princely background, although I'm four years older. Do you know, sir, I think he had a premonition. The night before we talked of England. I've been there. But he said, rather wistfully, I thought, that he'd never see it. When I asked why, he said simply that he couldn't imagine it. I asked what he meant and he said that a black curtain seemed to fall before his mind's eyes and this he believed meant that he'd never leave India, however much he'd looked forward to seeing other countries. This was something quite new and he believed it meant death. Then we talked of reincarnation, you know, and we promised we'd communicate somehow if one of us was killed and lived beyond. I haven't heard from him yet, but who knows? I think he had a real premonition, at any rate. The Chinese were so beastly well armed. All the same—"

"He died so quickly," Jagat said. His throat was tight with tears.

"Like that." The young captain flicked his finger against his thumb. "He was leading the men up the hill after I fell. A Chinese threw a grenade at him at short range. In an instant he was gone."

"I'm glad of that—if death was his karma," Jagat said.

"He was brave," the young captain said. "I could count on him to take my place."

"Yes, he was brave," Jagat agreed. "Not that he didn't know fear, mind you. I used to take him tiger hunting, and he was afraid—oh yes, I could see that. But he never yielded to fear."

"That's bravery," the young captain said faintly.

"Think of yourself now," Jagat told him. "Think only of yourself—"

He left after a few minutes. The young face showed quick exhaustion. And what was there more to discover?

"But how can you accept this?" Brooke demanded.

They were leaving the hotel and the car was passing through the narrow alley at the far end of Juhu Beach. At the other end was the hotel, its luxurious suites, its terraces fringed with palm trees, its vistas of the sea. Here were the squalid huts, hidden among tangles of thornbush. The sun was relentless, shining upon every ragged child, every tattered woman. The scene was deplorable in its poverty, and yet somehow it was not sad. This, she perceived, was because of the people, beautiful in spite of their emaciated bodies. Under tangled hair their eyes shone enormous and sparkling with a strange vitality that was strongly sexual. Once when she had lingered in Rio de Janeiro she had met at a dinner dance a famous scientist. There had been a brief attraction between them, immediate and short-lived because the sympathy had not been strong enough. While they danced they had talked, he beginning the conversation by asking what she had done that day.

"I visited the villages," she said.

His look had grown wary, as this handsome Indian's had done a moment ago, this prince, whom she was beginning to think of only as Jagat.

"Very horrible, were they not?" the Brazilian had asked boldly.

She understood the defensiveness of the question. Let her dare to defend his people!

"Very horrible," she had agreed calmly. "But their eyes!"

"What about their eyes?" he had demanded.

"So vivid," she said. "So powerful—"

"Sexual power," he had declared. "All starving people are strongly sexual. It is nature's way of assuring continuing life. The body, starving, knows it will die soon. Therefore it must reproduce early and often. This explains the overpopulation in poor countries, about which you and your well-fed compatriots are always complaining."

"What are you thinking about?" Jagat asked now.

She recounted the incident of the Brazilian scientist. "Do you think he was right?" she asked.

He shrugged. "Perhaps! Also, however, we believe in life. The act of sex is holy because it creates life. That is why even in our most sacred temples you will see scenes of love between the gods and goddesses. And you will see phallic symbols, sacred because they represent the organs of creation. For us sex is beautiful and joyful and without sin."

She listened, conscious of an unwilling excitement, and glancing at him, saw him in profile, arrogantly handsome. How strange a man and how difficult to understand! She felt a surge of emotion and restrained herself from putting out her hand to touch his hands, those strong dark hands clasped upon his lap. She changed the subject abruptly, finding the emotions distasteful.

"Look at that exquisite boy—a pity, isn't it, that he is naked and half-starved? And no chance for an education?"

"Whatever he is, it is his karma," Jagat said firmly.

She felt a sudden resentment against him. How dare he be so attractive to her and yet refuse to agree with her? "It is easy enough for you to accept such fate for others!"

"I accept because I must," Jagat said. "Yet I do not forget them. These people are also my countrymen in their own fashion."

"What are they?"

"Fishermen—and bootleggers."

"Bootleggers?"

"Don't you know that we have here, although for a different reason, what you Americans used once to call Prohibition? Liquor is forbidden by our religion."

She was still angry with him. "Yet I saw your other countrymen, the rich ones, there in the hotel, making friends with everyone from the west in order to share their allowances of liquor. Even I was approached! At first I thought it was because I was—attractive." She paused to laugh. "I soon learned better. It was because I was allowed a certain quota of liquor."

Jagat was gallant. "Both reasons, doubtless!"

She returned to her mood. "But to accept these hovels —is it necessary?"

"They have been here for a thousand years. Destroyed by wind and storm and rotting with age, they are rebuilt again and again."

"Why?"

"For simple shelter. It is reason enough here. Wait until you see Calcutta. People are born, they die, without a roof over them from birth till death."

"But why accept it?"

Jagat shrugged. "We are artists at accepting life as it comes to us."

"You put me off. And your wife does not accept your son's death. So you contradict yourself—"

They were on edge this morning, the two of them. He wondered if she knew why and decided that she did not. He knew very well, however. They had parted early last evening after he had given up hope of further acquaintance at that moment. He had perceived the wary manner in which she defended herself by frequent silences and had himself withdrawn.

"We must make a very early start," he had said. "I will not allow myself to keep you up late. Tomorrow will be a long day. There is plenty of time to talk."

She had risen from the table so quickly that he saw that she was relieved by his decision. What, therefore, had she been contemplating if he had not cut short the evening? Nevertheless, they had lingered over the parting at her door, he holding her hand between both of his. Looking down into her eyes, he had not been able entirely to restrain himself.

"What is this between us?" he had demanded. "It is as though I had known you forever."

"A friendship," she had said. "And friends are always sure they have met before—reincarnation and all that."

"Do you already believe in reincarnation?"

"Perhaps I have always believed," she said, her frank eyes uplifted to his face.

He stood, unwilling to release her hand, to allow the door to close between them. A fragment of the Bhagavdgita which his mother had often used to teach him came from his memory. He repeated it now, his voice clear and sonorous.

" 'Never to an evil place goes one who does good. He goes to the regions of the righteous where he dwells for untold years and is born again into a fortunate family . . . Being born again, he recalls the knowledge which formerly was his and he struggles the more earnestly toward perfection.' "

She listened, entranced, and upon her face he caught a first glimpse of adoration. It was new to him and intoxicating. Moti had never adored him.

"Good night," he had said gently. "Sleep well. Tomorrow we meet again—tomorrow and tomorrow and tomorrow."

Yesterday he had been amazed at the tenderness he felt toward her. Was this to be a new sort of love? Or was it that he had never before known love? This morning however, he felt changed again, distant and even perhaps slightly irritable, a mood corresponding, he discovered, to her own, but himself he interpreted always simply. He had last night been sexually stirred and had slept restlessly. In the early morning hours he had even toyed with the idea of knocking on her door, or at least waking her by a telephone call. Accustomed as he was to going at once to Moti when he was in similar mood, he felt a touch of hostility or perhaps it was no more than impatience that this American woman should pretend that there could be only a friendship between a man and woman. His irritability wandered among the varied problems of his life, the unending reconstruction of the lake palace, Veera's absurd and willful reluctance to marrying Raj because he had hair on the flanges of his ears, Moti's strange religious bond with Father Frances Paul, the burden upon him of the villagers in his domain, that region no longer his responsibility in any sense except that the villagers refused to release him from their hereditary affection, thereby forcing him to feel for them and care whether they starved; and now above all, that Moti insisted their son was not dead. Jai's death had been heavy enough to bear, and his sorrow, which he endeavored to bury, was only resurrected by Moti's refusal to accept the fact that their son was dead. All of these annoyances, wavering between irritation and deepest sorrow, were sharpened because his feelings were made acute by this new emotion for a western woman. It was an emotion edged by a determination, of which he was secretly ashamed, not to allow her, or at least not to wish her, to see the less pleasant aspects of his people who, however repulsive they were to him at times, must not appear repulsive to strangers, especially to this one who was also a beautiful woman with whom he did not wish to be in love.

They had left Juhu and were proceeding by car toward the airport from whence a rickety Viscount would fly them northward to Mussoorie. Certainly there was no use in going to the refugees at Darjeeling and Kalimpong, removed as they were from the scenes of battle with the

Chinese, but somewhere in the Tibetan camps near Mussoorie, he might hear news from a lama.

As though she read his mind Brooke now spoke. "Have you a plan of where we must go?"

"There is an encampment of Tibetan refugees in the north," he said, "and among them are lamas who will have recent news from the border."

"Did you visit Darjeeling before?"

"Not for my son's sake, but for my daughter's. Her school is near there, a famous school, founded by the British long ago in the days of empire for their own children, but now used by Indians also. Veera has been there for several years. I am not sure she will finish. She is to be married, and now, the time being short, she does not wish to leave her mother."

"Is she not very young for marriage?"

"We believe in early marriage, especially for girls."

"Is she in love?"

"I have not asked."

She stopped. They were walking now in the airport, on their way to enter the craft that waited for them, pulsing with power, its wings trembling. Behind them a fragile porter staggered under their bags sweat shining on his thin black body.

"You have not asked," she repeated, incredulous.

"It is an arranged marriage," he said shortly. "Like my own."

"You mean you didn't—you weren't in love with your wife when you married?"

"Of course I wasn't," he retorted. "It would have been indecent of me. My wife comes of a very high family, almost as noble as my own. We have learned to—to appreciate each other since marriage. We have been happy, I think. She has been a good wife to me, and I have fulfilled my part, I daresay, with equal satisfaction to her."

They hastened their steps, urged on by the surrounding crowd. She was learning the difference between a crowd in India and one elsewhere in the world. Here the people moved with joyous delight in mere moving, in being alive, and in communication. Each seemed intent on his own direction and yet each was aware of every other human being, which is to say that each had within himself the contrast of detachment and connection, a particle single and independent and yet imbedded in a whole. She had the wish to express this fresh perception to Jagat and was prevented by his hand urgent upon her elbow.

"Hurry," he said. "We have reserved seats but I cannot swear for how long. We'll be sure of them only if we are in them."

They entered the aircraft and took their places. It was already full, and children were crowded in with parents and other relatives.

"Is it safe?" she inquired with doubt.

"Of course not," he replied, laughing. "Nothing in India is safe. We carry our lives in our hands."

He was strapping the belt about her. One end of the clasp was gone but someone, perhaps a stewardess, had supplied a large safety pin.

"There," he said, leaning back in his own seat. "Now nothing can happen to us. We are here, we are together."

She glanced at him to see if the last three words had special meaning and decided they did not. His handsome face was bland and composed, his eyebrows, always alert and quick to move, were for the moment at rest. He caught her glance and laughed again.

"Yes, I am quite myself, thank you! I am merely stating two facts. We are here, we are together. It is as far as I will go at the moment. Let the future take care of itself."

A peculiar gaiety suddenly infused them both, and she felt warm and even lighthearted.

"About reincarnation," she began irrelevantly. Indeed she had not been thinking of that at all, and the word came out of her mouth of its own accord, so startling that she paused.

"What about reincarnation?" he asked.

"Simply that today somehow I am ready to believe in it totally. It's the effect that India has on me. Here I believe anything!"

"Perhaps it's the effect that I have on you!"

If he expected coquetry or hoped for it, he was disappointed. She looked at him, frankly considering.

"Perhaps it is only you," she agreed.

He was stopped by that small word *only*. Her little hand, lying loosely open upon her lap, had been under his eyes ever since they sat down side by side. He had kept his own hands tightly clasped lest he reach for it and cherish it between his palms. Now, impelled to reach for her hand in spite of himself, a stewardesss in a green sari prevented him. Smiling, she held a tray before him.

"Your Highness," she said with naughty emphasis. "We are delighted to welcome you aboard, with your beautiful companion. May I offer you a sweet? Very nice against airsickness!"

He turned to Brooke. "A sweet?"

She shook her head but he helped himself to two honey-colored bits. Meanwhile the stewardess stared at Brooke so avidly that she forgot to move.

"Come, come," Jagat said sharply.

"Oh, sorry," the stewardess murmured, smiling.

She moved away from them then, and their eyes met with meaning.

"She knows you," Brooke said.

"Now she also knows you," he replied. "Do you mind?"

She considered. "I'm not sure what it means that she knows me."

"Whatever it means—do you mind?"

She met his eyes again. "No. Didn't I say you are a sympathy?"

The engines were whirling now and the plane was moving slowly, then swiftly. It paused at the end of the runway, trembling for a long moment while the engines roared.

"This is the moment I dread," Brooke said, her lips close to Jagat's right ear.

He turned and smoothed the soft straight hair away from her left ear, a small pretty ear, he took time to observe, and he leaned toward it.

"It is the moment I love," he said, "the moment of danger."

He hesitated and she felt his warm lips touch her ear as he withdrew. The next instant they had left the earth and were soaring into the sky.

Night fell in New Delhi with an enormous moon magnified by pre-monsoon dust. At the Ashoka they lingered over dinner, both conscious of the sidelong looks cast at them from other tables and both determined to ignore them. Men made a point of passing their table when they rose from their own and accosting Jagat as they passed.

"Good evening, Highness."

"Glad to see you looking so well, Highness."

"Stopping here for long, Jagat, old boy?"

To all such salutations he replied with a cool smile and a wave of his right hand.

"They want to be introduced to you," he told Brooke, "and I have no intention of doing so."

Women, on the other hand, passed at a distance, giving Brooke a stare across the tables.

"There'll be no privacy here," Jagat said at last, "nor can I come to your suite or you to mine without servant gossip. Let me see—"

He meditated a moment and then snapped his fingers. "I have it—we'll do what we did before—we'll visit the Taj Mahal again by moonlight. It's a pleasant drive to Agra—remember? I'll ring for a car."

She hesitated. Did she dare so to utilize the night's moon and the Taj Mahal? This time it would also be dangerous. Already she was aware of impulses she had never felt before toward any man, emotions rising far beyond a sympathy. There was every reason not to be impelled by his emotions or her own. For that was the root of the sympathy and now the attraction. They were, in spite of intelligence and a certain intellectual arrogance, both persons of emotional capacity so profound that they could be destroyed if emotion became overweening in its power—that is to say, if it went wrong. She could not at this point, however, define either rightness or its opposite.

"Why do you hesitate?" he demanded.

"I am wondering if I am perhaps—tired."

"Nonsense," he said. "You're no more tired than I am. You look like a rose. And if I went to bed now I'd not sleep until dawn. Besides, I want to see the Taj again, with you. It'll be different this time."

She yielded, half alarmed that she enjoyed his male domineering, she who all her life had been solitary and independent and who had until now scorned dependence in other women

"Fetch a wrap," he was saying. "We'll want to sit on the marble bench and see the Taj reflect itself in the lagoon. Meet you here in fifteen minutes and mind you change those high heels to sandals!"

"Yes, Highness," she said, with sudden laughter.

And fifteen minutes later she met him, her feet bare in Indian sandals and over her arm her white ermine stole, feather light and lined with satin. The car was waiting, the brown chauffeur at the door, and they were rolling out of the city and along the highway to Agra. The day's dust, constantly in stir from slow bullock carts and flocks of black long-legged goats and caravans of camels pushing among the honking automobiles, settled upon the road, now almost empty of travel. In the scraggy trees on both sides of the highway the sleeping vultures she remembered were still hanging like black bags while the effulgent moonlight shone upon the dry and arid lands surrounding. The scene was all of quiet and the end of day. They sat side by side, not talking, and now Jagat reached to her and with his right hand took her left hand and held it gently. She was startled and for the moment made no movement to withdraw it.

"Let us test ourselves," he said. "Let us see if we are strong enough to say to ourselves 'thus far and no farther.'"

She did not reply and they sat hand in hand not looking at each other but at the moon now rising from the horizon toward zenith. Let it not be she who would reveal to this man the depth of her heart! Were she to withdraw her hand it would be to confess that she was not strong enough to govern herself. Yet she was scarcely strong enough. Strange, she thought, how easily and even care-

lessly she had held hands with men and boys who had
taken her to dances and dinners, theater and football
games. It was nothing, it was the least she could do of
what they hoped for, or expected, and it had meant nothing. Now, she woman and Jagat man, the touch of hand
to hand was danger. And how much did it mean to him,
an Indian? She remembered that once she had met a
Chinese girl in Washington, the daughter of an ambas-
sador from China, and that lovely Asian had refused to
touch the hand of an American male.

"Because," she had explained to Brooke, "when palm
meets palm the heart wakes."

At this moment Jagat moved and as gently as he had
taken her hand he laid it on her lap again. He made no
explanation and when, after some moments, he did speak
it was of the Taj Mahal.

"For us who are Indians, not only a tomb, but the temple of love itself. Each makes it his own temple. Yet I
wonder if for Shah Jehan it was not also a gift of contri-
tion. His wife died in her fourteenth childbirth, remember? Perhaps he had not sufficiently praised her in life.
That is the lesson for us, perhaps—not to wait too long
before we speak."

He waited for her to reply, and waited so long that she
felt compelled.

"What shall I say?" she asked.

"What do you wish to say?" he asked.

"I don't know," she told him. "In all honesty I don't
know."

"We have come too soon," Jagat exclaimed. "I should
have known better."

To which she had no answer—

It was nearly midnight when they passed through the
gate of the tomb. Her memory was still vivid of her first
visit, yet its full beauty had not revealed itself to her until
now. There it stood, suffused and softened by the moonlight, so full, so glowing, that the marble building, shining
white, seemed to float upon the landscape. No, more than
moonlight, it was their awareness of one another which

inspired beauty with new meaning. They stood speechless, gazing at the scene and slowly they walked beside the still waters, approaching the tomb and at last stopping at a distance to sit upon the marble bench facing it. Now, instinctively, their hands clasped. He bore this closeness until tension could endure no more and he was compelled to break it. He stood up, he put her hand into the crook of his elbow.

"Come," he said. "Let us go near. The moonlight is so bright that we can see the detail of the carving. It is all of flowers, petal by petal perfect, the centers colored gems—true, not the valuable gems the Shah put there. No, rude British soldiers long ago dug out most of them, remember? But an Englishman, a viceroy, had them replaced by semiprecious stones."

"You told me before," she said.

They were walking toward the tomb. Now they entered. She felt of the marble, warmed, she imagined, by the golden glow of the moonlight. But it was cool and smooth. They walked slowly in light and in shadow, and at last descended into the crypt, where an oil lamp burned. There the Shah and his beloved lay side by side, he compelled to share her resting place, and perhaps glad to share it at the sorrowful end of his life, instead of lying alone in the magnificence of the tomb he had planned for himself.

Death too recent made Jagat grave and Brooke shared his silence. They mounted the steps again and walked side by side, but no longer hand in hand, back to the car which had brought them there.

At the outer gate she paused to look back, a lingering gaze so long that Jagat inquired of her.

"What are you thinking?"

Here he paused, embarrassed. "No—no—I have no right to invade your thoughts."

She gave him, however, the simple truth. "I am thinking that this moment I must remember, whatever comes to me in my life, whatever disappointments."

He hesitated and then replied. "And I am thinking of Akbar, who lost two sons while he was here at Agra. Let him be called The Great—I agree. Shall I tell you of him? He was a contemporary of Queen Elizabeth the First."

"Who else will tell me if not you?" she replied.

"Very well—let us get in the car. Are you comfortable? Now then, Akbar! He was a man of middle height, only about five foot seven, and he hated cruelty but used it when necessary. He was immensely strong and very brave—killed tigers on foot, rode mad elephants no one else dared go near. He was dark but his eyes, it was said, 'were like the sea in sunshine.' He was a true king, hot tempered and loud-voiced. Once he found a lamplighter asleep on duty and he ordered him thrown from the battlements. But he could control his temper when necessary, and he had charming manners. He could be great with the great and lowly with the lowly. He wanted always to be first, but his mind was scintillating and so brilliant that it was hard for him to be patient. He loved machinery and to work with wood and metal and he made cannons and matchlocks. A great administrator—I remember studying how he controlled every detail—a lesson to me! He slept only three hours a night, but he wouldn't learn to read or write. He learned through listening—and was a mystic all his life and given, as most brilliant people are, to melancholy. He tried to found a state religion with himself the head. When his two sons died, he was told by a Muslim holy man who lived among the rocks at Sikri that he would have three living sons. So he built Fatehpur Sikri, the town of victory. It is not far from here."

"Take me there," she said.

He was amazed. "Now? At this hour of the night?"

"I don't want the night to end," she said.

Hours later they saw the dawn rise over the red sandstone walls of Fatehpur Sikri, and she gazed, awestruck, at the mighty structure.

"Why was it deserted?" she asked.

"Because there was too little water to support the people," he replied. "It was the capital for only fifteen years, between 1570 and 1585. But Akbar's heart was already broken. Two of his beloved sons, born here, died young

of excesses in living and he could not save them. So much
for sons—death and disappointment!"

She longed to comfort him and could not—not yet.

"Whether your son is living or dead is not the question,
Highness," the lama told him. He was surprisingly young,
this lama. She had somehow the idea that all lamas were
old, but this one was very young, twenty-four, he had replied, when Jagat asked him.

"Forgive me," Jagat said, "but is twenty-four not very
young for a wise man? You are scarcely older than my
son was. Yet you were recommended to me by your
superiors in Mussoorie." They had stopped in the high
mountain town to inquire of the lamas there in the make-
shift lamasery which of them could speak further of Jai.

"None of us, Highness," the chief lama there had replied. "We are not reincarnations. It is best if you will
travel north for another fifty miles. There you will find a
young lama who is a reincarnation. He lives alone with a
serving monk in a wayside temple."

So directed, they had found him, had accepted his invitation to enter his dwelling and now sat upon cushions
in his presence.

"I am the reincarnation of a famous lama in Tibet,"
the lama replied. "Moreover, since I was born, I have
made a study of death and of life again." The lama spoke
so surely and quietly that it seemed an echo from afar.

They were in a small new temple on the outskirts of a
village at the foot of the Himalayas. Over those mountains
the lama had walked with his fellow lamas and their people to find refuge from the Chinese who were seizing
Tibet. Men, women, and little children, they had come
over high and dangerous passes, already deep in snow
and ice. With them, their leader and their inspiration, was
the young Dalai Lama himself. Among his followers had
been this young lama.

"What is 'life again'?" Brooke asked.

The lama gazed at her with mournful eyes—eyes shaped
long, as the eyes of Mongols are, not Indian eyes, she recognized, not wide and liquid and the lashes curled. Here

were mysterious eyes, the irises impenetrably dark, the white clear and free of bloodshot, the lashes thick and straight. Indian eyes were too often clouded and feverish, the white congested, but the Mongol eyes were calm.

"It is to be born anew into another human body. It is reincarnation."

He did not look at her now, his gaze no higher than her hands folded on her lap. The serving monk offered them hot buttered tea, and she tasted it.

"Rather good," she whispered to Jagat, surprised.

The lama did not drink. He held the silver bowl in his thin pale hands, warming them. Time passed in silence and they waited for him to speak. Suddenly he turned to Jagat and his high, colorless voice floated upon the air.

"It is too soon for you to find your son in his new body. He must first pass through the three stages of death."

"What are these three stages?" Jagat asked.

He was uncomfortable in the eerie presence. The lama sat cross-legged in the buddha position, on a rug spread on a low wooden dais. In the bare poor room the hand-woven rug glowed with the colors of garnet and sapphire and jade. His robe was of a rough orange wool, a dark rich hue against which his waxen skin showed a pale gold, even his shaven head, and in his skeletal face his eyes burned. He set his tea bowl on the low table in front of him and placed his hands also in the buddha position. Then he spoke.

"The first stage of death is to die. When the one who dies is young, as your son was, and when death is untimely and violent, as your son's was, then the one does not know at first that he is dead. He still hears the voices of the living, he still sees them alive, and he thinks that he is still one of them. He cries aloud to them, he demands that they hear him. But they cannot hear him for he is dead. They hover over his dead body, which at first he does not recognize as his own. Then when they give him no answer, however loudly he may call to them 'This is I!' he looks closely at the dead body and recognizes himself as he was and is no more. Now he knows that he is dead. This is the first stage of death—to know that one is dead."

The lama paused. He took up his bowl and drank and set it down again. Jagat did not speak, nor did Brooke. They watched the lama's face, fascinated, half afraid. Jagat thought of Jai, hovering over his own mangled body lying on the snow. And Brooke—what was Brooke thinking? He glanced at her. She sat as though she were in a trance, gazing at the lama, her eyes intense, her lips parted.

"Brooke!" He cried out sharply, not knowing that he spoke her name.

She turned to him, unseeing. "Tell him to go on—"

The lama proceeded before Jagat could urge.

"The second stage is one of great melancholy and fear. Your son, knowing himself to be dead, feels himself lost in loneliness. To whom now can he speak? He can only flee away from the dead body lying on the ground."

The lama closed his eyes and was motionless for a time. Then he sighed deeply. "I see his body." His voice was a whisper. "Ah yes, a beautiful young man—but sadly wounded. Yes—his head—it is half blown away. Only the face remains untouched—very beautiful but lifeless —a mask of death. Too young, too young! So he flees from his own body—he cannot bear to see it lying there already half frozen in the snow. It is of no use to him now."

Jagat groaned. "How do you know he died when I have not told you?"

"I see—I see," the lama whispered.

"Then tell me," Jagat demanded. "Where did he go?"

The lama opened his eyes. The look on his face was almost tender. He stared into space. "Anywhere! He does not know where to go, but he is thinking only to get far away from that ruined body. He wanders, floating like a cloud. This is the second stage, a time of fear and grief. The loneliness is too heavy to bear and yet he must bear it for a time—for a time."

Jagat leaned forward. His hands on his knees were clenched and white at the knuckles.

"For a time," the lama repeated, "but all times end. When the close of the second stage draws near, then he hears words of comfort. Whether these words come from within himself or from others he does not know. But the voices comfort him. 'Be not afraid,' the voices tell him, 'for, lo, we are with you always. Take comfort, for your sorrow is over.' Now comes the great choice. It is the third stage of death."

The lama paused again, searching the distance in his mind.

"Choice?" Jagat asked, puzzled.

"The voices direct him," the lama went on. "They tell him that he may choose whether to be born again. If he chooses not to be born again, then he must proceed on the eternal way toward the godhead. If he wishes to be born again, then he must search the world of mankind. He must find two lovers in the divine embrace of conception. When the male element meets the female, at that very instant he must enter the union by force and claim the embryo as his dwelling place for another lifetime. There are forty-nine days from death to reincarnation."

"And may he choose what he shall be born?" Brooke asked, breathless.

The lama shook his shaven head. "He may choose only whether he wishes to be born again or whether he will proceed to the godhead. There must be no delay, for his substance changes. He must seize his chance, wherever he finds it. Male or female, he will be born by the chance of his choice. He must accept what life he can seize upon, with all its joys and burdens."

"How shall we recognize him if he is born again as an infant?" Jagat demanded.

"You must search," the lama said firmly. "Search first the countryside surrounding his home. He has fled the place where he died. He does not wish to see his dead body again. He will return to the places he knows best, when he was a child."

At this point the lama looked at Jagat with a new and extraordinary affection.

"Your blood is scarcely flowing and your heart is all

but stopped, for sorrow. Let me address the dead and take comfort. May I so do?"

"Please—" Jagat replied.

The lama thus addressed Jai:

"O nobly born, hear me! Now you are in the clear light of pure reality. This is its true nature. It has no form or symbol or color, and in the true reality of the All-Good, it is empty. Your intellect, which now is empty, is not the emptiness of nothingness. Rather it is pure intelligence, light-giving and blissful. It is the true consciousness of the All-Good . . . Your own consciousness, lucid, empty and inseparable from the great body of light, has neither birth nor death and is itself the unchangeable light. This is the final truth—the gods themselves are but the light and luster of your own soul."

Jagat was not comforted. He cried out, "O Holiness, you rob us of our gods!"

"Ah, you man," the lama replied. "Can you not understand that your own soul is the light of the godhead, and God is your own soul? Ah, you man! Where is your knowledge of life? It is so much easier to believe that things happen to you rather than to see how you yourselves compel them to happen! The animal part in man fights against recognizing the truth—that he is himself the creator of the conditions of life."

With this the lama closed his eyes and continued to speak but now his voice was faint, as though it came from very far. "It is not likely that your son has wandered to unknown countries. Spirits tend to linger where their bodies lived most happily. And since he is so young it is also not likely that he has chosen not to be born again. It is the old and weary, those who die of age and sickness, who refuse life and, accustomed to loneliness, proceed to the godhead. But your son has never known the joy of manhood, he left no child behind him, and he is not fulfilled. Therefore he will come back, he will be impatient to live again, and so he will not wander. He will enter the first union that he finds, in a hut or in a palace."

"How shall we find him?" Jagat inquired again. He was intent but puzzled, half believing, though skeptical.

"You have your talismans," the lama replied. "You know his childhood secrets. What food did he like to eat when he was in your house? What language did he speak? Had he some small accident to remember? Did he love one color above another? Can you remember the places where he liked to play? Did he hunt tigers with you, Highness, and when did he kill his own first tiger? These are your talismans."

The lama drifted into silence, which after a while they saw he would not break, and so they rose, they made pranam, their palms folded together, and they went away. Outside in the chill of the mountain air they walked the rough and narrow path, Jagat leading, Brooke following, each reflecting upon the mystery of what the lama had said. They could not believe in his faith, and yet the loneliness of these mountains, the stillness of the high air, the deep shadows of the valleys at the foot of yawning cliffs and precipices, lent credence to the possibilities of the unknown. When Jagat spoke, however, it was of something altogether different.

"I have a wish to go after this—what shall I call it, séance?—and visit the headmaster at Jai's school. He is an Englishman whom I respect, and one who did much once for Jai when he was a lad at that school. A perceptive chap, that headmaster! I've an idea that he knew more about Jai than I did. I saw Jai only as my son. And Mr. Cranston will balance the lama and all that mysticism, too. I'm disgusted with myself for being affected by it. It's too Indian of me."

"But why not?" Brooke replied. "I'm affected, as you call it. In fact, I'm ready to believe that Jai will return again—unless—"

She paused, her eyes inquiring.

"What?" he asked.

"Would Jai go on to seek the godhead?"

Jagat laughed, uncomfortable. "Oh, come now—I went to the lama to know if he'd heard any rumors of Jai— these monks always hear everything. I didn't expect a lot of—rubbish."

"Don't call it that!" she said sharply.

"Why not?"

"Because we don't know! There's so much we don't know—"

He was surprised to see tears in her eyes.

"Come," he said. "We'll visit the Englishman. Wonderfully comforting, the English! So realistic—so everything we Indians are not! No wonder we love them in spite of hating them. Why? Because we need them!"

"Yes," Mr. Cranston said. "Jai came to see me before he left for the front. I was surprised, for he had not been a communicative lad—proud in bearing, you know. One never forgot he was your son, Highness."

They were sitting in the headmaster's office, in a building perched on the side of a mountain and clinging to the cliffs like an eagle's eyrie. From the window near which she sat Brooke looked far away down upon the curling corkscrew curves of the narrow unpaved road along which she and Jagat had been driven by a reckless scrawny fellow whose only means of livelihood was a derelict American jeep, a relic left behind by American troops after the Second World War. Seated in this vehicle and moving along the edge of the abyss down which she gazed with fascinated horror, Brooke had held tightly to Jagat's hand.

"Look here," he said, astonished, "your palm is wet!"

He had turned her hand over and gazed at her wet palm.

"I can't help it," she had murmured. "I'm terrified. I've always been afraid of heights. It means something—doesn't it? I don't know what. But telling myself that I shan't fall does no good—my body acts on its own. It's afraid, no matter how I try to control myself."

"Ah, now," Jagat had murmured, soothing her. He put her hand to his breast. "Ah now, you're safe. Remember the British built this road—it's traveled by British parents even now, and the children walk halfway down the mountain to catch a bus."

The cheerful driver had been of no help.

"Highness," he had chirruped. "Let her be afraid! Only

last week a jeep went over the edge. As for me, I only pray that I do not meet another vehicle."

They had met none, fortunately, and had arrived here in time for an English tea with buttered crumpets and small watercress sandwiches. She ate and drank and listened, always mindful of the journey down the cliffs again.

"What did Jai tell you when he came to see you?" Jagat was asking the headmaster.

Mr. Cranston, as dry and English as though he had never left his native Sussex, stirred his tea and reflected. "I remember that I told him I was surprised that he had volunteered instead of waiting to be drafted. To this he replied that as your son he might never be drafted and so he had volunteered, because he wanted to offer himself. There was in him a deep mysticism which I had never suspected. You'd brought him up as a sportsman and a tiger hunter, Highness, and I thought of him as that— very British, in a way."

"We Rajputs are ancestrally tiger hunters, sir," Jagat retorted.

"Quite," Mr. Cranston agreed. He drank half his cup of tea and put the cup down. "And Jai was proud of having killed his tiger. But he spoke then of his mother. I didn't remember his having spoken of her before. I've met Her Highness several times, of course—a very beautiful, gentle lady. But it was only on that last visit of Jai's that I saw he was also her son. She had spoken to me once, I remember, of his other side. She told me that he had not yet found himself, that she suspected that he might become someone quite different from what he was then—I remember she mentioned the mandala, the universe, flowering into many forms, but always The One. I could see that she's a mystic—believes in reincarnation, you know —indeed, she had quite an influence on me. She set me to searching for myself what truth there might be in reincarnation."

"And were you convinced?" Brooke asked eagerly.

Mr. Cranston hesitated as he spoke. "I can't say I'm ever quite convinced—of anything, you know, Miss Westley. One doubts as one breathes—if one is intelligent. One sees that what one doesn't know is so much more—so infinitely more—than what one does know. But speaking as a skeptic, albeit a hopeful one, I might say that the subject has concerned so many great minds throughout the ages that one can scarcely dismiss it altogether, you know. In this way I began to study the Bhagavadgita and the Upanishads—and by Jove, you know"—he paused to make half-embarrassed laughter—"I confess that I was so struck—so overcome, in fact—with the wisdom of those writers that I felt it impossible that in a single lifetime, much of which is necessarily wasted in childhood and adolescence—not to mention sleep and the inevitable bodily functions such as eating and washing and so forth —these men could have accumulated such wisdom, whoever they were."

"Had you come to this conclusion before you saw Jai for the last time?" Jagat asked.

He was listening with concentration, leaning forward in his chair, his hands gripping the arms.

"Well, yes, in fact I had," Mr. Cranston replied. "I remember that Jai said something rather odd. He said that he felt quite certain that he would be killed in action. He spoke with such calmness that I was alarmed! 'My dear boy,' I said, 'I hope that you will take every precaution against being killed. You are your father's only son.'"

"And his reply?" Jagat demanded.

"He said, 'Of course I shall not try to die. But if I do die'—no, no, he said, 'when I do—I shall simply go on my way, whatever it is.'"

From outside the building the cry of boys at play rang through the pure mountain air. School was over for the day and children ran into the garden, walled against the cliffs. Watching them, Brooke saw a little boy, perhaps eight or nine, leap to the wall and run its length. She cried out.

"Oh, no—look at him! He'll fall to his death!"

Mr. Cranston rose, opened the window, and called. "Begley—off the wall—instantly!"

He waited until the boy jumped down and then closed

the window and sat down again. An Indian manservant refilled the teacups and passed the sliced pound cake.

Brooke felt her heart still beating fast with fright. "Has no child ever fallen?"

"None," the headmaster replied, "except for a little boy who was visiting his parents during a weekend several years ago. Their house is even higher than the school and he was walking their garden wall, taking advantage, poor little chap, of being free from school rules. That's a fact I remember about Jai—he never walked the wall."

"Not because he was afraid," Jagat said.

"No, he simply saw no reason to do so." Mr. Cranston ate his cake in small bits, remembering, and he went on. "I was quite surprised to find that Jai had read the Upanishads and somewhat amused that he had read in English translation. So typical of modern Indians! They are searching their own beginnings, but they don't speak their own languages. They must use the strange new English which they have been taught."

"I suspect his mother," Jagat said. "She read aloud to him from sacred books when he was small and willing to listen. Then for a time he turned to me and against her. But perhaps he returned to her again."

Mr. Cranston put aside his teacup and touched a linen napkin to his lips—a serviette he would have called it, Brooke thought, taking note. But he was already talking, half in meditation: "In the Katha Upanishad—Charles Johnston's translation, by the way, and very well done—there's a bit that goes something like this." He closed his eyes and clasped his thin pale hands across his slightly protruding stomach. " 'The knower is never born nor dies, nor is it from anywhere, nor did it become anything. Unborn, eternal, immemorial, this ancient is not slain when the body is slain.

" '. . . Smaller than small, greater than great, this Self is hidden in the heart of man . . . Understanding this great lord, the Self, bodiless in bodies, stable among the unstable, the wise man cannot grieve.' "

The mellow English voice, the perfectly enunciated English words, speaking in such Indian spirit, fell with musical rhythm upon the quiet air of the room. The children's voices were distant now, they had gone elsewhere to play, and only an occasional shout or burst of laughter could be heard. Mr. Cranston looked at his guests.

"I think that is all I have to say, Highness—if it is comfort to you, I tell you that Jai was older than he seemed, and while he was full of life, he considered death. Indeed, he looked death in the face while he yet lived, and to him the two were one."

He rose and held out his hand. Narrow and fleshless as it was, his grasp was strong and downright, an English handclasp. "Good-bye, I mustn't keep you. The sun sets quickly in the mountains and darkness follows immediately. I don't like your being on that rough road in tricky twilight."

He led the way then to the veranda, and there paused with them to gaze at the western sky. The golden rim of the sun was a crescent above the jagged peak of the mountain opposite. A twilight darkness already half hid the pit of the valley between and Jagat was about to hurry Brooke down the stone steps to the driveway when Mr. Cranston put a hand upon his arm.

"Highness, you have another son?"

Jagat paused, surprised. "Only my daughter."

"Veera of course," Mr. Cranston said. "And now I remember that Jai spoke of her to me, too. She is engaged to be married, I believe?"

"Yes—to an excellent young man."

"Jai only said it was not a love match. He said he hoped you would not compel her to marry against her wish. Let me remember exactly what he said—" Mr. Cranston put a pale hand to his brow. "He said life was too short—no, too precious, that was the word—too precious—to spend with lovelessness."

"Jai said that?"

"I assure you he did—here on the very steps where you stand. We'd said good-bye and he was running off—you know how he always ran up and down steps—when out of nothing, it seemed, since we hadn't talked of his sister, he stopped and said he doubted she'd go back to school at Woodstock and I said I was sorry for I'd been told she's very intelligent, and he said she was marrying instead, but without love, and this he felt was wrong."

"I am surprised that he spoke of her," Jagat said stiffly. "Her marriage is a family arrangement, of course, but she has been consulted. We are modern, at least to that extent."

"Ah, well," Mr. Cranston said peaceably, waving his hand at them. "I merely tell you what Jai said."

They left him, Jagat thanking him again. In the jeep he did not hesitate or wait for Brooke to put out her hand. He reached for hers and held it in both his own. When a sharp turn in the road all but suspended them over the cliff he pressed her head down upon his shoulder.

"Hide your eyes," he commanded. "I will look for both of us."

On the terrace of the lake palace Veera and Bert Osgood were talking as they stood leaning upon the marble balustrade. It was midnight and across the water her mother lay asleep, imagining while she had let herself be undressed that Veera already lay in her own bed in the room in the west wing. But Veera, waiting until she heard her mother's door close, and the old ayah's long sigh as she laid herself down on her mat before that door, had wrapped herself in a white shawl, had run down the inner staircase, that secret passage through which male ancestors, generation after generation in their youth, had escaped parental knowledge to enjoy themselves in the city at night. Like them, except that she was a girl, she opened the door of the boathouse to slip into a waiting boat—not one of the noisy motorboats but an ancient dory, manned by a boatman whom she bribed to silence. Noiselessly he had rowed across the still waters to the lake palace and there Bert was waiting for her—only half waiting, he told himself, disturbed by a sense of guilt, although he never knew when she was coming, and certainly would not invite her. After all, she was the daughter of his employer. He could not prevent her from coming if she chose, but he would not ask her to come. Nevertheless, after weeks,

such meetings were approaching rendezvous, not every
night as a certainty, but any night that she could get away,
and she had taken to waving a white silk scarf from her
window when she was coming. Yes, and let him be
honest. Every night before darkness fell, he watched for
the white flutter of the scarf.

"I am not in the least like Jai," Veera was saying now
in her positive fashion. "Jai molded himself to each person he was with, whereas—well, I expect people to mold
themselves to me!"

Bert laughed. "You're spoiled!"

She opened her eyes, suddenly serious. "You think so?"

"Yes, but I like it," Bert said. "It makes you seem
American."

"Is that a compliment?"

"For me it is. American girls are all spoiled. They
insist on having their own way. But I like them independent. I'm not used to the submissive type. If a girl
says yes to everything right away, a man doesn't have
anything to talk about."

He was well aware that discussion of male and female
was dangerous when he was with a girl whom he had no
intention of marrying and yet who was of a class that
would accept no less. This was true anywhere.

"Girls in India today are also not submissive—not all
of us," Veera said. She was provocatively near him, their
shoulders touching. He saw her small pretty ear with its
dangling ornament of gold and ruby, her soft pale cheek,
her profile, the lower lip slightly fuller than the upper,
and all this surrounded by her dark and curling hair. She
was talking.

"We even like to dance with men—"

He interrupted. "Hey, why don't we dance, here on the
terrace? I'm planning it as an outdoor dance place for
the guests, using that covered parapet—a marble gazebo
I guess I'd call it—for the band. I have the electricity
already laid on up here—wait, I'll get my recorder."

In a few minutes they were dancing to the music of a
rhumba. He was acute enough to catch to the full the
contrast, so bizarre, between the age-old setting, the seat

of kings, and the music alien and modern. Yet the contrast was not greater than he himself was in contrast to the princess of a hundred generations in his arms. His sense of romance, always alert, rose to passion. The soft female body, the beauty of the marble city in the distance, white under the moon, combined to make him suddenly dizzy, and stopping abruptly in the midst of the dance, he lifted her face, his hand under her chin, and placed his lips upon hers in a long and lingering kiss.

Across the water Moti woke, for no reason whatsoever, she thought, afterward, except that the gods warned her. What gods she did not know, since without rejecting any of her old deities she had also accepted the three gods of Father Francis Paul: Father, Son, and Holy Ghost. Now she rose out of her bed as though someone had taken her by the hand and going to the window, she gazed across the lake. There on the terrace of the lake palace she saw two white figures outlined against the hot moonlit sky. They were in each others arms, dancing! Male and female they must be, but what female except—

In horrid fear she opened the door, stepped over her sleeping ayah, and made haste to Veera's room. It was empty, the bed undisturbed. Then it was Veera! She hastened back again to her own room and wakened the ayah at the door her bare foot digging into the old woman's ribs.

"Get up," she ordered. "Dress me—then take me down to the boathouse. No questions! Do as I say."

All this she did without rousing anyone else, nor had she so much as lit the lamps in her own room, the moon being so bright. Therefore when she reached the terrace, neither Bert nor Veera was prepared for the white figure who appeared suddenly before them as they stood in close embrace.

"Veera!"

The sound of her mother's voice, which never before had she heard raised, startled Veera with violence. She drew away frow Bert but only slightly, stared at her mother, then defiantly hid her face upon his shoulder.

"Now then, honey," Bert said gently. He led her to a marble bench and helped her to sit down. "Leave this to me," he whispered.

Standing very straight, he faced the Maharani. "Your Highness," he said, his voice firm, "whatever has happened is my fault. It was I who suggested dancing. This is to be the dance terrace, and I thought we'd try it out."

Moti paid him no heed. "Veera, return to the palace at once."

"Not until you tell me you know it is my fault, Your Highness," Bert insisted.

She did not look at him. "Veera, I have often told you—whatever happens between a man and a woman, it is her fault. This I have taught you always."

Veera was silent, her head bowed.

"Come now, Your Highness," Bert said. "I won't be relegated like this."

Moti continued to address herself to Veera. "Did you come here by his invitation?"

Veera lifted her head in sudden rebellion. "No. I came because I wanted to come."

"Not for the first time!"

"No."

"Nevertheless for the last time, I promise you! Come with me instantly."

"No! I am not a child."

"Then I too must stay," Moti declared. She wrapped the white shawl closely about her and sat down on a marble bench. Bert looked from one white figure to the other. Now he went to Veera and stood beside her, looking down upon her beautiful sullen face.

"Honey, she's your mother."

Veera lifted mutinous eyes and did not reply.

"You must go home, honey," Bert insisted. "There are other ways of doing this."

"Doing what?" Veera demanded.

"Whatever we want."

"What do we want?"

"Honestly I don't know. We'll have to find out. But go home now. Maybe when your father comes—"

"He always does what my mother says—about me, that is."

"Maybe you and I will know by then—"

She rose unwillingly but yielding and Moti rose with her. Bert followed them in silence but with grace, and helped them into the boat.

"Good night," he said, but neither answered him. He stood looking after them. Halfway across the lake he saw Veera wave her hand, and he waved back. It was all he could do, he thought helplessly. Maybe it was all he would ever do.

There was no use pretending that they could sleep. Mother and daughter faced each other, Moti outstretched upon the chaise longue in her room, exhausted from within, and Veera seated cross-legged upon a floor cushion.

"Of course Raj must be told," Moti declared.

"What is there to tell?" Veera demanded. "You forget I am not of your generation, Mamu. In Bombay—"

Moti interrupted, "Nor is this Bombay! Moreover, you are of royal blood—"

"Oh, royal rot!" Veera cried. "All that is ended."

"Nevertheless your father has made guarantees to Raj's family."

"My father!" Veera said with scorn, and savagely she went on, using her most cruel weapons.

"What's he himself doing, off somewhere at this very moment with an American woman? Oh, yes, I know you cover it all up—you are so very Indian—saying that Jai is not really dead. Instead of its being a love jaunt, it's supposed to be a holy search! But you know as well as I do that it's not holy at all—she's in love with him, and he with her, and you—you won't face it. You won't face anything, not even that you're in love too with that English priest—he's so very holy!"

Moti was aghast. She felt faint and beaten. "I agree with you on one point," she said at last, her voice very weak. "I should never have let your father go with her. You young people—this wicked generation—there is noth-

ing pure, nothing religious in your minds. You would
—I daresay you would even have accused Gandhiji of—
of wrong thoughts about his handmaidens—"

"Indeed yes!" Veera said with utmost impudence.

Moti stared at her and tears welled into her eyes. "Incredible!" she murmured. "You cannot imagine that a
human being would do something because it is good and
right. But only to the pure are all things pure—"

Veera broke in impetuously. "Even impurity! I agree
with you now, Mamu! So we are agreed after all!"

She rose as she spoke, towering above her mother.
Moti stared up at her daughter with fear in her wet eyes.

"This is too much for me," she said faintly. "I shall
send for your father."

Veera turned. "As for Raj, I will tell him myself."

"What will you tell him?" Moti asked.

Veera paused at the threshold door. "I don't know," she
said uncertainly and closed the door behind her.

Jagat was in his room at the hotel in Mussoorie, dressing for dinner. The ride back from the school had been
worse than he thought possible, darkness falling upon
them, and the chasm yawning blackly beneath them.
Brooke had clung to him, frankly and helplessly in terror,
and tenderness had welled up in him as he had never
before felt it for any human being—though, yes, once, for
a wounded tiger, helpless against death. He had blamed
himself, as he watched the proud, helpless beast, for dealing death so clumsily. And now would he one day be as
clumsy with this beautiful western woman? Of course
they were in love, but of course he would not have given
up his kingdom, if he had one now, for love. Then,
furiously, he remembered, Moti had never seemed afraid
of anything, nor had she ever clung to him. Strange contrast, he thought, that Brooke, so modern, so American,
should be the one to cling!

"Close your eyes, my dear," he had whispered. "Don't
look! It will soon be over."

She had laid her head on his shoulder obediently and

had closed her eyes. He held her clenched hands in his
and felt them wet again.

"Oh, my stupid body," she had murmured. "I don't
want to be afraid, but I tell you my body is afraid in
spite of me."

Only when it was over, when they were in the plains
again, high but no longer mountainous, did she cease
murmuring upon his shoulder, her eyes closed. Then she
had lifted her head and wiped her hands on her handkerchief.

"It almost makes me believe," she said.

Her voice came out of the darkness and he could not
see her face.

"Believe what?" he had asked.

"Believe what the lama said, about the separation of
spirit and soul and body. The *I* of me stands quite apart
when I am on a height. The *I* of me is not afraid. It's
really scornful of me—the *me* of me. But the two are
separate. I feel it. Each has its own life. Oh, there's a
great deal of truth in what that lama said. I begin to
understand something."

"What?" he had asked again and now inclined to smile.

"I don't know—I don't know."

Her voice, speaking out of the darkness, had been
troubled.

It was at this instant of his remembering that he heard
a knock on the door. It opened as usual without waiting
for his call to enter. He recognized Rodriguez, the Portuguese butler.

"What are you doing here?" he demanded, amazed.

For answer the man held out a sealed envelope to him.

"Her Highness sends this."

"But why you?"

"I am Goan, Highness, I am very safe. I am not talking lightly to other peoples not Goan like me. Hindu
people, Muslim people talk always. Not me!"

He tapped his breast proudly, but Jagat was opening
the envelope. Within it was the sheet of thin silky paper
that was Moti's choice. She wrote in English to make it

more difficult for anyone to read, a few lines, brief and cryptic.

"It is necessary that you return at once. I have seen what I do not like. The American and Veera need you immediately, and I am not strong enough. As for the search, it can continue later, but I do not know what—or how to—"

It was like Moti, the English, precise but imperfect, the letter conveying her troubled being, and the last line unfinished. So often she ended even her conversation with a sentence unfinished! He folded the letter and turned to Rodriguez.

"Pack my bags and hire a car. We will leave early in the morning."

He was about to dismiss the man, and then remembered that, Goan though he was, he lived among other servants.

"Wait," he commanded. "Tell me all you know."

For this moment Rodriguez had been waiting for many days. He hated the redhaired American who was ruining the lake palace and destroying the past thereby. True, though times were changed, and this Maharana was not the equal of his father and grandfather, he was the Maharana, nevertheless, and though he, Rodriguez, was getting old, his knees aching mercilessly when he squatted over charcoal stoves, yet he himself would not change. He would serve this royal family until some night he died in his sleep. That was the way he wished to die and so he would die. But not before he had told the Maharana the evil that the American was doing.

He came near to Jagat and knelt on the floor beside his chair. "Highness," he muttered, wetting his lips, "I have sickness in my heart. What I see, night after night—" He shook his head and sighed.

"Well, well," Jagat said impatiently, "what do you see?"

"Your daughter, Highness—she bribes the boatman's son and he takes her to the lake palace where the American—it is too shameful for me to tell you." He hid his head in his arms.

"Go on," Jagat said harshly.

Rodriguez lifted his head and wiped his face with the end of a towel he wore over his shoulders. "Highness, they sit on the terrace, side by side. They lean on the balustrade looking at the moon."

"How do you know this?"

"In two ways, Highness. I borrowed—only borrowed, I swear it—the German spyglass from your grandfather's desk. I look through."

"And you ran and told the Maharani, making confusion in my palace! I daresay everything is innocent, although of course my daughter should not have—but she is willful enough so that perhaps the American had nothing to do with it. Wait—you said two ways?"

"The boatman's son, Highness," Rodriguez went on eagerly. "I threatened him. I said I would tell you unless he told me."

"And gave you some of the money, I daresay," Jagat put in.

"No—no—at least to no avail. Am I not here, telling you? And I did not tell Her Highness. She saw for herself. She sent me here—I swear it!"

"How did she know exactly where I am? I have not written her."

Rodriguez rose. "Highness, let me confess all. I bade your servant tell me whenever you went to a new place. I foresaw—"

Jagat burst into loud and cynical laughter. "So you spy on me, too!"

"For your own good, Highness!"

Rodriguez paused, considering. Should he tell his suspicions about the Maharani herself and the English priest? No, he had said enough. Let him reserve this further information until he had seen more. Indeed he did not wish to see more. When the ladies of a royal household allow themselves freedoms it is the end of everything. Hotel or palace, when honor departs from women, decay sets in. True, he had full information about the Maharana and the American woman also. Women one must expect and the palace had been full of women in the old Maharana's day, but many women were safer than one, and this one an American! Not since the times of the Greek girl, which he had so often heard about, had there been such danger in the family. And this American—could it be expected that she would hang herself as the Greek girl had done? No, it could not be expected.

"I will prepare everything for tomorrow, Highness," he promised. "Trust me—I will do all."

"Very well," Jagat said brusquely. He was accustomed to the mistaken zeal of loyal servants. One must balance the nuisance against the loyalty.

"Now I will go to dinner," he said.

Whether to share with Brooke this family news he could not at first decide. The meal was Indian, and he occupied the time of indecision by commenting on the dishes. She ate with lively interest and he marveled that this young woman, so frankly enjoying food, could be the same one, the woman who discussed the philosophy of life and death and who held in check, with the sureness of maturity, her own and his increasing passion.

"Why is the food so highly spiced?" she asked.

"Poor materials," he said ruefully. "We have no beef industry—not really—and our fowls are small and dark and the lamb—well, call it mutton, and dwarfed at that. Long-legged goats really, as you know."

"I have never eaten better breads."

"Well, yes, I admit that, not the thick bread but those thin sheets—yes, they do very nicely. But I foresee that food will be my problem when guests really begin to come to the lake palace hotel. I shall have to start more farms of my own, and increase my stock from England and America and Australia. And American farmers to teach my people how to breed—that will take some force on my part."

"I hope you will keep the cuisine Indian."

"Both sides will want both. I suppose that's good. When peoples like each other's foods, it's the first step to international understanding. Try the fresh cocoanut on your curry."

When the meal was over, however, the dining room

almost empty and the small cups filled with thick black coffee, the talk failed. He was thinking of what Rodriguez had told him, and forgetting all else for the moment, he felt his gaze drawn across the table to meet her eyes.

"Tell me," she said gently.

"Tell you what?"

"What troubles you?"

"What makes you think I am troubled?"

"I know! You are troubled and you are asking yourself whether to tell me."

He hesitated, tried to laugh, and then began to tell her.

"It is Veera. Strange that today the headmaster should have spoken to me of her, should have told me what Jai had said about her marriage! It is that which troubles me. My servant came today, the Goan butler who is the head of the palace staff. He has brought me a letter from my wife, telling me that Veera and Osgood are meeting secretly. I must return at once."

"I will return with you," she said.

"It is only a family matter." He tried to protest and then broke off. "It would be insupportable to me if you left me."

Across the table their hands met and clung for a long moment. Comfort flowed through his blood and warmed his body. But only for a moment, for a servant entered with fresh coffee and they snatched their hands apart.

Was it that involuntary parting that clung to his memory, even after they had said good night? They sat only a short while longer at the table, and then, rising, they glanced into the chill drawing room. The stiff English chairs were not inviting and the small English grate was empty of coals. She had shivered and he had become resolute.

"You must go straight to your room. We start at dawn and it is already late. These Indian servants can never get a dinner ready on time. You're tired—I can see it."

She seemed willing, she smiled, she bade him good night at her door. Through it he had a glimpse of her things, her silver brushes on the dressing table, a rose satin robe thrown over a chair, her slippers side by side on the floor, and he was shocked to feel his blood quicken. He held himself upright, then bent his head and lifted her hand and kissed it.

"Good night, my dear," he said. "Sleep in peace."

But there was no peace in his own room when he returned to it. He undressed and bathed in a tub of hot water—thank the English for tubs and hot water—and then put on a pair of silk pajamas and went to bed, fully determined to sleep, in spite of Veera, Moti, and all other problems. Alas, sleep was impossible. Annoyed first by a crack in the curtains, the moonlight streaming through in a narrow bar of gold, he rose to adjust the curtains and saw that the window was in reality a door, the upper part of glass and that this door led to a long narrow veranda, stretching across the garden side of the hotel. He had insisted on being away from the street and the noise of its squeaking bullock carts. This meant that the veranda was in fact a corridor to other rooms, Brooke's room. He was horrified at the next thought that occurred to him and he put it sternly away and returned to his bed. Two hours later a torture of longing beset him and he yielded. He wrapped himself in his dark silk robe and, sandals on his feet, he walked noiselessly down the long veranda to her room. The moon had almost set. It hung near the horizon, enormous and fiery gold, its light enough for him to see at the end of the veranda the figure of a servant curled asleep upon a mat. But in this dark robe he would not be seen from a distance.

Her door was open, he discovered to his horror. So carelessly she went to sleep, so trustfully, as confident as though she were in her own home! The light of the moon, dim as it was, revealed her as she lay, her hair tossed upon the pillow, one hand under her cheek. He knelt down beside her, and gently he put his arms about her. She stirred and sighed and he bent his head and put his lips to hers. He felt her waken without moving, coming to consciousness out of a dream. Then, feeling his mouth upon hers, she sat up suddenly and pushed back her hair.

He rose and stood, looking down at her, and she

looked up at him, surprised, as he could see, and more than that, bewildered, unbelieving. He sat down beside her and drew her to him.

"Shall I go away?" he whispered.

She gave a sharp sigh. "Oh—I was dreaming of you."

"I need not go away?"

She hesitated an instant. "Is it fair to put all the decision upon me?"

"I wish to be accepted. I am not forcing you."

The moment hung between them, tense and silent. His eyes were fixed upon her face, upon her lovely mouth, then straying, moved to her breasts, revealed by the slipping shoulder straps of her nightgown.

"The only question—" his mouth went suddenly dry and he could not go on. His desire for her burned too hot in his veins.

She lifted her head. "The only question—"

"Whether you love me. I will not take you without love. That I will not—"

Cruel memories cut across his desire, the memories of many times when he had taken women without love. This time, with her, could not be like one of those. It must be all that he had never had—or nothing. This desire was not like any other. He could not be content, not this time, with mere physical satisfaction.

"I want complete union—with you—"

His voice was husky in his throat and he was silent, waiting. What was she thinking, what was she remembering while he waited? He did not know.

She was thinking only about love. Yes, she loved this man, this stranger. Their worlds were not the same, their very history was different. In their two lives they had been and were completely separate. Then how was it that now in this alien room, in this alien place, a remote town at the foot of the highest and most formidable mountains in the world, their snows eternal, how could it be that here, among people she did not know, she felt no fear, no hesitation? She was aware only of the need for union with him. All else was nothing in comparison, their difference, their strangeness one to the other, faded into one great fact that, he a man and she a woman, had met, had found each other, and now desired, above all else, union. Lovers, she supposed, always dream of having met in some other life, but she did not dream, she knew. How else explain the sympathy, the instinctive understanding, the total comprehension each of the other's nature, except by reincarnation? In which, she thought with honorable justice, she still could not say she believed, since she could not explain it rationally, nor was this important, for explanation was not necessary, nor was belief. The simple fact was that here the two of them met together in a strange and distant place in the early hours of morning, by the light of a setting moon. Since nothing could be explained, since they could only act out of their deepest feeling, what else remained but to act? She felt herself swept clean of all reasoning and indecision and she turned to him and put her palms on his cheeks. His face was held between her hands, and for the first time of her own accord she kissed his lips and said not a word.

No word was needed. He went to the door and locked it and closed the curtains. In the darkness he lay down beside her, and drew her gently toward him until her head rested on his shoulder. He felt no need for haste. Instead he waited for the guidance of desire, the purest he had ever known because it was hers as well as his. Since union was his heart's wish, then union must come to them as one. Slowly, slowly, they came near, she shy, he gentle until he knew the instant, electric, intense, was here for them both. Yet the decision was his.

"Now," he muttered through set teeth.

"Now," she whispered.

When it was over he lay back overwhelmed by his discovery.

"But you did not tell me," he said under his breath.

Her cheek was warm on his breast and all her hair covered him softly as he held her. "Tell you what?" she asked.

"That you are—virgin!"

She lifted her head. "Why should I have told you?"

"I'm not sure I would have—"

"Then I'm glad you didn't know. I'm so proud—so proud—"

"Of what?"

"That you are first!"

The next day, compelled to silence in the presence of Rodriguez and the driver, they could not speak or even touch hand to hand under the Goan's sharp, observing eyes. They feigned indifference and cheerful talk, and she was glad, in a way, to be thus isolated, so that she might remember with inner calm what had taken place in the night. Did she regret? No more than one could regret the reaching of a mountaintop, from which the world can be surveyed! It was a different world today but the difference was in herself. Yesterday the woman that she was had possessed no guiding knowledge. Today she knew, not how or what but where her life was to be spent. She must be always near him, not with him perhaps, but near. Place was decided. Other guiding knowledge would be revealed, not by gods certainly but by her own inner conviction.

Later, when they were alone at the dinner table, still neither felt the need to talk. They were at peace, separately and together, and small talk, playful and in fragments, was enough. Near the end of the meal, however, the place the half-empty dining room of the airport in a terminal town, she felt suddenly swept with joy.

"I've never known happiness until now," she said, "although I've not thought of myself as unhappy. But I suppose that one never knows unhappiness, without first knowing its opposite."

"Nor I," he said. He let the moment fulfill itself and then went on. "I shall not allow myself to think beyond what has come about—at least, until we reach the end of this journey. Then, I suppose, we shall have to—to think."

"Yes," she agreed absently, only half hearing.

"Are you dreaming?" he asked.

She answered him straight out of her thought. "Why were you so—surprised—last night?"

He understood her at once. "It did not occur to me—that you were—what you were—"

"Why not? Have I ever behaved otherwise?"

He laughed, embarrassed. "No, but I supposed all American women, you know—"

"Are not?"

"Are not," he agreed. "We are led so to believe by your movies and magazines and so on. That you—"

"Were—"

"Was simply—unbelievable."

She mused. "Why is it so important—to a man? Are men all egoists?"

"I know nothing about all men," he said with decision. "I know only myself. Yes, it is important that I am the first—with you. I want you to know—you must know and never forget—that I am different now, a different man. I have only once known—perfect union—and it was —it is with you. Whatever our future is—I shall never again be satisfied with incompletion."

She received this with silence, pondering its meaning.

The first signs of the monsoon coincided with their return to Amarpur late at night. He had seen her to her rooms in the lake palace hotel, observing sharply that Bert Osgood and his decorators had been busy at work, whatever else had been his occupations. The hotel lobby, complete with porters and desk clerk, was finished except for the old chandelier which he had ordered to be left untouched until the birds nesting there had reared their young offspring, a nest, however, that they must be gently prevented from rebuilding. Carpets were laid along the corridors, not wall to wall since the floors were marble, but providing a pathway safer than the polished floors.

The desk clerk had exclaimed at his coming, obviously surprised.

"Highness, shall I wake Mr. Osgood?"

"No," Jagat had said shortly, "but tell him I shall be here at ten o'clock tomorrow morning."

"Yes, Highness."

"Miss Westley has her old rooms, has she not?" Jagat asked.

"Certainly, Highness."

He had accompanied Brooke and the luggage porters, had himself dismissed them and closed the door and drawn the curtains. Then, with a pang he realized that he must leave her. He took her hands in his, and stood looking down into her upturned face.

"I don't know—I don't know what lies ahead. There is only this one knowledge in me—I love you."

The words which some use so casually came from him with shyness. He had never used them truthfully until now. Between him and Moti the words had never been used, nor had they seemed necessary. He would have said, if asked, that they took love for granted. Therefore it needed not to be spoken. Now he knew that where there was love it must, it would, be spoken.

"I love you," Brooke said.

"Once in a while, whatever our life is to be," he told her, "we must say these three words—"

"I know," she said.

Upon this he had left her, had returned to his own palace and, without waking Moti, had gone to his rooms, to find upon his desk a pile of papers left for him to study. These were the important papers, those less urgent being left upon his desk in the palace offices. He glanced at them, put them aside, and went to bed, but was sleepless. After an hour of tossing he rose and went to work until the door opened and a servant brought him his morning tea. Then when he had bathed and dressed, he sent word to Moti that he would come to her rooms as soon as she wished.

When he entered an hour later she was having her frugal breakfast at a small inlaid marble table on her private veranda. He bent and laid his cheek against her hair for an instant. They had never kissed at any time, except at the most intimate moments. Now he wondered if he would ever kiss her again. But that was among the questions he could not answer. He was even grateful that it need not be asked, that at first he must attend to the problems of others.

"You look pale," Moti exclaimed.

"Of course I was sleepless," he replied. "I found a heap of papers on my desk, all requests from the city elders, the panchayat, and I worked until morning."

"You should have waked me," Moti said.

"And made you sleepless too? How foolish!"

"Had I known you were coming last night I would have waited."

"I purposely did not tell you the hour of my arrival." Instinctively he noticed that he did not say "our."

"We have a great deal to discuss," he went on. "First let me say that I got no farther in my search beyond a lama north of Mussoorie. He talked only of reincarnation."

Moti lifted her head. "Reincarnation? That means Jai is dead!"

"Or lives again," Jagat said.

Tears welled into Moti's eyes and she let them flow down her pale cheeks. "Is it only *that*? But I have no interest in someone else's child."

"Yet you believe in reincarnation, don't you?"

Jagat heard his own voice, hard and pressing, and he let it be so. He had no wish to take up the search again. In the problems of the living, she must forget the dead. As though she knew his thoughts, she did not reply. Then, after a moment she lifted the free end of her sari and wiped her eyes. "Father Francis Paul speaks of the resurrection of the dead," she murmured.

Jagat laughed a harsh bark. "Oh, come now, Moti! Let's not take on these foreign myths! We've enough of our own. At any rate, I shan't go off on any more such expeditions. Jai would be the first to—"

"Never speak his name again!"

Jagat stared. "Moti, you are beside yourself—"

"If I am, it is you who make me so." She gave him a strange sidewise look.

He continued, resolutely refusing her mood. "We were

—about to push on when Rodriguez reached me. Of course I returned at once."

"The American woman was with you?"

"Yes—at your invitation, remember!"

"Is she here?"

"At the lake palace hotel, of course."

"Ah, yes."

A moment hung between them, as fragile as a fluttering butterfly. He crushed it.

"Among the many problems the first is Veera. Have you anything more to tell me before I speak to Osgood this morning?"

"I would like you to speak to her first."

She touched a silver bell and her servant stood in the doorway. "Tell choti memsahib to come at once to her father," she commanded.

"Yes, Highness," the woman said and withdrew.

"Meanwhile," Moti continued so calmly that it seemed indifference, "what are the other problems most pressing?"

He sat down and she poured coffee and handed him the cup. "The usual ones," he replied. "I had asked before I left for a report on the dacoit situation. Some of the Bhils have been implicated, and I thought I would seek help from the English priest. While I've been gone the villagers have been attacked in several places, but there have been some fine brave repulses, too. In one village particularly the head man led a defense and the villagers fought off the robbers. Two dacoits were killed and four captured. I shall see that the head man gets a gun and five hundred rupees as reward. Perhaps it will encourage others to like bravery. Nevertheless, I must see to the strengthening of the police force everywhere in the state. It's not just a matter of numbers, but of esprit de corps. A modern community can't be at the mercy of dacoits, whatever tribes they come from—Minas, Bhils, Basries, Kanjars, Raisihks —whatever they are. Backward tribesmen all—"

He found relief from inner tension in speaking of the affairs of government, but was here interrupted by Veera's entrance. She looked extremely pretty, as he saw with disapproval and was somewhat amused that he should now dislike the beauty of which he had always been proud.

"You're back, Bapu," she said and brought her palms together in greeting. "I won't say I'm glad for I know you want to scold me. You needn't, for Mamu has already done it."

"Sit down," he commanded. "I shan't scold you for you're no longer a child. I shall merely ask what are your intentions."

She laughed and shook her black curls. "Isn't that usually asked of the man?"

"I shall talk later with him, but I must know first what you are thinking. Do you want to break your engagement to Raj?"

She was immediately serious. "I don't know, Bapu. I was hoping you'd help me to decide."

"Do you love Raj?"

"He hasn't tried to make me love him."

"What sort of answer is that?"

"Well, you know how it is, Bapu. We're engaged by our families, and we go through with it, wondering whether we will—you know."

He did know, very well. He himself had made no effort to love Moti or help her to love him before marriage. Indeed he would have considered it premature, not to say vulgar.

"I do not know," he replied. "When I was a young man and your mother a young woman, customs were entirely different. Our families had very little contact with the West except through official Englishmen, and it would not have occurred to me to address myself to any young woman of my own class, and certainly not your mother, thus compelling her to speak to a young man."

"Certainly not," Moti murmured over her coffee cup.

Jagat continued. "Now I am aware of many changes. For example, I may myself be somewhat to blame in bringing an American here to set up the hotel in the lake palace. I thought of it merely as a matter of business since Americans do this sort of thing very well. It did not occur to me—"

"It didn't to me, either," Veera said.

"Then why—"

"I don't know, Bapu!" Veera's voice was impatient. "Things just happen, don't they? Like your meeting Miss Westley!"

He received this barb and ignored it. In honesty he could not reply and he replied with unusual patience.

"What am I to do about your marriage then, Veera?"

"Oh, I don't know," she replied in the same sulky voice.

It was obvious that she would say no more. A lifetime of reserve on sexual matters could not be broken in a few minutes.

Jagat sighed. "Well, I shall talk with Osgood. It may be he has no intentions of any kind. American men are very lax, I'm told. But I suppose I shall have to tell Raj."

Veera looked up, startled. "Oh, no—he'll be raging!"

Moti put down her cup. "Better to rage before marriage than after!"

To this Veera said nothing. In the silence a bird called raucously from a peepul tree and a servant ran out to shout him away. They watched the small drama without seeing it. Then Jagat rose.

"Very well. Veera, without your advice or direction or whatever it is called nowadays, I shall speak with Osgood, and depending upon what he says, I will or will not speak to Raj. Is this your wish?"

"I don't know, Bapu," she said still sullenly.

"She doesn't know what she wants to do, Osgood," he said an hour later. He was in the manager's office in the lake palace hotel and assuming his place behind the desk, he had sent for the American and had been pleased because immediately the chap had begun talking about Veera, taking all blame upon himself.

"I suppose that's my situation too, sir," he said now in his forthright fashion. He was pale, as Jagat noticed, the freckles standing out oddly on his colorless face. He was still talking. "I do love her, though—at least when I don't remember the problems! She's the most beautiful girl I've ever seen, though I've always liked brunettes, you know, I suppose because I'm so disgustingly blond myself. Opposites attract, they say. Then I get scared. I remember who she is, a princess, and I'm nobody much. My father's a dentist in a small town. I'm the only one in our family who's ever left that town—I don't know why except I always wanted to travel. Still, in the end, I expected to go back to my home town and marry and settle down. Now this has happened to me and in India of all places. She wouldn't be happy with my family, sir, I can tell you that. I don't know as I'd be completely happy with hers, either, if you'll excuse my saying so."

"It's very honest of you to say so," Jagat replied. "The only question is what do we do? Either you stop seeing her or else we must accept—change."

He had been about to say catastrophe and then because he liked this young man he modified the word.

Bert's round young face was troubled. "I could go away of course, Your Highness, but—it would be hard. I guess I could do it only if she chose the other fellow. I mean, if she should tell me, for example, that she—loved me, you know—I don't think I could—just go away forever."

Jagat made no reply to this, watching that honest, troubled face.

"On the other hand," Bert continued, "I have my work here to think about. I'm not through—that is, I feel responsible for finishing up what I've begun."

Here was a moment's respite and Jagat seized upon it. "Just how much have you finished?"

Bert went to the second desk in the room, opened a drawer and took out a thick folder. "I've kept myself informed up to the last detail, thinking you'd ask me that question. Let me just run over the list . . . The decorating is done, the plumbing is all installed. I'd say the mechanics are finished with the exception of a few odds and ends I have to attend to myself. I had to call in an American firm—I hope you don't mind the extra expense, but I felt the generators weren't reliable. I do feel the local laundry service—if you can call it that—is totally inadequate, and

I'd like to suggest a good modern laundry installed in the cellars, which are enormous, as you know, sir, and now pretty well empty since we've used so much of the stored stuff. I'm proud of the suites, sir. They're handsome. You ought to charge well for them. About the laundry service, even if we have our own setup I wish you could stop the pounding of the women on the steps by the city gate, sir. I don't think tourists will like being waked up at five o'clock every morning. I don't myself."

"I wouldn't think of changing it, even if I could," Jagat said promptly.

"You mean it's got to go on forever?" Bert's too expressive face was a mask of disbelief, if not dismay.

"It's gone on for centuries," Jagat said.

Bert sighed. "Well, sir, you know your own people. Like I said, I've about finished my part, but I wish, whatever happens of a personal nature, to finish the job up properly. I've made up a folder of suggestions for you, and I'm taking the liberty of establishing certain departments—organizational operations, you might say. For example, the Front of the House—that means security, uniformed service, housekeeping, engineering. Catering—well, there's beverage, food, and coordination with other departments. Personnel and Accounting—well, those speak for themselves. Sales of course is terribly important—the rooms, public space, promotion of the services, and so forth. I've put down the names of men who could be employed—in case you'd like some American organizers. They'd come in and study the total situation and make recommendations. Whether you want more of them would be up to you."

He had been riffling the papers as he spoke, and now he put them together with an elastic band. "I wouldn't have to stay to see all that done, of course. It's just that it doesn't matter how beautiful your hotel is, you're sunk if you haven't the right personnel and services to carry on."

"Thank you," Jagat said. "I will take the material and study it."

He liked this man very much, and had there not been the matters of his unfortunate coloring, his distant family, his entire difference, all made more important because Veera's family was what it was—changed, of course, with the times, but with royal history and stance—well, it was all too difficult. One day at a time.

"I wonder," he said abruptly, "if I had better not send for Raj, Veera's fiancé. I suppose he should be given a chance to speak for himself."

Bert sat down suddenly. "Whatever you say, sir. Anyway, I want to be fair."

"We all do," Jagat said. "It is simply that we do not know how. Well, we must search."

He put out his hand abruptly and shook hands with Bert and went away.

"You are to find my son-in-law-to-be," Jagat told Rodriguez. "He is in Bombay with his parents, I daresay. Or they will know where he is. Bring him to me."

"Yes, Highness," the man replied.

"Tell him it is of the utmost urgency—a crisis concerning him."

"Indeed yes, Highness," the man replied.

"And I want no talk in the servants' houses," Jagat said sharply.

Rodriguez pretended hurt. "Have I told anything? Highness, I serve only you."

"Then continue to serve only me," Jagat retorted, "and go to the overseer in the old palace. He will give you traveling money."

He returned to the papers on his desk. It was difficult to concentrate upon them when all his thoughts kept flying across the lake. He had not seen Brooke alone this first day of his return, and as yet he had found no way of seeing her. Moti had invited the English priest to dinner tonight with a brief explanation. "He wants to see you about somethng urgent, Jagat, and I can't put him off any longer." He must devise some way of communicating with Brooke, especially on days when they could not meet. He clapped his hands and a servant came running into the room.

"Take this to Her Highness," he said, scribbling a note. "Bring back an answer at once."

He waited impatiently until the man returned with her reply. It was sealed. To his scribble, "Shall we invite Miss Westley tonight? She is quite alone in the hotel," Moti had replied, "Whatever you wish—but do not leave me alone with her."

And what, he inquired of himself, did that mean? He pondered whether he should go to Brooke himself or send a letter by messenger, and then threw down his pen. He could do nothing until he could see her alone, could talk with her and plan at least the next few days. Then perhaps he might be at temporary peace. In minutes he was in a motorboat.

"No," he told the boatman. "I will go alone."

And in minutes again he had crossed the lake glittering under the sunshine and tossing into rippling waves under the rising wind from the southeast. He docked, and throwing the rope to a waiting servant, he ran up the steps. In the lobby the two decorators were preparing to leave, their bags piled in the middle of the floor. He had scarcely seen them, occupied as he had been, and now he felt hurriedly that at least he should thank them. It occurred to him also that he would make the inspection his excuse to invite Brooke to go with him.

"And though I have not so much as inspected the rooms since my return," he said contritely, "I shall do so immediately."

Alpha Barron was overwhelmed by the presence of the Prince himself. "Oh, Your Highness," she gushed, "we've tried to do everything as we thought you might like it done. If anything is wrong, you have only to let us know —we'll come straight back, won't we, Ronnie?"

"Indeed we will, Your Highness," Ronnie Barron said. He was a pallid young man, effeminate and attenuated, his smile listless and his handclasp slack.

Jagat found himself in haste to escape them. "Thanks —thanks—thanks," he said heartily, "and good-bye— good-bye!" He turned them over to Bert Osgood, who appeared at this moment and hurrying to a telephone at the other end of the corridor, he rang Brooke's rooms. He heard her voice with a rush of relief. There was always the possibility, in spite of all, that she might simply slip away from him. Independent and elusive as she was, one could never tell. He was not accustomed yet to this woman, so new to his world.

"Will you make a tour of inspection with me?" he asked, pretending and casual.

"Of course," she replied.

"I'll meet you here in the lobby."

Better to be entirely open, he thought. By the time he reached the lobby the decorators had gone, and Bert was at his desk, reading mail.

"Our first tourist party is on the way, Your Highness," he called.

"Are we ready?" Jagat asked.

"Ready," Bert said, "and I'm glad to see the place in operation—partial, at least, before I go. I've hired a chef —he's coming in from New Delhi today. Shall I go ahead with a staff, sir?"

"The key people, yes," Jagat replied. "I'll engage the ones to work under them. I'm moving Rodriguez to the hotel, I think—just now he's gone to Bombay for me. He's been butler in the palace since my grandfather's time. He's honest and a wonderfully good tale-bearer. He'll see everything that goes on and report to me. He loves intrigue and gossip, but he's loyal."

"Aha," Bert said. "So he's been the line of communication!"

Jagat laughed. Why need he like this American so much? Irrepressible! Deep in trouble, Bert Osgood could laugh in the morning.

"I hope we won't have too many guests during the monsoons," he said. "I shan't know how to amuse them, if you go."

"These people are staying only a week," Bert replied. "Friends of mine, actually, from New York. I've told them so much about the hotel that they're curious. But they'll bring good publicity—they are all travel agents or reporters."

"Take good care of them, then," Jagat said.

As he spoke he saw Brooke at the far end of the corridor coming toward him. She was all in white, as she so often was, her fair hair shining. She was happy, he could see when she came near, and at peace, her eyes clear.

"I'm taking Miss Westley on a tour," he continued.

"Shall I come with you?" Bert asked.

Jagat shook his head. "You have all you can do to get the place finally ready. Besides, I know my way about in spite of changes."

He led Brooke up the wide marble stairs to the suites facing away from the city. Marble halls stretched from one suite to the other, and each suite had its own terrace, the water lapping gently at the base.

"Does the lake never rise?" she asked.

"Not since I built the dams," he said. "We can control the flow absolutely."

They were constrained and yet free. Never before had he waited until a woman made a sign to him, and yet he preferred to wait now until she made the sign, which she did, in the third suite to which he led her. It faced the island where Shah Jehan had been so long imprisoned and as they stood looking across the lake, she went to the door opening upon the hall and closed it. Then she turned and came to him and put her head on his breast, and he enfolded her.

"What shall we do?" she whispered.

"I don't know."

"If you don't know," she murmured, "how can I ever know?"

He watched her too sensitive face. "It is impossible for us to talk here, is it not? We must meet in some far-off place where there are no palace ears. Let me think—" He frowned. "I have it—tomorrow we will go to Chittor, you and I. We will go alone—not from here, but from the town. You will take an early boat, say at sunrise, and I will find you. Just walk along a street—Chittor, yes, that's it. I want you to see it—it's ancestral, my ancestors fought there, great warriors, though they lost and swore they and their descendants would never enter Chittor again, until it was restored to us, which it was, by the Prime Minister himself, you know."

"I don't know," Brooke said, laughing, "but you'll teach me tomorrow."

"A whole day alone," he said under his breath.

In the cold of the dawn she was rowed across the pearly lake, the boatman shivering under the strip of coarse gray cotton cloth over his shoulders. The women were already at their washing and she passed them as she mounted the flight of marble steps to the water gate. Then, in all but empty streets, she walked slowly as she waited. In a few minutes she heard the subdued roar of a motorcar and Jagat drew up beside her, stopped, and opened the door to receive her.

"Here's this rug," he said, and wrapped her in it, a soft multicolored handwoven blanket. "The nights are chill, but the sun will soon change everything. We Indians live by the sun."

It was true, she observed, for as they left the city behind they passed through villages awake but not alive. The men were sitting on their haunches outside the mud houses, wrapped in homespun cotton shawls, their faces somber with cold, while within those houses women bestirred themselves to make the morning meal. As the hours wore on and the sun mounted higher, the villages woke, men went to the fields, women and children to the wells, and mangy dogs were everywhere. Even the gray monkeys woke to chatter in the trees, and blackbirds busied themselves on the backs of scrawny cattle, searching for insects on their matted hides. She saw everything while she listened to Jagat's monologue.

"Chittor is three and a half miles long. It's built on a flat-topped mountain of solid rock—about 1303 A.D. I think. The walls enclose vegetable gardens, lakes, everything for survival. My forefathers thought it was impregnable, alas! Chittor was our ancient capital, sacked three times by the Muslims, the last one the great Akbar. The fort was once surrounded by deep forests—wonderful tiger hunting! It's said there were even lions, once—"

She heard history unrolled before her during the hours

before noon as they drove on the narrow road between fields that looked like brown suede in the barren spring.

"Nothing blooms or bears fruit until the rains come with the monsoon winds," Jagat told her. "Only those yellow flowers that look like what the English call St. John's wort and the thorn bushes you see everywhere. Ah, there's the fort. I'll park the car and lock it and pay a villager to watch it. Here, give me that basket."

For they had stopped at noon at the foot of the flat-topped mountain and she had tugged at the lunch basket.

"Under other circumstances," Jagat said as they climbed the rocky ascent, "I'd have brought Rodriguez and a couple of bearers to wait on us. But today I wanted you to myself."

In spite of which they were followed by a ragged crowd of village children and idlers, who left them only when Jagat shouted at them. Alone then they reached the top. He put down the basket in the shade of a ruined temple and, her hand in his, he led her through empty temples and palaces, pausing a moment before a tall pillar, its carving crumbling in the desert air.

"Impossible to show you everything or tell you all," he said. "There'd be no time left for us. But this—this we'll linger over—Padmini's little palace, surrounded by water, so that she was safe from attack. She was so beautiful that the Maharana dared not let dry land be the approach to her palace . . . Stand there, darling, against the background. I can see your reflection in the water, as hers must have been—ah, my love!"

He stepped forward, impetuous, and put his arms about her. She stood enfolded, then after a moment she lifted her head from his breast.

"What became of Padmini? When the conquerors came."

His arms dropped. "She waited until her lord was killed and the fort about to be lost. Then, still loyal, she led her ladies into a dark passageway and ordered her servants to set a fire and light it. Thus she died."

"Sad—sad," she whispered and hid her face again upon his breast.

The hours passed too swiftly and they were compelled to face the sinking sun. It was a day apart from all other days in all her life, a day strangely quiet and without love-making. They shared silences and moments of talk and laughter.

Only one strange incident marred the day. It was at noon. They sat on a bright hillside, in the midst of ruins, and eating their sandwiches as they talked. In the near distance a tower stool bleakly stark among fallen walls and broken terraces. He was speaking of the tower.

"A watchtower," he said, "and there my ancestors entrenched themselves for a last stand against our enemies."

He held his sandwich in his right hand, staying to eat it because he was talking. She, though listening, was suddenly diverted by a large bird that seemed to drop from the sky.

"A hawk—" she cried.

As though she had called it, the bird swooped low. So close it came that the whir of its wings fanned their faces, it stretched its claws and snatched away the sandwich that Jagat held in his hand.

He gazed at that empty hand. "Did I not have food in my hand?"

She laughed. "You did!"

But Jagat did not laugh. "Such a thing has not happened to me before! Bread in my hand, and it is gone! A sign of ill fortune—my son? No, he is already gone. Am I to be robbed again? But of what? Of whom?"

He muttered to himself as though she were not there and she was compelled to recall him.

"Jagat, darling! It's only a hungry hawk—"

"But bread out of my hand!"

"Never mind. Here's another sandwich—we've plenty. It's only that your birds and beasts are so spoiled. They're convinced that they're human beings—"

But it was a full five minutes before she persuaded him to eat, and half the afternoon was gone before he was himself again. Then all too soon it was nearly time for sunset.

"Shall we ever have such a day again?" she asked wistfully.

"We must—we must," he insisted.

She had paused, halfway down the hill.

"But how?"

He took her chin firmly in his right hand.

"Speak my name," he commanded.

She had seldom used his personal name. Now she still did so diffidently. "You do not answer my question— Jagat!"

"My name sits sweetly on your tongue," he said softly, and released her. Then he made his voice brisk again.

"We must think only of one day at a time, one day, one night. Tomorrow will you come to dinner at the palace?"

She lifted her head to look him in the eyes. "Must I?"

"Yes! We cannot miss any chance of meeting."

"Then promise me—don't leave me alone with her."

"No. She has asked the same of me."

"Has she? Does she know?"

"I don't know."

"I am so sorry for her."

"Sorry?"

"Because you love me."

"Ah yes—well, the two of you are different."

"Different?"

"You belong to different worlds."

"But you—where are you? In which world?"

"Dearest One, I don't know. That is what we must find out. Only be patient with me."

"Yes," she said.

And in silence they descended the mountain.

The next evening on the terrace, she understood what he had meant. It was much like the evening she had spent before and yet totally different. She was not the same woman. For her the search was ended, whatever the decision must be. They sat in the drawing room after dinner, the terrace impossible. The wind had risen to a gale, very nearly, the trees were twisting and tortured, and the lake was rocking with whitecaps.

"In a few days the rains will fall," Jagat said.

The under-butler brought coffee and rose wine. Rodriguez was already in Bombay tonight.

"Liqueur, Miss Westley?" Jagat asked.

"Yes, if you please, Your Highness."

She was impatient with these surfaces. All during dinner it had been difficult to make talk, Jagat absorbed in his own thoughts and Moti almost entirely silent. Had it not been for Father Francis Paul the meal would have been impossible to endure. But he had talked with his usual enthusiasm of his work among the Bhils. It was obvious that he had a purpose in his visit, and now he made frank use of Brooke as part of his unselfish scheme.

"Do you know the Bhils yet, Miss Westley?"

He moved across the room as he spoke and took the chair near hers.

"I don't, I'm afraid, except that they are one of the tribes, as you have told me."

"An attractive people though volatile," Father Francis Paul said, declining the liqueur with a wave of his right hand. "They are short and wiry and very brave. Among the most ancient of the primitive tribes, they live in the hills of Banswara and Dungarpur and very much as they have for centuries, although I'm trying to persuade—I hope to persuade—His Highness to make some improvements. They're very loyal to him still—loyalty is one of their traits."

"Hear, hear," Jagat said absently.

"We British did too little for them," Father Francis Paul went on. "Though Rajasthan was under British suzerainty for a hundred and thirty-seven years, and for eighty-two under the British Crown directly, they're not much better off for it."

"At least the Crown protected my ancestors from all dangers, and we protected the Bhils," Jagat put in. "Now the states are thrown to the wolves."

"Not at all," the priest retorted. "You've an extraordinary constabulary, you know. I do admire those fellows, living in the desert in rude tents or cabins, traveling ten or twelve days for water and food. Dacoits and smugglers and cattle robbers are not so difficult for them, I daresay, as the endless loneliness. No, no, Highness, your treasure is in your people. I confess that my Bhils contribute their share of criminals, too. Your Highness, I repeat, we'll never solve the problems of these tribes until we have schools and more wells. I know the irrigation wells have made good headway under your direction, but it's not enough. I have a plan—Your Highness, I beg you to remember that the Bhils have been given the least improvement, so far, among all your peoples. That is, in education and health."

"I've built over a thousand houses for them," Jagat began.

The priest interrupted. "Not enough, Your Highness! What we need is to arrange for resettlement around the newly watered areas."

"That will be done in due course." Jagat was irritated now. This Englishman preaching his gospel! He continued sharply. "The state is divided into four zones, as you may know. Where the irrigation is most needed depends entirely on rainfall. Subsoil water is brackish, although we've dug as deeply as four hundred feet. Only canals will serve in such areas. Look at the Gang Canal, for example, which brings water from the Ferozepore weir and transforms thereby the whole district! And give us credit, if you please, for the Naurangdesar tributary."

"I do give you credit," Father Francis Paul said warmly, "and I am reminded of the inscription on the cenotaph of Queen Semiramis of Assyria. Have you seen that cenotaph, Miss Westley?"

"I remember the inscription," Brooke said. "It goes like this, doesn't it?"

She paused an instant and then repeated the words in her soft clear voice. " 'I constrained the mighty river to flow according to my will and led its waters to fertilize lands that had before been barren and without inhabitants.' "

"Exactly," Father Francis Paul exclaimed, "and how well you say it! What has been done before, Your Highness, must be done again and again in many places."

"It shall be," Jagat retorted with energy. "But you must remember the costs. We can go no more quickly than we have the money. For example, the loss of water in transit is serious. In the long run it will be cheaper to line the passages with bricks, but the immediate cost is formidable."

Father Francis Paul proceeded with fervor, nevetheless. "Meanwhile we must plan for reforestation, Your Highness. The people have been allowed through centuries to cut off even the brush from the hills. I give full credit to what you have already done, Your Highness, in the area of forest management, but—"

Brooke rose. It was obvious to her that Jagat could bear no more and the Maharani made no move to deliver him. She had sat listless and silent throughout in her gold brocade chair.

"Your Highness," Brooke said, her voice high and clear. "I should like to see the storm. I've been watching the trees blow hither and yon through that window. It must be a sight."

"Ah!" Jagat's answer was a sigh of relief. "I'll take you up to the tower. Will you excuse us, Moti—and you, Father?"

The Maharani nodded but the priest was persistent.

"If you will give me fifteen minutes when you return?"

"Granted," Jagat said.

They left the room and for a minute or two neither Moti nor Father Francis Paul spoke. Then she lifted her head.

"Father, I wish to confess."

"Yes, Your Highness."

"Please let me forget the title."

"Very well."

Father, I cannot endure my life."

"There are times when none of us can."

"I am not speaking of times. I speak only of now—this instant, when we sit here alone in this room, in this palace, you and I."

"What can I do to help you?"

"Let me forget that you are a priest. May I?"

He did not reply. He looked at her half-startled, and she went on quickly, changing before his very eyes. Her listlessness was gone, she leaned toward him, her voice urgent.

"I have never loved anyone before—no one, you understand? Now I know I love you. It is not my wish to love you. It is not my wish to love anyone. I know, from my own mother, that it is a misfortune to love anyone, but especially for a woman to love a man."

He was overwhelmed with horror and with pity.

"My dear soul, do you not love your husband?"

"No, and never," she said.

"He is kind to you."

"That is not love."

"Does he love you?"

"How can he love me when I do not love him?"

"Is it not your fault then?"

She threw her fan on the floor in a gesture of impatience. "Can I help it?"

"You can pray that you will be enabled to love him."

She laughed bitterly. "How little you know about love!"

She rose impetuously, this woman whom he had never seen impatient, and crossing the floor swiftly, she knelt at his feet and folded her hands on his knees.

"Help me!"

For the first time in his life he looked into a woman's eyes and was made helpless by her love.

"Help me," she repeated, "help me!"

He put his hands over hers, trembling as he did so. "My dear, my dear," he murmured. "I wish I knew how to help you."

Then he summoned his strength and gently put her hands away so that they fell into her lap. He rose and drew her to her feet so that she stood beside him. "We are what we are," he said. "You are the wife of a great and good man, I am a priest of God. This is our destiny. If we are to meet again—and if we are not to meet again it would break my heart—it must be only because we do God's work together. What does it matter if your God is Krishna and mine is Christ? There are those who say that the two are one—that Krishna is called Kristi by some—who knows? Let us work together for the good of your people, who are mine also. I have made them mine."

He crossed himself; then, hesitating, he took her right hand and kissed it and let it fall again.

"I shall never forget what you have told me. I am honored. And now will you make my excuses to His Highness? He needs you very much in all the plans he is making for his people. Remember this always—my-my friend. My dear friend."

He bowed and hastened away, his robes flying behind him. And she stood there in the middle of the floor, the tears flowing down her cheeks.

Two days' search did not reveal Raj anywhere in Bombay and Rodriguez was ready to return without him until in the underground regions of the city where he had Goan friends he heard that Raj was infatuated with a new young actress who was making a film at the most famous of the several famous motion picture studios of Bombay.

At first he was highly indignant as a good Catholic that his master's son-in-law should be engaged in such idle pursuits. Upon reflection, however, he decided against increasing present family difficulties by adding this, a new misfortune. On the third day about noon, at which time he understood that the young star appeared for work, he arrived at the studio and made inquiry not of Raj and his whereabouts but of the star herself, who was no other, he discovered when he approached her, than Sehra Lall. He did not know of course that Jai had known Sehra, and would not have known now except when he made clear his presence, saying that he was the head servant and butler of the palace of the Maharana of Amarpur, he saw the beautiful girl burst into tears. She was in her dressing room sitting before her mirror while her maid was combing her long hair, and her dresser was at the same time putting on her the heavy gold jewelry necessary for her part in filming an ancient historical play.

"Why do you weep, lady?" he asked.

"Because Jai was my friend," she sobbed, "and until now I have not met one who knew him."

"Surely the young Raj Sahib knew him," Rodriguez exclaimed, "since he himself is betrothed to the sister of Jai."

At this the young woman's eyes dried quickly with anger and she screamed for Raj to be brought to her.

"Raj! Raj—where is he?" she cried.

Everyone searched for him in all likely and unlikely places and it was discovered that he had only just arrived and was waiting for her on the set. She gathered up her red and gold robes and swept out of the dressing room, Rodriguez following her, and so he came face to face at last with the young man he sought.

"Raj," Sehra wailed. "How is it you have not told me that you are engaged to be married and to Jai's sister?"

The young man flushed darkly red and the hairs on his ears flared. "Should I have told you?" he parried.

"Certainly you should," she cried, now very indignant. "Do you think I'd have wasted my time with you if I had known? In the first place, Jai's sister—shall I hurt her by allowing you to follow me like a dog? In the second place, but I am not sure that it is not the first, why should I accept a love affair from you instead of a marriage? Be gone—be gone!"

Suddenly against her will tears flowed again. She cried too easily since she had heard of Jai's death. He was hero to everyone, but to her he was also the perfect lover, the man she could never marry. In despair she had rebelled against her parents and had entered the motion picture studio here in Bombay, shamelessly using her father's well-known name as a multi-millionaire. Fortunately she also had talent and was the imperious star in a new and modern film, *The Woman Wins*.

She was able to forget Jai most of the time nowadays. but, reminded, she still wept and tears ruined her makeup just as she was ready for the scene, adding anger to grief. She gathered her wide skirts in her two hands and went after Raj as if he were a fowl that had wandered through the door. He could only turn and run away, Rodriguez following.

It was opportune, the Goan thought, for Raj was angry enough for having been thus dismissed before the laughing onlookers, and so he was the more ready to transfer his anger to the American, when Rodriguez told him the story.

"What!" he cried. "I am to be disgraced by the girl to whom I have promised myself! All this"—he nodded toward the studio door—"is play and nonsense! Come—let us return at once to Amarpur. I will face this American and send him home to his own country."

In less time than Rodriguez could have thought possible they were indeed on their way and at nightfall were in Amarpur by airplane. It was almost midnight, Raj having delayed only to eat a large dinner at the airport inn, when he burst in upon the American, who had already gone to bed.

"Up, up!" he shouted. "Out of your bed, thief!"

Bert sat up, dazed, and lit his bedside lamp. Like most young American men when he slept he was good as dead. Now faced by Raj's wild eyes, the hair on his ears flying with the impetus of rage, Bert was alarmed.

"Sit down, fella," he said. "Let's talk this thing over."

"What is there to talk?" Raj demanded. His English was excellent but in moments of excitement he reverted to Indian idiom. "You have wounded me in the deepest parts of myself! Like a thief, a dacoit of the heart, indeed you have stolen into my life!"

Nevertheless he sat down on the nearest chair, and drawing a large yellow silk handkerchief from his pocket, he wiped his face and hands. Bert found his slippers and put on his bathrobe. He tried to stifle a mighty yawn and failing, gave himself up to it, then shook himself like a dog just out of water."

"Now then," he said. "What's up?"

Raj stared at him. "You don't know?"

"I honestly don't," Bert replied. "Unless you—yes, you are—Raj!"

"Ah, now the guilt conscience strikes!" Raj bellowed in triumph. "You are right. I am Raj!" He beat his breast

with both clenched fists. "I am come to demand repent-
ance!"

"For what?" Bert asked mildly.

"For the affections of my fiancée, Veera, my betrothed,
my beloved!"

"Look," Bert said. "Let's be reasonable. If she chooses
you, she's yours. If she doesn't, well—fair play's the
thing."

"No choosing is possible," Raj declared in the same
loud tones. "It is too late for choosing. Our families have
decided. Formalities have been completed. Die is cast."

"Let's go and have a drink," Bert said.

"Where?" Raj asked.

"Downstairs in the bar. There's not much there yet but
a couple of whiskies will clarify our thinking."

In silence he led the way down the corridor, waking
two sleeping nightwatchmen on the way. In the bar he
mixed the drinks and, inviting Raj by a gesture, the two
of them sat down facing each other across the small
marble table. Almost immediately Raj was softened by
alcohol.

"You love her?" His piercing dark eyes fringed with
foolishly long lashes emphasized the question.

Bert was cautious. "Put it this way. She's a mighty attractive girl. If she were free, had her own way and all
that, I could love her."

"Even as an American you find her attractive?"

"Very much so."

"I take it as compliment, thank you." Raj made a large
gesture with his right hand. "To me, she is surpassingly
exquisite. I love her."

"I can understand," Bert said. For all his cautious
words, he left a pang. Obviously it was all going to be too
difficult. He'd better go home as soon as possible, his
commonsense told him, and yet there was something about
this beautiful Indian girl that he would never forget.
Whomever he married, and however long he might be
married, he'd know romance was here in this palace.

"It is not to say that I also was aware of my own passionate love for her until now," Raj was saying. "I thank

you for showing me this fact of loving. Had it not been so, it might have taken me many years, if ever, to know my love."

"She must also love you," Bert reminded him and filled the glasses again.

"Of course, of course," Raj said carelessly. "That I accept as fact. But Indian girls are very nicely cultivated in such matters by their mothers and older women. They are taught to love their husbands promptly."

"You're a good fellow," Bert said.

It was true, too. Under the ebullience and effervescence, Raj was a good fellow. He'd want to please his wife. Besides, he'd bet on Veera. She'd have her own way with him. And there was money, he supposed; Raj was expensively dressed in English clothes and he wore a large diamond ring on the little finger of his right hand. Years from now, if ever he came back to India, they would meet, he and Veera, and she would be a handsome Indian matron with a flock of dark-haired children, the boys all with flanges of hair on their ears.

"You know, Raj—" he said and paused.

"Yes, yes," Raj said eagerly. "Tell me all what is in your heart."

"I'm awfully glad you came."

"Thank you—why, please?"

He put out his hand and Bert clasped it and felt it feverishly hot but damp.

"If you hadn't come, I might have gone on imagining something foolish. As it is—"

"As what is, please?"

"We'll always be friends. And I'll wish you happiness on your wedding day. And please let me wish Veera happiness tomorrow, for the next day I am going back to America."

"Certainly I insist you must see her and wish her our happiness. We are marrying very soon—I think two more weeks or so, according to the lucky day of the horoscope."

"Good! And now let me take you to a room where you can sleep."

The next day he went to the palace and asked to see

the Maharana. When he was ushered into that presence, His Highness as usual behind his grandfather's desk in the palace offices, but alone, fortunately, Bert was direct.

"Your Highness, if you will allow me, I should like to return to my own country tomorrow."

"Why are you in such haste?"

"Your prospective son-in-law came in last night, Your Highness. We had a long talk. I see it would be very wrong of me to interfere with his life, for that would be to interfere with your daughter's life. The time has not yet come when—certain barriers—can be removed. She would not be happy in my country, and I would not be entirely happy to remain here. Ours would be a floating sort of existence and I am a man who likes my roots. I can make them for myself but I couldn't make them for her, and I don't think she could make them for herself—in a strange country, that is. You have a framework here for the individual that is—helpful. I don't want to be responsible for breaking it down, especially for one who is your daughter."

Never had the two men liked each other so well, and the same emotion swelled in the heart of each. Jagat rose and shook Bert's hand.

"You speak like a decent, honorable, wise man," he said warmly. "I thank you for myself and for my family. Now what can I do for you?"

Bert hesitated. "If I might see her for a few minutes, just to tell her myself—"

"Of course."

He touched a bell, and a servant entered.

"Tell my daughter to come here at once," Jagat ordered.

While they waited they were ill at ease and yet silent. All had been said and it was time to part while emotion was at its height. When Veera entered, beautiful in a sari of pale blue and silver with silver rings on her fingers and toes, Jagat rose, relieved.

"I will leave the two of you," he said. "In fifteen minutes I will return."

"We won't need that long," Bert said.

"What is it?" Veera whispered as the door closed.

He went to her and took her pretty hands. "Honey, it won't work."

"What won't work?"

"You and me, honey. Raj is here."

She pulled her hands away and stamped her foot. "I'll send him off!"

"No, you won't, Veera. He loves you. He wants you to marry him."

"The big stupid!" Her eyes filled with tears.

"It's not only him," Bert said. "It's the families. Your father has been wonderful to me—a great man. I can't hurt him."

She was sobbing now, and coming close to him, she leaned against him. He did not put his arm about her. No more of that—

"We don't care for families now," she sobbed. "It is too old-fashioned. Girls in Bombay—"

"You're not a girl in Bombay," Bert said. His voice was steady. "You're a princess. You have to act the part. And I can't help you there. I'm no prince but Raj is. The two of you together will make a wonderful couple. You'll have wonderful, beautiful children and they'll grow up in palaces, the way you did. We don't have palaces in America. I don't know as I could live in one myself."

Veera, her great eyes fixed upon his face, suddenly stamped her right foot and screamed, "You are a big coward!"

Her sandal flew off her bare foot and Bert stooped and taking it, he fitted it to her foot, such a pretty foot, so soft in his palm. Looking down upon him, she began suddenly to sob. He rose and she stepped back from him and wiped her eyes on the end of her sari.

"Here," Bert said, "take my handkerchief. You don't want to spoil your pretty dress."

She wiped her eyes and looked at him reproachfully, her long lashes wet. He smiled at her, a sad wry little smile.

"Good-bye, Veera," he said, and giving a stiff short bow, he left the room.

She stood there alone, the tears running down her cheeks, and thus Jagat found her.

"There, there," he said, and put his arms about her shoulders. "There now, don't cry, little one. He's a good man—a very good man, American though he is. He will always make me love America for his sake. But he is not for you, little one. What would we do without you here? And Raj we know so well and he will adore you and give you jewels and saris and take you to Paris and London. No more tears, Veera."

But she tore herself away and stamped one foot and then the other. "I wish to cry!" she screamed.

Jagat, accustomed, shrugged. "Cry then, child! Tears wash away sorrow. But I have no time for you. Go to your mother."

She ran out wailing, but she did not go to her mother. Instead she went to her room and clapped her hands for her ayah. When the old woman came running she scolded her.

"Where are you always when I need you? Find me the gold sari that I wore on Divali day. My fiancé has come and I must look my best. In two weeks I am to be married."

The monsoons were delayed and day after day came and went, the sun shining like silver in a white, hot sky. The lake palace hotel was filling slowly with guests from here and there around the world, a Greek princess and her husband on their honeymoon, three American senators from Washington, two old-maid sisters from London, and a retired British colonel and his wife. The official opening would not take place however until after the big party of American travel agents and reporters were to arrive. Twice they had been delayed at Jagat's request, for with Bert's departure he had been hard put to it to find anyone to take his place. Nor had he been able to set up the laundry service and the deep-freeze room he had ordered from America until after the commotion of Veera's wedding and her departure for her new home in Bombay.

"I don't know what I would have done without you," he told Brooke again and again.

For she had come forward quietly when she saw his

predicament and had offered her help. "I'm not a trained businesswoman," she said, "but I can answer letters and see that the rooms look well for the guests."

"I can't make a secretary and housekeeper out of you," he had said bluntly.

"No, no," she replied. "It's only temporary. You'll need professionals. Please let me, Jagat! It makes me happy to be useful to you."

Their relationship had changed and yet had not. Not once had they met again in the night and she wondered sometimes if they ever would. The daily bustle of a hotel occupied their time and apparently their thoughts. But there were moments, precious and rare, when alone—by accident or his design she was never sure which—he caught her hand and held it in both his own hands, or in passing brushed his lips against her hair. Then she knew that nothing had changed. It was only a question of what hour, what place. It did not occur to her to go away. He was here and if she slept alone at night, it was only to dream of the morrow, when she would see him, talk with him, know whether he was well or weary. He was her deepest sympathy, her secret joy. She trusted him wholly, and when he named the hour and the place she would be there at his command. Until then, she told herself, she would live alone.

And alone she did live. They could never be seen alone together. He could never enter her rooms, nor could she close the door of his office if both were there. She was aware that Rodriguez, now installed as the head servant here, was loyal to Jagat in his own way, and yes, to Jagat's wife. This loyalty compelled him to watchfulness of Brooke, since he trusted no Americans. He had been triumphant after Bert's departure, convinced of his own victory, and boasted that in fact the American had been dismissed. And Brooke did not doubt that he would work for her dismissal, as he would call it, if he saw any connection of a private nature between her and his master.

Therefore, secure in her inner peace and the knowledge of Jagat's unchanging love, she came and went to the hotel, enjoying its beauty and creating beauty of her own.

The gardens in the courtyards bloomed under her direction and each morning she spent hours in arranging bouquets in the public rooms and the guest suites. Sooner or later she and Jagat would meet, but now he only smiled at her in passing, or gave her a few words of greeting. In the late afternoon he returned of course to his own palace and she dared not telephone him, for listeners were everywhere, and the rest of the day was long. She took to walking in the city and for a while she used one of the boats and rowed on the lake until Jagat heard of it and forbade her to be alone in a small boat.

"The crocodiles are cruel," he told her. "I have not been able to have them killed. Their scales are like steel. Even a bullet slides away without wounding them. Spears are the best weapons, but even a spear must be cast by a huntsman who knows the small vulnerable space where the yellow of their underbellies begins. I have not found a spearsman, even among the Bhils who carry spears, who knows how to kill a crocodile. These are very old reptiles and they are sacred and my people are not prepared for their death. Though they are caged by the strong steel net at the lower end of the lake, it is always possible that the men did not catch them all." He paused to hold her with his intense gaze. "If anything happened to you, I would end my life." Even so he spoke in a whisper, so impossible, so dangerous it was to speak of love.

She had nodded briefly. "I won't row alone," she promised.

She did not tell him, however, of her long walks in the afternoon, nor did anyone else tell him. For in her loneliness she sought companionship among the people, though she did not speak their language, nor they hers. Yes, even from the birds and beasts she sought companionship. A flock of pigeons, hundreds upon hundreds, swept her into the sky upon their way, swallows in their mud nests upon an ancient wall in some village, a favorite cow decorated with spots of gold paint, tiny donkeys, their slender legs trembling beneath too heavy loads, a village lad, squatting beside a calf and patiently finding it grass he had pulled from some damp spot in the desert, all such small sights assuaged her loneliness.

It became her habit, then, when luncheon was over, when she had spoken pleasantly here and there to a guest, she went to the docks and beckoning a boatman, she was carried across the lake to the marble steps of the city. There she went ashore, and holding up two fingers or three, she signified how many hours hence she was to be met. Then she went her way, people staring at her at first but accepting her as the weeks went by as the eccentric American woman whom nobody knew but whom everybody recognized. She was a guest at the hotel, they said, a guest who never went away, it seemed. She was kind to children, they said, for wherever there was a child, a small child, an infant in the mother's arms, she would pause and turn the tiny face to the light of a street lamp and examine it carefully. Then she would give the mother a rupee or two and send her on her way. But sometimes she would take two or three small toys out of her handbag and place them before a child sitting in the dust of the street, but always it was a little one. Even two years was too old for her interest.

"Have you anything that belonged to Jai—something he loved especially?"

This she asked of Jagat one day in the lobby as he entered. He smiled at her. "You aren't believing what the lama said!"

"Yes and no," she replied. "If you ask me whether I believe, I would be compelled literally to say I do not. If you ask me if I feel it may be true, I would say it is not true. That's the agnostic's creed, isn't it? I cannot know, therefore I do not know. Yet, if I do not know, then nothing is impossible, however improbable. I wait for more light."

He had not replied, as they walked together into his office, but the slight smile had not left his lips. He was rummaging in his desk meanwhile and he took from a secret drawer three objects—a small ivory elephant, the dried forepaw of a tiger, and a tiny ape carved from a ruby.

"These were Jai's talismans," he told her. "The tiger's paw came from his first tiger. We were in my shooting box in the Aravalli hills. I would like to take you there someday—if ever there is such a day." He sighed and passed his hand wearily across his forehead and went on. "The ape belonged to his mother. I forget how she came by it. The elephant—he picked up somewhere—at school—I don't know."

She carried these small objects now in her handbag and took them with her on her walks. It was true that again and again, but not every day, she stopped to look into a boy's baby face. On one such day she paused at a doorway in a village outside the city where a mother sat nursing her little son. She was a simple woman, her sari of faded blue cotton and her feet bare, but she had a fresh, sweet face, and her long black hair was braided over her shoulder. The child turned from his mother's breast to gaze at the stranger as though he recognized her. She sat down beside the mother, and the child pushed away the breast which nourished him and put out his arms to her.

"He knows you," the mother exclaimed, and though she spoke in her own tongue, Brooke knew enough now to understand.

"Perhaps I also know him," she replied, and opening her bag, she took from it the toys that had once belonged to Jai. The child leaned from his mother's arms to look at them as she held them on the palms of her hands. He examined them and then with care he took in his tiny fingers the tiger's paw, and clasping it in both hands, he held it to his breast.

The mother laughed. "He will be a hunter of tigers," she exclaimed. Then she tried to take it and give it back to Brooke, coaxing the child. "Let the stranger from over the Black Water have the tiger's paw. dear little one," she said.

The child however would not yield it. He held the paw more tightly and hid his face on his mother's bosom.

"Let him keep it," Brooke said, "but see to it that he does not lose it. Someday it may have meaning for him."

So saying she went on her way again and by twilight

she was back at the hotel. There to her surprise she found Jagat in the lobby, waiting for her return, with an open letter in his hand.

"Where have you been?" he demanded. "I have been impatient for your coming and I would indeed have sent men in search of you except that Rodriguez tells me you are often away in the afternoons, but you come back always at sunset. Now it is an hour past sunset."

"I was outside the town," she said. "But why do you ask?"

"Here is this letter," he said impatiently. "What am I to do? Some Americans are coming next week. Without regard as to whether I am ready for them, they simply announce their coming, twenty-seven of them, to stay three days. Among them is a friend of yours." Here he consulted the letter. "Jerome Burnett," he added.

"I've never heard of him."

She sat down on a brocaded satin sofa and put up her hand to take the letter.

"Jerome Burnett, the recently famous novelist, will be one of our party. He particularly wishes to interview Miss Brooke Westley, who, we understand, is a guest in your hotel."

"No, I do not know him," she repeated and gave the letter again to Jagat.

"At any rate," he said, still impatient, "we must prepare for them. As usual there are all sorts of odds and ends which the workmen have left unfinished. Come into my office. We will discuss everything. Twenty-seven Americans! My god, what shall I do with them? How keep them amused? Three days! Cameras, film—they want to take pictures. Damn Osgood for having left me to meet this moment!"

He led the way into his office as he talked and sat down behind the huge ebony desk. "Now," he began. "How many suites are altogether ready?"

"Those on the second floor," she said, "and four of those on the east terrace. No—wait! I have not checked the bathrooms. I will do so in the morning. Of single rooms

we have at least fifteen ready except for small things—
cushions, pictures, curtains to be hung."

"Can you superintend?"

"Of course."

The door was open and anyone passing could see them
as they talked. Twice she saw Rodriguez pass. The third
time Jagat looked up irritably and saw the Goan, his face
turned inquisitively, and he got up and went to the door
and slammed it shut.

"Damned nosey old Goan," he muttered and sat down
again.

He gazed at her, half-absently, his chain of thoughts
broken, and she met his eyes frankly, waiting—for what?

"I ought not even to ask if you are happy—or unhappy,"
he said abruptly.

"I am happy," she said quietly.

"God knows why!" he muttered.

She opened her handbag and took out a small sheet of
paper. On it were lines of her compact handwriting.

"I copied something out of a book," she said. "There are
many wonderful books here—did you know, Jagat?"

"I've had no time to know," he said. "And perhaps,"
he added honestly, "perhaps I am not a reader, as my
grandfather was. He was in his way a philosopher, both
east and west. He read English and French as easily as he
did our own languages, of which he knew several well. So
he has communicated with you? Let me hear what he
says."

"Someone asks the questions," Brooke explained, "and
someone answers them. I don't know either of them,
except that the one who asks is a searcher, and the one
who answers is a wise man."

"Begin," Jagat commanded.

She began then to read softly and clearly.

"One asks: 'What is it that does not let me find peace?'

"And one answers: 'Desire.'

"One asks: 'But I desire only peace.'

"And one answers: 'Give up even that desire.'

"One asks: 'What then brings peace to the mind?'

"And one answers: 'Love.'

"One asks: 'Love of whom?'

"And one answers: 'Can you ask this lamp to shed its light here and not there? For whom does the light burn if not for all?'

"One asks: 'Does peace lie in burning?'

"And one answers: 'Does it lie in extinguishing the light? No, peace waits in the core of the burning light.' "

Jagat listened with attention and then shook his head. "It is meaningless to me. I am a new man in a very old country." Then suddenly he rose and went to her swiftly and took her in his arms.

"I am hungry," he whispered. "I am thirsty. I am restless. I cannot live like this—without you!"

"But I am here," she protested.

"We are as divided as though the lake were an ocean between us," he insisted. "I look out of my windows at night and wait to see if your light is burning. Only when it is dark do I go to sleep. Sleep? I have not had a night's sleep since we came back."

He pressed her hard against him then, and bending back her head with his right hand, he kissed her full on the lips. There was a scratch on the door. They sprang apart. The door was flung open and Rodriguez stood there.

"Highness!" he said loudly. "A new American is at the dock. He says he is the forerunner of those to come. He is sent to inspect the rooms, to report if they are ready or not."

"I must go," Jagat said hurriedly.

Left alone in the middle of the room, she met the dark and baleful eyes of Rodriguez. He gave her a long look and then softly closed the door.

In his small house high in the Aravalli hills Father Francis Paul was at his desk. It was late but only in the night had he time to work on his history. In his meticulous handwriting he was covering large sheets of yellow paper.

"The transition between early and medieval India was marked by the emergence of Rajput clans, not heard of previously, but beginning from the eighth century to play a part. Nearly all the kingdoms were ruled by Rajput families or clans. They were warriors, but aristocrats, of diverse descent, mostly foreigners, perhaps Scythians, who entered India during the fifth and sixth centuries. In ancient times the Brahman, or learned caste, often intermarried with the Rajput Kshatriyas or warriors."

He paused to consult a text and read of Raziya, the daughter of Sultan Iltut-mish, who appointed her to rule after his death because his sons were worthless. "She was a great sovereign, and sagacious, just, beneficent and learned, a dispenser of justice, the cherisher of her subjects, a woman of manlike talent, one who was endowed with all the admirable attributes and qualifications necessary for kings. But, as she did not attain the destiny in her creation of being computed among men, of what advantages were all these excellent qualifications unto her? Alas, she ruled only three years and was killed."

Pausing to ponder this woman's fate, he thought of Moti. Who knew what talents were lost, because she, too, was a woman? And she was only one of many, all beyond his knowledge. He continued to write.

"By the tenth century, Rajput houses ruled not only in Rajputana but in all the great cities of northern India. Clansmen, their loyalty did not go beyond the clan. Family pride and jealous temperament made union impossible. When centuries later the Muslim Arabs and Turks won easily, the Rajputs withdrew from the central plains of Hindustan, but they kept the enemy at bay. Nevertheless the Rajput clans remain the present specimens of the Aryan race in India. They are rulers and overlords, own the land but do not till it. They think it a disgrace to do manual labor."

He heard at this moment a scratching on the inner door of his study. He lifted his head to listen—yes, someone was there.

"Enter," he called, expecting to see a Bhil face.

The door opened slowly and a head peered in. It was not a Bhil. He recognized instead the face of the Maharana's Goan butler.

"Come in," he said. "What brings you here so late? For that matter, friend, what brings you here at all?"

He motioned to a low wooden stool, and Rodriguez sat on the edge of it and wiped his face with a towel he had knotted about his neck.

"Father," he said. "I come to confess. You know I am not a good Catholic. In Goa we learned about God from our captors, the Portuguese. Nevertheless, I have not made confession for many years. Now I am compelled."

He crossed himself and dropping his head, he muttered a Hail Mary in order to convince the English priest of his sincerity.

Father Francis Paul was amused. He had noticed the man when he was at the palace but of late he had not seen him. "Have you left the palace?" he asked.

"I am promoted, Father," Rodriguez said proudly. "I am now head servant at the new hotel. His Highness trusts everything to me."

He drew a deep breath and prepared for confession. "I am in fault, Father, deep fault. I have kept a secret which is not mine to keep. But what can I say? I am loyal to my beloved master, the Maharana, as I was to his father. I honor his family. I am proud to serve him. Yet long ago I should have come here to tell you a secret. But I have waited until I saw it with my own eyes. I could not believe without seeing. It is my duty, now I know, to save this great and honorable family from a deep sin. otherwise this family will be scattered to the wild winds, east and west. Is this not sin?"

"I have no idea what you mean," Father Francis Paul observed. "If you have a sin, then speak of it concretely."

Rodriguez cleared his throat and spat into a bit of paper he took out of the wastepaper basket by the desk. Then he put it back into the basket. He spread his knees apart and placed a hand on each knee.

"To this point I come," he said. "I saved the family from the American who would have spoiled the marriage of the daughter of the Maharana. Yes, I confess it—I went to Raj, her fiancé, and I told him the American was spoiling her."

"By wanting to marry her?" Father Francis Paul inquired.

"Marriage or no marriage,' Rodriguez retorted, "how would it look to have a red-haired child born into our honorable noble family? Raj came and the American went away."

"Is this your sin?" Father Francis Paul asked.

"No, no," Rodriguez said with some impatience. "I am coming to the sin. This is my sin—I have known and refused to know. I have seen and refused to see that even the Maharana himself can be spoiled." He leaned forward to whisper through black and broken teeth. "Two nights ago I saw him call the American woman into his office. After a few minutes he shut the door. When I opened it, first quickly scratching, she stood within his arms!"

He made this announcement with eyes opening wide, and his voice dropped. Father Francis Paul coughed.

"Perhaps it was only a sudden emotion," he said. "Had there been anything serious, I am sure the Maharani would have sought my counsel."

Rodriguez was silent. Should he or should he not mention the fact that the Maharani herself was in a strange mood? He decided not to risk the loss of an ally. "The American will not be a concubine," he said. "She is very proud."

"What do you wish me to do?" Father Francis Paul asked.

"Father," Rodriguez said, sputtering in eagerness to convince the priest. "I pray you will advise the American. Talk with her. Tell her she sins when she comes into a man's house and into his very arms when he is an honorable man, a great prince, married to a high lady, who has given him a son. Is it her fault the son is dead? I am not a good Catholic, sir, but I cannot see such things before my face."

Father Francis Paul did not reply at once. He pondered for a space of time. Then he lifted his head.

"I will go to the American," he said. "I will plead with her. But first I will ask her if what you say is true."

"Is it true?" Father Francis Paul asked.

He had traveled three days later to ask Brooke Westley this question. He found her in the living room of her suite overseeing the placing of a piano in a certain corner where she had a view through a wide window of the island of Shah Jehan's imprisonment.

"A gift from His Highness," she told him gaily. "A surprise for my birthday! He ordered it months ago but it's only just come. I didn't realize how much I had missed a piano. Suddenly this morning the bearers brought in an enormous crate. It's a German Steinway of the sweetest tone—"

She sat down before he could speak and began to play a rippling melody and broke off to whirl on the piano stool and face him with her joy. "I'm so happy," she cried softly.

He recognized the quality of her voice. Only love, rejoicing, reciprocated love, could infuse such music into a woman's voice, could add such light to her eyes. Therefore he put the question.

"Is what true?" she asked, and this was a very different voice, half-alarmed.

"That you and His Highness—that there is something between you that ought not to be there."

She closed the piano and faced him again. "Why should I lie to you? We love each other."

They were alone now. The bearers had gone and the door was shut. From across the lake came the rhythmic beat of the women washing clothes. Father Francis Paul sat down, suddenly exhausted. What could he say to this beautiful and willful woman? What could he say except that he too knew what it was to love someone who must not be loved by him? Long ago in England, before he had ever met or dreamed of meeting the Maharani, he had fallen in love with his older brother's wife, a simple, pretty girl too young for his brother. Not yet dedicated, he had lived in hope and misery until he found his love returned. Then, faced with decision, he had made confession to the abbot of the monastery where he was in training. The old man had made instant decision.

"You contemplate a grave sin, my son," he said.

In the despair of his youth he had cried out.

"But what shall I do with myself? I think of her day and night."

"I know—I know," the abbot had replied. "What man does not know torture? But spiritual growth comes only when the vow of chastity is observed. The Protestant church has produced no great saints."

"I fail to see the connection," he had said stubbornly.

The old abbot had yielded not a bit.

"There is profound connection through prayer and meditation. Thus the most powerful force in the body is transmuted into spiritual energy. The force so transmuted is stored in the brain. It has been lifted from the lowest to the highest. The lure of divinity, the divine drawing, makes the fishermen of Galilee leave their nets and the princes of the clan of Shagia give their robes, their jewels, their princely estates . . ."

"Is the body then an enemy?" he had demanded.

"The body is not an enemy," the abbot had replied. "Chastity is the disciplining of the will. So is fasting. A vow not kept does more harm than good. Spirituality brings life, power, joy, fire, glow, enthusiasm, all beautiful and positive qualities, never dullness or weakness."

These words had burned into his young brain, and strengthened, he had left England forever. But what he had learned he had learned forever, even for the Maharani. And he now had the resources of his consecration to God, and Brooke did not. Nor could he instill them in her. She must find them for herself, perhaps create them.

"My child," he said, "I cannot tell you not to love this most lovable man. I can only ask you to love him more."

"That," she said, "is impossible."

"What do you contemplate?" he asked.

"I don't know," she said. "I only know that we will come to some decision, but not now. He is expecting a large party of guests tomorrow. After they are gone, perhaps—"

"What do you yourself contemplate?" he asked.

"I will do whatever he asks me to do," she said.

"I ask you for a greater love," he replied stubbornly.

"I don't know any greater love," she retorted.

"Then I must teach you a greater," he said.

He pressed his lips together, closed his eyes, and prayed for inner guidance. Then opening his eyes and fixing their calm gaze upon her, he began to speak.

"I am sure that he loves you as much as you love him. Therefore he will do anything you ask him to do. This is the nature of true love between man and woman. I will not direct you beyond this. In the end the decision is not mine, for your lives are your own, to use as you wish. I will only tell you of him."

"I know him already," she said, interrupting.

"You know him as a woman," he said, correcting her. "I know him not only as a priest but as a man. I know him as the ruler of his people. Yes, he is still the ruler of their lives. In spite of the new government, it is to him that his people look."

"I am not responsible for them," she said.

She was aware of a strange new rebellion within herself, a jealousy so vague that she could not define it. She felt a fear, as though the priest were about to wound her in some tenderest part of her being.

"Quite right," he said. "You are not responsible for his people. You are responsible only for his happiness, because you love him. In order that he may be happy you must know his dreams."

"I know his dreams," she said quickly.

Father Francis Paul held up his right hand for silence. "Only some of them—those regarding you. A man has other dreams, his own dreams, quite apart from any woman, even the one he loves. Granted that you love each other, granted everything you want to say, I ask only that you consider his other dreams."

"I don't know what you are talking about," she said, her voice very low.

Father Francis Paul replied briskly, clearly. "You will forgive me if I am selfish enough to begin with my Bhils. There are a million Bhils who look to His Highness for life. Poverty is their problem. Yes, I know that the central government must provide for them, but His Highness must dream for them, too. Governments do not dream. They fulfill the dreams of others. Therefore he must dream of better methods of agriculture and of village crafts to give them work. They have only two hospitals—two hospitals for a million people! And schools—they need many schools. Most of all they need water—deep wells and irrigation canals. These must be the dreams of His Highness. He must fight for the Bhils, Miss Westley. No one else can do it."

"Someone else can do it," she said stubbornly.

Father Francis Paul ignored this. "It is not enough to dream of material benefits. There are the greater dreams. Poverty breeds filth and ignorance and immorality. My Bhils need help to become good people. There are many good Bhils, but there must be many more. True, these higher dreams will have their base in material improvement. Take mining, for example. In the last ten years there has been improvement here, of course, but we need much more and much more very quickly. This state is wonderfully rich in minerals. Yet the people starve. Marble everywhere, but beside marble there are—"

He counted off the minerals with his long pale fingers: "Tungsten and manganese, graphite, gypsum, garnet, glass sand, lead and silver, iron, fluorite, limestone for making cement, fuller's earth, cyanite, calcite, zinc, lignite—"

"Spare me," she broke in.

He laughed. "All dreams, waiting to be fulfilled!"

"I don't believe he's thought of such dreams," she declared.

"He has thought of them," Father Francis Paul insisted. Then his eyes twinkled. "If there are some he has not thought of, I will introduce them to him."

She tried to laugh above the dread in her heart. "I thought priests were supposed only to save souls!"

"Ah," he said, "that's where you're mistaken. We're very practical, we priests. We know that the body has to be saved first."

He studied her beautiful rebellious face.

"I shan't keep him from fulfilling all these dreams," she said at last. "In fact, I approve of them. I will help him."

"Ah," he said again. "What if you can help him best by leaving him? By not destroying his family life? By not destroying his leadership of his people because his people no longer respect him?"

She covered her face with her hands. "Oh, don't," she whispered.

But he was relentless. "It is not only he who must dream. The people must dream, too. They must believe him to be great and good. They must trust him. They must know he is devoted to them. Then they will be happy because they have hope. But if you remain here, they will cease to believe in him. And without their belief do you think he can be happy? Power will go out of him, that mysterious force which gives a man the attraction that only goodness gives. 'And I, if I be lifted up,' the Savior of people once said, 'I, if I be lifted up, will draw all men unto me.'"

"Oh, don't," she moaned behind her hands. "Don't—don't—don't!"

He had finished what he came to say, or very nearly. He went to her now and put his hand on her head. "I bless you, my child. I leave you with my blessing. My peace I give to you."

And so saying he did leave her and he returned again to the hills.

She was sleepless that night, and the next day she did not see Jagat even to thank him for the piano. He was harried with last-minute arrangements and it was night-fall before he came to her door. She heard his knock and the door opened but he did not come in. Instead he looked about the room.

"Did a gift—"

"Yes, yes, yes," she cried. "It is here. I have been playing on it. I have been waiting to thank you."

He came into the room then and closed the door and leaning against it, he swept her into his arms. "I can't stay, not an instant, Rodriguez is distraught with excitement. I must stand by until the guests come. Dinner is waiting for them. Are you not dressed?"

"Am I to be present? You didn't tell me."

"Of course, of course! Put on a long frock—that green and silver one. You will be the most honored guest, our first guest. And you will give me courage, my darling—"

He was so handsome, so gay, so filled with enthusiasm, that her heart hardened against Father Francis Paul. This was no longer old India, India of ancient tradition. It was an India new and young, led by such men as the one she loved. Old customs were dead, old loyalties useless—a new India.

There was a sudden commotion in the lobby, loud American laughter, fresh American voices.

He released her. "Quickly, quickly!" he cried and was gone.

In the same excitement she made herself ready for the evening, in and out of the shower, brushing her long bright hair, the light touches of makeup, the clasping of an Indian bracelet and earrings. She went into the lobby and saw a brilliant crowd of people, Americans, all of them exclaiming, or so it seemed by the noise of their voices, over the beauty with which they found themselves surrounded.

"Oh, look—everything is marble—the floors—"

"That painting is on marble—"

"What is it—a goddess of some sort?"

"Is that a bird flying into the chandelier?"

"Did you see the gray monkeys in the airport? Running around like people! They're cute—"

She stood uncertainly aside. It had been so long since she had been among her own people that now they had become strangers to her. No, it was more than a matter of time—far, far more, Through her love for Jagat, one Indian man, she had become a part of India. His people were hers, and forever. She stood apart, waiting, watching these transient folk and was seized by terror. They were strangers. If she left Jagat she would be among strangers! She must never leave him, lest she be lost. Whatever the price, she must stay with him, for she had not the courage to live without him. How should she break into this crowd?

Even as she wavered a man came toward her, a man older than herself but still young, a young man with golden hair and dark eyes, strikingly handsome, not too tall but taller than she, and strongly built.

"Miss Westley," he said warmly, his hand outstretched. "I have waited so long. I didn't know where you lived or even that you had left America, until I corresponded with Bert Osgood."

She let her hand be clasped and held. "But we have never met, have we?" she asked, wondering.

"Ah, yes, we have," he said. "We've met through your grandmother. She was my dearest friend and my name is Jerome Burnett."

"You must be one of the men she loved," Brooke said slowly, her gaze upon his face.

"Yes," he said simply.

Through the long week, each day stretching longer than she could endure, for her glimpses of Jagat were rare while he came and went across the lake, she found herself lost in long spaces of time when there was no hope of meeting him or even of hearing his voice. Once in mid-week he stopped to explain. They passed in a corridor and, uncontrollably longing, she put out her hand and caught his. He stopped instantly.

"Dear One," he whispered. "You must forgive me. These Americans—they have so many wants! But it is going well, is it not?"

"Wonderfully well," she agreed, clinging to his hand.

But he was wary, she could see, his eyes on either end of the corridor and she withdrew her hand.

"It is not only the Americans," he continued. "But this week of all weeks, the village panchayats are meeting. Until now they have been content, these old men, to do no more than see to the school buildings, if any, or to take care that the drinking water wells are kept clean and the roads passable and such small duties. Now they are suddenly inspired to do much more. They are talking of self-government, of building industries, more schools, and of no longer being ignorant and poor. Where does this talk come from at this moment?"

She kept her suspicions to herself. Father Francis Paul, of course! "But does this make you happy?" she asked.

"These are my dreams, too," he said earnestly. And pressing her hand again, he released it, smiled, and hastened on his way.

She walked slowly and alone then to the marble parapet that overlooked the lake. There she sat down and watched him step into the boat that was ready to carry him between his offices in the old palace and these in the new hotel. She waved but he did not see her. On the far shore she saw a crowd of villagers waiting for him and she watched until he had stepped ashore and was lost among them. Then she heard her name called, and saw Jerome Burnett approaching.

"I've been waiting all day for a chance to talk with you about your grandmother," he said, seating himself beside her. "How lucky to find you here and alone! What a mob, all these Americans, eh? We've fallen in love with the place. I must say the Prince has done a magnificent job. The detail is perfect. Of course the cuisine will improve. It's somewhat weighted just now with curries and chutneys but that won't last. I've suggested to him an American chef in addition to his Indian cooks."

"You spoke of my grandmother," she said.

"Yes," he agreed. "In a way I have a debt to fulfill to her. She died so suddenly that I wasn't able to pay it to her directly, and in a vague sort of fashion I've been looking for you ever since. I know you are her sole heir and —oh god, I don't mean that the way it sounds! I've tons of money myself—no, no, I mean she had no family, it seems, except you, and she used to talk about you and yet she never introduced me to you. Not that I cared— oh, here I go again saying absolutely the wrong thing! But what I mean is I was so in love with her that I didn't care if I never met another woman, whatever her age!"

"You were in love with my grandmother?"

"Certainly! Don't be so surprised! She was the most fascinating, beautiful woman I ever knew and I'll never forget her. I loved her madly. I'd have married her in a minute, whatever our ages, but I never had the courage to broach the subject of marriage to her. She might have laughed. That I couldn't have borne."

"She would never have laughed," Brooke said.

"No? Well, I missed my chance, then. If she'd lifted a little finger I'd even have become her lover. But she never lifted it, and I could only go on adoring her and do adore her at this very instant. I wonder if she knew?"

"She did know," Brooke said.

"How do you know?"

"She told me—about love."

"Good god," he said under his breath.

He was silent then, gazing out over the water and she was silent, too, glancing now and again at his intent face.

"Was she wrong?" she asked at last. "Would it have been better now if she had—lifted her little finger or even spoken of marriage?"

His eyes came back to her face. He was searching his soul, she could see. "No," he said at last. "No, I don't think so. I think she was right to do as she did."

"Why?"

He put his hand over his mouth, thinking before he spoke. "I am asking myself. If she had—no, she was too wise. She knew what I needed then. I wanted to adore. I needed to believe in someone's pure goodness. I can't explain it all to you now but perhaps sometime when we know each other better—you see, I'd had terrible disappointments—in people, I mean. My mother, whom I trusted, suddenly went away with another man and my father—shot himself. I was the loneliest person in the world because I'd loved them both and never knew they were—not happy. And then I found her, someone I could trust and could adore. And if she'd been—of the earth just then—I don't think I could have stood it. But she wasn't. She was delicate about me, understanding that I had to have a dream, I suppose. I can't explain."

"I hate explanations," Brooke said. "Either one knows the meaning or one doesn't. Either one understands or there is no possibility of understanding."

He looked at her as though he saw her for the first time. "Now that is what she would have said!"

"So when you leave here," Brooke said so slowly that she felt someone was compelling her to speak. "When you leave here," she repeated, "I think I will go, too—back to America, I mean. I'm just beginning to understand that I don't belong here, after all. I love it and I'll always love it—but I don't belong, and if I stay I'll lose my love. As it is—I can't explain—myself."

"Don't," he said. "She never explained herself. That's why I was always in love with her, and still am, though her lovely bones are dust."

He looked at her as though he had not seen her before. Then he spoke, but slowly and feeling for the words he needed.

"It's odd—you make me think of her. Yet you don't look like her. But I've an idea you are like her—inside, I mean."

"I never knew her—not really," Brooke confessed.

"I can understand that," he said, nodding. "I was too young, too—but somehow just loving her made me a man."

"Now it's I who understand," she replied.

She meditated upon the possibility of telling him that she, too, knew the power of love, for love had made her a woman. But, no—it was too soon. Later, perhaps, in another country than this, she could explain, or would, although, in general, she distrusted explanations. Silence was best, certainly at this hour of her life.

Distrusting explanations, then, she left none behind her. On a certain morning some few days later—and one day did not matter to her now more than another—she merely wrote Jagat a short letter which she sealed with wax so that no one else could read it. Inside there were a few lines which, if he understood them, would bind them together across the world, and if he did not, then he remained what he had been, a sympathy between them, east and west.

"When I am gone," she wrote, "I wish you would find

a certain little child in the village just outside the city to the south. I found him there one day and he chose the tiger's paw. He still has it. You will recognize him. He is about nine months old. Was it only nine months ago that your son was killed?

"As far me, I keep with me a joy that none can take from me, a gift I gave you, as a virgin gives, and which you received as a prince receives. You alone, my life long, are that prince."

She paused, and inexplicably, or so it seemed to her, she thought of the Greek girl long ago, who had hanged herself—for love, doubtless for love, a love from which she had been separated, perhaps? Who knew the end of that story, or the end of any story? And swiftly she wrote:

"Love burns on—forever. And peace waits—in the core of the burning light."

"But why?" Jagat groaned. "What did I do to make her want to leave me?"

He had drawn the plans for the new village schoolhouses for the Bhils, and Father Francis Paul had pored over them, had suggested improvements here and there.

"Very exciting, Your Highness," he had said. "When Miss Westley returns—"

"Is she returning?" Jagat had demanded in excitement. "Is she not?"

Jagat threw up his hands in question. "How can I know?"

"If she does not?" Father Francis Paul inquired gently.

"If she does not," Jagat said with decision, "then I shall devote myself to my people—lose myself."

The two men looked at each other in question, the one asking what the priest knew, if anything, and the other deciding how much he should tell, if anything. Each decided to let life rest as it was.

Father Francis Paul rose. "Then if that's all, Highness—"

"I don't know of anything else," Jagat said. "I shall simply push on with the plans and bring them to reality."

"Dreams," Father Francis Paul said.

Jagat lifted inquiring eyebrows, and the priest continued. "In the dreaming and the vision is your next step, Highness. Isn't that true?"

"I don't know," Jagat said, and then laughed with an edge of bitterness. "That's all I seem to say these day—I don't know!"

It was perhaps a month later when he was in a village to the south of the city that he saw a woman coming along the dusty path from the drinking-water well. She did not hold her brass jar on her head, however, but instead rested it on her left hip. With her right hand she steadied a huge brass tray on her head. Upon the tray sat a baby boy, cross-legged like a tiny Buddha. The woman was young and strong and smiling, her face brown with the sun, her hair orange with desert dust. She wore the full skirt of the Rajasthani village women but she had embroidered this skirt in gay colors. Jagat stepped aside to let her pass, and as he did so, the baby turned his head, saw him, and laughed aloud, showing small white teeth.

The woman, surprised, stopped where she was, her feet deep in the dust. "Does my son know you, High One?"

"What has he in his hand?" Jagat asked.

"It is a tiger's paw that a foreign lady gave him."

"How did she give him such a toy?" Jagat asked.

"To speak more truly," she said, "he chose it. The lady had a small white elephant and also a small monkey made of red stone. But my son would have the tiger's paw and he will not allow anyone to take it from him, even when he sleeps."

She watched Jagat's face with surprise as she spoke. A strange look came over his face, a look half frightened but half smiling.

"Have you seen my son before, High One?" she asked.

Believing and unbelieving, he gave a great sigh. "I do not know," he said and, believing and unbelieving, he went his way.

THE INCREDIBLE STORY
OF A MAGNIFICENT REBEL
WHO WOULD LIVE FREE...
OR NOT AT ALL!

THE INTERNATIONAL BEST SELLER
NOW A POCKET 📖 BOOK

"A tale of adventure such as few of us could ever imagine, far less survive."—<u>Book-of-the-Month Club News</u>

▼ AT YOUR BOOKSTORE OR MAIL THE COUPON BELOW ▼

Mail Service Department, POCKET BOOKS, Dept. 97.
A Division of Simon & Schuster, Inc., 1 W. 39th St./N.Y. 10018
Please send me the following:

NO. OF COPIES	AMT.	IBM #	PRICE	
———	———	78528	$1.95	PAPILLON

Plus 25¢ ....for mailing and handling. Please enclose check or money order. We are not responsible for orders containing cash.

TOTAL
AMOUNT ....   (PLEASE PRINT CLEARLY)

Name ....

Address ....

City ....State ....Zip ....

P 3271